PRAISE FOR ROISIN MEANEY

'A wonderfully woven, beautiful book full of hope,
love and characters so fully formed I feel like I know them. I adored it'
Emer McLysaght

'A warm, insightful story about new beginnings and the power
of kindness'
Rachael English

'A cracking yarn . . . Meaney can excavate the core of our human failings
and present it to us, mirror-like on the page . . . Which makes her utterly
credible, utterly authentic, utterly irresistible' *Irish Independent*

'Roisin Meaney is a skilful storyteller' **Sheila O'Flanagan**

'A real treat . . . Meaney wraps her readers in the company and
comfort of ordinary strangers'
Sunday Independent

'Meaney weaves wonderful feel-good tales of a consistently high
standard. And that standard rises with each book she writes'
Irish Examiner

'This book is like chatting with a friend over a cup of tea . . .
full of all the things that make life interesting'
Irish Mail on Sunday

'Delightful . . . a cosy read for any time of the year, be it in your
beach bag or sitting curled up in front of the fire'
Swirl and Thread

Roisin Meaney was born in Listowel, County Kerry. She has lived in the US, Canada, Africa and Europe but is now based in County Clare, Ireland.

She is the author of twenty-one novels and has also written books for children.

www.roisinmeaney.com @roisinmeaney

Bluesky: @roisinm.bsky.social

ALSO BY ROISIN MEANEY
A Winter to Remember
Life Before Us
The Book Club
It's That Time of Year
The Restaurant
The Birthday Party (a Roone novel)
The Anniversary
The Street Where You Live
The Reunion
I'll Be Home for Christmas (a Roone novel)
Two Fridays in April
After the Wedding (a Roone novel)
Something in Common
One Summer (a Roone novel)
The Things We Do for Love
Love in the Making
Half Seven on a Thursday
The People Next Door
The Last Week of May
Putting Out the Stars
The Daisy Picker

CHILDREN'S BOOKS
Puffin Paulie (with illustrator Louisa Condon)
Don't Even Think About It
See If I Care, co-written with Judi Curtin

Moving On

ROISIN MEANEY

SPHERE

SPHERE

First published in the Ireland in 2025 by Hachette Books Ireland,
First published in Great Britain in 2025 by Sphere

1 3 5 7 9 10 8 6 4 2

A CIP catalogue record for this book
is available from the British Library.

PAPERBACK ISBN 978-140-873173-4
TRADEBACK ISBN 978-140-873172-7

Typeset in Arno Pro by Palimpsest Book Production Limited, Falkirk, Stirlingshire

Printed and bound in Great Britain by Clays Ltd, Elcograf S.p.A

Papers used by Sphere are from well-managed forests and other responsible sources.

Sphere
An imprint of
Little, Brown Book Group
Carmelite House
50 Victoria Embankment
London EC4Y 0DZ

The authorised representative
in the EEA is
Hachette Ireland,
8 Castlecourt Centre,
Dublin 15, D15 XTP3, Ireland
(email: info@hbgi.ie).

An Hachette UK Company
www.hachette.co.uk

www.littlebrown.co.uk

For Emily Moriarty, with love

Life itself is the most wonderful fairytale

– Hans Christian Andersen

GALWAY
OCTOBER 2019

Anticipation

HER TEA HAS GONE COLD. SHE WONDERS HOW MANY cups she's wasted over the years, made and then forgotten as she's tapped the keys of her laptop or sat lost in thought, trying to puzzle her way through a roadblock in a plot while tea has cooled in a cup.

Today she's not typing or sitting; she's standing in the littlest bedroom that became her writing room after the girls moved out, and she's preparing to pack up the contents of her bureau, a task she's left till last. She found the bureau in a charity shop over twenty years ago, and its drawers and cubbyholes harbour many memories.

Packing again, moving house for what she hopes – no, she knows – will be the last time. Tomorrow she will leave the home she loved best, of all the places she's lived, and today she's lost in the past, and her tea cools.

She sets the cup back on the windowsill and makes a start. From one of the little nooks in the top of the bureau she takes a notebook, its cover dark green with a flowery print. She traces the inscription on the flyleaf, its ink faded with age. They were children, two children playing at love.

In the pocket inside the notebook's back cover are letters written in different hands, all precious, all folded and stored there over the years. She unfolds them carefully and rereads them now, tears brimming as the words conjure long-ago emotions.

In the same pocket is a newspaper clipping of the Irish fiction bestseller list from almost twenty years ago, her first book sitting at number ten. Seeing it listed there prompts a stir of the old excitement. Its publication had been the beginning of something, when she'd thought herself too old for any more beginnings. So much still ahead, and she'd had no idea.

In a week she'll be fifty-nine. At twenty she'd considered herself so grown-up. She shakes her head, smiling. How little the young know, and how wise they fancy themselves to be.

She returns the clipping and the letters to their pocket. She closes the notebook and places it into a waiting box. In the next nook is a cork, which she lifts out and sniffs. *Keep the cork,* she hears Alf saying, and she did keep it. Her first-ever champagne, popped open to mark a bittersweet day, years before any of the books. She adds it to the box.

In a small drawer she finds a page from a magazine that she meant to frame and never got around to. Her first-ever press ad, for a yogurt aimed at weaning babies. She remembers buying extra copies of the magazine, sending the page to Danny and Frances and Joan and her mother.

An hour or so later, as she's closing the last box, her phone rings. She pulls it from her pocket and sees Juliet's name.

'Hello, darling.'

'Mum – we're just leaving now, see you soon.'

'Wonderful. Drive carefully.'

'I will. Any word from Grace?'

'Not yet.'

Her last phone conversation with Grace had turned into a row. At twenty-seven, Ellen's younger daughter could still be volatile – and when she told her mother that Tom wanted to take a year out to travel the world, Ellen made the mistake of saying that it sounded like a good idea.

'A good idea? Really? It's fine for Tom – he can take leave of absence. What am I supposed to do with my clinic, pack it up until we come back?'

Ellen should have backed off and left it at that, but she didn't. 'Maybe you could get someone to stand in.'

Another mistake. 'Right – like vets are floating around just waiting for a job offer! Have you forgotten when I tried to find someone to go into partnership with when I was starting up? You haven't a clue!'

And on she went, taking her frustration out on her mother, like so often before. Since then there's been no response to any of Ellen's voice messages – were they even listened to? Will Grace show up this evening?

After saying goodbye to Juliet, Ellen brings the boxes downstairs and stacks them with the others in the hall, and then she push-pulls the empty bureau out to the landing. A lot of the furniture has already been moved; the rest will be transported tomorrow. Now the house feels hollow when she walks through its rooms.

She enters the bedroom that used to be her aunt's and looks down at the back garden. She remembers her first sight of it in 1981, and Frances on her knees, digging weeds out of the rockery. How strange it will be to see a different garden when she pulls apart other curtains every morning.

She's just out of the shower when her phone rings again. She looks at the name and smiles.

'Hey.'

'Hey yourself. How are things?'

'Great. I emptied the bureau.'

'Finally. Don't dream of trying to move it.'

'I just pulled it out to the landing.'

She hears his long sigh. 'I can't turn my back for an instant.'

'I'm fifty-eight, not ninety-eight. I'll have you know I'm still young enough to move furniture.' But she's laughing. Every day he makes her laugh.

'Just don't come crying to me when you slip a disc. You all set for this evening?'

'Why? Is something happening?'

'Very funny. You're hilarious. When can we expect you?'

'About half an hour.'

'Love you,' he says.

'Love you more. See you soon.'

Her heart is too full for all the happiness. It spills over; it fills all the spaces in the hollow house. Tomorrow they are moving into the cottage closer to the sea that they came across six months ago and instantly, jointly, loved. They are going to live there for the rest of their lives, and they are going to be monumentally happy. Abundantly happy. Stupidly happy.

She dries her hair and pins it up with the big tortoiseshell slide Juliet had taken off and given her, one time Ellen admired it. She dusts powder on her face and adds lipstick, and gets into the black dress Juliet had insisted she splash out on. As she slides her feet into red shoes she hears Claire saying *At least one pair of red shoes should feature in every woman's wardrobe.* Claire, who knew it all, or thought she did.

In the kitchen Ellen checks that she switched off the cooker before phoning a taxi. As she hangs up, her eye is caught by the cardboard box on the worktop. She looks at the books inside; twelve copies, all the same. She lifts one out and runs a hand over the cover. Her happiest book yet, every word flooded with love.

Ten minutes later, a car horn sounds outside. She pulls on her coat and leaves the house.

GALWAY
SEPTEMBER 1981
THE FIRST MOVE

Freedom

'I CAN'T BELIEVE YOU'RE ACTUALLY GOING,' CLAIRE said.

'Oh, I'm definitely going.'

All morning she'd felt fluttery with excitement, for once not able to eat breakfast. At the age of twenty, Ellen Sheehan was finally leaving home, making a start on a life that she knew would be filled with amazing adventures.

Her one tiny regret – well, maybe not that tiny – was that Claire wasn't coming too. That had been the plan, for both of them to escape together, but that was before Claire's only brother had skipped off to London to work on the building sites for the summer, leaving Claire trapped behind the counter of her family's pub.

'The minute Martin comes back you'll follow me, right?'

'I've told you I will. Can't wait.'

Claire had turned twenty in February, five months before Ellen. They were grown-ups now, ready for the world and all it could throw at them. They rounded a bend and there was the bus station, causing Ellen's stomach to flip again. Another few minutes and she'd be on her way – and this time tomorrow she'd have begun her new job, surrounded by books all day, meeting people who loved them as much as she did. Could things get any better?

At the station they found the Galway bus and stood at the open door. 'Behave yourself,' Claire said. 'And obviously I'm joking.'

Claire never behaved herself if she could help it. She believed in having fun, particularly if it meant breaking rules. Ellen knew she'd never be half as brave – and so did Claire. She called Ellen her rock of sense, but Ellen didn't want to be anyone's rock of sense. She wanted to have fun too, without worrying about it.

Ellen's mother didn't think Claire was brave. *That girl is a bad influence,* she'd said more than once. *I'm glad you're getting away from her.* She didn't know that Claire was following on: Ellen had thought it best to say nothing about that.

'Here,' Claire said, fishing a long blue box from her pocket. 'A little going-away present' – and inside, Ellen found a silver pen.

'Wow, I love it. Thanks a million.'

It crossed her mind that it might be stolen. Claire was an experienced shoplifter. *The trick,* she'd told Ellen, *is to buy something small, and look them in the eye when you're paying for it, and smile like mad and talk about the weather.*

There had been a time, a horrible time, when Ellen had stolen from shops too, but it hadn't lasted.

The bus was filling up. 'Find a proper boyfriend,' Claire said. 'You'll have plenty to choose from in Galway. Stop being so fussy.'

Claire wasn't fussy. She'd lost her virginity at seventeen, in the back seat of her then boyfriend's car, and she'd had plenty more sexual partners since then. *It's just physical,* she'd say. *It's fun, and no big deal* – and that was the problem, because Ellen wanted the big deal.

She wanted the drama, the deep passion of all the lovers she read about, the Cathys and the Heathcliffs, the Elizabeth Bennets and the Mr Darcys. She wanted someone who would die for her, someone who would kill for her. She wanted nothing less than a soulmate, and she was happy to wait for him.

And she would meet him in Galway. She was convinced of it.

For one thing, she was bound to encounter lots of readers in the bookshop: right from the start, they'd have that in common. Plus, if she could lose ten pounds by Christmas, and stop biting her nails, and let her hair grow, she'd feel so much better about her appearance, and that confidence would definitely attract more attention.

Yes, she was hopeful. Very hopeful.

'Are you getting on?' the bus driver called.

'Just a sec.' Claire flung the rucksack into the luggage compartment and threw her arms around Ellen. 'Phone me,' she ordered. 'I want all the news. If your aunt doesn't allow you to use her phone, wait till she goes out.'

At the mention of her aunt, Ellen's excitement dimmed. Moving in with her mother's older sister, a relative she hardly knew, wasn't the start she'd have chosen for her new life, but it would only be for a short while, until she and Claire found a flat together.

'See you soon,' she said. 'Tell Martin he has to come home.'

'I will. Have a ball. Go wild. Now get on before they leave without you.'

Ellen hitched her small bag higher on her shoulder and boarded. From her window seat she waved at Claire until the bus pulled out of the station. Watching familiar streets as they flashed past, she wondered if she would ever live in the town again – and this thought stirred a memory of another uprooting when she was eight, the family leaving their old town when her father had been offered a better job here. It must have been momentous at the time for her and Joan, but they'd been young enough to adjust and make new friends.

And then, eight years after that—

No. She would not think about it, not today. She switched her thoughts to the man who was going to be her new boss, and whom she had yet to meet.

Ben McCarthy, he'd said at the start of their phone call two weeks earlier. *Manager of Piles of Books. Coming back to you about the job you applied for.*

Oh . . . yes. She hadn't expected to hear so quickly – hadn't she only posted her letter two days ago?

What's your favourite book?

The question had caught her off-guard, but was an easy one to answer. *Lolita.*

Ah, the great Nabokov. Could you live without reading?

Another unexpected question – but again, one she hadn't had to think about. *I couldn't go a day without reading.*

The right answer, he'd said, sounding pleased. *Which dead author do you wish you'd met?*

She'd almost laughed. This was crazy. *Dickens.*

And what are you reading now?

Housekeeping.

Marilynne Robinson?

Yes.

Like it?

Yes, I'm really enjoying it.

A brief pause had followed, and then: *You'll do.*

Pardon?

Six pounds an hour, half nine to half five, Monday to Saturday, with one flexible day off in the week. How does that sound?

She'd hardly believed it. Was he actually offering her a job based on a conversation lasting less than a minute, and involving no more than a few bookish questions? He hadn't asked anything about the typing pool, wasn't even looking for a reference.

Is that a yes? Are you thinking about it?

Yes, she'd said hastily. *Yes, please. Thank you.* She'd already forgotten the terms and conditions he'd rattled off, but she hadn't cared.

Great. How soon can you start?

She'd thought fast. *I need to give two weeks' notice where I am.*

Two weeks. That brings us up to . . . Friday, September fourth. So let's say you start here on Monday seventh.

OK.

Good, all settled.

Um . . . is there anything else I need to know?

Yes. Wear comfortable shoes – you'll be on your feet a lot. Be here at half nine sharp, or I'll have to fire you.

She'd waited for a laugh, but none had come. *Thank you,* she'd replied, but he'd already hung up.

Half nine sharp, in comfortable shoes. No mention of a dress code, or what her duties would be. No information about the shop or who else worked there. It had certainly been an odd interview, but it had ended with an offer of work, and it had enabled her to hand in her notice at a job she'd hated, and now she was on her way.

She wondered what he'd be like face to face. Hopefully he'd be a bit less . . . unpredictable. Some people just didn't suit the phone.

On the other hand, what was wrong with unpredictable? Might make life more interesting, working with someone who didn't do the expected thing. From now on she must be open to every possibility, willing to embrace the unknown, the unexpected. Willing to be brave.

She rummaged in her bag until she found her book, and the apple she'd snatched from the fruit bowl on her way out of the kitchen. She began to read, and the world outside the bus window fell away.

Arrival

THERE WAS NOBODY TO MEET HER IN GALWAY. HER mother had said Frances would collect her, but her aunt was nowhere to be seen. Ellen hadn't set eyes on her since Granddad's funeral six or seven years ago, and only intermittently before that. She thought she'd recognise her, just about, but there was no sign of anyone who looked remotely like her.

After hanging around for fifteen minutes she found the address she'd tucked into her jeans pocket, just in case, and showed it to a ticket clerk, a tired-looking woman with colourless hair and holes in her ears but no earrings. She glanced at the address and shook her head.

'Ask Paddy,' she said, indicating a stocky uniformed man by the door. He took glasses from his pocket and peered at the paper. 'That's right across the city,' he told Ellen. 'Too far to walk with luggage. You can pick up a bus at Eyre Square: show the address to the driver.'

Forty minutes later she stood outside her aunt's house. Number 9 was a semi-detached in a row of identical others, or nearly identical. Different colours on the doors, windows curtained or left bare, but basically the same house repeated, two-storey with red brick below, pebbledash above. Twenty or so houses in total, the end ones curving in towards each other to form a cul-de-sac.

A few skinny boys kicked a ball about on the road, ignoring Ellen. Two women stood talking over a low straggling hedge a few doors up from number 9, one with arms folded, the other dragging on a cigarette. They'd broken off their conversation to stare at Ellen as she'd trudged past, and now she could sense them behind her, still watching.

She studied the house. They'd come back here after her grandfather's funeral, but she didn't remember it. Its front door and window frames were dark green. Two metal gates, a narrow cement path leading from the smaller one to the front door, a rectangle of neatly mown lawn to one side of it, gravel to the other. A blue Volkswagen Beetle was parked on the gravel, its body scratched and dented in several places, some of the dents rusting.

She pushed open the gate and walked up the path to the front door. There was no doorbell or knocker so she rattled the brass letter-box. Up close, the green paint was flaking.

No response. She tried again, and still nobody came. She took the address from her pocket – yes, number 9, and the road's name displayed on the first garden wall she'd passed. It was the right house, but nobody appeared to be home.

Or had her aunt changed her mind, decided not to put Ellen up after all? Was she inside right now, waiting quietly until her niece went away? But where could she go? She knew nobody else in the city, not a soul. She stifled a flutter of alarm. She set her rucksack on the doorstep and crossed to the side passage. She saw a metal dustbin, a big black bicycle attached by a chain to a drainpipe, and a huddle of coal bags.

She stood uncertainly, biting a nail until she remembered she was trying to stop, and whipped it from her mouth. She didn't want to go around to the back in case her aunt was hiding from her there, but what choice did she have? She took a deep breath and walked down the passage and rounded the corner.

And stopped dead.

The garden was magnificent. Filled with colour, even this late in the year, a riotous mix of flowerbeds and rockeries and shrubs, with a crazy-paving path taking a winding course through it. A shed on one side, its door ajar, was completely covered in some vigorous climbing plant.

A strip of concrete ran along behind the house, three-foot wide or so. It held a wooden seat, silvered with age, on which a pair of fur-trimmed slippers sat. Birds darted at a feeder suspended from an overhanging branch of a neighbouring tree.

It was a haven, rich in fluttering and buzzing, and heady with scent. In such a busy space it took her a minute to spot the figure in a wide-brimmed sunhat kneeling by one of the rockeries, her back to Ellen. The ridged soles of wellingtons showed beneath a substantial backside. Brown corduroy trousers, a checked shirt tucked in. Ellen heard the small clank of metal against rock.

'Aunt Frances?'

The head swung around to reveal a face, weatherbeaten and beakish. 'Yes?' The word barked out, and accompanied by an expression of deep suspicion.

'I'm . . . Ellen. I'm . . . coming to stay with you.'

The suspicion was replaced by outrage. 'Today? You were to come tomorrow! Your mother clearly said Monday!'

'Oh . . . I'm sorry. There must have been a mix-up. My job is starting tomorrow.'

The frown didn't budge. 'How did you get from the station?'

'I . . . took a bus.'

Her aunt tutted, looking even more put out. 'Why didn't you ring me?'

Ellen felt under attack. Everything sounded like an accusation, when she had done nothing wrong. 'Sorry – I didn't have your number, just your address.'

More tutting. 'Your mother has my number – why didn't she give it to you?'

'. . . I don't know.' *Because you were supposed to pick me up*, she shouted in her head.

'Where's your luggage? You must have luggage!'

'I left it by the front door.'

'Well, go and get it, for goodness' sake!'

Ellen scuttled away. At least it looked like she had a roof over her head – but how on earth was she to get on with this snapping creature? Would she have to spend all her time out of the house, just to avoid her? Thank God it wasn't going to be for long.

When she returned, her aunt was heaving herself laboriously to her feet. 'Can I help?' Ellen asked, stepping forward – but she was flapped away impatiently: 'I can manage!'

Once upright, her aunt walked in a swaying, waddling way to the garden seat and lowered herself onto it, pulling off the hat to reveal yellow hair that sprang from her head in peculiar little tufts – had it always been that colour? 'I have arthritis in the hips,' she pronounced, somehow making that sound like Ellen's fault too. 'I refuse to let it stop me doing what I want.'

She was short, with pouched watery blue eyes, and a pointed nose that looked like it had strayed there from a larger face, and a small pale mouth. Apart from a broad midsection, her figure was neat.

She didn't resemble Ellen's mother in the least. Not one common feature could Ellen see, except for a shared eye colour, although her aunt's were a paler blue. They even dressed differently; Ellen had never once seen her mother in trousers.

There was twelve years between them, which would make Frances sixty-eight now. There were two brothers younger than the girls who'd emigrated to Australia years earlier and never returned home.

Her aunt shucked off her wellingtons and wriggled a foot into one of the waiting slippers. A smudge of earth sat on her left cheek. 'When did you eat?' she asked.

Ellen thought of the apple on the bus. 'Er, I had lunch.'

'What *time*?'

'. . . Around two o'clock.'

'Dinner is at half six. You'll have to wait till then.'

'I can go out and eat if you like. Seeing as how you weren't expecting me, I mean.' She was starving, and half six was ages away. She could get fish and chips somewhere.

Her aunt pushed on the second slipper. 'No need for that. I roast a full chicken on Sundays so I have leftovers for other dishes. There'll be plenty for you.' She threw Ellen another sharp look. 'I hope you're not a fussy eater. I can't abide fussy eaters.'

'No.' Not that she'd dare admit it if she was.

'You can empty those weeds into the bin at the end of the garden,' her aunt said, pointing to a blue basin by the rockery, 'and then put the things back into the shed, and follow me in.' Without waiting for a response she levered herself off the seat and disappeared into the house, wellingtons standing where she'd left them.

The kitchen was small and painted apple green. A chipped white sink under the window, a cooker in a corner, a tall slim cupboard, a square table against a wall with a single chair tucked under it. A yellow Formica counter ran along the opposite wall, a fridge and a twin-tub washing machine beneath, along with open shelving on which crockery and pots and pans were stacked.

The table was draped in dark blue oilcloth. A newspaper was folded open at a crossword. A calendar with a picture of a mountain hung crookedly from a nail, still showing August.

Her aunt was chopping an onion at an alarming rate. A frying pan waited on the cooker, a wedge of yellow fat pooling on it. 'You might as well go up and unpack,' she told Ellen. 'Your room is next to the bathroom.'

Ellen hauled the rucksack up a narrow staircase with a brown strip of carpet running along its centre. She stood on the landing and located the bathroom, and opened the door beside it.

The walls were papered in grey, with twining green vines and purple grapes. One strip of paper had peeled away from the top and dangled above the window. There was a single bed with no headboard, a small heap of blankets and a flat pillow sitting on the bare mattress. A large wardrobe, ludicrously big for the room, was crammed between the foot of the bed and the window. A kitchen chair, the partner of the one downstairs, was the only other furniture. The floor was wooden, with a thin blue mat by the bed.

There was nothing else. No locker, no reading lamp, no mirror, no dressing table or chest of drawers. The ceiling bulb had no shade; the window was uncurtained. Ellen lifted the bedclothes and found a tan stain in the centre of the mattress. She opened the wardrobe – the door stuck until she tugged sharply – and a musty smell rushed out. Three wire hangers hung from a rail, a single black sock dangling from one of them.

She sat on the edge of the bed and thought of the bedroom she'd been so delighted to leave, with its bookshelves and matching wardrobe and dressing table, and its armchair and frilled bed linen. This one was definitely a step down, but it would have to do until Claire came.

The bathroom next door wasn't much better. A large cast-iron bath had a damp towel slung over the side and a short rubber hose attached to its taps. Two pairs of enormous grey knickers hung from a makeshift clothesline above the bath. A bar of cracked soap sat in a small puddle by the sink taps. A faint but definite smell of urine hung in the room. Ellen did what she had to do and hurried out, shaking her hands dry.

Back in the little bedroom she propped her toilet bag on the windowsill and stacked her books beside it. She dropped her rucksack on the floor by the wardrobe – did she dare to ask for more hangers?

She turned her attention to the bed. She threw off the bedding and heaved at the mattress until she managed to turn it over. No stain on this side, at least. She went out to the landing and located the hot press and rummaged among a jumble of linens until she found single sheets and a pillowcase. The blankets were threadbare: just as well she'd be moved out long before winter.

But in the meantime she had to eat – and a savoury smell was drifting up the stairs now and making her mouth water. She made the bed and lay on it and read until her watch said twenty-five past six, and then she ran a comb through her hair and went downstairs.

'I was just going to call you,' her aunt said, carving chicken. 'Fill that jug with water and take out the butter.'

The table had been set with mismatched crockery, and another chair had joined the first. Ellen did as she was told while her aunt lifted plates from the rack above the cooker with a tea towel. 'I assume you can cook,' she said.

Ellen's heart sank. Another reason for a scolding. 'I've never really had the chance. I mean, Mam does the cooking.' She could hear how pathetic it sounded. Twenty years old, and her mother still making her dinner.

Her aunt regarded her grimly. 'Every girl should know how to cook. I'll teach you while you're here,' and Ellen's gloom deepened, imagining orders being rapped out while she scurried about, scalding herself and burning everything else from sheer nervousness.

But her aunt knew how to cook, no denying it. The chicken was wonderfully tender and succulent, its stuffing flavoured with something tantalising Ellen couldn't identify. Cauliflower was cloaked in a rich cheese sauce; potatoes were golden and crunchy outside, fluffy within. At least she'd eat well while she was here – although losing weight might be difficult until she and Claire had their own place.

'It's delicious,' she said.

'Don't talk with your mouth full,' her aunt responded, but without the sharpness that had accompanied every other remark. Ellen gave up and ate hungrily, wondering if she dared ask for a lamp for her room.

'More chicken?' her aunt asked eventually. 'Another potato? More carrots?' and to every enquiry Ellen said yes please.

She waited until they'd both finished eating before venturing her request. 'Aunt Frances, I wonder if – would there be a lamp anywhere I could take for my room?'

Her aunt stared at her. 'A lamp? There's one on the locker. Didn't you see it?'

What locker? Could her aunt's mind have started wandering? She'd already got Ellen's arrival day wrong, and now she seemed to be imagining bedroom furniture where none existed. 'I didn't see a locker, just the bed, and a big wardrobe, and a chair.'

'Oh, for goodness sake – that's the wrong room!'

It was Ellen's turn to stare. 'You said beside the bathroom.'

'The *other* side! I meant the other side!'

Ellen felt a sudden flare of anger. 'Well, I wasn't to know that,' she said, as forcefully as she dared. 'I'm not a mind-reader.'

Dead silence followed. She'd overstepped. She decided she had nothing more to lose. 'Aunt Frances, I'm sorry. I'm grateful for your offer to keep me, but since I arrived I've been feeling that maybe you don't really want me here, so I can tell you that it won't be for long. A friend is moving to Galway soon, in the next few weeks, and we're going to find a flat together. If it's OK, I'll stay here until then, but I'll try to keep out of your way as much as I can.'

More silence followed. They regarded each other across the small table, and then her aunt gave a long sigh.

'Listen,' she said wearily, 'I'm sharp. It's my way. It comes out like I'm cross, but the only person I'm cross with right now is me. It's clear I made a mess of things. Your mother wouldn't have got the day wrong, so I was the one who muddled it, and you had to find your way through a city you don't know. I'm very cross about that, and I'm sorry that you felt I was annoyed with you. And then

I sent you up to the wrong room, and that was my fault too for not making it clear.'

'Well, maybe I should have—'

'But the thing about me,' her aunt went on, as if Ellen hadn't spoken, 'is I always speak the truth, and I'll own up if I make a mistake. I have no problem with you staying here – it makes perfect sense when I have the room. I expect you to help out a bit in the house, clean up after yourself and that, and I would be happy to teach you to cook, if you're willing to learn – but you're young, and you're out on your own for the first time, so you need to make the most of that too.

'Now,' she went on, pointing her fork at Ellen, 'I'm not your mother, so I won't be watching out for you. I'll give you a key and you can come and go as you please, as long as you show up in time for dinner when you're eating here and you don't wake me if I'm in bed when you get home. And if you get yourself into trouble – I think you know the trouble I mean – you needn't come crying to me. Is that all understood?'

'Yes.'

'Good. Now, have you anything to say, anything to ask me?'

Ellen searched for something, and found it. 'Your garden is beautiful. I'd really like to help out there, if you let me.'

There was a further small softening in her aunt's face. 'I would like that very much.' She set down her fork and put her hand out. 'Will we start again?'

Ellen, feeling slightly ridiculous, shook the offered hand – and the gesture, foolish as it seemed, brought a kind of change into the room. It felt like a settling, and the beginning of an understanding. Her aunt had opened her home to a niece she scarcely knew. Maybe she'd felt obliged, but she'd still taken Ellen in.

'Welcome to Galway,' she said now to Ellen. 'I hope you'll enjoy your time here.'

'Thank you.'

'And call me Frances – Aunt Frances makes me feel like a dowager in pearls.'

Ellen had to suppress a smile. Her aunt, still wearing her gardening clothes, a trace of earth faintly visible yet on her cheek, was as far from a dowager, pearls or no pearls, as it was possible to be.

Afterwards they washed up together, listening to the radio. 'Those men sound like girls,' Frances complained when the Bee Gees came on, and Ellen told her that her friend called them cats in a sack, and this prompted a sudden bark of laughter from her aunt, and more tension disappeared.

When the kitchen was tidy Frances brought her up to the bedroom that was bigger and brighter and altogether more inviting than the other. The bed, a double, was already made, and swaddled in a thick eiderdown. There was a wardrobe with lots of hangers, and a chest of drawers, and a small armchair in the corner.

And sitting on a bedside locker, along with a lamp, was a transistor radio. 'Is that for me?' Ellen asked.

'If you want it. It's old, but it still works.'

'I'd love it.' She could listen to Radio Luxembourg every night.

'And the other room is there if any friend wants to come for a night.'

'Thank you.' It wouldn't be needed, not once she and Claire were sorted.

'I leave the house at half seven in the morning,' Frances said, 'so make your own breakfast, and tidy the kitchen after you.'

'I will.' She wondered what work her aunt did: she had no

recollection of her mother mentioning it. That enquiry could wait for another day. Instead, she named the street the bookshop was on. 'How long should it take me to walk there in the morning?'

'Half an hour if you don't dawdle. I'll say goodnight then. Good luck with the new job – I hope it's to your liking.'

'Thank you.'

Left alone, Ellen opened her rucksack – and sitting on top was the package her mother had given her that morning, which Ellen had completely forgotten about. *To wish you well with the job,* her mother had said. Ellen pulled off the wrapping – and found, to her amazement, a Sony Walkman.

They'd cost a whopping two hundred pounds when they'd come out two years earlier, and she didn't imagine they'd got much cheaper in the meantime. She thought of the scrimping and saving it must have required for her mother to afford it.

She took the Walkman and its accompanying earphones from the box. She pressed buttons and opened the compartment to hold a cassette tape. She turned it over, this magical thing that allowed you to listen to your music wherever you went. Pretty much the best gift she could have been given – and it had come from her mother, of all people.

She thought of how things had been between them since the worst thing had happened, how she'd quietly shut her mother out, and how her mother had never challenged her on it. So much left unsaid, so much piled-up hurt and anger.

Leaving her this morning, it had been all Ellen could do to give her the briefest of hugs – and now here was this unexpected extravagance. What was she to make of it? How was she to respond?

She set the Walkman on the locker. She would get batteries for it tomorrow. She'd ask her sister Joan to find someone travelling to Galway and give them Ellen's box of tapes to bring along.

She would send a thank-you card to her mother. She couldn't move beyond that, couldn't consider the possibility of forgiveness. Not yet. Maybe never.

She switched on the transistor Frances had given her, careful to keep it low. She listened to Debbie Harry singing about a heart of glass. The reception was tinny, but she didn't care.

She unpacked, stowing her clothes in the wardrobe, arranging her shoes under the window. She shook the creases from the shirt and skirt she'd decided on for her first day of work and draped them over the wardrobe door.

The thought of the following day brought a return of her earlier excitement. She was here, she had arrived – and after a shaky start, she felt she could cope with living with Frances.

She was ready for whatever Galway had in store for her.

Bookshop

IT WAS SMALLER THAN SHE'D BEEN EXPECTING, wedged between a pub and a tobacconist on a street a few blocks back from the main thoroughfare. It was painted dark green, with the name spelled out in yellow above a single window that was full of books, most of which she'd read. Newspapers were stacked by the door, tied in bundles.

It was twenty minutes past nine. The walk from Frances' house had taken just under thirty minutes. An hour of walking a day should go some way towards burning off the calories of her aunt's dinners.

Closed, the sign on the door read. Should she knock? Was anyone inside? She caught sight of her reflection in the window. She jiggled her hair about, wishing as she always did that it wasn't quite so red. Why couldn't she have got Claire's mass of blonde curls?

As she bared her teeth to make sure they were free of lipstick, the door flew open, startling her.

'Hello there!'

She saw a sandy-haired man beaming at her. The sleeves of his white shirt were rolled, his jeans faded and patched. No tie.

'I spied you coming,' he said, thrusting a hand at her. 'Ellen Sheehan, I presume.'

'Yes.'

He didn't look any older than her. Surely he was too young to be a manager? His hand was warm, his clasp firm. 'Ben McCarthy, you're welcome. Good to have you on board.'

'Thank you.'

She felt tongue-tied, and acutely aware of how little she knew about working in a bookshop. She wondered how long it would take for him to realise this.

He held the door open – 'Go on in, I'll just grab these papers' – so she stepped across the threshold and gazed around at her new workplace.

It was perfect.

Narrow and meandering, with a low beamed ceiling and an uneven wooden floor whose broad boards were shiny with age. A third of the way down was a spiral staircase that climbed to an upper floor, and it was wooden too.

And everywhere she looked, there were books.

Covering the walls, stacked on tables, filling every space they could. Books as far as the eye could see. She inhaled her favourite smell, the heady scent of glue and ink and new pages not yet turned. She would never grow tired of that smell.

She felt the promise of stories and characters waiting to be discovered, and a smile came unbidden to her face. She was actually employed here. This was where she would spend all her working hours. She itched to explore the place further, to delve into all its nooks and crannies.

'You like it,' he said, jolting her out of her reverie. She had almost forgotten him.

'I love it. I love all bookshops, but this one's especially nice. How old is it?'

He dumped the paper bales onto a desk with a thump and began cutting their strings. 'Well, the building has been here as long as Galway has, but it's only been a bookshop for about eight years. Before that it was a shoe shop.'

She couldn't see it as a place where shoes were sold. It looked like it had been a bookshop since the beginning of time.

'Let me show you around before the others arrive. Staffroom up here,' and she followed him up the spiral stairs. The first door had *Manager* on it. 'My office, obviously,' he said as they passed, and again she thought him too young for the position.

The staffroom held a small table and four chairs, a fridge and a sink. A little window above the sink overlooked the street. Mugs were stacked on a shelf, along with a jar of instant coffee and a tea caddy. Teaspoons were propped in a mug. There was an electric kettle on the table.

He leant against the sink and crossed his arms. 'You have a fifteen-minute break in the morning, and another in the afternoon, and half an hour for lunch. There are just four of us here, including you. Jasper likes an early lunch, so he takes his at twelve thirty, and Edwin waits till one thirty because he starts work later. How does one o'clock sound for yours?'

'Fine.'

Jasper and Edwin. They could have come straight out of Dickens. Ellen should be called Dorrit, or maybe Estella, to fit in.

'The timings for the shorter breaks you can decide between yourselves.'

'That's fine.'

He jiggled at the window fastening. 'I have a confession,' he said. 'I may as well come clean.'

She felt a small prickle of alarm. Confession was rarely good.

He propped the window open and turned to face her again. 'I'm not really the manager,' he said. 'Well, I am, but I'm an accidental one. The real manager had a tumble on a mountain in Switzerland a few weeks ago and broke just about every bone in her body, so there's no knowing when she'll be back, or if she will.'

'Oh . . . that's awful.'

'Yes, poor old Muriel. She's not in any danger, apparently, just out of action for the foreseeable future. The owner, who runs his own shop in Dublin, persuaded me to take over in the interim, even though I only started here in January, but Jasper, who's been around a lot longer, isn't really manager material – you'll understand when you meet him – and Edwin is even newer than me, so I said yes, but I haven't a clue. I have no managerial qualifications. I'm literally making it up as I go along.'

His candour was disarming. She felt herself relaxing. 'As far as I can see, you're doing OK.'

'That's what everyone thinks. You were the first person I interviewed – I mean ever. I'm sure you guessed.'

She risked a small laugh, not sure if he expected her to be equally candid. 'It wasn't your typical interview,' she ventured. 'You didn't ask any of the questions I was expecting.'

He looked pleased, as if she'd complimented him. 'True. I decided I'd just look for a book lover.'

'Well, you found her. Was I the only one who applied for the job?'

'No, there were others. You just happened to be the first one I rang.'

So it had been a matter of blind luck. Any other reader would have passed his literary test as easily as she had. 'I did think it strange that you didn't ask for a reference.'

He grimaced. 'I forgot about a reference. See? No clue. I suppose I'm too late to ask for one now.'

'No, I'm sure I could—' She broke off, seeing his grin.

'Happy to take my chances with you,' he said. 'You look honest. Now I'd better go down and open up – and Jasper will be along any minute. Take your time, settle in. Your things will be quite safe in here: we're all trustworthy.'

Left alone, she peeked in the fridge and saw a half-full bottle of milk, and opened packets of Lincoln Cream and Marietta biscuits, and a sugar bowl and an apple, and a glass-topped butter dish with no butter in it. She was hanging her jacket and bag on a hook by the door when a man appeared.

'Oh – hello,' he said, stopping short on seeing her. Deep-voiced, forties or fifties, she wasn't sure. Dark hair above a face so completely bloodless it might never have seen the sun. Rumpled pinstriped suit, black shiny shoes. Tall, thin, solemn. Cradling a brown paper bag.

'I'm Ellen,' she told him, putting out a hand. His was shockingly chilly, given the mild weather. 'I'm starting today.'

'Yes, we were told. Jasper is my name. Pleased to meet you.' His words were slow and deliberate. A kind of earnest, melancholy air seemed to hang about him. 'I work in the storeroom at the back of the shop, unless I'm needed on the floor.' He made a small movement with his mouth, gave a little toss of his head. 'To be entirely honest, I'm happier out of the public eye, so I'm very glad you're joining us.'

Not manager material, Ben had said, and she could see what he meant. Probably ran the storeroom beautifully. Kept it as neat as a new pin, she guessed.

He deposited his brown bag in the fridge. 'Well,' he said, 'I'll be off then,' and disappeared. Ellen gave a last finger-rake through her hair, squared her shoulders and followed him down the stairs.

Ben was at the cash register, emptying coins into compartments. 'I man the desk until Edwin arrives at ten,' he told her, 'but once you've got the hang of it, I'll let you do this first half hour.'

'Right. By the way, what should I call you?'

'Ben's fine. We don't stand on ceremony here. Why don't you have a look around while it's quiet, familiarise yourself with the layout?'

She wandered about, taking it all in, trying to memorise where everything was. A children's section was brightly lit, the book-shelves painted in primary colours. A section of cookery books reminded her of Frances promising, or threatening, to teach her to cook. She wouldn't mind learning how to make a few dishes, handy for when she and Claire had to fend for themselves.

When she returned to the cash desk, someone was talking to Ben. They turned as she approached.

'Edwin,' Ben said, 'meet Ellen, our newest recruit.'

'Hi,' he said. 'Welcome.'

He looked about sixteen. Rumpled blond hair, casually dressed like Ben, and as smilingly cheerful as Jasper was lugubrious. 'Edwin will show you the ropes,' Ben told her. 'Pay attention: there may be a test – and if you haven't made lunch plans it's on me, a first-day tradition I've just made up.'

'No plans,' she said. 'Thank you.'

'Great, see you at one. Now I must go and pretend to be a manager.'

With a wave of his hand he made for the spiral stairs and disappeared.

She spent the remainder of the morning with Edwin, who she learnt was eighteen, and who had been working at the bookshop since he'd left school at the end of May. 'It's been great since Ben became manager,' he said. 'I mean, Muriel was OK, but she was a bit . . . official.'

'Why do you start at ten?' Ellen wanted to know, and he told her of his invalid grandmother who lived with them.

'Mum mainly looks after her, and Dad and I help out after work, but when Ben took over he said I could start half an hour later if it helped, so I give Gran breakfast now before I leave, and Mum gets a lie-in. And he didn't even reduce my salary.'

The accidental manager might be making it up as he went along, but he had also put his own stamp on the job by taking it on himself to make life easier for a member of staff, something Muriel hadn't done. And treating Ellen to lunch on her first day was a sweet gesture too.

He brought her to the pub next door, where they ate decent sandwiches and drank excellent coffee. 'I only ever have coffee when I'm out,' he said, stirring too much sugar into his. 'I'm rubbish at making the proper stuff, and I can't abide instant.'

He took a bite of his sandwich – 'cheese and more cheese' was what he had ordered – and then sat back, regarding her as he chewed, while she tried not to feel self-conscious under his scrutiny.

'Tell me,' he said eventually, 'about the typing pool. You've come from one, right?'

She was surprised he'd remembered, with no mention made of it during the phone interview. She described the job she'd taken after leaving school, and the stultifying monotony of it.

'What made you go for it, and why did you stay for two years?'

Good questions. She couldn't tell him the truth, that after what had happened she'd been aimless, hadn't seen any point in looking for anything better, hadn't felt herself worthy of being happy. 'Laziness, I suppose. Complacency.'

And then she'd seen his ad, idly leafing through the newspaper one evening, and she'd imagined working in a bookshop – and the thought had been so intoxicating, so tempting, that she couldn't think why it hadn't occurred to her till then. She would apply, before she died of boredom in the typing pool. She'd found her mother's writing pad and written on the spot, and posted it on her way to work the following morning, and here she was.

'Where are you living now?'

'With my aunt, just temporarily.'

'Good,' he said. 'Family connections, but not parental, so she can't boss you around too much.'

'No, she says she's not going to be responsible for me. I'm free to do as I please, as long as I'm not late for dinner – half past six on the dot. Oh, and as long as I don't wake her when I come in after a night out.'

'No falling up the stairs then. And do you know anyone else in Galway besides your aunt?'

'Just you so far – and Jasper and Edwin.'

'You won't be long making friends. So who's in your family?'

'A mother and a younger sister,' she said – and quickly, before he could ask about a father, she threw the question back to him.

'Two parents, one brother, one sister, both older than me. My brother's in his final year in UCG. He's the one with the brains.'

'What's he studying?'

'Law – and how to solve the problems of the world. He's a real activist, supports every cause going.'

'So you'll soon have a lawyer in the family.'

'Not that soon: he's planning to do some travelling when he graduates next summer.' He seemed about to say something else, but stopped.

'And your sister?'

'My sister's the eldest. She's a hairdresser, married with one little daughter. First grandchild on both sides, spoilt rotten by everyone, but a little poppet.'

'And are you from Galway?'

'I am – born and bred. Love it.'

'And do you live at home with your parents?' Immediately, she caught herself. 'Sorry – I'm being nosy.'

'Not at all, ask away. I was living at home until I was made manager, and then the owner offered me the tiny flat above the shop that nobody was using, and I said yes. It needed a small bit of smartening up – I gave it a few coats of paint and begged bits of furniture from various charitable souls, and it's basic but fine. I felt a manager should have his own place, to go with the prestige of the job.'

He was joking. Already she'd cottoned on to the impish expression, the barely suppressed laughter contained within it.

Yes, she would enjoy working with him.

Encounter

LATER THAT AFTERNOON, AS SHE WAS HELPING A
mother choose birthday books for her toddler twins, she became
aware of a figure hovering nearby. Waiting with a question, maybe.
When the woman had left, she looked at him enquiringly. 'Can I
help you?'

He advanced with a tentative smile. 'Sorry,' he said. 'Sorry for
staring.' He lifted a hand to sweep his long hair back. Softly spoken.
Tall. Around her own age. 'It's just – I might be wrong, but you
look like someone I used to know.'

She waited. He didn't seem familiar.

'You're not, by any chance – Ellen Sheehan, are you?'

She stared at him. 'I am, but—' She stopped. It wasn't – was it?
Could it be?

'Danny?'

He gave a wide smile. 'I thought I might be hallucinating.'

'I don't believe it,' she said.

Her best friend before they'd moved from their old town, living just
three doors from the Sheehans. It was surreal, seeing this grown version
of the boy she'd known so well, once upon a time. He was a full head
taller than her now – hadn't she always been the taller one?

'Wow,' he said, 'it's like time travel or something, isn't it? I can still see you with your hair in pigtails.'

'I never wore my hair in pigtails. You must be thinking of Joan.'

He laughed. She liked the sound of it. 'No, not Joan, definitely you. I used to pull them when you made me cross. Remember poking my chin dimple, just to annoy me?'

'Oh, I do. You hated when I poked it.' Still she was trying to reconcile him with the long-ago boy. The same person, chin dimple still in place, only all grown up now.

He folded his arms, narrowed his eyes at her. 'Now that I come to think of it, you were actually incredibly annoying.'

'So were you. It's a wonder we got on at all.' They stood there, taking in their adult versions as people walked around them.

'How long's it been?' he asked.

'Twelve years. We were eight.'

He was a week younger than her, so every year they'd had a joint birthday party on a day between the two dates, their houses hosting in turn. She'd forgotten that until now, hadn't given him a thought in so long. He'd been tucked away, along with the rest of her old life.

He gave a low whistle. 'My God. Twelve years. More than half our lifetimes.' A beat passed while that sank in. 'I hardly know where to begin,' he said. 'Have you lived in Galway long?'

'Moved here yesterday, started this job today. You live here too?'

'For now I do. I'm three years through a course in UCG, one more to go. Electronic engineering.'

'What on earth is that?'

'It's a new course. Basically, it's all about computers.'

'Computers? That's a surprise – you always wanted to be a vet.'

'A vet? I did not!'

'You did, or an explorer. You wanted to sail the seas like Christopher Columbus. You were going to build your own boat.'

'What? Now you're just making things up.'

'No, it's true.' She thought of something else. 'I wrote to you after we left.'

'And I wrote back, and I never heard from you again.'

'Oh, really? I'd forgotten that part. I suppose we moved on.'

'You moved on, you mean. Forgot your old friend in five minutes.'

'Sorry. I replaced you with a girl.'

'Typical.'

Already they were falling back into old familiarity. She liked his hair long. He looked like a fairer version of Neil Young. Amazing they'd both landed in Galway.

'We must have a proper catch-up,' he said. 'When do you finish?'

'Half five.'

'Could we grab a coffee then?'

'We could, in the pub right next door.' As long as she left by six, she'd be home for dinner.

'Great – see you there.'

Danny O'Meara, of all people. Wait till she told Joan. She wished she'd kept his letter.

'You're a natural,' Ben said at closing time. 'I made a good choice.'

'And you're a big improvement on my last boss. Miss Arthur never bought me lunch.'

'Now don't get ideas. I did make it clear that was a one-time occurrence, didn't I?'

'Very clear. I have no expectations.' She enjoyed his humour. What had seemed disconcerting on the phone was much better face to face.

'See you in the morning. Half nine sharp, or you'll never darken this door again.'

'Half nine sharp.'

Danny was waiting on a high stool in the pub. 'Coffee, or something stronger?'

'Coffee's fine, thanks.'

Time slipped by as they caught up. Sheila, his eldest sister, was married with a four-year-old daughter, and two other sisters were engaged and planning a double wedding next summer. His two brothers, both still single, were working on building sites in England. She used to envy his big noisy family, with him the youngest of the six.

'What about you?' he asked. 'How are your parents, and Joan?'

The question wasn't unexpected. He wouldn't have heard about what had happened. She said what she hated to say, what she avoided saying if she could, but there was no avoiding it now. 'My father walked out four years ago, the day after my sixteenth birthday. We haven't seen or heard from him since.'

His face fell. 'What? He just left?'

'Just left.'

'Are you OK?'

If anyone else had asked, she would have said she was fine and quickly changed the subject – but she wanted to tell him the truth. Sensed, even after all this time, that the truth would be safe with him.

'I'm . . . I try not to think about it. It was a huge shock for me and Joan. We had no idea it was coming. I mean, he and Mam had . . . drifted apart, I suppose, but it never once occurred to us that he might leave. He didn't say goodbye, just went one night after we were in bed. He left us a note that explained nothing.'

'Jesus, that's . . . And no contact at all since then?'

'Nothing, not even a letter or a phone call.'

He shook his head in sympathy. Would he have had any idea how close she'd been to her father, how much of a hero she'd considered him? Of course not – eight-year-olds didn't notice things like that.

'I blamed Mam,' she said slowly. 'I still do. I felt she pushed him away.'

He made no response, and she regretted saying it. He hadn't needed to hear that. 'I'm living with my aunt now,' she said, to change the subject. 'Mam's sister.' She told him about the previous evening, exaggerating the mishaps to make them funnier.

He knew where Frances' road was. 'Not too far from us, about half a mile.'

'Who's us?'

'Two pals from secondary school, both in college as well. We're sharing a house.'

'And how do you like student life?'

'Good. I'm enjoying it.'

'Met anyone nice?' she teased, and he grinned and said a few, and didn't elaborate. She thought he would be popular. Nice looking, good personality.

'If you have three years of college done, you started young.'

'I skipped fourth class in primary,' he said. 'Left school at seventeen.'

'Brainbox' – and he laughed, but he was. He must be. She told him about Claire, soon to join her in Galway. 'I'll start looking for a flat, once she lets me know when she can come.'

'I'll keep an eye out,' he promised. 'Spread the word.'

'Thanks.' She glanced at the clock above the bar and got up. 'I have to go – I've been warned not to be late for dinner.'

'I'll walk with you,' so he did, until their paths diverged at a roundabout. 'Come to the college some evening,' he said. 'We can have drinks in the bar – I can get you in as a guest. How's Wednesday night?'

'Perfect.' Any night was perfect, with no plans and nobody to make them with.

'Might as well meet you here – eight o'clock?'

'Fine.'

Unexpectedly, he stepped closer and bent to give her a swift hug, over before she had time to react. 'Amazing,' he said, 'to meet you again. See you Wednesday.'

His shampoo, or something, smelt of lemons.

She got home as Frances was setting the table. 'Sorry,' Ellen said, 'I meant to be back in time to help, but I bumped into an old friend and we got chatting.'

'Wash your hands,' Frances said, 'and fill the water jug. You can help another night. How was your first day?'

'Great. The shop is lovely. Have you ever been in it?'

'I have not. I get my books from the library. Cold chicken we're having, and a bit of salad.'

'Lovely, thank you. My boss took me out to lunch for my first day.'

'Well, that's a good start. And you met an old friend too.'

'He came into the shop. I knew him years ago – we were neighbours before we moved. Now he's in college here.'

'Small world,' Frances said.

Small world indeed. Danny O'Meara, of all people.

Friends

ON HER WAY HOME FROM WORK THE NEXT DAY SHE called Claire from a phone box, reluctant to ask Frances if she could use her phone. Not yet, not till they were better acquainted.

'How's the job?' Claire asked.

'Great. I love it.'

'How's the weird boss man?'

'He's lovely. He's our age, and not a bit weird.'

'Well, that's a relief. Good-looking?'

She considered. 'Not drop-dead gorgeous, but not bad.'

'Fancy him?'

She laughed. 'Claire Sullivan, you have a one-track mind. I'm too busy settling in to fancy anyone yet. But guess what – I ran into my old best friend.' She described her encounter with Danny and their arrangement to meet for drinks during the week.

'Forget your boss,' Claire said. 'This is much more promising.'

'Not Danny – he's like a brother. Anyway, he might well have a girlfriend.'

'So what? All's fair in love and war.'

'No, I wouldn't do that. You wouldn't either.'

'Course I wouldn't. What's your aunt like?'

'She's fine. I've told her it's just temporary, until you come up.'

'I miss you.'

'Me too. Danny is keeping an eye out for a flat for us.'

After dinner she worked for an hour in the garden with her aunt, digging bindweed from the herb patch while Frances talked.

'I'm the housekeeper in a family-owned country house hotel three miles out. Mornings only, Monday to Friday. I've never worked anywhere else – I started there as a chambermaid when I left school, and after that I was in the kitchen for years.'

'You were the cook?'

'Eventually. I worked my way up.'

'That must have been interesting.'

'It was demanding, and interesting too. I was on my feet all day, from breakfast to dinner, but I met some lovely people.' She shook earth from a weed root and dropped it into her basin. 'There was a man from Ghana working in the kitchen with me for a few years, Isaac his name was. He had a heart of gold, and so diligent.'

'How did he come to be living in Ireland?'

'His mother was an Irish missionary. When his father died she brought Isaac back here.' She chased a strand of bindweed and eased up the root. 'Anyway, when I turned sixty I decided I'd had enough and I asked if they could give me something part-time, so they made me housekeeper. I'm happy enough with it. It gives me more time in the garden.'

She stopped then and sat back on her heels. 'How are you getting on,' she asked, 'since your father left?'

Ellen teased bindweed from around a herb whose name she'd been told but had forgotten. 'We're managing,' she said, hoping Frances would leave it at that, but she didn't.

'Your mother is doing the best she can.'

The sisters must have talked about it in their weekly phone calls. Ellen's mother must have told her sister of Ellen's coldness towards her since the split, and Frances had taken it upon herself to fix it.

'I know you found it hard, but so did she, left with two teenagers on her own. It wasn't easy for her, having to find work again after years of staying at home to raise you and Joan.'

She hadn't had to find work: it had been handed to her. In the days that had followed her husband's departure, the parish priest had called to the house and spoken with her in the sitting room. *He's offered me a job*, she'd told the girls after he left. *He's chairman of the school board, they need a secretary*, and Ellen had hated that too, the thought that she'd been taken in out of pity by the very school, a boys' primary, where her husband had been principal. She was now the deserted wife, a charity case who needed help to support her daughters.

Ellen's father had left his job as well as his family. He'd left his entire life behind, and nobody from his side – his parents, his cousins – had made contact since then. It was as if he'd packed them up too, with the rest of his belongings.

'She's doing the best she can,' Frances repeated, and again Ellen ignored it. A short silence fell, but it didn't last.

'Growing up, she was different,' Frances said. 'Distant, moody. Wouldn't look at any of us some days, and none of us could figure out what we'd done. But we always made allowances: being the youngest she was indulged, so we'd say nothing and wait till she came out of it.'

Ellen sat back on her heels. 'Frances, I really don't want to talk about her. Can we please not?'

A beat passed. 'As you wish,' Frances said, 'but if the time comes that you want to know more, you can always ask me. Go in and get scissors from the kitchen drawer,' pointing to a clump of chives, 'and cut a few of those. I'm doing stuffed tomatoes to go with the fish.' And that was that.

After dinner on Wednesday Ellen made her way to the nearby roundabout, where Danny was waiting with two others.

'James and Fergus,' he said, 'my housemates.'

'You're the long-lost friend,' James said. Shorter and broader than Danny, curly dark hair, a beard on the way. Fergus was boyish, clean-shaven, brown hair past his shoulders. His T-shirt read *Get Up Stand Up* beneath a picture of Bob Marley. His jeans hung loose on his slight frame.

On the walk to the college they told Ellen that they were studying law, like Ben's brother. She asked if they knew a McCarthy student in his final year.

'Everyone knows him,' Fergus said. 'He's very active in the Students' Union, always fundraising for something. A few weeks ago he organised a big march against apartheid. It made the news.'

'I saw it on telly.'

'What's his brother like?' James asked.

'Friendly. Very nice.'

They were easy to talk to. They asked about the bookshop and said she must come to dinner at their house some night. 'We might even rise above beans on toast,' Fergus told her. It felt good to be out for the evening: shame Claire was missing it.

The college bar was small and plainly furnished, and full of students even on a Wednesday night. Ellen was introduced to a few more, male and female, and one of the girls perched for a while on James' lap, and Ellen wondered if they were together until she got up and wandered away again.

Everyone was drinking beer, which they told her was mandatory for students and which was all they could normally afford. She bought a round for her three companions, ignoring their protests. 'I'm in paid employment, I'm earning money,' she told them, although the employment hadn't actually paid out anything yet.

It was fun. Despite her non-student status she felt like she belonged, like she'd been accepted. At ten she got up to go, conscious of work in the morning, and Danny said he'd be off too. 'I have a nine o'clock lecture,' he said. 'I'll be sensible, not like these reprobates.'

'You should see him on a Saturday night,' James put in. 'He's the worst of us,' and Danny laughed and didn't contradict him.

'We should make this a habit,' he said on the way home. 'Wednesday-night drinks.'

'I'd like that.'

'I told my folks about meeting you. They said to say hello.'

'Tell them I said hello back.'

What did she remember of them? His mother smelling of apples, colour in her cheeks, hands warm in winter or summer, sending Ellen home with a wedge of cake or half a dozen homemade biscuits in a paper bag. His father, tall and dark-haired and grey-suited, worked in the post office. They'd had a blue car with a tartan rug on the back seat. Bit by bit, it came back to her.

She wondered if he'd told them of her father's departure. She didn't ask. At the roundabout he took her road, telling her he'd feel better if he saw her home. He hugged her again at Frances' gate. Light, quick, like the last one. 'Same time next week,' he said, and off he went.

The house was in darkness, no sound from within. She let herself in quietly and tiptoed up the stairs. Lying in bed, she heard rain begin to patter against the window. She closed her eyes, but still felt wide-awake. She hadn't slept through the night for a year after her father had walked out on them, and four years later she still had some broken nights. They would ambush her out of nowhere, and here came another.

She reached out in the dark and fumbled for the little transistor and switched it on low, and listened to Barbra Streisand singing about a woman in love.

Not yet, she thought. Still looking. Still hopeful.

Pub

'HELLO, STRANGER,' CLAIRE SAID, HOPPING OFF
the bus, flinging her arms around Ellen. 'You're a sight for sore
eyes.'

'Took you long enough to get here.'

'I know. Sorry. I had to practically donate a kidney to Dad before
he let me go.'

She wore a red coat Ellen hadn't seen before – 'on sale in A
Wear' – and platform patent boots that added three inches to her
height. Her eyes were ringed with black, her lipstick the same shade
of red as the coat.

She wasn't here to stay. This visit was just for the night. Martin
hadn't come home at the end of the summer as he'd promised,
opting instead to stay in London for as long as his job lasted, which
meant that seven weeks after her arrival in Galway, Ellen was still
living with Frances, and there was no way of knowing when Claire
would be free to join her.

It was a blow, but not the end of the world. She had a job she
loved, and Danny and his friends for nights out, and she and
Frances were getting on OK. She'd survive until Martin finally
showed up and freed his sister to come to Galway.

'So tell me,' Claire said, linking arms with Ellen as they walked to the bus stop, 'who we're meeting tonight.'

'Danny and his gang will be in the pub, and you'll meet others at the college disco.'

'Can't wait. And which man do you have your eye on, so I can leave him alone?'

'Nobody. None of them. You're welcome to any of them.'

'Oh come on – there must be someone.'

'There's nobody. I'm still biding my time.'

'What about Danny? Hasn't he made a move yet?'

'Claire, I told you, we're friends.'

Good friends, as close as they'd been before life had pulled them apart. Did she want it to change, to turn into something more? She honestly couldn't say. For now, she was happy as things were.

'Ellen Sheehan, you will die a spinster. And worse, a virgin.'

She'd heard it all before, many times. 'Biding my time,' she repeated, and Claire gave up.

At the house she presented Frances with the box of Black Magic she'd brought on Ellen's advice. 'Thank you so much for letting me stay the night. I've heard great things about you.'

'Have you.' There was a brief pause. 'Your skirt is very short.'

Claire laughed. 'Isn't it? It must have shrunk in the wash. I'm mortified.' Ellen had to bite her lip to stop smiling as she watched Claire pulling down the skirt, or pretending to.

Frances wasn't fooled. 'Don't come crying to me if you go home with pneumonia.'

'I'll keep my coat on all night,' Claire promised, and Frances made no response to that. She'd got the measure of her, Ellen thought. She saw the wildness in her friend, right from the start. Clever Frances.

After dinner they went upstairs to make Claire's bed and freshen up. In Ellen's room Claire pushed open the window and poked her head out. 'Just checking I'll know the one to throw pebbles at when I come home in the small hours.'

Ellen laughed. 'That won't be happening, because you'll be coming home with me.'

Claire pulled in her head. 'Say I meet someone, though.'

'But what if you don't remember the way back to this house?'

Claire pushed up a sleeve. 'Write the name of the road there,' she said, and Ellen found a pen and wrote it on her arm.

'Just stay safe.'

'I will of course. Frances is a howl, isn't she? The fierce looks she gives.' Claire pulled a small silver flask from her bag and unscrewed the top. 'Here, take a swig of that.'

'What is it?'

'Brandy, to keep the cold out.'

Fifteen minutes later they came downstairs giggling like school-children, and Ellen was relieved that Frances was already installed in the sitting room for the evening. 'Goodnight,' they called, and through the closed door they heard her response. Frances didn't take a drink, and Ellen wasn't sure what she'd make of them getting a bit tiddly before they even went out.

They pulled the front door shut and walked up the path. 'We need to be quiet coming in,' Ellen said. 'She'll be cross if we wake her.'

'We'll be like the grave.'

The pub where she'd arranged to meet Danny and the others, like many Galway pubs on a Saturday night, was filling up with students. Claire took off in search of stools while Ellen went to the counter. By the time Danny showed up alone, they were halfway through their second round of gins.

'Finally,' Claire said, getting to her feet as Ellen made the introductions. 'The mysterious Danny from Ellen's past.'

'Not that mysterious,' he said.

'Let me be the judge of that. What are you having?'

'I'll go—' but she planted palms on his shoulders and pushed him down onto her stool.

'You can go next,' she said. 'Keep my seat warm.'

She made it seem effortless, Ellen thought. She knew just what to say and do, and just how to look as she said it. *It's easy*, she'd tell Ellen, but it wasn't easy, not for everyone.

'Where are James and Fergus?' she asked Danny.

'On the way' – and as Claire returned they appeared with a few more, and in the ensuing reshuffle of seating Ellen found herself separated from Claire. By now the pub was properly full, people without seats standing in knots, talk becoming louder. Claire would be in her element, out for the night with nobody to answer to. Ellen would track her down before they left for the disco.

In what seemed like no time at all, another drink that she hadn't looked for appeared. 'From Danny,' Fergus told her. At some stage, she felt the room sway a little. When she needed the loo she stumbled as she made her way through the crowd. She cast around for Claire, but saw no sign. Could be anywhere.

After that, time took on a new and uncertain rhythm. Faces came and went before her, spatters of laughter erupted, cigarette smoke made her eyes sting. She caught snatched remarks that seemed to slide away before she could grab them. Someone was singing

'American Pie'. No, the entire place was singing 'American Pie', including her. Belting it out, making up words to replace ones she'd forgotten.

'Right,' a voice said, 'time to get you home.'

James, placing a glass of water in front of her. 'Here, take some of this.'

She looked around blearily and realised that the pub was emptying out. She had no idea what time it was. She could see no sign of Claire or Danny.

'They went off,' James said when she asked.

'Off?'

'Yeah, a little while ago.'

'Why didn't she wait for me? I have to find her.' The words slurred into each other. Her tongue refused to cooperate.

'Danny will look after her,' James said. 'She'll be fine. Drink some water.'

Suddenly it was all too much. 'I need to go home.' She struggled to her feet and fell back onto her stool, the room spinning, the world spinning. She grabbed the table to steady herself and the glass toppled, water splashing.

'Steady on,' he said, 'I'll take you home. Let's get your coat.'

Outside, the cold air hit her like a slap. She clung to him and he led her away.

Hangover

SHE WOKE WITH A POUNDING HEADACHE AND A mouth that felt like it had been carpeted during the night. She opened her eyes and lay still, afraid to move as she revisited the evening before, or tried to.

She couldn't remember coming home. She cringed to think people might have, must have, seen her in such a state. Imagine if she'd met Ben, or either of her other colleagues. It didn't bear thinking about.

She turned her head slowly and saw her jeans and top crumpled on the floor. She lifted the blankets and saw that she was still in her underwear. She felt under the pillow and discovered her pyjamas. Her alarm clock said 8.15.

She had no idea what time she'd got back. The room was freezing, her window still open from last evening. The curtains were open too. She climbed slowly out of bed, wincing at the stabbing pain in her head. She bent and retrieved her clothes, which stank of smoke. Grimacing, she let them fall to the floor again.

She'd drunk more than she should with Claire before – they'd often got giggly and silly – but this was a new level. This was blackout territory, and it was terrifying. Anything could have happened.

Claire. Where was Claire? She shrugged on her dressing gown and tiptoed out, planting a palm against the landing wall when the floor seemed to sway beneath her – was she still drunk? She eased open the door to the small room and saw an unused bed and the contents of a make-up bag strewn over the eiderdown.

Claire hadn't come back. It was morning, and she wasn't here. Where was she? Ellen sank onto the bed, head continuing to hammer, trying to push down a rising panic. The last thing she remembered was Danny coming into the pub, and nothing after that. Had they gone to the college disco like they'd planned? She had no idea.

In the bathroom mirror she looked at a ghost-white face, and mascara smudges, and hair all over the place. She removed her make-up with a hand that shook and gulped water from the tap and brushed her teeth twice. She ran a wet comb through her hair and pushed and pulled it until it was some way presentable.

Back in her room she dressed, telling herself that Claire was fine, she'd gone home with some man and fallen asleep. Or had she come back here at some stage and thrown pebbles at Ellen's window, and had Ellen slept right through it?

There was no sound from her aunt's room. Frances liked to sleep in on Sundays. Ellen hoped fervently that she wouldn't appear before Claire showed up. If Claire showed up. Of course she'd show up.

She pushed her feet into slippers and went downstairs, every step hurting her head. She opened the front door as quietly as she could, and saw the grass gone white with the first frost of autumn. She walked to the gate, shivering, and looked up the road, as if simply by wanting it badly enough she could conjure up her friend coming towards her, but the place was deserted.

Back in the kitchen she filled a glass with water and gulped it down, and made tea. She sat at the table and sipped the hot liquid, trying to think what to do. Should she hang around here and wait for Claire or go out and try to find her? But she had no idea where to look.

Would Danny know where she'd gone? She couldn't ring him, their house had no phone, but he was only ten minutes away. She'd walk there, just to feel like she was doing something. If Claire came back in the meantime she'd have to concoct a story for Frances, which she was well able to do.

Ellen got into her jacket. She slung a scarf around her neck and jammed Frances' dark green knitted hat on her head and opened the front door again – and there was Claire coming up the path, pink-cheeked from the cold, rubbing her hands.

'Oh good,' she said cheerfully. 'I was hoping I wouldn't meet auntie. I'd kill for a cuppa – I'm frozen solid. Jesus, I was so drunk last night. You must have been as bad.' She walked past Ellen into the house.

'I can't remember half of it. I had visions of you wandering around Galway, looking for this house.'

'Not at all – you wrote it on my arm, remember?'

'I'd forgotten that.'

'I told you there was no fear of me.' She made for the kitchen. 'Come on, let's get that kettle on before I get frostbite.'

'There's tea made,' Ellen told her. 'Where were you?'

Claire took a mug from the draining board and filled it. 'You want some? You might need to boil the kettle again.'

Ellen took it to the sink. 'Where did you spend the night?'

Claire poured milk, yawning. 'With Danny. I think I told one of his pals to tell you. I need to brush my teeth so badly. Is Frances up yet?'

'No – shh.'

Claire and Danny. Her two friends had spent the night together.

'He's sweet,' Claire said. 'I can see why you like him. Any toast?'

Claire and Danny.

They were adults and free spirits. They could sleep with whoever they wanted. Ellen wasn't interested in him that way, she'd said so to Claire. Just friends, she'd said.

After breakfast they went out, the day having softened a little, the frost melted away. Still no sign of Frances. Staying out of their way, maybe. Letting the young people have their space.

Or maybe too mad at Ellen, if she'd woken her last night. She felt a creeping sense of dread and wished she knew.

'I'll bring my bag,' Claire said, 'so we won't have to backtrack.' At her insistence, Ellen brought her into the city centre to see the bookshop – closed on Sundays, of course – and then they wandered around until they found a café that was open, and sat with coffees and sugar doughnuts. 'For the hangover,' Claire said, biting into one.

She didn't act like she was hungover. Ellen wrapped hands around her mug, still feeling rough. 'Will you meet Danny again?'

Claire licked sugar from her fingers. 'Probably not. A bit too soft and gentle for me.' She looked at Ellen. 'You're not mad at me, are you?'

'Of course I'm not mad.'

'You're acting a bit funny.'

'I'm hungover, that's all. Never give me alcohol again.'

'Never' – but at four, when the pubs reopened after the holy hour, she dragged Ellen into one. 'To warm us up,' she said, ordering two hot ports. They drank them by a roaring fire, and Ellen began to feel slightly more human.

'Tell Frances I'm sorry I didn't get to say goodbye,' Claire said as the bus pulled in at the station. 'Do you think she knows I didn't come back?'

'I don't know.'

'I probably won't get up again anyway – Dad hates having to replace me.'

'We'll just have to hope Martin comes home soon.'

'He'd better.' She gave Ellen a hug. 'Thanks for having me. See you soon.'

Back at the house, Ellen found Frances tipping potatoes from a saucepan into a colander. 'Your friend is gone.'

'She is, I just left her at the bus station. She said to say thanks.'

'Wash your hands and you can make a start on the carrots. You had a good night?'

'We had.' Ellen pushed up her sleeves and reached for the bar of soap by the sink.

'I heard you coming in,' Frances said, returning the drained potatoes to the saucepan.

'Oh.' Ellen felt her face reddening.

'You made a bit of noise on the stairs.' She shook the saucepan so the potatoes tumbled about.

'Sorry. I had too much to drink. Sorry, Frances.' She dried her hands and found the carrots.

Frances opened the oven door and took out the roasting dish with the chicken in it. She tipped in the potatoes, and Ellen heard little sizzles as they hit the hot fat. Was she going to tell Ellen that she'd have to find somewhere else to live?

'I had to get up for the toilet a bit later,' she said, closing the oven door with a smart click. 'I looked in to check that you were both home.'

Ellen's heart dropped. She'd seen Claire's empty bed. She opened her mouth to speak and closed it again, having nothing to offer.

'She got back safe so,' Frances said.

'She did. She spent the night with . . . some friends I introduced her to.' It sounded like the evasion it was.

'Did she.' The way she said it left Ellen in no doubt that she knew Claire had gone off with someone. It didn't take much intelligence to figure that out, and Frances had plenty of intelligence.

'Be careful,' Frances said, putting two dinner plates on top of the cooker. 'Be careful of her, Ellen.'

'What do you mean?'

'I know she's your friend, and I can see she likes her fun. Just make sure she doesn't get you into any trouble.'

'Trouble?'

'By association, I mean.'

Ellen gathered up the ribbons of carrot peel and threw them into the bin. 'I know she can be a bit reckless, but I was glad to have her when my father left. I didn't handle it well, and she . . . looked out for me.'

'That's good, that's what friends are for, but you have to be your own person, Ellen. Know your own mind. Don't do anything you don't want to do, just because someone else is doing it, and calling it fun. That's all I'll say.'

Maybe looked out for Ellen wasn't entirely accurate. Claire had happily gone along with her various rebellions, covering for her when she bunked off school, supplying the cider they drank in the park behind the shopping centre on weekend afternoons, praising the shoplifting Ellen had briefly indulged in. And Ellen *had* been glad of her, glad to have an ally while she lashed out at a world that had stopped making sense.

'I hear James got you home on Saturday night,' Danny said when they met on Wednesday at the roundabout.

It was news to Ellen. She cringed at the thought of them talking about her and how drunk she'd been. 'I was pretty bad.'

He grinned. 'Don't worry, we were all pretty bad. It was one of those crazy nights.'

He made no mention of Claire. She wondered whose idea it had been to go back to his house. Maybe the decision had been mutual, the logical conclusion to an evening of flirting.

It didn't matter to her. It didn't matter in the least.

Break

SHE WAITED WHILE HE MADE HIS TEA. IT WAS MID-way through November, a few weeks after Claire's visit. The staffroom window was tightly shut against a biting wind. A pathetic two pounds Ellen had lost since arriving in Galway, thanks to Frances' dinners. Just as well she had the walk to and from work every day.

'I've been thinking,' she said when he'd settled across the table from her.

'Thinking is good,' Ben replied. He'd taken to joining her for her morning break, saying he hated to drink alone. He reached for the sugar bowl and she caught a whiff of his aftershave, a salty under-tone to it that always put her in mind of the sea. Today he was in her favourite check shirt, olive green and maroon and chocolate brown. By now she was acquainted with all his shirts.

'I think we should start a weekly children's storytime,' she said.

He scratched his chin. He always did that when he was thinking. If he was impatient, he pulled on an ear. 'A children's storytime. Interesting. Are you offering?'

'Well, I've never done it, but I'd be happy to give it a go.' She took a Lincoln Cream from its pack before remembering that she'd sworn off them. She dunked it in her tea. One wouldn't kill her. 'When I started school there was a library close by, and our teacher would bring us there for storytime every Friday. I loved it.'

'We were never brought anywhere from school, too bold. I don't know how our first teacher survived us. Poor Mrs Dolan.'

'She should see you now, bookshop manager.'

'Chancing his arm, she'd say, and she'd be right.'

When he smiled, the left side of his mouth tilted up, lending a delightful mischief to his face. Boyish mischievousness. She imagined him aged eight, shinning up neighbours' apple trees or ringing doorbells and racing away.

'The children's section is pretty small,' he said. 'Would we have the space?'

'Oh, I think so – little children don't take up too much room.'

He crunched on a biscuit. 'Age group?'

'I'd say three to six.'

'Duration?'

'Not sure. Maybe half an hour? Might have to be trial and error.'

'OK. I'll have a think.'

They clicked. They worked well together. She was very fond of lovely Edwin – who wouldn't be? And Jasper had his own shy charm – but with Ben, she felt perfectly in tune.

He was a year older than her. His star sign was Scorpio. He'd had curly hair as a young child. He detested the texture of tapioca. Every day she learnt a little more.

He checked his watch and got up. 'Right, back to the lion's den.' He left his mug in the sink as he always did, knowing she'd wash it.

She didn't mind. A manager had to have some perks.

Post

Dear Ellen

I hope you're keeping well. All is fine with me, but three of the teachers are out with a bad flu, along with several of the children – it's doing the rounds, so I hope I don't catch it. I suppose it's not surprising, with the cold weather we've been getting. Make sure you wrap up well when you go out, especially if you're still walking to work – the early mornings can be chilly. Yesterday we had very heavy rain, I don't know if Galway got it too. There was flooding on the Limerick road.

I hope the job is going well. You didn't seem that happy in the typing pool, although you never said very much about it. Frances tells me you're a great help to her, and I'm sure she's glad of the company too.

She mentioned Claire Sullivan was up for a night before Halloween. I was surprised to hear it. I thought you might have cut ties when you left for Galway, especially as you're probably making lots of other friends now. I see her mother got a new car. I don't know the make but it's red, and a little flashy for my liking. They must have money to burn with that pub.

You'll be sorry to hear John Dalton died on Thursday. He hadn't been well since the summer. He'll be missed around the place, always out on the bicycle, even after he turned eighty. There was a good turnout at the funeral. That house will be up for sale now. It needs a lot of work, but it has the bay window and the converted garage.

This house is very quiet during the week without you and Joan. It's good to have Joan at the weekends. She's hoping to find a job here in town when she graduates next summer. It'll be nice to see you too, when you're able to take a break. Pity you don't have Saturdays off.

I'll stop now and get this into the post. Drop me a line when you get a chance. It would be nice to hear your news.

Mam

Ellen read it through, her face expressionless.

I thought you might have cut ties when you left for Galway. She hadn't a clue. Wait till Claire finally made it here.

It's red, and a little flashy for my liking. It was a Toyota Starlet, Claire had told her. Hardly flashy.

It's good to have Joan at the weekends. The only reason Joan went home every weekend was to see Seamus.

Ellen had written to her mother twice since moving to Galway. The first had been to thank her for the Walkman; the second, a month later, had contained nothing of any consequence. Job going well, making friends, Frances nice, weather changeable.

Her mother's letters arrived every two weeks. She dropped this one into the wastepaper basket in her room.

She'd write back next week, or maybe the week after.

Theatre

'I WON TWO TICKETS TO *RIDERS TO THE SEA* FOR Friday night, if you fancy coming along,' Danny said.

'I'd love it.' She'd never been to a play – her only theatre outings had been pantomimes as a child, sometimes with Danny. 'How did you win them?'

'A raffle that your boss' brother was running for the Vietnam boat people. First thing I ever won.'

It was December. They were in the college bar for their usual Wednesday drinks. They'd missed just one week since they'd started, when Danny had gone home for the mid-term break. They met other times too, at the disco Ellen sometimes turned up for on Saturdays, or at his house for dinner, or a game of Trivial Pursuit. There were always other people around then – this would be their first time going out alone.

It wasn't a date. You couldn't call it that. He'd won the tickets; it was pure chance. They might hug on meeting and parting, she might wonder sometimes what he'd be like as a boyfriend, but there was nothing more to it. He'd never asked her out, and he wasn't doing it now. Still, the following night she changed into her favourite dress, and the boots she hadn't been able to resist.

'You look nice,' Frances said. 'Enjoy yourself.'

'It's only Danny.'

'I know it's only Danny. You can still have a good time. Put on a scarf, you'll catch your death.'

They met at the roundabout. She smelled toothpaste when he leaned in for the usual hug. She tucked her arm into his for warmth as they walked. 'So who'll be at home for Christmas dinner?' Her words came out in soft clouds that drifted away.

'Everyone. My brothers are coming from England, and Sheila will be there with husband and daughter – they went to his folks last year – and Connie and Nora are threatening to bring the fiancés. It'll be bedlam, but my mother's thrilled.'

'I'm sure she is. You'll have a great day.'

'How about you?'

'Oh, just me, Mam and Joan – and Seamus, Joan's boyfriend, will show up after dinner with a bottle of Baileys. Very exciting.'

She said it lightly but he squeezed her arm, and she knew he was thinking of her father not being there and guessing how she felt about it. Their fifth Christmas without him.

'I won't see you for a while,' Danny said. Tomorrow he was going home for the holidays, and in January he was beginning three months of work experience in a computer company in Dublin.

'I'll miss our Wednesday nights,' she said, 'and the rest of it.'

'Me too. It's been fun getting to know you again.'

They walked easily together, their paces similar. He wore a blue woolly hat she hadn't seen before and a fur-lined denim jacket she knew well. She *would* miss their nights out.

The theatre lobby was warm and bustling. Smartly dressed people milled around, everyone looking happy and expectant. 'You want a drink?' Danny asked. 'We have a few minutes.' But she shook her head so he went off in search of a programme. As Ellen was leafing through it a bell rang to summon them to the auditorium. They climbed the stairs to their balcony seats and settled in, and after a few minutes the lights dimmed.

A hush spread then, conversations halting until all was silence. Ellen took in the set, the interior of an old Irish cottage. Table, dresser, fireplace with kettle suspended, spinning wheel. A cough sounded loud in the dark silence. It felt like they were poised on some brink.

The play began, and from the opening lines of dialogue she was transfixed. This was no panto; this was something with its own kind of magic. This was a story with life breathed into it. She sat enthralled until the curtain came down, and then she got to her feet with the rest of the audience as the cast took their bows, trying to pull her head from the little cottage with all its sadness, and move back to reality.

'Thanks so much,' she said as they filed down the stairs. 'That was amazing.'

'Glad you enjoyed it. Let's get a quick drink on the way home – a hot whiskey to keep the cold out.'

'Good idea.'

His arm rested lightly on her back. Looking at them, a person would assume they were a couple. They got to the lobby and shuffled with the crowd towards the exit – but upon reaching the door they saw rain pelting down outside, streetlights reflected in the wet stone.

'Damn,' Danny said. 'Looks like we'll have to find a taxi.'

'Let's give it a few minutes; it might lighten off.'

'Ellen?'

She turned to see Ben – a jolt of recognition – with a woman she didn't know. He introduced her as his sister Ruth. 'This is the Ellen I was telling you about,' he said.

'I escaped for the evening,' Ruth confided, and Ellen remembered the little niece Ben had mentioned. A poppet, he'd called her. She introduced Danny, and the four of them regarded the rain.

'Looks like it's here to stay,' Ruth remarked. 'Are you driving?'

'No – we walked. We're going to get a taxi.'

'I have a car,' she said. 'Sit in with us.'

'We're fine—'

'Come on, it's no trouble. We're just around the corner' – so the four of them hurried to the car, with Danny being dropped first. No hot whiskey after all, and no chance for Ellen to react to the kiss he gave her – a soft brush of her cheek, no more – before he opened his door and got out.

'I'll drop a line,' he said, 'when I'm landed.'

'Do. Happy Christmas. Good luck in Dublin,' and he was gone. On the way to Frances' house she told Ben and Ruth about their early friendship, and their years apart. 'We ran into each other again, just after I started in the bookshop.'

'Stranger things have happened,' Ruth said. 'Is this your road?'

'Yes, just up here on the left.' The rain hadn't been there to stay after all; now it was gone, and the moon shone down on the wet street.

Ben got out of the passenger seat and opened her door. 'I've been thinking,' he said. 'We should do a storytime for Christmas, to kick-start it. Ruth said she'd come and bring Sadie, so at least you'll have an audience of one.'

'She'd love it,' Ruth called from within.

'I thought you'd forgotten about it,' Ellen said. She'd almost forgotten her offer herself.

'Not in the least, just other things getting in the way. It'll have to be Saturday of next week, to give us time to get the word out.'

'Last Saturday before Christmas. People will be busy.'

'Let's give it a shot anyway. We'll need a poster for the window. Can you do it?'

'I'm not sure . . . I could word it, but I'm not arty. My lettering mightn't be great.'

'Let's do it together – between us we should be able to come up with something presentable. Could you stay on for a bit after work on Monday? I'll buy you a bag of chips to say thanks.'

She feigned shock. 'What – no overtime?'

He thought. 'You can come in half an hour later on Tuesday.'

'Deal.'

Lying in bed that night, she arranged the poster wording in her head. *Christmas Storytime at Piles of Books* as the heading. Eleven o'clock would be a good time. She'd wear a Santa hat if she could find one. She could read the sweet story of the little girl who met Santa that she'd been leafing through the other day.

And they could give out little goody bags as the children left. A colouring book, a box of crayons. Maybe a bag of jellies.

This is the Ellen I was telling you about. He'd been talking about her.

Dinner

AFTERWARDS, LONG AFTERWARDS, SHE THOUGHT, *That was where it began. That Monday night was where we started.*

'Come with me,' Ben said, appearing in the staffroom at closing time, a rolled-up chart under his arm. 'The table in the flat is bigger.' He led the way up a narrow steep staircase to the building's top floor and opened a door.

'My kingdom,' he said, and she entered a slope-ceilinged, white-walled room that held a trestle table and two chairs, a fridge and a glass-fronted press. A hotplate with two rings sat on the table, a kettle and a small saucepan perched on top. In the press she saw a cereal box, stacked cans, a tea caddy, a bowl of oranges, a bag of sugar.

And also in the room were books, lots of books. Piled on top of the press, stacked on one of the chairs. Towers of books, some climbing almost to waist height, were lined up by the far wall.

He unplugged the hotplate and transferred it to the top of the fridge. 'I have a bedroom and a bathroom too, and a laughably small sitting room that I ignore.'

He unrolled the chart and spread it on the table. He took markers and pencils from his pockets and pushed up his shirtsleeves, even though the room felt a little chilly to Ellen.

She produced the wording she'd written out. 'Does this sound OK?'

He scanned it. 'Fine. What's the free surprise?'

She explained her goody-bag idea.

'Great. I'll leave you to organise that. Take money from the kitty.'

'OK – and I thought I'd write a letter from Santa and bring it in to read to them.'

'Wonderful.'

'And maybe we could offer a discount on the book I've chosen, just for that day? I could announce it at the end.'

'Go on, why not? I'll order in a few extra copies – remind me tomorrow. So how do we do this?'

'We'll need a ruler,' she said, 'and a rubber.' He thumped down the stairs and got them from his office, and she ruled faint pencil guidelines on the chart. They stood side by side looking down at it.

'You go first,' he said. 'You do the heading.'

She took a marker and held it poised. 'I'm afraid I'll mess it up.'

'I'll start so' – but his spacing was off, and he ran out of paper halfway through *Books*. He made another trip to his office and came back with a fresh chart.

'You go this time,' he said, and she added more guidelines to contain each word, but when she'd finished it looked too cramped.

'We should drop the heading,' she said, 'and just go with *Christmas Storytime*,' so he found a third chart.

'Let's write it in pencil first,' she suggested, 'to be on the safe side,' and after much rubbing out it was all set down and correctly spaced.

'You go over it in marker,' he said.

'Why me?'

'Because of the two of us, you're slightly less terrible.'

'That doesn't exactly inspire me with confidence.'

'Go on, you'll be grand' – so she worked cautiously with the marker and got to the end, and stepped back to check it.

'Oh no,' she said.

A dark smudge in the lower corner. She checked her hand and saw the marker stain on the side of it. 'Sorry,' she said, and went to wash her hands in his bathroom while he got another chart.

By the time the poster was finally completed, an hour had gone by. 'I'm in need of a lie-down,' he said, rolling up the rejected sheets. 'Talk about trauma.'

'No lying down before you get me the bag of chips I was promised. I told my aunt not to include me for dinner.'

'Ah yes, the chips. Right, I'll dispose of these and meet you at the front door.'

He didn't get her a bag of chips. He brought her to a little restaurant on the next street and she ordered chicken and he ordered fish, and as they ate, he told her he'd done two years in college before dropping out.

'What were you studying?'

'Science. Bad choice, wasn't for me. I'd like to go back some fine day and do what I should have done.'

'What?'

'Don't laugh. I play a bit of piano, so I'd like to see what a music degree might feel like.'

'That sounds great – but why wait? Why not go now, when you're young?'

He shrugged. 'Things to do, promises to keep – and I'd rather not ask my folks to fund it, after I wasted two years of fees. It'll happen eventually, though, when the time is right, and I can pay for it myself.'

She told him about Joan studying to be a teacher.

'You never considered college yourself?'

She hesitated. How much should she tell him? 'I thought about it in school, but . . . well, our circumstances changed.'

'Sorry,' he said immediately. 'You don't have to tell me any more.'

But suddenly she found she wanted to. 'I don't mind. My father walked out when I was sixteen, and after that, well, I . . . lost interest in college and got a job instead.'

'Tough,' he said, and she saw the sympathy in his face.

'But I'm happy now, so it's fine.'

'Glad to hear it.' He topped up their wine glasses, and she was glad too that he hadn't made a big thing of it.

Towards the end of their meal a woman at a nearby table gave a sudden little cry, and they turned to see her companion on one knee by her chair. They watched as he took a small box from his pocket, and they saw her put hands to her face as he opened the box, and they watched her eyes fill with tears as she nodded wordlessly, and they clapped along with the other onlookers as he placed the ring on her finger and kissed her to seal the deal.

And Ellen saw that they were oblivious to the rest of the room, and she thought, yes, yes, this, and felt her own tears threaten, and blinked them away. She turned back to see Ben watching her and was embarrassed. 'I'm a softie,' she said, laughing.

He smiled. 'You're a romantic. Nothing wrong with that.'

They finished their main courses. When she turned down an

offer of dessert he called for the bill. 'So,' he said, 'where will Ellen Sheehan be in ten years? Any dreams you want to fulfil, like me and the piano?'

To be married, she thought. *To be married and in love and happy.* She searched for something that sounded a little more practical. 'Actually, I wouldn't mind trying to write a book sometime.' She waited for him to laugh.

He didn't. 'Fiction?'

'Yes, definitely fiction. I enjoyed creative writing in school.'

'So what's stopping you?'

'I suppose I'm nervous. What if I try and fail?'

He propped elbows on the table. 'What if you try and don't fail? What if Ellen Sheehan was born to write?'

She laughed. 'I suppose the idea terrifies me. It can't be easy, writing an entire book.'

'Probably not – but if you really want something, it's worth a try. And look at all the people who tried and didn't fail.'

'True.'

He tipped his head to the side and gave her that considering, narrow-eyed look she had come to know. 'I think we should make a pact, you and me. You have a go at a novel, and I'll give a music degree my best shot. Deal?'

'Deal.'

'Shake,' he said, and she shook, hoping nobody was watching.

He held on to her hand. 'Any questions?'

'Are we putting a time limit on it?'

'Let's just say when the time is right. Promise me you'll try.'

'I promise.'

Afterwards, he put her into a taxi. 'I can walk,' she said.

'No you can't, it's too dark.' He paid the driver, again ignoring her protestations. 'See you in the morning, half nine sharp.'

He'd forgotten he'd said she could come in later. She didn't mention it. Probably would have gone in at her usual time anyway – and he *had* paid for dinner, and her taxi home.

After that, she was aware of a shift in her awareness of him. She took to studying him when he wasn't looking. She memorised all the features of his face – the splotch of black in the iris of his left eye, the pupil bleeding into the hazel. The eyelashes a shade darker than the sandy hair on his head. The front tooth that projected slightly in front of the other. The two small pale freckles on his nose, another beneath his right ear.

She recreated them in her head, conjuring up his face as she lay in bed each night. She fell asleep to the remembered sound of his voice.

He appeared in the children's section just before the start of the Christmas storytime. He gave a short welcome speech and handed over to Ellen before disappearing – and halfway through, something made her look beyond her audience, and she saw that he'd returned and was propped against the wall, a half-smile on his face as he watched. Their eyes met for an instant, and his smile broadened into a grin, and she had to pull her attention back to the story and try to forget he was there.

Yes, that was where it began. The night of the poster.

Christmas

'NICE TO HAVE YOU HOME,' HER MOTHER SAID. 'You've lost weight.'

'Just a few pounds.'

'Your hair is getting long.'

'I'm letting it grow.'

'Still biting your nails, I see.'

'I'm trying to give up.'

There was no depth to their conversation, just a ping-pong of remark and response. They might have been casual acquaintances sitting together in a doctor's waiting room, forced into polite small talk. *She's doing the best she can*, Frances had said – but what good was her best now, after she'd been responsible for the departure of the parent Ellen had loved more? There was no getting past that.

Still, she must try, if only for Frances' sake. 'I'll cook dinner some night,' she said, 'if you like.'

'Frances said she was teaching you. That would be nice.'

Christmas Day came and went precisely as she'd expected it to. Eggs and bacon for breakfast – their father would make French toast on Christmas morning, the only dish he'd mastered – followed by mass. The usual invitation to Seamus' house afterwards for coffee and his grandmother's mince pies.

'You're enjoying Galway?' Seamus' father asked, and Ellen replied that she was.

'Met anyone nice?' the grandmother enquired.

'I've met lots of nice people,' Ellen replied, ignoring the image of Ben's face that popped into her head.

'Anyone special?' the older woman persisted, and her daughter, Seamus' mother, told her not to be so nosey, and Ellen, colouring, said no, nobody special.

'Plenty of time for that,' Ellen's mother put in. 'Your mince pies are as good as ever, Pearl,' and the subject was dropped. Ellen caught her eye for an instant and gave her a tiny nod of gratitude.

They ate dinner back at home, in the late afternoon as usual, with gifts exchanged after the plum pudding. Scarves from their mother to her daughters, earrings from Joan to Ellen. Ellen gave books to both, Agatha Christie for her mother, Margaret Atwood for Joan. Seamus turned up as they were opening a box of Milk Tray to dip into while they watched *It's a Wonderful Life*.

Next day the phone rang, and Joan went out to the hall to answer it. 'For you,' she said to Ellen. 'Danny O'Meara.'

'Just thought I'd give a ring,' he said. 'Nice to hear Joan. How did yesterday go?'

It was the first time they'd spoken since the night at the theatre over two weeks ago. He must have found her number in the phone book – was it still in her father's name?

'It went fine,' she said. 'Same as usual. How was your day?'

'Just as bedlam as expected. I never want to see turkey again. When do you go back to work?'

'Wednesday.'

'Four more days – not much of a break.'

It was plenty of a break for Ellen. It was more than enough. 'Are you all set for Dublin?'

'Nearly. I had a good time,' he said, 'at the play. Shame we didn't get to have that drink after,' and she remembered the kiss that had brushed her cheek before he'd got out of Ruth's car.

'There'll still be drink in Galway when you're back,' she said, and he agreed that there would be, and shortly afterwards she heard his mother's voice calling him to dinner.

'Happy New Year,' he said. 'See you in 1982.'

'Happy New Year. Hope Dublin goes well.'

'So, you and Danny,' Joan said when Ellen returned to the kitchen.

'What about me and Danny?'

'Well, he's ringing you here, so I'm assuming you're more than just friends. That was definitely fate, bumping into him again.' She was making a turkey sandwich, buttering bread, laying slices of meat on top.

'Can't he ring me as a friend?'

'I doubt it,' Joan said, dipping a spoon into the cranberry sauce jar. 'Only a matter of time. If we hadn't moved house, you'd prob-ably be engaged to him by now.'

Ellen felt a dart of anger. Just because her sister was all sorted with Seamus, she was the expert on love. 'You're making a lot of assumptions, and none of them are right. Danny and I *are* just friends.' The swift kiss flashed into her head again; she nudged it away.

Joan cut her sandwich in half. 'Have it your own way.'

After dinner Ellen walked to Claire's house, located next to the family pub on the corner of the town's main street. Claire answered the door already wearing her red coat, temporarily freed from nights behind the counter by Martin's return from London for Christmas. 'Let's do a pub crawl,' she said, pulling the door closed behind her.

She hadn't been back to Galway since her first visit. Ellen had mixed feelings about it. On the one hand she missed her friend; on the other, she didn't want to give Frances any more reason to distrust Claire. Probably best to wait till Martin finally came home, and they could move on with their own plans.

They sat by the fire in Doherty's Bar, a group of old men at the counter checking them out over their pints. 'Has Martin given you any idea when he's coming back?'

'Summer, he says. He wants to give it a year. I've told Dad I'm leaving then, even if Martin stays in England. I'll be twenty-one in February – there won't be a thing he can do about it.'

Summer seemed so long away, with winter hardly halfway through. Then again, living with Frances was no problem at all. Living with Frances was infinitely preferable to living at home.

She'd flatly turned down Ellen's tentative offer of rent from her first pay packet – 'I wouldn't dream of taking money from family!' – so Ellen quietly replenished toilet rolls and firelighters and washing powder before they ran out, and slipped various foodstuffs into kitchen cupboards, and if her aunt noticed, no mention was made.

Thanks to Frances, she could now name flowers and herbs with confidence. She knew when to prune and how to deadhead, and which plants thrived in shade and which needed light and sunshine, and it was thanks to Frances too that she was finding her feet in the kitchen.

They did crosswords together – or rather, Frances called out clues and Ellen guessed wildly, and usually wrongly, leaving most of the solving to Frances. Ellen borrowed Frances' big bicycle on her days off to explore the Galway countryside. When rainy Sunday afternoons made gardening impossible Frances made a cake, and put half into an old biscuit tin for Ellen to take into work on Monday morning.

Over the months of living together they'd grown closer, finding a wholly unexpected friendship that Ellen was grateful for.

'Hang on,' Claire said. She went to the counter and spoke with one of the old men, and came back with a lit cigarette.

'I thought you'd given up.'

'I have, I just fancy the odd one.' She propped her feet on a rung of Ellen's stool. 'Guess what: I have a new plan for us.'

Ellen regarded her warily. Claire with a plan could be dangerous.

'Stop looking so scared. I just think we should move to London in the summer.'

Ellen stared at her. 'London? What's wrong with Galway?'

'Nothing's wrong with Galway, but London would be bigger and brighter and more exciting. I'm sick of Ireland. I want real adventures.'

London. A whole other country. It would mean giving up a job Ellen loved, having to start all over again in a new place, saying goodbye to Ben and the others, and leaving Frances. 'But I'm settled in Galway now. I like it. I have friends there, and my job is there.'

'Oh, come on, it's not as if London's at the other side of the world. And you'd get another job no problem: I'm sure it's full of bookshops. At least think about it. Think of the craic we'd have.'

'I know . . . but accommodation could be expensive.'

'So what? We'd both be working.'

The idea didn't appeal to Ellen. She was happy in Galway, happy to make it her home for the foreseeable future. She had no appetite to uproot herself, even for a while.

Claire stubbed out her cigarette and drained her glass. 'Come on, this place is dead. Let's go to Casey's, it'll be a bit livelier. Look, just think about London, OK? Don't rule it out.'

Ellen finished her drink and pulled on her coat. 'I won't rule it out,' she said, but in her head she already had.

Falling

THE MORE TIME SHE SPENT WITH HIM, THE MORE Ellen felt herself drawn to Ben. They never ran out of conversation. They talked about books, and swapped books, and argued about books. They compared notes on films that had come from books. Their tastes in modern music were similar, apart from Supertramp (she loved, he didn't) and The Doors (he loved, she didn't).

On the Mondays she brought cake to work, he complained. 'You want to turn us into Billy Bunters.'

'Nobody's making you eat it' – but he always did, and usually came back for more, telling her they couldn't insult her aunt by ignoring it.

He teased her about her confessed crush on Dustin Hoffman. 'You could hang a poster in the staffroom,' he said, and she told him she'd think about it.

She produced fresh copies of crosswords that she and Frances had already completed and innocently beat him to every answer. He threatened to teach her chess, so he could get his own back. When she took him up on it he produced a chess set the next day and began, each lunchtime, to coach her.

And she would watch his hands as he moved the pieces, and

she would try hard to concentrate on what he was saying, but his hands . . . his hands bewitched her.

And every so often, she would come up with a new idea for the shop.

'Secondhand books.'

'Secondhand? How would that work?'

'Customers could return ones they'd bought – in perfect condition, and with their receipt – and get a small discount off their next purchase.'

'I like it, but where would we put another section? We're completely full.'

'Not sure, but it's worth thinking about. You'd be selling the same books twice.'

'Definitely worth considering. I'll put my lateral thinking cap on.'

And another day: 'How about special offers tied to occasions?'

'Go on.'

'Discounts on all books by Irish writers for a few days around St Patrick's Day, and on American novels for the fourth of July or Thanksgiving. Things like that.'

He thought. 'Discounts on books that have been adapted for the screen in the run-up to the Oscars.'

'Yes – and what about a free draw around the time of the Booker? The prize would be the winner, obviously.'

'Genius.'

He sought her out one day as she was leafing through picture books, trying to choose a story for the following Saturday.

'I've just had an idea,' he said, 'about where we could put the secondhand books. Come and see.' He caught her arm and led her to the spiral staircase. 'Here,' he said, indicating the underside of the steps. 'I've got a carpenter pal who might be able to make some kind of shelving to project from them. It wouldn't be very big – we could only use the middle section, half a dozen shelves – but it's better than nothing. What do you think?'

She looked at the boyish eagerness in his face. Her arm tingled where he had caught it. She wasn't sure – could it be a hazard, would people risk bumping into projecting shelves? But she couldn't bring herself to dampen his enthusiasm. 'Great idea,' she said, and he rushed off to phone the carpenter.

Next day he brought a magazine to the staffroom. 'Help me out with this,' he said, flipping pages till he found what he wanted. '*I'd love to win a year's subscription to* Time *magazine because . . .*' He looked up. 'Finish it in ten words or fewer. Something snappy.'

She'd seen competitions like that. There had been one on the back of the Weetabix box when she'd been home for Christmas. Six cars to be won, just by finishing a sentence with the right words. It hadn't occurred to her to enter.

She thought for a minute. 'What about *because I could really use some free Time?*'

His face lit up. 'Brilliant!' He pulled a pen from his pocket and scribbled. 'Capital T on time?'

'Definitely.'

'I knew you'd be good at these things. If it wins, I'll up your wages.'

It won – and true to his word, her pay packet swelled by a fiver a week. From then on she entered every similar competition she came across, and she won a cuckoo clock that she and Frances hung in the kitchen, and a box of biscuits that she brought to work, and a red sweater that she passed on to Joan, and a woolly hat that she saved for Danny's return to Galway.

'I take full credit,' Ben said. 'You'd never have started this lark without me.'

'I owe it all to you,' she agreed. 'I do give you lots of ideas for the shop in return, though.'

'True.'

It was the start of April, just on closing time. They were in his office, she having brought up the day's takings. He tipped back his chair as he often did, even though she'd told him it terrified her to see it, imagining him toppling over and breaking his neck.

'I'm afraid to say you're wasted here in case you leave, but you should be in marketing. You've got the perfect brain for it – and you're a whizz at the snappy slogans, so you could work an idea up into an ad no problem.'

'Well,' she said, 'something to think about.'

The notion of getting paid to come up with ideas all day was intoxicating, and also daunting – what if they didn't come? What if her brain refused to cooperate? – but she couldn't imagine leaving the bookshop. Leaving him.

She would look at the back of his neck when he bent to retrieve a book from a lower shelf, and she would want so badly to reach out and touch the soft hairs that grew there. If their fingers brushed when they were engaged in a common task – pricing up new books, say, reaching together into the box that held them – she would burn. He was all she thought about when they were apart. He filled her dreams when she slept.

And now and again, maybe while they were sitting over the chess board, he would look up and hold her gaze, and she'd think he was about to say something, and then he wouldn't – and she would wish with all her heart that he would. Because she felt, she was convinced, that her feelings were returned. All she needed was a word from him.

Did it matter that they worked together? Not in a bookshop, surely. And it wasn't as if he was older and might be seen to be using his position as her superior to take advantage. She knew from Ruth that he was single: *my bachelor brothers*, she'd called her siblings once, chatting with Ellen after a storytime. There was nothing that could be seen as an obstacle.

The world with him in it was beautiful. She loved everyone, not just him. At work she went out of her way to help customers. She conversed and laughed with regulars, returned fallen toys to chubby hands, shushed babies while mothers browsed. Love made her a higher-voltage version of herself, spreading goodwill wherever she went.

She brought little treats home to Frances: a bag of favourite mints, a pocket book of crossword puzzles, a box of notecards. She even took to writing more regularly to her mother, although her letters remained formal and remote.

She was the clichéd heroine of every love song, every mushy, slushy film, every romance novel. She imagined them making a life together, opening a chain of bookshops in . . . Paris: why not? Three children they would have, two sons who would inherit their father's sunny disposition, a daughter who would adore him as Ellen did. Readers, of course, every one of them. The most contented family there ever was.

One word from him. That was all it would take for her happy ever after to begin.

Declaration

HE'D CUT HIS HAIR: NOW IT SKIMMED HIS shoulders. His jacket was new.

'Not new,' he told her when she admired it. 'Got it in the Dandelion Market, a huge warehouse full of hippies off Stephen's Green. Clothes, antiques, record players, paintings, furniture, you name it. And buskers.'

'Sounds great.'

It was after Easter, and they were back in the college bar, their first Wednesday night since his return from Dublin. No Fergus or James this evening, so it was just her and Danny.

'How was the job?'

'Great. They've offered me full-time work if I get the exam results.'

'Danny, that's wonderful. Will you go for it?'

'I sure will. They're one of the top computer companies in the world.'

'Funny that you chose that degree. I mean, I know you're the expert, but computers seem so complicated, and so huge. What exactly is the attraction?'

He laughed. 'They're the future, Ellen. They might be big and awkward now, but they're getting smaller and smarter all the time, and it's so exciting to be involved at the start like this. Everyone will have a computer soon – wait and see.'

'You mean every workplace?'

'I mean everywhere. They'll be in every home. They'll change the world.'

She doubted this, but said nothing. There had been a photo in the paper not so long ago of one in California, completely dwarfing the men in white coats who stood before it. They'd want to get a hell of a lot smaller.

'So what did you bring me from Dublin?'

'Nearly forgot.' He reached into a pocket and drew out something wrapped in tissue paper. 'For you,' he said, 'from the market.'

'Oh God – I was joking! You didn't have to bring me anything!'

'But I did. Open it.'

It was a cameo brooch, peach on cream. 'That's really sweet. Thanks so much.' She pinned it to her shirt. 'You shouldn't have.' She told him about the woolly hat she'd won and earmarked for him that she'd forgotten to bring along.

'Ellen,' he said then, and the way he said it told her what was coming. She'd known it was coming, hadn't she, ever since the barely-there kiss before Christmas? And then the phone call to her home, and the few calls since then from Dublin to Frances' house. She'd known, from the things he almost said, that he was waiting to return to Galway so he could say them face to face.

And maybe, if there was no Ben, she would have been glad to hear them.

'Danny—'

'Hang on,' he said, 'just let me say this,' so she listened as he spoke of feelings that had developed since they'd met up again, feelings he'd only realised were there in December. 'I mean, we got on so well, it was like we picked up where we'd left off, and I just thought it was great to have my old friend back – but I know now it's more than that. For me, anyway. It's more than friendship, Ellen.'

She had to stop him. She put a hand on his. 'Danny,' she said again, and he must have heard something in her voice, because he stopped.

She searched for the kindest words. 'I'm sorry,' she said. 'I'm really sorry. You mean the world to me, I love that you came back into my life, and I hope I'll never lose you as a friend again, but . . . I just think we might ruin what we have if we try to make it something more and it doesn't work out.'

It was lame, she could hear how lame it sounded, but it was the best she could do.

She couldn't mention Ben, not with nothing declared between them. She hadn't told anyone, even Claire, of her growing feelings for him, in case they weren't returned. 'I'm sorry,' she repeated, and he shook his head and said no, don't be, he was glad of her honesty. He looked anything but glad.

They limped along for another while, as she prattled about the storytimes in the bookshop, and Joan's exams before Easter, and the basil in Frances' garden that the slugs had eaten, and he threw in a few comments along the way, but she could see how she'd dampened his spirits, and it was awful to see.

Afterwards he walked her back to the roundabout and hugged her as usual. 'Same time next week?' she asked, and he said sure, but she knew it wouldn't be the same between them after this, and there was nothing at all she could do about it.

Disclosure

'LET'S GO TO LUNCH TODAY,' BEN SAID. 'MY TREAT, next door. There's something I need to talk to you about.'

For once he wasn't smiling. His expression was thoughtful, unreadable. Instantly she was alarmed: had she done something wrong? For the rest of the morning, as she went about her usual tasks, she cast back to find anything he might have objected to, but nothing came to her.

It was the last week of May, the days long, the weather softening finally after a bitterly cold spring. The racking cough that had plagued Frances for over a month was drying up at last. Joan had got good results in her Easter exams.

Claire remained set on London, despite Ellen's continuing reticence. *July*, she'd said on the phone two nights ago. *Martin's finally coming home. He says he can have a word with his landlord, see if we can rent his flat. You'll love London, Ellen – wait and see.* Claire never took no for an answer, but this time she might have to.

Lunchtime came. They took a table in the corner of the pub. Ellen ordered a salad sandwich she didn't want, and coffee she did.

'So,' Ben said, tenting his fingers, then deciding against it and placing his palms on the table. He seemed ill at ease. Again she puzzled over possible wrongdoing on her part.

'OK, right. So, here's the thing. The thing is—'

He broke off as their coffees arrived. He waited until the barman had left. 'My brother,' he said then. 'Rory, in UCG. I've mentioned him.'

His brother? He'd brought her here to talk about his brother?

'He's in his final year. I think I told you that.'

'You did.' The activist, he'd called him. Supporting every cause he could find. Where was this going?

'I mentioned he was planning to travel after he graduates.'

'. . . Yes.' He had. She'd forgotten that.

There was a little pause. When he spoke again his voice was gentler. 'The thing is, Ellen, I'm going with him. It's all arranged, it's been arranged for ages.'

She stared at him, the information dropping like a stone inside her, plummeting down like a broken lift shaft, yanking all her hopes and dreams down with it.

She found her voice. 'Oh,' she said. 'You're going too – that's . . . good. Nice for him, to have company.' Over-bright, horribly false. Fixing a smile, or a grimace trying to be a smile, on her face. 'How long will you be away for?'

He hesitated. 'A year. Possibly more.'

No. No. No.

She gave up trying to pretend. She let the smile, or whatever it was, slide off her face. She pushed aside her coffee, the smell suddenly nauseating her.

'Ellen,' he said, and the sound of her name, so softly spoken, was more than she could take. She sank her head into her hands and let the tears fall silently.

'Look at me, Ellen.'

She couldn't look at him.

'Please,' he said. 'Ellen, look at me.'

She drew in a ragged breath. She lifted her head, tears still streaming. If he hadn't been sure how she felt about him up to this, he knew now.

'I'm mad about you,' he said, so quietly she just caught it. 'You must know that. I've been mad about you for ages, but I couldn't act on it, not when I knew I'd be going away. I couldn't . . . start something I wouldn't be here to continue.'

He sighed, ran a hand through his hair. 'God, this isn't – this wasn't supposed to happen. I can't back out now, Ellen. I couldn't do it to him. He's got nobody else. I mean, he knows lots of people, but he's never been good at making friends.'

She stopped listening to the words. They didn't matter. Nothing mattered now that he was going away. She took another shuddering breath, tried to swallow the lump in her throat. He looked deflated, defeated. Not a trace of his usual merry smile.

'When?' she managed.

'First of June.'

Less than a week away. She felt a fresh wave of despair. He was leaving her, leaving Galway for who knew how long.

'I'm sorry, Ellen,' he said. 'I'm so sorry. Our timing is rotten. I'm going to say it to the other two this afternoon, but I wanted to . . .

I had to tell you first. Muriel isn't coming back, but there's a new manager starting next week.'

She sat there, swiping at tears that continued to fall silently. Their sandwiches arrived. 'Could you pack them up?' he asked the barman as she blotted her face with a serviette. 'We have to go.'

At the door she halted. 'Can I have the rest of the day off?' She must look a fright – crying always left her blotchy. She couldn't face going back, couldn't work in the shop all afternoon as if nothing had happened.

'Yes, of course. Ellen, I'm sorry. Here, take your sandwich—' but she'd already turned away, not wanting food, unable to listen to any more, needing to be alone so she could make sense of this, or try to.

She walked without purpose, her only objective to get far from the bookshop. She ended up in a park she passed on her way to and from work. She found a vacant bench and sat hunched, feeling utterly miserable. Today was Wednesday, tomorrow her day off. On Friday she'd have to go back to work and endure two days with him, pretending in front of the others that nothing was wrong, when everything that could be wrong was wrong.

Wednesday. Drinks with Danny. She couldn't, not tonight.

She rummaged in her bag and found one of the crosswords she and Ben had done together. She scribbled on the back.

Danny, sorry, not feeling well, will skip drinks. Next week, hopefully – Ellen x

It was three o'clock. She prayed he wouldn't be home from college. She hurried to his house and posted the note through the letter-box, relieved that nobody came out at the sound. She made her way back to Frances', where she found her aunt arranging lupins in a vase.

'A headache,' Ellen told her. 'I'm going to lie down. Count me out for dinner.'

Frances gave her a searching look. 'Has something happened?'

'No' – but she knew something had. Frances didn't miss things. Ellen spent the rest of the day curled in bed, her book for once unopened.

At some stage, Frances tapped on the door and appeared with a steaming mug. She looked down at Ellen's tear-stained face. 'Chicken soup,' she said, setting the mug on the bedside locker. 'You don't have to tell me what's wrong if you don't want. But whatever it is, it won't last. Things never last, Ellen. They really don't.'

She was wrong, of course. This would never stop hurting. Never.

Sorrow

WAITING FOR SOMETHING TERRIBLE TO HAPPEN, SHE discovered, was every bit as hard as dealing with its aftermath. Struggling through Ben's last two days in the shop, she was reminded of her devastation in the wake of her father's departure. The mammoth effort it required to appear cheerful at work left her drained. She wanted and didn't want to see him, to be around him, knowing that every minute was bringing their parting closer. They kept up their normal banter in front of the others, but underneath she was in pieces. She avoided the staffroom during her breaks, inventing errands that kept away the danger of being alone with him.

She caught Edwin studying her now and again. Sensing something, she was sure, but nice enough not to pry. Jasper seemed oblivious during his brief appearances on the shop floor.

On his last day Ben closed the shop for an hour in the middle of the day and took the three of them to lunch in the pub, and they presented him with the pen they'd clubbed together to buy. *Safe travels*, they'd had engraved on it, Jasper's idea. Ellen forced herself to eat, to smile, all the time wishing to be anywhere else.

At closing time she hung back as Edwin and Jasper shook his hand and wished him well and left. When they were gone, Ben turned to her. It was the first time they'd been alone since his announcement.

They regarded one another wordlessly for what felt like an eternity. Her heart was beating so hard it hurt. 'I want . . .' she said, and stopped.

'Ellen,' he said, and broke off too. She crossed on trembling legs to where he stood by the door and locked it, and turned the sign to *Closed*. She switched off the lights, and the narrow low-ceilinged space dimmed, lit now only by what daylight came through the small window. She reached for his hand and he gave it.

'I want to be with you,' she whispered, and in response he pulled her away from the doorway and took her in his arms and kissed her, a kiss that started softly and grew in fervour until she drowned in it. They clung to each other, mouths exploring hungrily, bodies pressed together. Her blood pounded, desire rising until she could bear it no longer. She drew back, her breathing ragged, and saw the same hunger in him.

'Are you sure?' he whispered, and she said yes, and he brought her upstairs, and up the next stairs, and into his small bedroom, where they undressed and climbed beneath the covers of his bed.

'Your first time?' he asked and she nodded, and he was gentle and loving, and it wasn't his first time, and they murmured the words of all lovers, and she cried, and she thought he did too. And it didn't hurt as much as she'd been expecting, and the wonder of skin on skin, the touch of him, the scent of him, filled her and left room for nothing else. There was nothing else in the world but them.

'I'll write,' he said afterwards, but she said no, she didn't want that. She couldn't be the chain that kept him tied to Ireland. She couldn't spend the next year or more clinging to hope, waiting for something that might never happen. She'd done that with her father; she couldn't do it again.

'Let's leave it open,' she said. 'If we meet again, so be it. If not . . .' she found a smile from somewhere '. . . we were never meant to be.'

He squeezed her hand. 'No letters?'

'No letters.'

It had to be this way. It nearly killed her, but it was the only way she could survive.

She got dressed. He pulled on jeans and a T-shirt. Downstairs they left the shop lights off so passers-by wouldn't see. 'Wait,' he said, rummaging behind the cash desk for something that he slipped into her pocket. 'Open it when you get home.'

He unlocked the door. He squeezed her hand, put his other palm to her cheek. 'Don't forget me,' he said, and she wanted to wail aloud. She pulled away and rushed out and didn't look back.

She was late for dinner. Frances had already started. Ellen walked into the kitchen and sat across from her at the table and burst into tears, and Frances listened as Ellen sobbed out her heartbreak, leaving unsaid the final scene in his bedroom. When she'd run out of words and run out of tears, she propped her elbows on the table and held her hot, damp face in her hands.

'Sorry,' she said, 'your dinner's getting cold.'

In response, Frances rose and crossed to the cooker. She took a tea towel and drew from the oven a plate and set it in front of

Ellen. 'Careful, it's hot.' She lifted the saucepan lid that covered it, and the rich smell of shepherd's pie wafted up.

'Eat,' Frances ordered, and Ellen picked up cutlery and ate what she could as Frances resumed her own meal. When they had finished, Frances took their plates and set them on the draining board and returned to the table.

'Heartbreak is horrible,' she said, 'but everyone goes through it, and the world keeps on turning, and in time it becomes less hard to bear. You don't believe me now, but you'll see I'm right. I wish I could stop it hurting for you, but I can't. Only time can do that.' She got to her feet. 'Come on, let's wash up.'

'Can I make a phone call? Just a quick one.' Her first time to ask.

'Of course you can.'

She dialled the number of the pub. It wasn't yet eight, it wouldn't be crowded.

'I'll go to London,' she said when Claire answered. 'Let me know when I need to give notice.'

Later, in her room, she opened what he had given her. It was a little hardback notebook, its cover dark green with a flowery print. *To Ellen, for the book ideas*, he'd written in blue ink on the flyleaf – and below it, *All my love, B xxx*

She put it under her pillow. She waited for sleep, and eventually it came.

Leaving

'IT'LL BE GOOD FOR YOU,' FRANCES SAID. 'TRAVEL broadens the mind. I'd like to have seen a few different places, but it wasn't done in my day, not for women anyway. You'll always have a bed here if you need it.'

'Thank you, Frances. I'll miss you.'

'Come and see me when you're home on holidays.'

'I will,' Ellen promised.

'London?' her mother said, frowning. 'What put that into your head? I thought you liked the bookshop.'

'I did . . . I just felt like a change.'

'But you know nobody in London.'

Ellen let a beat pass. 'Claire's coming too.'

Her mother regarded her in dismay. 'Oh no – I was hoping you'd get away from her.'

Ellen smothered a stab of anger. No point in fighting now, not when she'd be gone soon. 'I know you don't like her, but she's my friend. We'll be fine.'

No comment. 'It'll be far more expensive than Ireland. I can't afford to pay London rent.'

'You won't have to – I have savings. I'll be OK till I get sorted with work.'

'Exciting,' Joan said, 'but mind your bag on those underground trains. Seamus' cousin had her wallet taken last summer – it was so crowded she hadn't a clue who did it.'

'Big change,' Danny said. 'I hope you'll still make my graduation.'

'Of course I will. I've said it to Frances.'

They'd managed to paper over the cracks his approach, and her rejection of it, had caused. They still met up on Wednesday nights, and often at the weekend too, and if she sensed a new small caution between them, she figured they'd get past that too, in time.

She hadn't told him about Ben. She'd told nobody apart from Frances. It was too raw to talk about, the wound still too open to probe.

'Every good wish,' Miss Fogarty said when Ellen was finishing up on her last day at work. Miss Fogarty was Ben's replacement, a very different kind of manager. Nothing accidental about her, with her tailored suits and clipboard. No discounts on books at any time of the year, and no secondhand section either: she'd soon put a stop to that.

'Take care,' Edwin said, looking mournful. 'Drop in anytime you're back in Galway.'

'Some fine bookshops in London,' Jasper said. 'Very fine indeed.'

Ellen intended to visit them all, every single one, particularly Marks & Co. at 84 Charing Cross Road, the one she most wanted to see. Helene Hanff's book had prompted lots of tears.

In the last week of July she turned twenty-one. Two days later, she and Claire took the Magic Bus to London

NOTTING HILL, LONDON
JULY 1982
THE SECOND MOVE

Flat

IT WASN'T INSPIRING.

A smell of onions hung in the air of the small living room whose sole item of furniture was a battered brown couch. It was set into a bay window, which let in plenty of light at least. A kitchenette ran along the opposite wall, a counter in front of it.

A windowless shower room had dark spots high up on the walls and half a toilet roll on the floor.

The two tiny bedrooms held nothing but a wastepaper basket in one, with a balled-up tissue in it. The wall between the bedrooms was paper-thin.

'Technically,' their landlord said, 'it's an unfurnished flat, but your brother and his friend left the couch behind, so you're in luck.'

'Fantastic,' Claire said. She'd told Ellen that Martin and Pat O'Connor had found the couch on a skip and hauled it back to the flat. Ellen wondered if there were things living in it.

'There's a launderette and a corner shop on the next street, and a big outdoor market on nearby Portobello Road. You'll get everything you need there, from furniture to kitchen things. A lot of it is secondhand, so you won't have to spend too much. You're late for it today, but you can go tomorrow.'

He told them he'd lived in nearby Hammersmith for the past thirty years. He looked in his fifties to Ellen, with thinning brown hair and a pale complexion, and an air of weariness about him. The fingers of his right hand were stained yellow. Even on this mild day he wore a coat.

'Down to business,' he said. He gave them a rent book and took their first month's payment, along with the same sum as a security deposit. Bring cash, Martin had said. He only deals in cash. Given the minuscule size of the flat, the rent seemed astronomical to Ellen. They'd better find work fast.

The landlord told them about the Notting Hill Carnival, held every August bank holiday. 'Two days of Caribbean music and dancing, parades and floats, loads of different stalls, gets huge crowds. You'll love it. Just out of college, are you?'

'That's right,' Claire said. 'Art college. Dress design. We're working on a collection for London Fashion Week.'

She was so very good at not telling the truth. After he'd gone, leaving them his phone number – 'only in case of emergencies' – and promising to see them next month, they gave their new home a more thorough investigation.

The bay window overlooked a rather pretty street. The flat was on the top floor of a three-storey terraced house, situated roughly in the centre of a long sweep of houses, all painted different pastel shades. There were six doorbells by the main front door. They'd already discovered that the bell for their flat – number 6 – didn't work.

A drawer in the kitchenette held three forks and two knives, a bent teaspoon, a can opener, a corkscrew and a bottle opener. There was a single saucepan and a frying pan in another drawer.

No sign of a kettle, toaster or bread bin, but on a shelf sat half a dozen intact pint glasses, with various pub names etched on them, and a pair of Tottenham Hotspur mugs, one missing its handle.

'Easily known lads lived here,' Claire said. 'At least we have a cooker.' She opened the oven door. 'That'll be fine with a good scrub.'

'The shower works,' Ellen said. 'We just need a new curtain.'

'I love the bay window.'

'Me too – and it'll be easy to heat a room this small when the weather gets bad.'

'We can stock up tomorrow at the market.'

There was a pause.

'We're in London,' Claire said. 'We're living in London. We're young and free and single. We can do exactly what we like.'

Despite her weariness after fifteen hours of travel and little sleep, Ellen felt duty bound to find another positive. 'We have a roof over our heads,' she said, 'and the location is good.'

'Come on,' Claire said, 'we need to eat. Everything else can wait.'

On the way downstairs they met a trio coming up, two galloping little boys of about four and six, and a woman in a brightly patterned dress and matching turban calling after them to slow down. She smiled an apologetic hello at Ellen and Claire as she passed them. The little boys stared briefly at them before resuming their headlong rush upstairs.

They followed Martin's directions to a street with lots of pubs. The grub is great in pubs here, he'd told them, and not too dear. So many skin shades, Ellen thought as they walked. So many forms of dress, so many different languages and accents in the snatches of conversations they heard. She wondered if the entire city of London was as colourful as Notting Hill.

She thought of Sherlock Holmes and Oliver Twist and Mrs Dalloway and Mary Poppins and Paddington Bear, all walking the London streets of her books. She thought of Dickens and Chaucer and Austen and Trollope, literary giants who had trod the same cobbles that she and Claire would tread.

In London, she would heal. In London, she would forget him.

They found a pub called The Laughing Lion, busy and noisy and smelling of food. They ordered fish and chips and two large glasses of red wine. They raised their drinks.

'Here's to our London adventures,' Claire said, smothering a yawn.

'And the fantastic jobs we're going to get tomorrow.'

'And our many, many love affairs.'

No more love affairs, Ellen thought. *Not for a long time.*

When they got back to the flat there was a plastic box by their door with a note on top. *Welcome to our building*, the note said, *from Jada, Ace and Delroy in number 5*. The box held squares of a deliciously soft, crumbly coconut cake that they washed down with tap water in wine glasses.

'I think I'm going to like it here,' Claire said.

Claudia

THE OUTDOOR MARKET WAS A MASS OF TRADERS and shoppers, and vast enough for Ellen to feel slightly overwhelmed – but it certainly sold everything they needed. By the end of the day they'd made several trips back to the flat with their purchases, including two single mattresses that the trader had rolled up with string. *On your heads,* he'd said, *only way,* so they'd trudged back feeling foolish, although nobody paid them much attention. At least, Ellen thought, they wouldn't have to sleep top to tail on the awful couch again – just as well they'd been too exhausted to care.

Their first dinner in the flat was poached eggs on bread – they'd forgotten a toaster – after which they returned to the pub of the night before. They sat at the counter and Claire ordered drinks before asking the barman if there were any jobs going.

'The manager isn't here,' he said. 'She'll be in tomorrow.' He looked younger than them, but his sideburns were impressive. 'You got a number?'

'No, I'll come back. What are her hours?'

Next morning Ellen left Claire scrubbing the oven in Notting Hill and set off on her own job hunt. She'd start locally, see if she could find any bookshops within walking distance.

Two blocks from the flat she came across her first one, located between an off-licence and a premises that called itself Notting Hill Sandwich Bar. As she pushed open the door of the bookshop, a sudden cry made her turn to see a load of packages tumbling onto the path from the arms of a dark-haired woman. Ellen darted about, helping to retrieve them.

'Oh, thank you so much!' the woman exclaimed in accented English. 'You are so kind! You wait, please – I open.' She set her armload on the window ledge of the sandwich bar and rummaged in a pocket and pulled out a key. *Opening soon*, Ellen read on a sign in the only window, which otherwise was covered with sheets of brown paper.

'Please,' the woman repeated, motioning Ellen to follow her inside. The interior was gloomy, the daylight denied access by the brown paper. 'You please put here,' the woman said, flicking a light switch to reveal a little table just behind the door. '*¡Ahí está!*' she exclaimed, sweeping an arm around. 'Look my new business! You like it?'

'It's lovely.'

It was. The walls were painted the same rich yellow as the shop name, with a fat red border above and below. The countertop was chunky and wooden, a glass-fronted display unit taking up half of it. A large blackboard was attached to the wall behind, a cash register and a coffee machine on a shelf underneath. Someone had written a giant *¡Hola!* in different-coloured chalks on the board, and a yellow smiley face beside it. The floor was wooden too, the boards smooth and pale.

It wasn't big enough to be a sit-down place. It had to be a take-away outlet, with a bench against one wall – for the queue, Ellen assumed. She wondered if it was just sandwiches on offer.

'The colours of the Spanish flag,' the woman said, gesturing towards the wall. 'The red, the yellow.'

'Oh yes, the flag, of course. Well, best of luck with it.' Ellen made to turn away.

'I am from Spain,' the woman said, abruptly thrusting a hand – short purple nails, a glitter of rings – in Ellen's direction. 'I am Claudia.'

'Pleased to meet you. I'm Ellen, from Ireland.'

Claudia clasped her hands in delight. 'You are from *Ireland* – that is wonderful! Ireland is so beautiful!'

'Yes, it is, but Spain has a lot more sunshine.' Again she moved towards the door. 'Well, I'd better—'

'You want job?' Claudia asked.

Ellen stopped. She was joking. It had to be a joke. She didn't look like she was joking though.

'A job? You're offering me a job here?'

'Yes, I offer you a job. My sister say she will come from Spain, but now she is not coming, so I need worker. I want to open next week. You have job?'

'Well . . .'

Unbelievable. Without knowing the first thing about Ellen, apart from the fact that she was Irish and could pick boxes off a path, she was asking her if she wanted a job. Ellen had considered Ben's phone interview unconventional, but Claudia hadn't even interviewed her, hadn't asked a single question, apart from enquiring if she'd like a job.

Did she want to work here? It wasn't a bookshop – but did that matter? Might a new work environment not be a good thing, given that she was bent on forgetting her last one?

'I'm actually looking for employment,' Ellen admitted. 'I've just arrived in London' – and again, the Spanish woman's face lit up.

'So we meet when you are looking for work! It is a sign, a very good sign! You *must* come and work here! I like you, Ellen. You help me in the street; it is the sign of a good person.'

An offer of work, simply because she'd done what any right-thinking person would surely have done in her place. Claudia must truly be desperate. Ellen decided it wouldn't hurt to find out more.

'You sell sandwiches here? Is that right, just sandwiches?'

'Yes, yes, and the potato crisps, and hot drinks. You will make the sandwiches and clean afterwards. That is all.'

Sounded easy enough. 'And how many days a week?'

'Five days, Monday to Friday, ten o'clock until four o'clock.'

She liked the sound of that. The late start would give her a lie-in, and weekends off would give plenty of time to explore the city. And it was five minutes from the flat, which meant no commuting costs.

'Um, what salary are you offering?'

Claudia named a sum. It was more than Ellen had earned in the bookshop, but here she had big rent to pay. With her savings pretty much eaten up already from her half of their initial outlay to the landlord and the cost of furnishing the flat, she needed to earn as much as she could to stay afloat.

'You take the job, Ellen?'

She crossed fingers, out of sight. 'If you could increase the salary a little – our rent is high, I'm not sure if . . .'

'I give you extra five pounds every week,' Claudia said promptly, just like that. 'OK?'

Not much of an improvement, but some. Should she check out bookshop rates of pay before she said yes?

No. Claudia had already shown herself to be impulsive – and with a week to go before opening, she needed someone fast. Ellen might lose this opportunity if she didn't grab it right away. And she thought Claudia would be fun to work with.

'You would be working with my mama, her name is Gloria. She is . . . strong woman, but if you work hard she will be OK.'

Oh dear. Gloria, not Claudia. Strong woman could mean anything. 'You wouldn't be here at all?'

'No – my husband and me have other sandwich bar in Ealing – we work there Monday to Friday. On Saturday we will close Ealing and come here, because Notting Hill is more busy on Saturday with the market. Mama is OK,' she assured Ellen. 'Really, she is OK.' So Ellen agreed to take the job, and Claudia gave a little cry of delight, and just like that, four days after leaving the bookshop, Ellen was employed again.

And when she met Claire later, it was to find that she was sorted too. 'Five nights a week, three lunchtime shifts, and more if I want them. Meals included at work, and I'll sneak home what grub I can. You might be able to swipe stuff from the sandwich bar too.'

'I'll have to check out Gloria first.'

Next day, Ellen gathered her coins together and made some calls from the phone box on their street.

'That's good,' Frances said. 'Any job is good to start you off. If you don't like it, you can always look around for another one. London must be full of jobs.'

'Ever heard of a sandwich bar?' she asked Danny in the next call.

'I've heard of a sandwich, and a bar.'

She filled him in quickly, conscious of the ticking seconds and her dwindling coins. 'Never know who'd drop in for a ham and cheese.'

'Sounds like fun.'

'A bar?' her mother said. 'Do they serve alcohol?'

'No, just sandwiches, and teas and coffees. Claire got a job in a bar – I mean, a proper bar.'

'Well, that's fine for her, that's all she knows, but I wouldn't like the idea of you working in that environment. I hope you're eating properly and getting enough sleep. Joan wants a word.'

'How's your apartment?' Joan asked, and Ellen told her it was basic but it would do them for the moment. 'Notting Hill is really colourful – and there's a big carnival here next month.'

'Sounds great – and I bet you'll meet someone nice soon.'

Not yet. Soon was far too soon.

Exploring

STRONG WAS ONE WORD FOR GLORIA. TACITURN, grouchy and disapproving were others. She only spoke when she needed to say something, and then she used as few words as possible, rapping them out like an order or an accusation, even if they were neither: *Your lace open! Where you put sugar? Knife on floor!* Ellen had a deep repect for Frances' sharp tongue and fearless outlook, but if Gloria and her aunt ever went head to head, Ellen's money would be on Gloria.

She did enjoy the job, though. She liked the bustle that made the hours fly, between the first trickle of customers soon after eleven and the latecomers who trailed in around two. During those peak hours she and Gloria worked like automatons, Ellen on sandwich-making duty – within a day she'd perfected her technique – and Gloria in charge of drinks and taking payment.

Best of all, it stopped her thinking about Ben. No room for anything else when you were continually slapping butter on bread, piling on fillings, cutting and wrapping and saying thank you before moving on, with a bright enquiring smile, to the next.

When things quietened down each day Ellen cleaned up while Gloria recorded the takings and made a list for Claudia of what food items needed to be replenished. These tasks were carried out mostly in silence, but after three hours of customer interactions, that suited Ellen too.

And living with Claire was great, as she'd known it would be. Their fridge was permanently full of the leftovers Claire brought home from work, saving them money that they spent on their shared time off. They explored the city together, quickly finding their way around the Tube network.

They walked through parks and strolled by the river. They visited the free attractions and discovered which pubs gave complimentary tapas with drinks orders, to save more money. Sadly, Marks & Co., the bookshop Ellen had longed to see on Charing Cross Road, had ceased trading over a decade earlier, but there were plenty of others to check out, some very old indeed, and all with the same intoxicating bookish smell.

When they ventured into the big department stores on the fancy streets it was mostly for a look, or to try out the make-up and perfume samples, pretty much everything on offer being beyond their budgets – but now and again Claire would produce something on the way home that she'd lifted: a tube of foundation, a pair of hoop earrings, a packet of joss sticks. Ellen lived in silent terror of her being caught – what was the penalty in London? – but Claire, as ever, knew no fear.

They went out on Claire's nights off too, as often as they could afford. Sometimes to the cinema, buying bags of chips on the way home, other times splashing out on a happy hour cocktail or two which they washed down with cheap wine back at the flat. When they were broke – frequently – they'd go to The Laughing Lion, and Claire would wangle free drinks from her colleagues when the manager wasn't around.

Ellen hungered for live theatre in a city renowned for it, but the prohibitive price of the tickets made the West End shows beyond her reach – until she discovered, to her great delight, the half-price ticket booth in Leicester Square. Still costly, but she resolved to treat herself to one show a month. Claire flatly refused to accompany her – 'I'm not spending money on that' – so on theatre nights she went alone, and didn't care.

Within a week or so of their arrival, she and Claire had met all their neighbours. In addition to Jada from Barbados and her delightful boys there was an Australian musician and a pair of sisters from Manchester who worked in the market. There was a young couple from Offaly, both teachers, and a trio of French culinary students who once a week put out a general invitation to share whatever they had cooked that day. *Supper tonight, 8.00pm*, a notice on their door would proclaim, and Claire and Ellen would bring along a bottle of wine and try out their schoolgirl French.

It wasn't long before Claire was dating. In the pub she had plenty to choose from, and more often than not, she fell into conversation on the Tube or in the parks too. Thankfully, she overnighted at her dates' places: 'I couldn't put you through it,' she told Ellen. 'I can hear you when you turn over.'

'And I can hear you snoring.'

It was a Saturday. They were washing up after breakfast. Claire dropped cutlery with a clatter into its drawer. 'I'll have to find someone for you. It's high time you discovered the joy of sex. I can't believe you haven't done it yet.'

Ellen lifted a cereal bowl from the sink. 'Actually, I have done it.' There, it was out. Maybe now she could pack it away. Maybe now he would begin to leave her.

Claire laughed. 'Doing it with yourself doesn't count.'

Ellen pulled the plug. Water rushed away. 'There was someone in Galway.'

'What? There was not.'

Ellen looked at her, and Claire's face changed. 'Seriously? I can't believe you didn't tell me. Who was he? Where did you meet him?' She stopped. 'Was it Danny?'

'Not Danny. It was my boss in the bookshop. He's gone away. He went off to see the world with his brother.'

'Was that why you came to London?'

'Yes.'

Claire studied her. 'He broke your heart.'

Ellen swallowed a lump in her throat. She hadn't thought talking about it would still be hard. 'Not on purpose.'

Claire set down the tea towel and put her arms around Ellen. 'Oh, poor you. You should have said. Poor Ellen. Why didn't you say?'

'I couldn't.'

'You could. You can tell me anything, you know that. Anything at all.'

'I do know that.'

She did – and still Frances was the one she'd chosen.

Idea

'A SWEATER,' ELLEN SAID. 'A CUCKOO CLOCK, A WOOLLY hat, a year's subscription to *Time* magazine.' She turned to Claire. 'What else?'

'Box of biscuits,' Claire said.

The barman whistled. 'Lucky.'

'Not lucky,' Claire told him. 'Clever. Very clever. I have a very clever friend. She's much cleverer than me.'

Ellen giggled. They were at the giggly stage of the night, on the second of what they'd sworn was their last drink – or was it the third? Tomorrow was Saturday, so who cared? 'To Gloria,' she said, raising her glass. 'The light of my life.'

'You should get a job in advertising,' the barman said to her. 'Sounds like it would be right up your alley.'

He was Irish, and working in The Horse and Carriage, two doors down from The Laughing Lion. They were getting to know the local pubs, and the barmen.

'Someone said that to me once,' Ellen replied, an image of Ben flashing briefly. 'Someone I loved and lost.' God, she must be drunk.

The barman gave a sympathetic smile. 'Been there, done that. Sorry to hear.' He was sweet.

'You're sweet,' she said, even though she knew he was eyeing up Claire.

'Seriously,' he said, 'my cousin works in an employment agency here. I don't know her number, but—' He peeled the top layer from a beermat and scribbled on the newly blank side. 'Here's where she works. You should give her a ring, tell her about the prizes, and ask if she has any jobs in advertising.'

'Thanks – I will.'

She tucked the beermat into her bag as Claire ordered another round. Next morning it took her befuddled mind a while to recall the conversation – and when she did, she almost threw the beermat into the bin. What did she know about working in advertising? Absolutely nothing. What agency in its right mind would hire someone with nothing to show but a few competition wins and zero qualifications – what qualifications did you even need?

On the other hand, a job in advertising sounded a lot more glamorous than working behind the counter of a sandwich bar or a bookshop. Pressurised, probably – ideas to conjure up, deadlines to meet – but maybe she'd be able for it.

She studied the beermat again. His cousin's name was Laura Redmond. Ellen could talk to her, ask her what her chances were. What did she have to lose?

Something Ben had said floated into her head, something about things being worth a try. *What if I try and fail?* she'd asked, and he'd said, *What if you try and don't fail?* They'd been talking about her writing a book, which was so daunting a prospect it might never happen – but this was something that might be a more realistic goal. *What if you try and don't fail?* She closed her eyes and saw his face as he'd urged her to be brave, to give things a go.

She would be brave. She'd give this a go.

Possibility

'THEY'RE CALLED COPY TESTS,' LAURA REDMOND said. 'All the ad agencies have their own – they're aimed at prospective employees, but they'll give them out to anyone looking to put a portfolio together. Basically, they're asking you to create imaginary ads – some for press, some for radio, maybe some TV advertising – so you can show what you're capable of.'

She wore a cream and navy striped blouse with a bow at the neck, tucked into dark wide-legged trousers. Her waist was tiny, her blonde hair big and shaggy like Farrah Fawcett's. She had a beauty spot on one cheek, and she was from Carlow.

She didn't seem fazed by Ellen's inexperience. 'There really isn't a normal path into advertising – and you don't need any kind of formal qualification if you're looking to work in the creative department of an agency. What you need is an aptitude for words and ideas. You need to be quick-thinking and versatile, and able to work in a team.'

'OK.' Ellen tried to look as if she was all those things. 'So my first step is to compile a portfolio?'

'Exactly. Do a round of the agencies – you'll find them all in the Golden Pages – and collect as many copy tests as you can, then basically work your way through them.'

'What about pictures to go with my words for the press ads? I'm not artistic.'

'Don't worry about that – anyone looking to hire you as a copywriter will be focusing on your words and your ideas.'

'How do I show a TV ad?'

'Do it like a comic, giving the rough sequence of events – and again, drawings won't really matter. If you get a job, you'll be working with an art director.'

If you get a job. She wasn't ruling it out. Ellen tried to quell a rising excitement. 'Thanks so much for your help.'

'Not at all. Come back to me with your portfolio and we'll take it from there. Best of luck.'

Ellen thanked her again and left. On the Tube home she made a list.

1. Find book on copywriting.
2. Collect copy tests.
3. Buy portfolio.
4. Fill portfolio.
5. Bring portfolio to Laura.

It looked simple on paper, a straightforward path to a better job. All she had to do was work through the steps – so the following morning she left the flat a little earlier than usual and called into the bookshop next to the sandwich bar. There she found three books on copywriting, and she bought the one that seemed to be written in the plainest English, and she read and reread it until it sank in.

After that she took the Tube into central London and located five ad agencies within a few minutes' walk of each other. All of them were glass-fronted and stylish, and she was hugely intimidated by them. All featured revolving doors through which she watched well-groomed men and women coming and going. Did she have the nerve to walk in, in her not very stylish clothes?

What if you try and don't fail?

She found the nerve, and went home with five copy tests.

Claire

Dear Frances,

I've just opened your letter, and I'm bowled over by your generous gift. I'd been saving up for the flights so there was no need, but I'm so grateful. Thanks a million.

See you next week – really looking forward to it. I land in Shannon at half six, so it'll be after eight when I arrive.

Thanks again, you're very kind.

Ellen xx

PS I'm bringing you spices from the big outdoor market near our flat. They're the real deal, a couple of brothers from Morocco run the stall. You'd love the market, like a giant charity shop.

She also dashed off a letter to Danny, telling him of Frances' unexpected cheque: *I'll be able to splash out in Galway!* she wrote. *I'd love to treat you to dinner on Saturday night if you're free.*

Sealing his envelope, she thought about seeing him again after nearly three months apart. She conjured up his voice, his laugh, the dimple in his chin, the way he had of sweeping back his hair. She imagined herself wrapped in one of his warm hugs.

Was it too late for them? Had that chance come and gone? Would it even be a wise move if they decided to go for it, or was she simply lonely after Ben, and needing someone to fill the void he'd left? She'd dated a few times in London, but hadn't encountered anyone who made her heart beat faster. Would Danny, given the chance? Maybe.

There should be a handbook, she thought. *Beginner's Guide to Love*, or *How to Avoid Absurd Romantic Mistakes*. Making it up as you went along was so hard. Claire never worried about things like that – she had no trouble making it up as she went along.

'Go for it,' she said when Ellen confided the way her thoughts were going. 'What's the worst that can happen?'

'I could break his heart – or he could break mine.'

Claire sighed. 'I've told you before, you take all of this stuff far too seriously. Hearts get broken, Ellen – yours did, remember? Mine did too, a couple of times – but people move on, and broken hearts mend. It's all part of the game.'

If only Ellen could look on it as a game. She decided to wait and see how she felt on meeting him again.

The days passed, and finally the eve of the graduation arrived. 'See you on Monday,' she said to Gloria, who gave a curt nod in return. Probably didn't approve of Ellen getting a day off. Tomorrow a cousin of Claudia's was stepping in: maybe she'd make a mess of things, and Gloria would be glad to see Ellen back.

Three days she'd have in Galway, or nearly three. All of Friday and Saturday, and an evening flight back to London on Sunday. The graduation wasn't until Friday afternoon, so Ellen planned to visit Piles of Books in the morning. It would be bittersweet, with Ben missing, but it would be lovely to catch up with Edwin and Jasper.

On Friday night she'd cook dinner with Frances, Danny being taken out for a post-graduation meal by his parents. He'd invited her along and she'd said no, not wanting to butt into a family occasion, but his parents were travelling home on Saturday so they'd have time to themselves after that.

After leaving the sandwich bar she sped back to the flat instead of going straight to the airport as she'd planned, having realised during the day that she'd left the spices for Frances on a shelf in the kitchen. She'd still make the flight if she didn't delay.

In the house, she dropped her bag at the bottom of the stairs and hurried up. Claire was gone to Cornwall with her latest man for the weekend, so the place would be empty – but it wasn't.

'You should be gone,' Claire said in an odd flat voice. She was in her dressing gown, face as white as a sheet, pouring water from the kettle into a mug. 'You should be on your way to the airport. Why are you back?'

'Claire, what are you doing here? What happened? Are you sick?'

Claire replaced the kettle. 'I had an abortion,' she said, leaning into the counter.

'What? When?'

'This morning. I'm just home. You weren't supposed to be here.' She tried to pour milk, but the bottle shook and the milk splashed onto the counter. 'Fuck,' she said quietly.

Ellen took the bottle and poured. She got a cloth and mopped up the spill. 'Come on,' she said, hooking an arm around Claire's waist, 'let's get you to bed. Lean on me if it helps.'

Claire winced. 'I think I need a fresh pad. Sorry to be gruesome.'

'OK.'

They went to the bathroom and did what needed to be done. Back in the kitchen Ellen filled a hot-water bottle, and then another, and brought them both to Claire, who was lying on her mattress on the floor with her eyes closed.

'Were you given painkillers?' Ellen asked, squatting to slip the bottles between the sheets.

Claire nodded. 'I took them. You should go – you don't want to miss your flight. Why did you come back?'

'I forgot something, but it doesn't matter. I'm not going. I'm not leaving you.'

Claire's eyes fluttered open. 'No, you're not staying. I'll be fine after a night's sleep.'

'Why didn't you tell me? I would have gone with you. You shouldn't have done that alone.'

'Because you're good,' she said, so quietly Ellen could hardly hear. 'I didn't want to involve you.'

'Don't be daft – I'm your friend.'

'Ellen, just go, please. Go and clap for Danny. I'll be fine.'

'I'm not leaving you on your own.'

'I'll go to Jada if I need help. Please, I want you to go.'

So Ellen went, still full of reservations. By now rush hour was well underway, the station full of commuters, her train too full to find a seat. She stood with her bag between her feet, hanging onto a strap. In a couple of hours she would be landing in Shannon.

She imagined seeing Danny tomorrow, watching him cross a stage in his robe and funny flat hat. She'd packed a pretty blue polka dot dress she'd found in the market, and borrowed Claire's red shoes. She'd take a photo of him with his parents after the ceremony, and put it into a frame for him.

The train arrived at the airport and people swarmed off. Ellen was swept along the platform, but as soon as she could she veered sideways and found a wall, and pressed against it until the wave of people had passed.

No. She couldn't do it. She couldn't go.

She hitched up her bag and followed arrows until she found herself on the opposite platform. By the time she climbed the steps to street level at Notting Hill Gate Station it was half an hour after her plane had been scheduled to take off.

She stopped at a phone box and dropped in coins and phoned Frances. She told her what had happened, and what was not now going to happen.

'I'm sorry, Frances. I've wasted the money you sent me. I'm really sorry.'

'Don't you worry your head about the money,' Frances said. 'I'm cross that you'll miss your trip. You're a good friend, Ellen. You're a better friend than she deserves.'

'She'd do the same for me.'

'She wouldn't have to,' Frances replied tartly.

Ellen let that go. 'I'll come and see you at Christmas,' she promised. 'I'll let you know when I book my flights.'

'Do. Look after yourself.'

She couldn't phone Danny, staying with friends in Galway tonight, so she phoned his family home and spoke with his mother. She told her a friend was sick and she needed to stay with her. 'Tell Danny I'm sorry to miss it,' she said. 'I'll write.'

His mother's voice was familiar. 'Oh lovey, we were so looking forward to meeting you again. Danny will be disappointed too, I know. I hope your friend gets better soon.'

She trudged back to the flat to find Claire asleep. As she made tea she spotted the bag of spices for Frances, forgotten for the second time. She took her tea across to the bay window. They'd covered the couch in a giant tie-dyed tablecloth and shifted it to another wall where they largely ignored it, preferring to sit on the wide sill to watch the goings-on in the street.

In a recent letter, Danny had told her he was going skiing at Christmas with workmates, so she wouldn't have a chance to see him then. It could well be next Christmas before they encountered one another again.

It was probably for the best. It might have been on the rebound.

Waiting

IT TOOK UNTIL THE MIDDLE OF JANUARY BEFORE Ellen was happy with her portfolio. Twenty ads, written and rewritten and polished, and culled from over thirty she'd drafted. Ads for bananas and light bulbs and charities and cars; ads for breakfast cereals and depilatory creams and toys; ads for whiskey and butter and painkillers.

Despite Laura in the employment agency having told her not to worry about accompanying imagery, Ellen wanted the ads to look as good as they possibly could, so Sandrine, one of the French culinary students in the house, had obliged with very competent line drawings and sketches.

Ellen had said nothing about exploring the possibility of a new career while she was at home at Christmas, and nothing either to Frances when she'd taken the bus to Galway for a night. Better wait until there was some kind of outcome, or until she gave up hoping for one. She'd hinted to Danny in a letter: *thinking of going in a different direction workwise – watch this space!*

Good for you, he'd replied. *Let me know.*

'You think it's ready?' she asked Claire, poring over the portfolio for the millionth time.

'As ready as it'll ever be' – so she took it to the employment agency after work the next day, and sat trying not to bite her nails while Laura leafed through it.

'These are good,' she announced. 'Some good ideas here, very impressive for someone with no formal experience. Well done.'

'You really think so?'

'Definitely. I'll send the word out that I have a promising young copywriter and see who bites.'

She took photocopies of half a dozen ads – 'to whet their appetites' – and got Ellen to complete a form that asked for a contact number.

Ellen explained about the sandwich bar. 'It's got a phone, but it's also got a boss who wouldn't take kindly to my getting calls – and anyway, I wouldn't have time to answer it once the lunchtime rush starts.'

'Any home phone?'

'No, sorry.'

'In that case you should call me, say twice a week.' Laura handed her a card. 'Best of luck, hopefully I'll find you someplace soon.'

'Thank you.'

How soon was soon? Was Laura talking weeks, or longer? Ellen left without asking, not wanting to sound too needy, and the waiting game began. She rang Laura every Tuesday and Friday, and had to push away the disappointment each time there was no news. Once again she was glad of the busyness of the little sandwich bar that had helped to distract her from the pain of losing Ben. Now it was keeping her from dwelling on the lack of interest from advertising agencies.

Every so often he still drifted into her head, but enough time had passed for her to be able to think about him with little more than a soft ache of loss. *In time it becomes less hard to bear*, Frances had said, and Ellen hadn't believed her, but she'd been right.

Still, it would be good to know where he was. Her own fault, saying she didn't want him to write – she could see now how stupid that had been. If her life was a Hollywood film they'd meet up again by chance in the unlikeliest place and ride off into the sunset together, but here she was in reality, with no serendipitous reunion to hope for.

With the lease of their flat running out at the end of January, she and Claire considered looking around for a better one, but on balance decided to stay put for another while. Despite its limitations they'd grown accustomed to the flat and liked their neighbours, and the location suited both their workplaces.

On a chilly Tuesday in March, more than six weeks after Ellen had presented Laura with her portfolio, she rang the agency as usual. 'Oh good,' Laura said, 'I was waiting for your call. How's Thursday for an interview?'

Hope

LOCATED IN WEST LONDON, FAR FROM THE GLITZY advertising agencies Ellen had encountered in the centre of the city, those of the glass frontages and revolving doors, Marketing Solutions was different.

It was a regular-looking building, painted cream, and its windows were regular too. Its name was displayed on a small brass plaque on the wall by its (non-revolving) entrance. It was at the end of a short street that also featured a café, a launderette, a bookshop and a pub called The Greedy Ostrich that advertised a beer garden at the rear.

The agency was just three years old, according to Laura: *Started by two friends who met in another agency and decided to go it alone. They've got a nice little client list.* She'd named brands, and Ellen had recognised two of them.

They were currently in need of a copywriter, and had agreed to interview Ellen. She glanced at her reflection in the launderette window and patted her hair, which was just about long enough to pin up – she hoped her clips would hold it in place till after the interview. She took a lipstick from her bag and refreshed what was already there.

She smoothed her skirt. She took a deep breath, and another. *What if you try and don't fail?*

She walked in and found herself in a reception area painted white. Behind a desk was a young girl in a check shirt whose sleeves were rolled to the elbows. Her dark hair was pulled off her face with what looked like, but couldn't possibly be, a giant clothes peg. She regarded Ellen with raised eyebrows and a wide smile.

'Hi! Can I help?'

'I have an interview with Mr . . .' for a second or two his name was gone '. . . Robinson.' Ellen gave an apologetic smile. 'Sorry, I'm a bit nervous.'

'Oh, don't be, he's not at all scary.' The girl lifted a phone and jabbed at a button. 'Someone to see you,' she said. 'What? . . . Hang on.' She covered the mouthpiece and said, 'I forgot to ask your name.'

'Ellen Sheehan.'

She relayed this. 'He'll be out in a sec,' she said, replacing the receiver. 'Have a seat.'

Definitely not the polished receptionist type Ellen had encountered in the other agencies. She was directed towards a green tweed couch that was more comfortable than it looked. She plucked a magazine from a table but didn't open it.

'I like your skirt,' the girl said.

'Thanks.'

'Have you been in London long?'

'About eight months.'

Before the girl could ask anything else a nearby door opened and a man emerged. Somewhere between forty and fifty, baggy jeans, white shirt with no tie. Tousle-headed, brown hair sprinkled with grey. A hint of stubble. She wondered if it was company policy *not* to be smartly dressed. Maybe they were a rebel ad agency.

'Ellen,' he said, hand extended. 'Tim Robinson, creative director. Call me Tim. Thanks for coming in.'

'She's nervous,' the receptionist said, to Ellen's mortification. 'Go easy on her.'

He threw her a look, but didn't respond. 'Follow me,' he told Ellen, and led her into the room he'd come from. It held two large desks that butted up together, with a younger man seated at one. Computer monitors sat on both desks: the sight of them made her think of Danny. *Everyone will have a computer soon*, she remembered him telling her. *Wait and see.*

The second man looked about Ellen's age. He had white-blond hair and brown eyes, a striking combination. His neat beard was a few shades darker than his hair. Like Tim, he was in open-necked shirt and jeans. There was a sketchpad on his desk and a scatter of felt-tip pens.

'Jeff,' Tim said, 'Ellen,' and the man nodded and didn't offer a hand. On the wall behind him were several framed ads. *Butter Up Your Bread*, she read, and *Don't Say Cheese, Say Cheddar*. One of her ads might be on a wall someday.

'Please,' Tim said, indicating a chair, and Ellen sat. 'Jeff's copywriter is leaving,' Tim explained. 'He's been poached by a rival agency that can pay more than we can, so we need to replace him.'

'I see.'

Was that his way of letting her know that the job was low-paid? She wouldn't let it stop her, if work was offered. She'd determined to accept any job in advertising, as long as the salary paid her bills. She'd got used to living on a shoestring here.

Tim's desk was practically hidden under piled-up paper-clipped bundles, higgledy-piggledy stacks of folders, scattered leaflets and brochures. He plucked, from the top of the clutter, what looked like Ellen's embarrassingly short CV.

'You win competitions,' he said, reading.

'Yes. I like coming up with snappy sentence endings.'

'So that made you think about working in advertising?'

'Pretty much, yes.' Was that enough of a reason?

'You enjoy playing with words.'

'I do. I love words. I'm a reader,' she added. 'I think it goes with the territory.'

'Certainly helps to broaden the vocabulary,' he agreed. 'How's your Scrabble?'

'Good – and I love crosswords too.' Thanks to Frances.

'I liked what Laura sent of your samples, so let's see the rest.'

She handed over the portfolio and clenched her hands into fists out of sight while he leafed through it slowly and silently before passing it to Jeff, who did the same. So far, Jeff hadn't said a word. If she was offered a job, she'd be his copywriter. She wondered what that would be like.

When he'd finished he returned the portfolio to her with a nod. No comment, no smile. Nothing at all to indicate what he'd thought of it.

She saw him exchange a look with Tim that she couldn't read. She waited to be told that she was no good. She felt they'd be nice enough not to put it in so many words, but the message would be the same. It was her first interview – she couldn't expect to strike it lucky right away.

'You're currently working?' Tim asked.

'Yes, in a sandwich bar in Notting Hill.'

'You definitely have potential,' he told her. 'Some nice ideas there – and the competition wins are a good indicator too.'

'Thank you.'

She waited for the but. The polite but. There was a pause, another silent exchanged look. 'The stuff in there,' Tim said, nodding towards the portfolio, 'is the fun part. Ads are where you get to play – but you'd also have to produce company brochures with all the waffle they want you to write, about their innovative this and cutting edge that. You'd have to come up with promotional ideas for supermarkets and other businesses. You'd be writing copy for price drops, and two-for-one deals, and introductory offers, and other equally scintillating things.'

To her it all sounded scintillating. Every bit of it. 'I wouldn't mind any of that,' she said. 'I'm pretty sure I'd enjoy it.'

He paused. Had that been a bit much, a bit over-eager? He drummed his fingers on the edge of his desk.

'We could do a three-month trial,' he said, 'and see how we go. Jeff?'

'Fine.' He didn't look like he cared, either way.

It took a few seconds to sink in. Ellen looked from one to the other. Really? *Really?*

'Wow, thanks so much, I'm completely . . . I mean, I didn't think—' She broke off. *Pull yourself together.* 'I'm a bit flabbergasted, as you can see. I wasn't sure whether you'd see any – but I'd love to accept. Thank you.'

'Don't thank me yet – like I say, it's a trial, and there's no guarantee it'll come to anything more. You might be ready to run away from us after three months.'

She smiled, her first real smile of the interview. Run away? Not a chance.

'Also, we can only pay peanuts, which is why we're looking for a newcomer. Here' – he rummaged in the pile on his desk and pulled out a brochure – 'you can read all about us, see what you're getting into. If you work out, and we keep you on, we might be able to do a small salary raise. I'll get a temporary contract drafted in the next few days and send it to Laura, and you can see what you think of our terms and conditions before you commit yourself. We're a friendly bunch here – and Jeff isn't half as fierce as he looks.'

At that, Jeff simply lifted his eyebrows a fraction. She was sorry she wasn't going to be working with Tim, who seemed altogether more amiable – but she would happily team up with Quasimodo for this job.

Tim swivelled to consult a desk calendar propped by his computer. 'Assuming you're OK with the contract, how would Monday the eleventh of April sound as a starting date? It's a week after Easter, just over three weeks away. Like I say, you'll have the contract in a few days.'

'Perfect,' she said. Everything was perfect, as long as the peanuts he was offering paid her bills.

'That's that then.' Tim got to his feet, and so did Ellen. Jeff remained seated. 'Well done,' he said.

'I look forward to working with you,' Ellen replied. Looked forward might be a bit strong.

In the lobby Tim shook her hand again. 'Welcome to the team.'

'You got the job!' the receptionist exclaimed. 'Congratulations!'

Tim looked pained. 'My daughter,' he told Ellen. 'Our proper receptionist is on honeymoon. Normal service will resume soon.'

'Well, there's gratitude for you,' the girl said. Ellen thought how nice for a workplace not to be too swanky to have the boss' daughter filling in.

On her way back to the Tube station she was unable to keep the smile off her face. Soon, in just a few weeks, she would be getting paid for playing with words all day.

'An advertising copywriter,' she'd say, if anyone asked what she did. She'd throw it out casually, as if it was just another job, and inside she'd be whooping with delight.

She couldn't wait to start. She imagined telling everyone at home. To think a chance remark from a barman had led to this – she'd have to call in and tell him, and bring him a thank-you gift.

'Fantastic,' Claire said. 'I'm so happy for you. You look like the cat that got the cream.'

'I feel like it.'

'I might be job hunting myself soon.'

'What? You want to leave the pub? I thought you loved it.'

Claire made a face. 'Not any more. It's too busy, too noisy – and it's got too many creeps trying to look down my top. I want somewhere more civilised.'

'You mean another pub?'

'I mean another something. I don't know what I mean.'

An idea struck Ellen. 'Would you consider the sandwich bar? Evenings and weekends off, and lunch included.'

'I'd consider anything, but what about Gloria?'

'Oh, you'd be well able for Gloria – her bark's worse than her bite. Will I say it to Claudia when I'm handing in my notice? She loves the Irish – she'd be delighted to be getting another one.'

'Go on then. Nothing to lose.'

In bed later, Ellen replayed the interview in her head, reliving the excitement she'd felt on her way back to Notting Hill. Tomorrow she'd exchange a fiver for coins from the cash register in the sandwich bar, and on the way home she'd phone everyone with the news.

She fell asleep smiling.

Plans

AS PROMISED, THE MARKETING SOLUTIONS CON-
tract arrived from Laura a few days later. Despite Tim's warnings
about the salary, Ellen was pleasantly surprised to discover that he
was offering a fair bit more than she was making at the sandwich
bar. Her working hours would be the usual nine to five, with a
straightforward commute.

She signed the contract and posted it back, with a note to Tim
saying she looked forward to joining the team, and then she broke
the news to Claudia.

As she'd expected, it wasn't well received. 'I am sorry,' her
employer said mournfully. 'I am very sorry to lose you. This is a
big disaster for me. We must find another Ellen.'

'Actually, I have a friend who might be interested,' Ellen said.
'She's Irish too' – so an arrangement was made for Claire and
Claudia to meet at the sandwich bar the following Friday.

'Well, that is wonderful news,' Frances said, 'just wonderful. I
know you liked the sandwich bar, but I was hoping you'd find
something a bit more interesting. You'll fly it.'

'Congrats,' Joan said. 'I didn't even know you were thinking of

looking for that kind of work. Mam isn't here; I'll tell her when I
see her.'

'That's fantastic,' Danny said. 'Delighted for you. When are you
home again? I forget what you look like.'

'I'm finishing up in the sandwich bar at Easter, and then I have
a week before the other job starts. If I can get a cheap flight just
after Easter I'll come home for a few days.'

'How about you fly into Dublin instead of Shannon? I could
pick you up at the airport and drive you home. You could admire
my jalopy.' His parents had bought him a secondhand car when
he'd accepted the permanent job from the company that had given
him work experience.

'That's a lovely offer, but I couldn't possibly drag you all the way
across the country.'

'I'm due a trip home. I haven't been forgiven yet for missing
Christmas because of the skiing trip. My mother's on the point of
writing me out of the will.'

'Well, if you're sure it would suit, that would be great. I'll check
out flights and let you know.'

On the appointed day, Claire showed up fifteen minutes early
to meet Claudia, and while she waited she turned her attention to
Gloria.

'I'd love to learn Spanish,' she said. This was news to Ellen.

Gloria closed the ledger she'd been writing in and folded her
arms. 'You want speak Spanish.'

'*Si*,' Claire replied – and to Ellen's astonishment, Gloria took up
a cup.

'*Taza*,' she said.

'*Taza*,' Claire repeated.

Gloria pointed to the milk. *'Leche.'*

'Leche.'

'Azucar.'

'Azucar' – and by the time Claudia arrived, Claire could say *Una taza de café con leche sin azucar por favor* in perfectly accented Spanish.

While Gloria finished doing the books and Ellen cleaned up, Claudia took Claire into the small back room. When they emerged shortly afterwards, both appeared satisfied.

'See you soon,' Claudia said.

'Can't wait,' Claire replied. *'Adiós,* Gloria.'

'Eight pounds a week more than she paid you,' she reported to Ellen on the way home. 'I asked for ten, she offered eight. I would have taken five.'

'Well done. Since when have you wanted to learn Spanish?'

'Since half an hour ago. Listen, it worked, didn't it? Gloria was flattered that someone was interested in learning her language, so she's going to be easier to live with. You just tell people what they want to hear. I told Claudia working in a sandwich bar was my dream job.'

Ellen laughed. 'You're shameless. You'd never have gone for it if I hadn't put the idea in your head.'

'True – but what harm is a little white lie if it gets you what you want? Anyway, I quite fancy learning another language.'

'You didn't kill yourself learning French at school.'

'That was different. Mrs Purcell hated me.'

'Because you never did a tap!'

Claire ignored that. 'Gloria's a native speaker, so I'll have the right accent – and I won't have to do dictation, or any of that rubbish. And you know what the best bit is?'

'What?'

'I don't have to give up the pub.'

Ellen stared at her. 'You're going to keep it on? I thought you wanted to get away from late nights.'

'Not if they're just Saturdays and Sundays. I'll keep those on, and drop the rest.'

'But that means you'll be working seven days a week. You'd have no day off.'

'So what? I'll finish at four on the weekdays and get a lie-in at the weekends, and between the two I'll have a nice little income.'

'That's true.'

Telling Gloria she wanted to learn Spanish, Ellen thought. Telling Claudia that working in a sandwich bar was her dream job. Telling them what they wanted to hear.

'It's all falling into place,' Claire went on, linking arms with Ellen. 'We're both getting what we want. Right?'

'Right,' Ellen replied. There was no harm in it. It was just Claire, doing things her own way.

A few days later she booked a return flight into Dublin and back from Shannon, and rang Danny to give him her arrival date and time.

'Wear a name badge,' he said, 'just in case.'

'Very funny.'

She phoned her mother, who'd written to congratulate her on the new job.

'You're coming home *after* Easter? Did you tell that to Joan when you phoned?'

'No – I just booked the flight today. I would have come for Easter but it was much dearer. Is there a problem?'

'It's just that I've arranged to go on a little trip.'

'Oh.' This was most unusual. When did she go on trips? 'Where are you going?'

'France. I wouldn't have planned it if I'd known you were coming.'

'*France?*' To the best of Ellen's knowledge, her mother had never been outside Ireland.

'We're leaving on the day you arrive. A pity I didn't know.'

We. She wasn't going alone. As far as Ellen was aware, she didn't have friends, or certainly not the kind of friends she'd go away with – people she knew were more casual acquaintances. After Ellen's father had walked out, not a single person from the town had called in to enquire how they were doing.

Then again, what did Ellen know? Clearly, there *was* a friend. Maybe she'd met her at work. 'When do you get home?'

'On Saturday.'

'I'm flying back to London that day.'

'Well, that's too bad. Joan will be here, of course. I'll let her know you're coming.'

'Have a good trip.'

She'd go to Frances, she decided. She'd stay one night with Joan and then travel on to Galway and spend the rest of her time there. Joan had Seamus; she wouldn't be put out.

She was losing touch with her family, moving further away as time went on. She'd always keep in contact with Joan, but she imagined the day would come when she stopped going home altogether, apart from weddings or funerals.

It made her a little sad. Not much, just a little.

America

ON HER FINAL DAY IN THE SANDWICH BAR GLORIA presented Ellen with a small packet. 'Good luck with new job,' she said gruffly. 'I am sorry you are going.'

'Thank you, Gloria.' She was deeply touched. In all the months they'd worked together, it was the most human interaction they'd had.

When Claudia showed up with her final pay cheque, she had a gift too. Also small, also wrapped. 'Is a thank you,' she told Ellen, 'for all your work. I hope I see you again some time.' She kissed Ellen on both cheeks and wished her good luck.

Back at the flat, Ellen opened her gifts. Gloria's was Spanish biscuits, and Claudia's was perfume.

Chanel No. 5 perfume, to be precise.

Ellen couldn't believe it. She and Claire were mad about it, spraying as much of the sample bottle as they could in the fancy department stores before a staff member descended. Now, thanks to Claudia, Ellen had her very own No. 5.

She opened it and dabbed it onto a wrist. She sniffed, and closed her eyes at the pleasure of it, and tucked the bottle away.

Three days later she flew to Dublin, and as she descended the steps from the plane the first taste of Irish air, clean and cold and misty, brought a lift to her heart as it always did. With just hand luggage she went straight through – 'Welcome home, Ellen,' the passport control official said – and emerged into the arrivals hall, where Danny was waiting.

And the sight of him after eight months apart caused her heart to perform an unexpected little flip.

'Good to see you,' he said, wrapping his arms around her in the way she remembered. 'You smell nice.'

'Got a present of posh perfume,' she told him. 'Special occasions only.'

He'd got his hair cut very short, and gained a little weight. He wore the black leather jacket he'd bought in the Dandelion Market. He led the way to his car, which was small and green, and dented in a few places. 'Just so you know, the dents are not mine. I inherited them.'

'So I'm safe sitting in with you?'

'Fairly safe.'

He drove her through the city, asking about London, and her imminent move to Marketing Solutions. It felt a little like when they'd met in the bookshop, after all the years apart. She felt slightly shy, which was crazy.

She wondered again if now was their time. However much she might wish him still with her, Ben was gone, and she needed someone to love, and someone to love her. It wouldn't matter, she thought, that they lived in different countries, not with regular flights.

They left the city behind and headed west along the dual carriageway. 'So how are things with you?' she asked. 'How's Dublin suiting you? How's the job going?'

'Good,' he said. 'All good, but . . . actually, I have some news.' He changed gear as he moved out to overtake a lorry. 'Big news.'

'What?'

'I've got a new job too. I'm going to be moving.'

'Moving? Where to?'

'California.' He gave her a quick grin. 'I'm off to the land of Stars and Stripes.'

California, thousands of miles from London. Moving away from her, just like Ben had. Was she destined to lose everyone she cared about?

'Seriously, you're moving to America?'

'I am. There's an area called Silicon Valley, not far from San Francisco, and it's the computer capital of the world. All the big companies are located there, including the head office of where I am now. I requested a transfer, and I got it. They want me to start in June.'

'Wow.'

Something in her voice must have sounded off. He glanced at her. 'You OK?'

She threw back a quick smile. 'Yes, sorry, well done, that's great. It's just . . . unexpected – and so far away. You said nothing.' They talked on the phone once a month or so. They wrote in between.

'I wanted to wait until it was all tied up. That only happened last week.'

'Don't you like your job here?'

'I do, it's great – but this will mean more responsibility, and a lot more money.' He laughed. 'Not to mention more sunshine.'

'And you don't mind the idea of living so far from your family, all on your own?'

He darted another look at her. 'Yeah. That's the other thing.'

'What other thing?'

'I won't be all on my own.'

'Someone's going with you?'

'Actually, she's already over there.'

She.

Oh.

'She was working in the company when I joined it in September. She's from California, a city called Palo Alto, right in the heart of Silicon Valley. She got a job offer there just after Christmas, and she started last week.'

'So that's why you're moving.'

'Yup.'

'You kept that quiet too.'

He laughed. 'Ah, you know what men are like, Ellen. They don't talk about that kind of thing.'

He sounded happy. She must be happy for him too. 'So tell me about her.'

She watched his profile as he spoke of Bobbi – 'with an i' – and her African father and her German mother. She heard about how he and Bobbi had met, when he'd walked into the office kitchen and skidded on yogurt from the tub she'd just dropped.

She listened as he talked about the project they'd been working on together for a month, and how Bobbi, not he, had finally been the one to suggest a date, and how she'd asked if they could go to the Botanic Gardens, because she was into plants.

She recalled the flip her heart had made when she'd walked into the arrivals hall and seen him. She imagined Bobbi waiting for him in California. She could see how perfectly obvious it was as he talked about her that he loved her.

She swallowed back the stupid tears that threatened, glad of the darkness outside the car. She was lonely, that was all.

Danny was her friend, her good friend. He would always be her friend.

Home

'NORMANDY,' JOAN SAID, CUTTING A SLICE OF TEA brack. 'They're going to travel around the war cemeteries.'

Ellen frowned. 'The war cemeteries? I didn't think Mam would have any interest in that.'

'She doesn't, but Kevin does.'

'Who's Kevin?'

'The man she's going with, of course,' Joan replied, as casually as if Ellen had just asked her the time. 'Do you want butter on that?'

'She's going to France with a man? But she's still married.'

Joan smiled. She actually smiled as she set down the butter dish. 'Are you serious?'

'What's so funny? She *is* still married, isn't she? Or did they get a separation without anyone bothering to tell me?'

'Of course not. They're still married, but you don't imagine Dad is going to appear over the horizon anytime soon, do you?'

For an instant Ellen felt pure rage. 'Don't make light of it. It's not a joke.'

'I'm not making light of it. I know it's not funny. I was there, remember? But you have to face facts, Ellen. He went, and he's not coming back. Do you really expect Mam to stay on her own for the rest of her life?'

'No. Yes. I don't know.' It hadn't for a second occurred to Ellen that their mother might be involved with another man. She had to be in some kind of relationship with him, and Ellen had had no idea. 'Why didn't you tell me about him? I'm part of this family too.'

Joan peeled the skin from a banana in strips, dropping them one by one into the bin. 'To be honest, I didn't think you'd be all that interested. You hardly ever come home, and when you do you're in your room reading, or out walking.'

'I'm still family. How long has it been going on?'

Joan shrugged. 'A few months, I don't remember exactly. Some time after Christmas.' She began chopping the banana into thin slices. 'Ellen, she's been on her own for over six years.'

'How does she know him?'

'He's teaching in the school. His brother owns the big garage on the Tipperary Road. To be honest, I think he's a bit dull, but Mam seems happy enough.'

'You've met him?'

'He's come to dinner a few times.'

'So everyone knows about them.'

'Well, it's not a secret, if that's what you mean. Look, it's no big deal, Ellen. He's not attached, and Mam may as well not be. They're not hurting anyone.'

It wasn't the point. It wasn't the *point*.

'I know you miss Dad,' Joan said, 'but I hope he doesn't come back. I hope he never shows his face here ever again. *Ever*. If he came here right this minute I wouldn't let him in.'

Ellen spread butter on the brack. 'I'm thinking of going to see Frances tomorrow,' she said, needing to change the subject. 'I promised her I'd visit when I was home, and with Mam gone . . . I'm thinking I'll stay a few days with her.'

Joan arranged the banana discs on another slice of brack. 'Fine.'

'You wouldn't mind?'

'No. Do what you want.'

And when Ellen brought up the matter of Kevin with Frances, it was to discover that she knew about him too. 'Let her off, Ellen. She might be lonely. She might just be looking for companionship, and you can't deny anyone that.'

Ellen made no response. They'd all known, and nobody had told her.

'You're not over your father leaving,' Frances said.

'I don't think I'll ever be over that.'

'I can understand. It was a terrible thing he did – and I can see you hold your mother responsible, rightly or wrongly.'

Ellen said nothing.

'But regardless of whose fault it was, life goes on. It's going on for your mam, and it's going on for you. Now tell me more about this new job.'

And so Ellen pushed down her resentment, and spoke of the future.

Copywriter

DURING HER FIRST WEEK AT MARKETING SOLUTIONS, she learnt three things about Jeff. The first was that his name was spelt Geoff. The second was that he liked his coffee black with half a spoon of sugar. She knew this because he told her, on her very first morning. 'Just so you know, when you make it for me.' No trace of a smile. Nothing to indicate whether he was joking or not.

'Take no notice of him,' Kit said. Kit was another copywriter. She was from the Isle of Wight and had a very fancy accent. Her clothes looked expensive – grey trouser suit, long jacket – and her dark auburn hair was caught up in a blue bandana, and her nails were long and black. 'He looks for attention: don't give it to him. And don't *ever* make him coffee.'

Geoff shot her a look of puzzlement. 'Why do you hate me?'

'Because you're impossible. Be nice to Ellen and I'll stop hating you.'

There were two others in the creative department. Alf was co-founder of the agency, bushy haired and bearded and jovial, and Tim's art director. They worked in the office where Ellen had been interviewed, right next door to the studio where she and the other creatives were situated.

Thomas, the sixth member of the team, was Kit's art director. In his free time he doodled cars, and sometimes he went on doodling cars while he and Kit tossed ideas back and forth. He wore glasses with thick black frames, and brought a dark brown bottle of ginger beer to work every day that he poured into a glass halfway through the morning and drank through a paper straw.

Ellen and Geoff sat facing each other across the two-desk arrangement that seemed to be the norm, with Kit and Thomas similarly positioned at the far end of the room. Ellen was given a computer to work on, which terrified her until Kit took her through the rudiments of the word processing programme they used, and by the end of the week she could tap the keys without feeling knotted up inside.

In addition to the creative department there were six account handlers who liaised with the clients, one accountant who managed the company finances, and Debbie the receptionist, returned from honeymoon in Sardinia by the time Ellen started.

Her first job, a press ad for a new yogurt aimed at weaning babies, terrified her. It was one thing coming up with ideas for her portfolio when she was alone in the safety of her room, and quite another to be sitting across from her art director, who was now waiting, with an open sketch pad, for them to hit on an idea.

The yogurt was called Babygloop. She couldn't decide if the name was ingenious or awful. She reread the bullet-point information she'd been given by the account handler. *Real fruit* and *full-cream milk* and *pureed for smoothness* and *the perfect first taste. Half-page press ad*, she read, *to feature in women's magazines.*

She was afraid Geoff would scoff at her efforts, or regard her pityingly if she said something stupid, but she was now a copywriter and this was what copywriters did. She scrambled about for something intelligent to say. Something creative. Babies. Food. Mess.

'Babies are messy,' she said, 'particularly babies who are just learning to eat solid food.'

He began to scribble. She watched a baby's plump face emerging. He added a headband with an L-plate stuck to it.

Encouraged, she searched for something else. 'Yogurt is slathery and gloopy.'

'So is every other baby food,' he pointed out, still sketching. 'Pureed everything.'

'True – but Babygloop is tastier. If you were a baby, would you choose yogurt or pureed carrots for your dinner?'

'Yogurt is dessert rather than dinner, though,' he said.

It was like they were playing ping-pong, she throwing something out, he batting it back. She decided she liked it.

'Would it matter with babies whether you fed them sweet or savoury? Yogurt is more fun than carrots. It's the perfect messy food. It gets everywhere.'

'All over the high chair,' he said, placing the baby into one. His pencil flew across the page. 'All over the floor.' Adding dollops as he went. Putting a baby-sized spoon into the dimpled little fist.

'It's impossible for a baby to eat tidily,' Ellen said, gaining more confidence. 'They just can't do it. Making a mess is their area of expertise.'

'No table manners,' he agreed, pinning a rosette to the baby's top, writing THE MESSIEST around it.

'Deplorable,' she said. 'Shouldn't be allowed near a spoon.'

'Never use a napkin.' He drew a crumpled napkin on the baby's head.

'Have even been known to wear dishes on their heads,' she said.

He rubbed out the napkin and replaced it with an upside-down dish. He studied it for a few seconds, and then reached again for the eraser. He replaced the dish with a yogurt tub.

Pause.

'But actually,' Ellen said slowly, 'the thing about Babygloop is that it's so delicious they'll want all of it to get into their mouths. So there'll be no messing.'

He looked up. 'No messing?'

'Minimal messing.'

'Yup.' He tore off his page and started a new one. The finished ad depicted baby, mouth agape, eyes fixed on an approaching spoonful of yogurt. The baby's face and clothing were pristine.

The ad read:

The treat your baby's been waiting for. No messing.

For all their cuteness, babies have deplorable table manners. They get as much food on them as in them – but that's about to change. Say hello to Babygloop yogurt, made specially for weaning babies, with lashings of real fruit and full-cream milk. Babygloop yogurt is so smoothly delicious, they won't want to waste a single blob. No messing.

Disclaimer: There might be some messing. Babies are unpredictable.

Tim approved it, and it was submitted to the account handlers for presentation to the client. If it got the go-ahead, it would be Ellen's first official ad. She couldn't wait to see it in print. She'd send copies to Frances and Danny. She might frame it.

The third thing she learnt about Geoff was that he drank real ale. She knew this because that was what he ordered when they all went to The Greedy Ostrich for drinks after work on Friday.

'I'd like to say it's to welcome you,' Tim told her, 'but we do this every Friday.' He bought her a white wine, and grumbled about having to pay for everyone else's drinks too, but Ellen guessed that treating his employees to the first round was also part of the Friday tradition.

'You've done well,' he told her. 'You've had a good first week. I hope you're enjoying it.'

'I really am.'

The ad made it into print, and Ellen bought six copies of the magazine. Thinking up ads *was* fun, like Tim had said – but she also enjoyed writing the company brochures and leaflets that followed Babygloop.

And Geoff slowly grew on her, once she got used to his laid-back way of communicating, his occasional sardonic comments, his bouts of silence as he scribbled in his pad. He was even-tempered, and patient when she was uninspired, and quick to praise her good ideas.

He was also easy on the eye. That never hurt.

In July she was summoned to the office next door, where Tim and Alf were waiting. 'You're a natural at this game,' Tim said. 'You've got a fine creative mind, you've come up with some very original work, and you're solid at the boring stuff too. You're coping with Geoff?'

'I am. I've got used to him.'

'Glad to hear it. That partnership's important. So,' he went on, 'your three-month trial is up tomorrow.'

'It is.' It hadn't escaped her notice.

'You'll probably be poached by the competition when word gets out, but in the meantime we'd both be very happy if you stayed on with us.'

'We certainly would,' Alf put in.

She'd half expected it, but still it was very welcome news. 'I'd be delighted, thanks so much.'

'Excellent. And we promised you a few extra peanuts a month.' He named a sum that was more than she'd been expecting, and she thanked him again and shook hands with both.

'Welcome to the team, Ellen – properly this time,' Alf said.

'Permanently,' Tim added. 'I'll have a new contract drafted up.'

Life was good. After a time, she and Geoff took to indulging in occasional mild flirtation, and she enjoyed it, and that was as far as it went. As far as she would allow it to go. The last thing she wanted was the complication of getting involved with someone she worked with. Not again.

All going great here, Danny wrote in a postcard from California. *Bobbi and I have moved in together. She says hi, and hopes to meet you some day. Are we all grown up now?*

The image on the postcard was a cartoon American bald eagle, looking stern against a Stars and Stripes background. Ellen found a postcard showing a cartoon Big Ben and wrote back.

Moving in together sounds pretty grown up. Hi to Bobbi – I'll be over for the wedding. Send sunshine, it's freezing here.

That might have been her. If she'd got together with Danny when he'd asked, she'd never have moved to London. If he'd told her he wanted to transfer to the head office in California she'd have said go for it, and gone with him. She could be sitting in the sunshine now instead of looking out at the London rain. She could be living a different life.

But chances were she wouldn't be working in advertising. She guessed a job in that sector would be a lot harder to come by in America, and there would be the hassle of looking for a work visa too.

She was happy in London. Her job was great, and the city was fascinating, and she and Claire had fun.

And if love wasn't part of it, it surely would be soon.

Paris

IN THE SUMMER OF 1984, AFTER ELLEN HAD WORKED at Marketing Solutions for over a year, Gloria announced that she was retiring from the sandwich bar and Claire took on the role of manager, with a salary hike and an option to take over the rental of the premises if and when she was in a position to do so.

'You want that?' Ellen asked.

'To be my own boss? Yes please. I'm aiming to afford it by the end of the year.'

She was still holding down two jobs, still managing to have a social life, still finding plenty of men to buy her dinner and bring her home with them for the night. Occasionally her date brought a friend along for Ellen, and occasionally the friend asked to see Ellen again, and now and again Ellen also slept in another bed, but nothing lasted, nothing came of any of them.

She and Claire stayed on in the flat, neither having the appetite to move. Some day, they kept saying, and maybe some day would never come, and so what if it didn't? They'd finally got the land-lord to repair the doorbell, and they'd managed, with the help of two of their male neighbours, to bring the couch downstairs and out to a skip. They'd replaced it with a futon and added a big red rug and a coffee table, and the living room was considerably improved.

At the Marketing Solutions Christmas party that year, Tim announced that he and Alf were taking the creative department to Paris for a weekend in January. 'Call it a late Christmas present,' he said. 'We've had a good year, and we'd like to say thank you.'

Paris, a city Ellen had dreamed of visiting for years. In celebration she bought a designer wrap dress that she found in the market for twenty pounds. 'Cost you over six hundred quid new,' the stallholder told her, and she had no idea if that was true but decided to believe him. She loved the way the dress showed off the right curves and hid the wrong ones.

'You and Geoff should have a fling in Paris,' Claire said.

'Hardly likely, with the rest of the creatives there.'

'See what you can do – and bring me back a Frenchman.'

Their hotel was small and old. The rooms were not ensuite. The bathrooms, three to a corridor, featured enormous cast-iron baths and toilets with dangling chains to pull for the flush.

Ellen's window looked out on a narrow cobbled street through which people darted, heels clip-clopping, snatches of French floating up to her. She stuck out her head and caught a whiff of cigarette smoke, and a waft of perfume, and a hint of garlic.

On the first night they went out to dinner, and everyone but Ellen ordered *moules*. She had chicken, not being a fan of shellfish.

'You can't come to Paris and not have mussels,' Tim said.

'I can actually. What will we do tomorrow? Who'll come to the Eiffel Tower and the Louvre?'

'I will,' Kit said. It was her first time in Paris too – but in the morning everyone apart from Ellen was hollow-eyed and exhausted after a night of throwing up, and in no position to go anywhere. The mussels, it turned out, hadn't been such a good idea.

'Sorry, Ellen,' Tim said. 'You're on your own. We'll see you this evening,' so she pulled on her winter coat over her new dress and left the hotel.

It was bitterly cold. She was glad of the fur-lined boots she'd got in a sale. She didn't fancy doing the Eiffel Tower or the Louvre alone, so she contented herself with wandering about the city for a few hours, dipping in and out of the shops and admiring the smartly dressed Parisians who hurried past.

She hadn't used a word of French since school, but when she stepped into a café with a black and white tiled floor and marble-topped tables she took a seat by the window and ordered *café crème* and a *pain au chocolat* without stumbling. When her order was delivered she cradled her cup, trying to decipher the snatches of conversations within earshot. Maybe next she would go to—

Someone bumped against her chair, causing her to lurch forward and sending an arc of coffee flying from her cup onto her untouched pastry. She swung around, expecting an apology – and was horrified to see a man rushing out, holding the bag she'd slung casually, stupidly, over her chair back.

She sprang to her feet – 'Stop!' she cried, causing heads to swing towards her. '*Arrêt!*' she called, and '*Voleur!*', the words coming back without thinking. She clattered her cup onto the table and dashed from the café, heedless of the hubbub and the coat she left in her wake, her only thought to reclaim her bag.

Almost immediately, she heard another set of footsteps pounding behind her – a waiter, chasing her for payment? No: a man raced past her, hopefully also in pursuit of her thief. She flew along in his wake, heart pounding, boots thudding on the path. Her wrap dress flapped open as she ran, sending cold air to her thighs. She ignored it, modesty not a priority.

At an intersection the man darted across the street, the thief still visible some way ahead. Ellen raced blindly after them, hearing a screech of brakes and a volley of horns.

The chase continued for another half block, until a painful stitch forced her to halt and bend double, panting heavily. By the time she could catch her breath, both men had vanished from sight. Maybe the second had been an accomplice, and not someone trying to help her after all.

Struggling not to cry, she tried to recall the bag's contents. Wallet with traveller's cheques, some French francs, around the equivalent of a hundred pounds in total. What else? Not her passport, thankfully – they'd surrendered those at the hotel reception last evening.

Her keys to the flat in London. The bits and pieces that every woman kept in her bag: lipstick, comb, pen, tissues. Her book, in case she wanted to read over lunch. *The Color Purple*, which Kit had lent her last week.

Her perfume. The last of the precious scent that Claudia had given her when she'd left the sandwich bar. Eked out, used only on the most special of occasions, brought along to Paris for its final outing. Kept in her bag so she could refresh when needed. For some reason, the loss of it upset her more than anything else.

The cold was biting through the thin fabric of her dress. She began to walk back the way she'd come. She'd stop at the café and tell them she'd return with cash to pay her bill. She'd have to get a loan from one of her group. She shivered, wrapping arms around herself. Hopefully her coat was still there.

'Excuse me.'

A voice behind her, not French. She turned to see a man approaching. 'Sorry,' he said, out of breath. 'I couldn't catch him. Not as fit as I used to be.'

Polished English accent. Navy jacket, dark grey sweater, pale grey trousers. Solidly built. Dark haired, clean-shaven. Definitely not an accomplice.

'Thank you so much for trying. I really appreciate it.'

'You're cold,' he said, taking off his jacket and placing it on her shoulders. 'I assume you left a coat in the café.'

'Oh . . . thank you.' The warmth of it was wonderful. She hugged it to her. 'Yes, a coat, unless someone's stolen that too.'

'Let's hope not.' He put out a hand. 'Leo Morgan.'

'Ellen Sheehan.'

They fell into step. 'Did you have much in the bag?' he asked.

'Some cash, keys that can be replaced, nothing much else . . . it's OK. I'm here with my work colleagues. They'll help me out.' But she felt somehow lost, exposed in some way, without the bag swinging from her shoulder.

They reached the café. 'Let me get you a brandy,' he said, 'just to be on the safe side. You've had a shock' – so they sat at the table she'd vacated by the window, and he spoke in what sounded like perfect French to the waiter, and her coat was returned to her.

The brandy was fiery, the first sip making her eyes swim. She was reminded of the last time she'd drunk brandy, the night Claire had come up to Galway and brought some in a flask. She felt its warmth radiating wonderfully through her, sliding into her extremities. 'This was a good idea,' she said.

'They're not charging for it, or for what you had earlier.'

'Oh . . . ' She smiled at the waiter, mouthed *merci*. 'That's nice of them.'

He drank an espresso. The small cup looked like part of a doll's tea set in his hand. 'You need to be careful,' he told her. 'Paris is beautiful, but it's also full of opportunist thieves. Tourists are sitting ducks.'

'I was careless,' she agreed.

'Your first time in the city?'

'Yes. Do you live here?'

'No – this is a business trip. I live in London.'

'Me too.'

'You're from Ireland.'

'Yes, the west.'

By the time the brandy was gone she'd told him about Marketing Solutions, and the flat she shared with Claire, and he'd told her that he worked in banking – 'Very boring, but someone has to do it.'

He was older than her, thirty or so. His eyes were almost black, very little distinction between pupil and iris.

'How is your French so good?' she asked.

'My mother's French. She lives in Nantes, where I was born. My father was English. Where else have you been besides France?'

'Nowhere, apart from Ireland and the UK.'

'Check out Rome when you get a chance; it's my favourite capital. Throw coins into the Trevi Fountain, and visit the Villa Borghese, and walk through the Forum. You can skip the Colosseum, it's overrated – and unless you want to stand in a queue for hours and then get rushed through the main event, forget the Sistine Chapel. But watch your bag in Rome too – every capital has its criminals.'

She liked his voice, rich and deep. A good voice for a radio presenter. His programme would be music, a mix of jazz and classical. She liked his hands too. They reminded her of Ben's, solid fingers with nails that he looked after. He wore a gold signet ring on the little finger of his left. His watch was gold too.

He smiled a lot. Not a wide beam, more a gentle smile that crinkled the skin slightly around those dark eyes. He was a step above the men she'd come into contact with so far in London. He was cool, cosmopolitan, cultured. Probably well-off too, working in banking.

She could see him going to the theatre. She bet he appreciated a good play.

'You should report the theft to the police,' he said when they were getting up to leave. 'The chances of your bag being found are tiny, but a tiny chance is better than none.'

When she agreed, he asked in the café for directions to a *gendarmerie*, where again he did most of the talking. She was lucky he'd been around. She felt taken care of.

'Right,' he said outside the station, 'I'm going to put you in a taxi and send you back to your hotel.'

She protested, saying she didn't mind walking, but in truth the experience had drained her, and the day was getting chillier, and she was glad when he insisted. He paid the driver, again ignoring her protestations, and settled her in.

'It was nice meeting you,' he said, 'despite the circumstances.'

'You too. Thank you for everything. You've been so kind.'

'My pleasure. I'll keep an eye out for you in London.'

He closed the door and stood on the path as they drove off. No doubt he thought her very naïve.

Back at the hotel, she found the rest of them sitting with cups of hot tea around a roaring fire in the bar, looking somewhat improved. She told them of the theft, and the man who'd come to her aid – and in bed later she heard again his beautiful accent, and saw again the dark, dark eyes.

She imagined the two of them in Rome, strolling hand in hand through the ancient streets, tossing coins into a fountain, gazing at Michelangelo's *Pietà*. They might stop in a doorway to kiss in the moonlight, his hands caressing her body as she tasted the limoncello he'd sipped after their shared pizza . . .

She pulled the bedclothes more tightly around her, smiling at her foolishness. She must really be desperate if she was turning a man she scarcely knew into a lover. Chances were she'd never lay eyes on him again.

That night, despite her calamitous day, or maybe because of it, she slept more deeply and soundly than she'd done in months.

Engagement

IN MAY, FRANCES FELL IN THE HALL AND LAY WITH
a broken hip all night till the postman heard her calling in the
morning. She spent a week in hospital and another in a nursing
home, and when she was deemed strong enough to be sent home
Ellen took a few days off work and made her way straight to Galway,
cooking meals and pulling weeds from the flowerbeds while
Frances issued instructions from her garden seat.

Towards the end of July, a letter arrived for Ellen from Joan. She
felt a prickle of alarm: Joan only ever slipped a letter in with their
mother's. Something must be wrong for her to send her own.

Dear Ellen
I hope all is well. I'm writing with good news. Seamus and I are
engaged, and we're getting married on the fourteenth of September.

What?
The fourteenth of September, not even two months away. Of
course she was always going to marry Seamus, but she'd said
nothing about planning a wedding in any of her letters.

I hope you can come. We're not bothering with printed invitations, so this is it. We're getting married in St Finian's, with a reception after at home. We're only inviting twenty-four, so we'll get caterers to do a buffet. Fingers crossed for a fine day, so we can use the garden too.

Just twenty-four guests, and a reception at home? Joan had always talked about having a big wedding, with the reception in Shannon's Hotel.

We're going to invite Frances as well. Please let me know if you'll be able to come, and feel free to bring a guest if you want.
    love Joan

Ellen read it twice. It was a lot to take in. 'Joan's getting married,' she told Claire.

'That'll be a big splash.'

'Actually, it won't. They're only inviting twenty-four and having the reception at home.'

Claire's eyes narrowed. 'When?'

'September.'

'This September?'

'Yes.'

'Pregnant,' Claire said immediately. 'Congrats – you'll be an auntie by Christmas.'

'I'll ring her' – and when she did, Joan confirmed it.

'I was on the pill,' she said. 'I'm just one of the unlucky few.'

'Since when were you on the pill? Don't you have to be married in Ireland to get it?'

'I've been on it for four years. Doctor O'Brien prescribes it if you say you have bad periods.'

Doctor O'Brien, who'd been their GP since the family had moved into the town. Doctor Imelda O'Brien, who must be near retirement, doing her bit for the sex lives of young single Irishwomen. 'When are you due?'

'January.'

Not quite an auntie by Christmas then. 'And how are you feeling – physically, I mean?'

'Rotten. I'm sick every morning. Just hoping it'll have stopped by the wedding.'

'Hopefully. And otherwise, how do you feel about it?'

'Well, we'd rather have waited a while, but we're going to do the right thing.'

Ellen thought of Claire's abortion. 'How did Mam take it when you told her?'

'She's OK now. We had to talk her around a bit, but she likes Seamus, and she's happy we're getting married.'

'Is she still seeing . . . that man?' She'd forgotten his name. There had been no further mention of him, no sighting of him on her trips home since Joan had told her about him over two years ago.

'Kevin? Yes, he's coming to the wedding. I hope you can make it.'

'Of course I'll make it. I wouldn't miss it.'

'Is there anyone you want to bring?'

Any boyfriend, she meant. Ellen would far rather ask Claire than try and find a man to keep everyone happy, but her mother wouldn't be impressed.

'Nobody,' she said. Nobody who interested her enough to issue that kind of invitation. Certainly not Geoff, whose offbeat personality had started to grate just a bit over the last few weeks. He was a solid work partner, that hadn't changed, but he really wasn't as funny or as cool as he thought he was – or maybe she was just a little tired of his quirkiness.

She wondered if it was time to look for another ad agency. She'd been at Marketing Solutions for two and a half years, and while it had given her a great start, she thought she might be outgrowing it. Was there something better that she should be aiming for? She felt more confident now, and she had a body of real work behind her.

She thought of Claire, who'd taken over the sandwich-bar rental at the start of the year as she'd planned, and who was busy and loving it – and making good money for the first time, enough to finally hand in her notice at the pub. Claire was steering an upward course: maybe it was time for Ellen to do the same.

At lunchtime she rang Laura from a phone box on the street. 'I think I'm ready for a change of job,' she said. 'Anyone looking for a copywriter?'

'I'll make enquiries,' Laura promised. 'Do up a new CV, put everything down that you can think of, and let me have copies of all you've done at Marketing Solutions. Tim will give you a nice reference?'

'Definitely.'

'Leave it with me. Check in like before, every few days, and hopefully it won't take long.'

It took until the first week in September.

'They're called Creative Ways,' Laura said. 'They're an American operation – Chicago, Los Angeles and New York – and they want to move into London. They're planning to open at the start of

November, and they're recruiting now. They've located premises in Battersea.'

Battersea. She knew where it was from her weekend wanderings. South of the river, relatively close to Notting Hill.

'I faxed them your CV as soon as they got in touch,' Laura said. 'They want you to come for an interview on Friday afternoon, four o'clock.'

'Perfect.' She could take a day off. She felt a rising excitement that she tried to quell. She shouldn't get her hopes up – it was an interview, not a job offer. It might come to nothing.

But for now, it was something.

Interview

She stood outside the building and counted six storeys. The frontage was pretty much a wall of glass, every pane looking out at the Thames. If she'd been searching for the polar opposite of Marketing Solutions, she'd found it.

It unnerved her. It reminded her of the big swanky agencies that had made her quake, back in the days when she was looking for copy tests and dreaming of working in advertising. She wanted to ring Laura and say she'd changed her mind, she'd stay put at Marketing Solutions, where everything was small and familiar and safe.

She imagined saying it to Frances, and she could hear her aunt's typically blunt reaction. *Nonsense – they asked for you, they want to see you. Don't be so cowardly!*

And then she heard: *What if you try and don't fail?*

She pulled herself together. She climbed the wide stone steps and pushed through a revolving door into the lobby, which had a marble floor and a wooden bank of pigeonholes set against one wall. A burly moustachioed man in a navy uniform sitting behind a large desk lowered his newspaper and regarded Ellen over his glasses.

'Can I help you?'

'I'm looking for Creative Ways,' she told him, and he got her to sign a register.

'Fifth floor,' he said, indicating a pair of lifts at the far end.

Fifth floor made things less terrifying. The idea that they occupied only one floor, or maybe even just part of that floor, gave her new heart. She tightened her grip on her portfolio – a bigger one than the original, full of actual ads, leaflets and brochures – and glided up in the lift, taking the opportunity for a final inspection in the mirrored wall.

She'd splashed out on a royal blue trouser suit, on sale in John Lewis at the end of the summer. Her first serious clothing purchase in London, and deemed the perfect interview outfit by Claire. *Hold your head up*, she'd said. *Shoulders back. Keep telling yourself they'll be lucky to get you.*

Easier said than done. Yet again, she wished for Claire's easy confidence.

The lift opened onto another smaller lobby. *Creative Ways* was written above double doors in orange lettering. No other company sign in evidence, so it looked like they did have the full floor. She pushed through the doors and found a reception desk with nobody behind it, and stacked-up boxes all over the place. After waiting a few minutes for someone to appear, she tapped on another door to the left of the desk.

'Hello?' she called, feeling foolish. 'Anyone there?'

Almost immediately she heard the rapid tap of advancing footsteps. The door was flung open by a teenage girl fastening a strap of her denim dungarees. 'Sorry,' she said cheerfully, 'I needed the loo. I take it you're Ellen.'

'That's right.'

'I'm Lucinda, lovely to meet you.' She pushed hands through long brown hair. 'Excuse the mess – we're not properly set up yet. We will be more organised then, I promise. Come this way.'

Ellen followed her down a corridor full of more boxes – 'Watch your step' – to a room that contained just a desk, a couch and a coffee table. A man behind the desk – thirtyish, clean-shaven, short-haired – got to his feet as they entered.

'This is Ellen,' the receptionist said.

'Thanks for coming along,' he replied, getting up to offer her his hand. American or Canadian by his accent; Ellen could never tell the difference. A shirt so white it had to be new, and white teeth too. He reminded her of the Mormons, ringing doorbells with fresh, hopeful smiles and Bibles under their arms. 'I'm Justin, and you've met my wife Lucinda.'

His wife? Ellen couldn't hide her surprise. Seeing it, Lucinda laughed.

'I'm twenty-five. Everyone thinks I'm younger. Runs in the family – my mum's forty-eight, and she could be my sister. Justin thought he was going to be arrested every time we went out in the States.'

They told her they'd met at Creative Ways in New York, where they'd both been working, and they'd been chosen to head up the new London branch because of Lucinda being English.

'So far,' she told Ellen, 'we've recruited three account handlers, no creatives yet. We're aiming for an initial workforce of twenty, with a creative department of eight. Justin's an accountant so he'll be managing the books, and I'm an art director, and I'll also head up the creative department. Why don't you tell us a little of your story and what you're hoping for?'

She made it easy; they both did. They were complimentary about her portfolio, and seemed charmed by her account of the prizes she'd won. 'I'll definitely keep you in mind next time I come across a competition,' Lucinda declared.

By the end of it, Ellen felt she'd given as good an account of herself as she could. They thanked her for coming in, and promised to let her know by the end of the following week. Too energised for the lift, Ellen bounded down the stairs to the ground floor, and gave the security guard a jaunty wave on her way out.

She walked in sunshine back to the Tube, stopping along the way to ring Laura.

'Well – did you like them?'

'I did. They were really nice. I think they liked me.'

'That's great. I'll be in touch as soon as I hear. Best of luck – my fingers are tightly crossed for you.'

The days of the week that followed crawled past. By Friday morning, Ellen had convinced herself that Justin and Lucinda hadn't after all considered her good enough to work with them. She trudged from the Tube station to work, weekend bag in hand, on her way to Ireland that evening for Joan's wedding the following day, trying to summon up enthusiasm for the trip.

In the late afternoon, ten minutes before finishing time, Debbie appeared from reception with an envelope and handed it to Ellen. 'Delivered by courier,' she said.

It was plain white, A4 size. There was more than one page in it. No indication of who had sent it – which meant it had to have come from Laura, who was being discreet. Ellen wanted to rip it open on the spot, but she couldn't, not with the others there.

She slipped it into her bag and waited for the clock to crawl to half five. When it did, she switched off her computer. 'Sorry to miss the Friday drinks. Have a nice weekend, everyone.'

'Enjoy the wedding,' Kit said. 'Don't forget to catch the bouquet.'

She lasted till she reached the Tube station. She stood by a wall and wedged her bag between her feet and ripped open the envelope. She pulled out the stapled-together bundle of pages and skimmed the note that had been paper-clipped to the top page as people streamed past her.

Ellen,

Congratulations, delighted for you! I'm going to courier this to your work so you get it as soon as possible. Have a read of the attached and think about it, and if you're happy with everything give me a ring on Monday, and I'll need you to sign and return the contract by the end of next week.

    Laura

She folded the note and tucked it into her pocket and found another handwritten communication beneath.

Dear Ellen,

We are delighted to offer you a copywriting job with Creative Ways. We were really impressed with you when we met last week: your track record at Marketing Solutions speaks for itself, and we feel that personally you'd fit right in here. You came across as capable and friendly, and not afraid of challenges and hard work – our kind of person!

*   As we mentioned at your interview, we're hoping to open for*

business in early November, and we'd love to have all our staff recruited by the end of next week. We're attaching your contract: please read carefully and make sure you're happy with everything. We'll be waiting for Laura to give us your response, and we really hope you'll come and join us in this exciting venture.

Best regards,

Lucinda and Justin

On the Tube she read the contract slowly, and then went through it a second time. The salary they were offering was almost twice what she was earning in Marketing Solutions. She would have twenty days' holidays a year, five fewer than her current job. She was perfectly happy to work five extra days for nearly double the money.

Nearly double the money. Real earnings, like Claire.

She slipped the contract back into the envelope and returned it to her bag, fizzing with excitement. She'd say nothing at home till after the wedding: tomorrow was Joan's day.

At the airport she checked in and went straight through to the departure lounge. For once she ordered a white wine, instead of her usual pre-flight coffee, and took it to a bank of chairs that faced the wall of windows. She lifted her drink and toasted herself silently. A new job. Moving on, moving up.

The future was bright and exciting.

Wedding

'WE INVITED GRANNY AND GRANDPA SHEEHAN,' Joan said. 'I felt we should. They sent a cheque for a hundred pounds, and said sorry they couldn't make it. We won't be telling them when the baby is born. They clearly want out of our lives, so let them be out.'

Their father's parents knew where he was, of course. He wouldn't have cut them off too. But they'd quietly drifted away from their granddaughters after he'd left. It used to hurt when Ellen thought about it, but not any more.

They still sent birthday and Christmas cards to Joan and Ellen, the messages always in Gran's writing. *From Gran and Grandpa Sheehan, hope all's well, everything fine here, love to your mam.* Better, Ellen thought, that they'd ignored those occasions too. The cards felt dutiful, nothing more.

'How do I look?' Joan asked.

'You look wonderful.'

They were about to leave for the church. Her cream dress with its full skirt hid her small bump. Ellen had tied her sister's pale brown hair into a topknot and persuaded her to sweep a little blusher onto her cheeks. The morning sickness hadn't quite abated.

'Thanks again for the perfume,' Joan said. 'It must have cost a bomb.'

She looked happy, Ellen thought. She'd found what she wanted. The little diamond in Seamus' ring winked as she tucked a strand of hair behind her ear.

At the church, as they waited for the ceremony to begin, Ellen was introduced to Kevin, her mother's . . . friend? Boyfriend? Partner? Nothing sounded right. Balding and shy in a pinstriped suit, he told her he'd been looking forward to meeting her. 'Patricia speaks very highly of you,' he said, nodding and blushing. It sounded like something a person would say to be polite.

Their mother walked Joan up the aisle as Joan's teacher friend Louise played the organ. For some reason, Ellen thought of Ben. Yes, the piano, the music degree he'd wanted to get. She allowed herself, just for a second, to imagine that she was the bride on her mother's arm, and Ben the groom waiting at the top of the church for her.

She watched the pair progressing slowly up the aisle, and thought how sad it was that their father was missing his younger daughter's wedding. How awful it was that he'd left them, and walked off into another life. What would Ellen say if she ever met him again? She had no idea.

The weather was kind to them. After the buffet meal, after they'd cut the wedding cake, and after Seamus' father had given an unexpectedly funny speech, guests drifted out to the garden and sat in small knots on borrowed seating under a clear blue September sky.

In the evening, when everyone had left, and the bride and groom had driven off to spend the night in Shannon's Hotel, and Ellen's mother had gone to bed, Ellen and Frances sat in dressing gowns at the kitchen table. Frances had been given Joan's room for the night, but she and Ellen weren't yet ready for sleep.

She'd be seventy-one in a week's time, the skin on the backs of her hands beginning to blotch and crimp. She'd retired from the country house hotel on her seventieth birthday.

'Did you never find someone, Frances?' Ellen asked. She'd had a few glasses of wine; it seemed like a question she could ask, and late enough in the day to ask it.

'I did, but it wasn't to be. Too many things went against it. That was a long time ago. It's history now.'

Silence fell. Ellen didn't press for more.

'By the way,' she said, just remembering, 'I got a new job, with a new company. It's a nice step up from the old one.'

'That's wonderful news,' Frances replied. 'Well done; I always knew you'd go far. You can tell me all about it in the morning. Now,' rising, 'I think it's time for bed.'

They walked together up the stairs. In her old room, Ellen sat on the edge of her single bed as memories crowded in. For twelve years she'd slept here. In this room she'd moved from a child to an adult, weathering life's small everyday challenges until a big one had upended everything.

Without planning to, she slid a hand between the base of her bed and the mattress. She pulled out an envelope, limp with age, just as she had done every night years earlier. She looked at her name in the familiar handwriting before slowly drawing out the single sheet. She knew what it said by heart, but she unfolded it anyway.

Ellen, my dearest girl,
It breaks my heart to leave you and Joan, but it's become impos-
sible for me to stay. Please look after your mother, and try not to
think too badly of me. I'm so sorry.
    Always your loving father

How she'd puzzled over it, wept over it, raged over it. What did he mean, it had become impossible for him to stay? How could he write that and not explain it? And why had he not kept in touch? Surely he knew how much his leaving, his unexplained leaving, would wound the daughters he'd professed to love?

Ellen had gone to pieces after he'd left. She'd become uncharacteristically rebellious, breaking every rule she could get away with. At weekends she'd stayed out later than she was allowed, often getting home not completely sober, shouting at her mother to leave her alone if she was challenged.

She'd taken up smoking, forcing herself to pull the hot smoke into her lungs, persisting until it began to feel like something she needed. She'd also begun to steal from shops, a thing she hadn't had the nerve to try up to this.

Everyone had made allowances. Everyone had felt sorry for her. Her mother lectured, but didn't punish. Nothing anyone said made a difference – until the day she'd felt a hand on her shoulder as she left a boutique with a silk scarf pushed up her sleeve.

That, and all that had followed – the arrival to the shop of a guard whose daughter was in her class, the mortifying journey home in a squad car, her mother's incredulous face when she opened the door – had brought her to her senses. She'd quit smoking and stealing and skipping classes, and life had limped along until she'd left school with mediocre exam results.

She'd found a job she had no interest in, just to keep her mother quiet, and her only happy times were when she was with Claire, experimenting with make-up in her friend's room, hitching their skirts higher on the way to discos, thumbing lifts to shop in nearby towns. In her determined pursuit of fun, and her insistence on Ellen accompanying her, Claire had made it easier.

She looked down at his note again. In the first awful weeks she'd been desperate for a letter, or an address, or anything at all that would connect her with him – but now she wasn't sure what she wanted. Joan had said she wouldn't let him in if he turned up at the house.

Ellen was beginning to be afraid she'd do the same.

Ending

'WELL, I'M DISAPPOINTED, BUT I CAN'T SAY I'M surprised,' Tim said. 'I knew you'd head for bigger and better things, and I'm happy for you. Our loss.'

'Second that,' Alf added. 'We're gutted to lose you.'

'I hope my new bosses will be as good as my old ones,' Ellen replied. 'I've learnt so much here. Thank you for taking a chance on me.'

Tim smiled. 'No chance was taken, Ellen. I could see you had what it took when I interviewed you.'

Word spread. 'Sorry you're going,' Geoff said. 'You're great to work with.'

'You too.'

'How could you leave me alone with all these men?' Kit demanded. 'Not fair.'

Ellen laughed. 'You managed fine before I arrived – and maybe they'll find a woman to replace me.'

'I'll live in hope. Excited about the new job?'

'Very – although I'll miss everyone here.'

'We'll miss you too.'

She'd had a note from Lucinda a few days after she'd accepted the job.

Ellen,
Justin and I are delighted you're coming on board – and I'd like
you and me to be a creative team, if you're agreeable. I think we'd
work well together. See you at 9.00 a.m. on November fourth.
Dress how you want – we're casual here.
   My best,
   Lucinda

She wrote to Danny with the news. He wrote back.

Hey, that's fantastic – and you're going in at the start, just like I
did in Dublin. Delighted for you, pal – won't feel it till you're a
big shot on the London advertising scene.

On her last day at Marketing Solutions they threw a surprise party for her in the reception area. She was presented with a giant card that everyone had signed, and a cake was brought out with *Best of Luck Ellen* on top, and they washed down the cake with champagne – the proper stuff, which she'd never tasted. 'Keep the cork,' Alf said when she told him it was her first, so she did.

Her first champagne. Even at the ripe old age of twenty-four, she was still having firsts.

Beginning

NOVEMBER FOURTH WAS COLD AND DRY. UNDER her sheepskin jacket she wore a green mohair sweater and her favourite Levi's, and tan fur-lined desert boots that were as comfortable as slippers. No need to be nervous, she told herself on the Tube. Everyone was new today, not just her.

The same moustachioed man sat behind the same desk in the lobby. 'I'm starting work at Creative Ways,' she told him, and he wished her well and got her to sign a different register to the one she'd signed before.

'Just for your first day,' he said, 'so we have a record of employees.'

'Nice to meet you,' the receptionist on the fifth floor said. 'I'm Bella, Lucinda's sister.' She was a darker-haired version of Lucinda. 'The studio's at the end of the corridor.'

The piled-up boxes had disappeared. There was a smell of fresh paint. The door at the end of the corridor was open.

'Ellen,' Lucinda said, 'come and meet everyone.'

Two Americans, one Australian, four English and Ellen, who was secretly pleased to be the only Irish creative. Everybody looked under thirty. Jamie, one of the Americans, wore two tiny studs, one gold, one silver, in his right ear. Briony, English, had a tumble of curls like Claire's and shiny black platform boots that extended to mid-thigh. 'I love your red hair,' she said to Ellen, the first time anyone had complimented it.

The studio was L-shaped, with three pairs of desks against the long wall, and Ellen and Lucinda's in the other section. A round table with eight chairs was positioned in the corner of the L. Appointment diaries and pens, branded with the company logo, sat on everyone's desk.

Lucinda gave a short talk, listing the clients already secured. 'We need,' she said, 'to deliver top-class advertising. We need to be original and cutting edge. We want people talking about us – and remember, even though you're working in a team of two, you're also a team of eight. The big table,' she said, pointing, 'is for when a job needs everyone to pitch in with ideas. It's there to be used, so let's use it.

'I should add that your pairings are not set in stone – because we're all new here, it remains to be seen how we work with our assigned partners. Let's see how we go for a month, and then review the situation.'

Her hair was tied up today in a ponytail. She looked even younger than Ellen remembered, in a blue and white gingham shirt over jeans, but her voice rang with confidence. She knew what she was doing.

It was thrilling to be part of it. Ellen loved that she was paired with Lucinda – she felt it gave her an advantage right off, like odds in a race. The eight of them spent the morning in their teams of two, reading up on the client brands. At noon, Bella appeared with menus from a local delicatessen and took orders for sandwiches and drinks, which arrived at one. They brought them to the staff canteen just down the corridor, and as they ate, they talked.

Stuart, the Australian, gave an account of the two weeks he'd spent volunteering in an elephant sanctuary in Namibia before arriving in the UK: 'We went on poacher patrols, and built protective walls around water sources, and reported elephant movement to the government.'

Briony told them of the rock band she'd joined age sixteen, to her parents' horror: 'I wanted to be the next Suzi Quatro. We lasted four months and got no gigs at all. There went that dream.'

'Ellen, tell them about the competitions,' Lucinda prompted, so Ellen, self-conscious, listed her wins, and the others seemed impressed, but she felt it wasn't half as interesting as working with elephants or being a member of a rock band, with or without gigs.

After lunch they returned to the studio and sat around the big table, and tossed ideas about for possible advertising angles for each client. Ellen listened to the contributions, and made some of her own, and pinched herself that she was in what felt like exactly the right place for her.

As four o'clock approached, Lucinda told them they were finishing early so they could meet the rest of the company. She brought them to one of the meeting rooms, where others were already congregating, and where the polished table was laid with bottles of wine and jugs of water and plates of cheese, and dishes of fat olives and mixed nuts and dried figs.

Justin gave a short welcoming talk. 'Momentous day,' he said. 'The first day of the London branch of Creative Ways. Lucinda and I are excited, and we hope you're excited too. Within our small company we have five nationalities, so we'll have a lot to learn from one another.' He raised his glass. 'Here's to our new venture, and all who sail in her.'

The wine tasted expensive. Ellen shook various hands, trying to remember all the names. She was careful not to drink too much, but on the Tube on the way home her head buzzed gently and pleasantly. She reached into her bag for her book, but for once she found it hard to concentrate on the story, her mind bent on replaying her first day.

'Excuse me.'

She looked up to see a man sitting directly across from her. Dark hair, navy overcoat, polished shoes. Cradling a bottle-shaped package. Something familiar about him. They'd met before – but where?

'I may be wrong,' he said, 'but did we meet in Paris, at the start of the year?'

Paris. The man who'd chased the thief who'd snatched her bag. She beamed at him, braver because of the wine. 'Oh, we did. You came to my rescue.'

He lifted a hand to dismiss it, giving the gentle smile she remembered. 'I tried.'

'You were very kind. Nice to see you again.' She hadn't thought about him in months. What were the chances of a second encounter in a city the size of London? She'd forgotten his name, and how good-looking he was, and how attractive his voice.

'Ellen,' he said, 'isn't it?'

She was inordinately pleased that he'd remembered hers. 'It is indeed, but I'm afraid—'

'Leo,' he said. 'My memory is embarrassingly good. So how have you been?'

They talked. She told him about the new job, hoping she didn't sound too animated. 'Just started today, actually.'

'Wonderful. I haven't heard of them.'

'They're American, new to London. Starting up in Battersea.'

'My stomping ground,' he said. 'Wishing you every success.'

'Thank you.'

A short pause followed. The train rattled along its rail. She wished she'd chosen less casual clothes this morning. Her beloved sheepskin felt suddenly shabby – and the desert boots, Lord.

The train stopped. Passengers got off. He crossed the aisle and took a newly vacated seat beside her.

'Would you by any chance care to have dinner sometime?'

Wow – he was asking her out. She felt herself flushing. 'Oh . . . well, that would . . . yes, I'd like that.' She wondered if he could smell the wine on her breath.

'Great. How's this weekend?'

She thought fast. On Friday she and Claire had planned to see *Desperately Seeking Susan*. 'I'm free Saturday night.'

'Saturday it is.' He took a little notebook from a pocket inside his coat. 'Let me have your address and I'll pick you up.'

She blinked. The conversation felt like it was galloping along. She recited her address, her thoughts spinning. 'We're on the top floor,' she said. 'Flat 6.'

'Shall we say half past seven?'

'Yes, fine.'

'Lovely. I'll book us a table somewhere nice.' He got to his feet as the train approached Bond Street Station. 'Well, this is me,' he said, 'off to a seventieth birthday party, for my sins.'

His smile. 'Enjoy,' she said.

The train stopped. The doors slid open. 'Bye, Ellen.'

'Bye, Leo.'

She practically skipped home. She had a date, and it was with by far the most interesting man she'd met in London, the most interesting man since Ben. He was booking a table. They were going somewhere nice for dinner. He was picking her up. She'd need something very swish to wear.

It felt like she was on the brink of something, teetering on a precipice.

And she was dying to jump.

Date

SHE WROTE TO FRANCES, JUST FRANCES, AND TOLD her.

Remember the man who tried to catch the thief who stole my bag in Paris? Would you believe I met him on the Tube going home from work on my first day, and he asked me out to dinner – wish me luck!

She knew what her aunt would say if they were face to face. *Be yourself,* Frances would advise. *Don't try to be anything you're not.* All well and good, but what if herself wasn't intelligent enough, or funny enough, or pretty enough?

He was older – she wondered how much older – and sophisticated enough to have a French mother. She was fairly sure he came from a wealthier background than she did; what would he see in plain old Ellen Sheehan, whose family was not in the least wealthy or sophisticated?

She wondered about his romantic history. He was sure to have plenty of it. In fact, she was surprised he hadn't been snapped up already. Then again, maybe he had: maybe he'd been married and divorced, or maybe he still had a wife he wasn't telling her about. Again, she found herself wishing for an instruction manual, one that would list five signs, say, that could identify a married man.

She welcomed the distraction of work, like she'd welcomed the busy times at the sandwich bar, when the pain of losing Ben was still sharp. Her first task with Lucinda was to create a full-page magazine ad to launch a new range of handcrafted fountain pens.

Make a point, Ellen's headline proclaimed in beautiful copperplate script, above Lucinda's close-up photograph of the working end of a pen, gold nib poised above a dot of ink on a sheet of textured ivory notepaper. The concept was approved by the client, along with Ellen's suggestion of a limited offer of a box of beautiful notepaper with every fountain pen purchase.

'Good start,' Lucinda said. 'I foresee great things for the team of us, Ellen.'

Taking the Tube home on Friday evening, she thought of the silk dress that was soft as a whisper on her skin, waiting on its hanger for tomorrow night, beneath the new red coat with cashmere in it. She'd spent her first month's wages before earning them, and she didn't care.

Saturday came, dry and crisp. She whiled away the day alone, Claire at work. She cleaned the flat and brought bedding to the launderette. She did a grocery shop and changed her library books, conscious of a persistent nagging anxiety.

Back at the flat she painted her nails and plucked her eyebrows and spread horrible-smelling depilatory cream over her legs and showered it off.

She heard the flat door opening as she was drying her hair. 'Only me,' Claire called, and water ran. A few minutes later she appeared at the door of Ellen's room in a low-cut top and black leather pants. 'That is one heck of a dress,' she said. 'Your banker will tear it off you.'

'I suspect he'll be too much of a gentleman.'

'You'll just have to knock that out of him. See you when I see you,' she said, winding a scarf around her neck. 'Good luck, have fun. You look great. Relax.'

Easier said than done. Ellen perched on the futon, afraid to move in case she creased her dress. Did silk crease? At two minutes after half seven, the front doorbell buzzed, causing her heart to give an answering leap. She pressed the buzzer and heard, three floors down, the front door opening and closing.

Calm down. Relax. She eased her feet into Claire's black stilettos. She dabbed Chanel on her wrists and at her throat and behind her ears. She ran her tongue over her teeth and took a deep breath.

There was a tap on the door. Her heart jumped again at the sound of it.

'Hi,' he said, giving her the smile that in her already nervous state caused a fresh flock of butterflies to rise up and whirl inside her. 'You look lovely.'

'Thank you.'

He looked lovely too. The same dark heavy coat, dark trousers beneath, an olive green scarf around his neck. The tip of his nose was pink with cold.

She took up her bag – Claire's bag – and lifted her new coat from the futon.

'Here' – he reached for it and held it while she put it on. She pulled the door closed behind her, and she felt his hand lightly on her back as they descended the stairs. She tried to walk as if she was used to stilettos. She could have done with more practice.

A taxi idled outside. He took her to a restaurant with widely spaced tables covered in white cloths, and no prices on the menu. They shared a starter of mixed nibbles – olives, nuts, pâté, cooked meats, warm bread – and both followed with the poached salmon. The dishes were simple, perfectly flavoured and beautifully presented. Every so often their waiter appeared and discreetly topped up their glasses with ice-cold white wine.

They talked. He told her of his upbringing, divided between England and France, and his father's death in a road accident when Leo was fifteen, and his mother's passion for sailing, and his two half-brothers from her second marriage. He was thirty-four now, he told her, and didn't enquire how old she was, and she didn't tell him she was ten years younger.

He'd been to Eton. He meditated, off and on. He was ambidextrous. He'd been skiing since he was six. He liked reggae and jazz. He worked for the same bank he'd started with after college. He found the work soulless, but it paid well and he was good at it.

He'd never been married. No children. 'My mother says I'm too particular,' he told her, laughing.

He laughed often. He gestured a lot when he spoke. His table manners were impeccable. He listened when she told him of her job in the bookshop in Ireland, and her days in the sandwich bar, and her move to Marketing Solutions, and from there to Creative Ways.

She told him her parents were separated, and he didn't probe. He didn't ask if she'd been married, probably assuming that she was too young to have a failed marriage behind her. He enquired about siblings, and she spoke of Joan. 'Thirteen months younger than me,' she said. 'We just missed being Irish twins.'

'What's that?'

'Children born into the same family less than twelve months apart. Holy Catholic Ireland,' she said, just to make him laugh, and it did.

She wondered what living arrangements he had. On the Tube he'd called Battersea his stomping ground, so he might live close enough to her workplace. She didn't imagine he shared with anyone. There was a good chance he owned the place he lived in.

'Dessert?' he asked, and she shook her head, so he took her to a jazz club with red lamps on the little tables and wonderful music, where she sipped her first cherry brandy, and said no thanks to a second, afraid of stumbling in the stilettos.

He brought her back to the flat in another taxi and walked her to the front door. 'I hope you had a good time,' he said, linking his fingers in hers. His skin was cool. He smelt wonderful; she kept inhaling him.

'I did, thank you.'

'I did too. I'm glad you said yes. Would you like to do it again?'

Oh. 'I would.'

'What about next weekend, same day, same time?'

A whole week to wait. 'Yes, fine. Great.'

He took a card from his wallet. 'My number,' he said, 'just in case you need to reach me. Do you have one?'

'Just at work – and I'm afraid I haven't learnt it off yet.' And unlike him, she didn't have a business card.

'Creative Ways, right?'

'Yes.' He listened. He remembered. What had he said on the Tube? An embarrassingly good memory.

He leant in and kissed her goodnight – a soft, gentlemanly kiss, more gentlemanly than it needed to be. He didn't ask to come in, and she didn't suggest it. What he'd seen of the flat must have looked terribly basic to him, and that was the most presentable part of it. She imagined his reaction to a mattress on the floor.

She entered the house in a kind of daze. Upstairs she cleaned her face and brushed her teeth. She took off her new clothes and hung them on the clothes rail that had come from the market. She fell asleep with the evening running on repeat in her head.

He'd enjoyed it. He wanted to do it again. She'd felt looked after by him, as she had in Paris. She felt chosen by him. She couldn't imagine why, but it had happened.

On Tuesday morning a card arrived to her work.

Ellen,
Thank you for Saturday. It was wonderful. See you next week.
  Leo x

Love

IN DECEMBER, AFTER THEIR FIFTH DATE, HE TOOK her back to his house – old and tall and narrow, located in a quiet square, and yes, he owned it – and they became lovers in his brass bed, and she felt like she was living in a Dylan song. She went on the pill, even though it hadn't stopped Joan from becoming pregnant. 'You don't have to,' Leo told her. 'I'm OK with condoms' – but she wasn't a fan of them, and this felt like it might last.

Please let it last. Please don't let him leave as well. She didn't know who she was asking – she'd stopped believing in God after her father had left – but maybe someone, or something, was listening.

Leo was the first man she felt deeply for since Ben. Now she could finally let her old love go, although she suspected he would live on, somewhere within her, maybe for the rest of her life. Did first loves always do that? Did they become after their departure an indelible mark, a small, silent presence in the other's heart?

Lying in Leo's arms afterwards, too full of emotion to sleep, she heard the pure song of a bird in the square outside, and wondered if it was a nightingale. She thought of magic abroad in the air, and angels dining at the Ritz on the night another pair of lovers had met. The song had been her grandmother's party piece, back in the days when they still met up.

Two days before Christmas they kissed goodbye in Heathrow, Ellen bound for Ireland, he for France. 'Next Christmas,' he promised, 'we'll spend together,' and the thought of her being in his future plans warmed her all the way home. On the plane she opened his gift, unable to wait, and found a white gold chain on which hung her first diamond, a perfect teardrop. Her gift to him was more humble, a just-published biography of Charlie Chaplin. They had different reading tastes, he sticking to non-fiction – history, politics and biographies – she only wanting to get lost in a novel.

In January 1986 Joan gave birth to a son. They called him Ivan after Seamus' father, and Ellen flew back for the christening and to become his godmother. *Bring your new man*, Joan said – but Ellen told her he was too tied up with work. She wanted his introduction to the family to be a thing in itself, not tagged onto another occasion – and anyway, she might scare him off if she suggested introducing him to her family too soon.

As it happened, he was the first to make introductions. In March, his French mother Marguerite came to stay with him for a few days, and he took both women out to dinner so they could become acquainted. Marguerite was trim and angular, with stiff beige hair swept into a chignon, and pale unpainted lips and slightly bulbous grey eyes, and she wore perfectly tailored jacket-and-skirt suits and an air of patient boredom, and Leo was nothing like her, physically or temperamentally. Ellen put her in her late sixties, somewhere between Ellen's own mother and Frances.

'Pleased to meet you,' Marguerite said, nodding coolly, and her hand when she offered it to Ellen was cold and dry. Everything about her lacked warmth. Her smile, on the rare occasions it appeared, was weary and humourless. During the single evening they spent together, Ellen formed the opinion that his mother was unimpressed with Leo's choice, and she tried not to let it hurt.

She and my stepfather divorced last year, Leo had told her. *She found it very difficult.* Widowed by her first husband, divorced from the second. Maybe she didn't have much to smile about. Ellen wondered what Leo's French half-brothers were like, and hoped to find out at some stage.

In May, a charity press ad that Ellen and Lucinda had created won a commendation at a newly founded advertising awards event. Leo accompanied her to the awards night, where he met her colleagues for the first time. 'I approve,' Lucinda told her afterwards. 'Definitely a catch.'

He met Claire a few times in the flat, when he turned up to collect Ellen. 'Not bad,' she said. 'Very suave, very man-about-town. Wouldn't be for me – I prefer them more rough and ready – but he's perfect for you.'

He *was* perfect for Ellen. She constantly wondered why he'd chosen her, when he could surely have his pick of women. She'd asked him once, in jest but not really, and he'd ticked off the reasons on his fingers.

'Because of your intelligence, and your creativity, and your kind heart, and your smile, and your accent, and your red Irish hair, and your pretty grey eyes. And because little things make you happy.'

'Is that all?' She feigned disappointment.

'And because of the way you read,' he said, 'as if you're eating up the words. And because of the way you kiss.'

'How do I kiss?'

'Generously,' he said. 'It's hard to explain; better if we have a demonstration. Pay attention now.'

He told her he loved her every time they were together. He whispered endearments when they lay in his bed, called her sweetheart and darling girl and poppet, and she closed her eyes and let his beautiful voice wash over her.

She tortured herself by asking about his past loves. He told her, when she insisted, of Caroline whose father was an earl, and who'd broken his heart in college, and Maria, a model who'd left him for an airline pilot. She thought he may well have broken his own share of hearts but didn't ask, preferring not to know.

She told him eventually of her father's departure, and how much it had hurt, and how rightly or wrongly she blamed her mother. She told him about Ben, and what might have been, and about leaving her best friend behind when she was eight, and finding him again years later. There was nothing she didn't tell him – apart from when she'd considered the possibility of her and Danny embarking on something, before she'd been told about Bobbi. He didn't need to know that.

He was the One. He was Mr Right. He was her second big love, and hopefully her forever one.

I've found him, she wrote to Danny at the start of July, when she felt safe committing it to paper. *Finally. Took me long enough. Have you and Bobbi set a date yet, now that you're almost twenty-five, old man?*

Delighted to hear it, he wrote back. *About time. Bobbi and I are in no rush, both busy with work, both happy with the way things are. One day we'll do it, just not yet – and may I remind you that you're a week older than me, and always will be, grandma?*

That's so ungallant of you, reminding a woman of her age. You've cut me to the quick, Daniel O'Meara.

Uh-oh, I know I'm in trouble when someone calls me Daniel. Please accept my almost sincere apologies. Twenty-five, though. Quarter of a century. We're moving on, pal. Enjoy the last of your youth with your French Englishman.

She wrote to Frances too.

He was worth waiting for, Frances. I know you'll like him when you meet him.

I'm sure I will, Frances replied. *As long as he's good to you, that's all I care about.*

Ireland

IN SEPTEMBER SHE ASKED LEO IF HE'D COME WITH
her for a few days to Ireland. 'They think I'm making you up,' she
said, and he said in that case he'd better go. They flew to Shannon,
where her brother-in-law Seamus picked them up, and within thirty
seconds he and Leo discovered a mutual love of rugby, and all the
way home Ellen sat back and left them to it, and willed her mother
to be nice to him.

She was. 'I've been looking forward to meeting you, Leo,' she
said, wearing an unfamiliar lilac dress that brought out the blue in
her eyes. 'Please call me Patricia. Do come in.'

She was like the Queen, leading him into the sitting room that
smelt of polish. She'd lit a fire although the day was warm, and
little dishes of olives, black and green, sat on the coffee table. Ellen
never remembered them eating olives.

Kevin was there, looking too warm in his suit. He stood as they
entered and Ellen made the introductions. He welcomed Leo to
Ireland. 'Your first time?'

'No – I've been to Dublin a few times on business. My first time
in the west.'

'Would you like a whiskey?' Ellen's mother asked Leo, and when he said yes a bottle of Jameson was produced, and a little bowl of ice, and paper serviettes. Watching her fussing about, Ellen realised her mother was nervous. Kevin must have been drafted in for moral support.

She was touched. It felt like an act of kindness, directed as much towards Ellen as towards Leo. She needed to let go of the past, now that she was looking to the future with Leo. Again she remembered Frances' words: *She's doing the best she can.*

Kevin proved a godsend. 'Twelve of us,' he told Leo, 'went to London one summer, working on the buildings. We would have been eighteen or nineteen, we all had a year of college done, and no building experience. Cricklewood,' he said. 'Twelve of us in a three-bedroom house. Good times. Great history in London. You were born there?'

This led on to Leo's English-French ancestry, and that in turn prompted an account of the trip Ellen's mother and Kevin had taken to Normandy, and with every minute that passed, Ellen could feel her own tension being elbowed aside by relief and happiness.

Seamus reappeared for dinner with Joan, Ivan having been deposited at his other grandparents' house for the evening. Ellen noted Joan's sidelong glances at Leo, and she felt a quiet pride. *Look who I got,* she thought. *Look who loves me.*

He loved her. She was loved, and she loved him.

Her mother put them in separate bedrooms, as Ellen had known she would. 'Better keep our distance,' she told Leo, who was highly amused but went along with it. In the morning they picked up a rental car and drove to Galway to meet Frances, who fed them bowls of carrot and coriander soup and warm brown soda bread.

'No Irish blood in you at all?' she asked Leo, and he said not that he knew of, and Ellen couldn't tell what Frances thought of him. Hard to know what impression she was forming.

She told Ellen she'd given up her big black bicycle. 'It was getting too much,' she said. 'I gave it to a friend.' Her job was already gone, and now the bike. Seventy-two at the end of the month: not old, but the years were showing. She still had the battered blue Beetle – Ellen hoped it didn't get out too often. On the few occasions she'd travelled in it with Frances to visit her grandparents' grave, she'd been very glad to emerge alive.

'You go and admire the garden,' Frances told Ellen afterwards. 'Leo will help me wash up,' and Ellen threw him an apologetic glance before obeying. The garden was looking better than ever, Frances having all the time in the world now to tend it. Some day, Ellen thought, she'd have a garden like this.

'Your aunt would have done well in the Gestapo,' Leo remarked on the way back.

'Was it awful?'

'It was very thorough. I thought she was going to look for bank statements. She made it clear how highly she thinks of you – and there was a veiled threat about all sorts of vengeance if I ever do you wrong.'

'Gosh.'

They were due for dinner at Joan and Seamus' house that evening. Ellen was dying to see the changes in Ivan, nearly nine months old now. Beginning to pull himself up to standing, Joan had reported on the phone, the youngest of her work colleagues' babies to do it. One day, Ellen thought, she and Leo would have a child. She couldn't wait.

They went to Rome for Christmas. 'I prefer it in the winter,' Leo said. 'Not so crowded.' Ellen was relieved he hadn't suggested they go to France to spend Christmas with Marguerite, although she would have liked to meet his half-brothers.

They stayed in a hotel that delivered breakfast in bed each morning, and afterwards they soaked in a sunken bath before piling on layers and going out.

They walked over cobbles grown shiny and smooth with age. They gazed at sculptures and frescos and paintings, and Ellen felt overwhelmed at the abundance of beautiful things to look at. They climbed ancient stone steps and flung a scatter of coins into the Trevi Fountain and walked through the Forum, and she insisted on waiting in line (not too long) to marvel, neck craned, at the glory that was the ceiling of the Sistine Chapel.

And one evening, as they strolled back to their hotel after dinner, she pulled him into a doorway and relived the kiss she'd fantasised about after meeting him in Paris, and the moon beamed down as it had in her imaginings, and his mouth tasted of cognac.

On Christmas Day they ordered room service and ate pizza in bed and watched *It's a Wonderful Life* with Italian subtitles on television. He gave her diamonds again, stud earrings this time that twinkled in the light, and she told herself it was too soon for a diamond ring, and they were in no hurry.

She gave him a hardback copy of *The Old Curiosity Shop* she'd found in a secondhand bookshop in Covent Garden. The edges of its red cover were frayed, its wafer-thin pages yellowed and blotched with foxing. *Matthew Goody 1848* was inscribed in neat handwriting on the yellowed flyleaf, the ink faded to pale brown, and even though she knew he would never read it, she simply hadn't been able to resist.

'Wonderful,' Leo said. 'Thank you, my darling.'

Discovery

IN FEBRUARY JOAN SENT PHOTOS OF IVAN TOTTER-
ing around the kitchen floor, arms extended, a look of fierce concen-
tration on his baby features. *We've had to put locks on the presses, and*
gates at the stairs, top and bottom. I can't turn my back for a second.

Ellen showed Leo the photos, and studied his face as he looked
at them. He'd held Ivan on his lap when they'd met in Ireland, and
had shown no sign of unease. She imagined a baby with his dark,
dark eyes.

In May Claire told Ellen she was planning to give up the lease
of the sandwich bar and find a place of her own. 'I've outgrown
it,' she said. 'It's time to move up to bigger and better.'

'Can you afford it?'

'I will next year. Big changes then.'

In June Danny and Bobbi flew to Ireland for a holiday, and Ellen
travelled to meet them. She went alone, Leo having been sent to
a conference in Leeds. She was sorry she couldn't introduce him
to her oldest friend, but looked forward to meeting the woman
who'd caused Danny to cross the Atlantic.

'I've heard so much about you,' Bobbi said. She was striking, with
a halo of brown curls and eyes almost as dark as Leo's, and clear

glowing skin, and teeth that looked too white and perfect to be real. She wore a short blue tunic with little bells around its hem, and flat brown sandals. Her toenails were painted red, with silver rings on both little toes and a thin chain around one ankle. She looked like she got plenty of exercise and ate foods that doctors recommended.

Danny looked good too, hair bleached and skin tanned from the Californian sunshine, making his teeth look whiter. His sweatshirt had Led Zeppelin on it. He gave her a Supertramp tape called *Brother Where You Bound*. 'Put that in your Walkman,' he said.

Ellen gave them fridge magnets of the Tower of London and Buckingham Palace, and a concertina of postcards showing London sights. They ate hamburgers, and Bobbi asked for ketchup for her chips, which she called fries.

They were very much a couple, jumping into one another's sentences, indulging in mutual gentle teasing, Bobbi taking chips from his plate when she'd finished her own. Ellen was sorry again that she didn't have Leo to present to them.

Towards the end of the meal, Danny showed her his mobile phone, which was roughly the same size and shape as a peat briquette. 'It doesn't work over here yet: I just brought it to show you. It can make calls all over the US.'

'Wow.'

'His new toy,' Bobbi put in. 'He calls me from a diner to tell me he's out to lunch from work. Like I need to know.'

Ellen envied them, living together. She was still dividing her time between Leo's house and the flat, not wanting to be the one to suggest a more permanent arrangement.

They both hugged her on leaving. 'Next time, you come to us,' Bobbi said.

'I'd love it.'

In July Ellen turned twenty-six, and Leo took her out to what had become their favourite restaurant, Italian and chic. After dinner, the chef, Giovanni, appeared at their table with a slice of tiramisu that held a single lit candle. 'For you, *bella*,' he said, placing it before her with a flourish. '*Buon compleanno*.'

Ellen hadn't ordered dessert. Leo must have arranged this. She thanked the chef, flushing with self-consciousness as heads turned in her direction.

'Surprise,' Leo said, and she laughed and thanked him too – and abruptly she remembered the proposal she and Ben had witnessed, on the one and only night they'd gone out to dinner.

She regarded the dessert with its creamy layers and powdered chocolate topping – tiramisu was one of her favourites – and felt a small hopeful fluttering. She'd heard of rings being hidden in desserts – was this what was happening now? They'd been together a year and a half – was it time for the question?

She picked up her spoon and pushed it in, meeting no resistance. She began to eat, feeling Leo's eyes on her.

'Good?'

She nodded, still fluttering inwardly. She tasted soft biscuit and coffee and mascarpone. She took another mouthful, and another. 'Want some?' she asked, but he shook his head.

He drank coffee and sipped brandy. She ate some more, telling herself there was still time, still hope – but she found nothing. She set her spoon down on her empty plate.

'Delicious,' she said, her smile just a bit too wide. He wasn't ready yet. She quashed her disappointment.

In the middle of August they flew to Ireland for Joan's twenty-fifth birthday, which was to be a grand affair. 'I missed out on a big wedding,' Joan said, 'so this will make up.' They erected a marquee in the family home's garden, which was considerably bigger than the little patch of green behind the house Joan and Seamus had bought, and forty guests sat down to eat.

Next day Leo and Ellen had lunch in a café on their way back to Shannon, and Ellen ate a chicken salad that caused her to dash to the nearest toilet when they landed at Heathrow and left her unable to countenance food for three days.

Six weeks later, following a missed period, she did a pregnancy test and got a positive result. She was still on the pill – but so had Joan been. Had it failed Ellen too, or had the vomiting at Heathrow caused a break in her protection? Not that it mattered. All that mattered now was that she was pregnant.

She lowered the toilet lid and sat on it, still holding the wand with its two clear lines. She was pregnant with Leo's child. They'd skimmed over the idea of children, in a kind of a sometime-in-the-future way. How would he feel when she told him the future had arrived?

She was having his baby. Despite being unsure of his reaction, hers was positive. He'd be happy too. He would. Next month they'd be together two years. It was time, more than time, to move forward.

She must tell him. She must tell him in person, which meant waiting for three days, with him gone to Manchester on business till the weekend.

But she couldn't keep it to herself, so she told Claire after work that evening.

'What? Are you serious? I never knew you two were trying for a baby – that's brilliant!'

'We weren't trying. This wasn't planned.'

'Oh . . . What did Leo say when you told him?'

'He doesn't know yet. He's away – I won't see him till Friday. Don't tell anyone, and don't ever tell him I told you first.'

'Credit me with some intelligence,' Claire said. 'Look, whatever happens, whatever you decide to do, I'm here for you.'

Ellen looked at her. 'What do you mean, whatever I decide to do?'

'You and Leo, I mean. Whatever you both decide.'

'There's nothing to decide. I'm pregnant, and I'm having the baby.'

'You mean with or without him?'

'What? No – I mean with him. Of course with him. Claire, we're in a loving, long-term relationship. We mightn't have planned a baby right now, but we'll have it. There's no question about that.'

'Right,' Claire said. 'In that case, congratulations. I'm very happy for you both.'

But what if Ellen was wrong, and Leo didn't want this accidental baby they'd made? What if he'd never really seen children in his future, or not for another few years? A baby undeniably changed things, complicated things – but a baby also turned a loving couple into a family. Surely he'd want that? And he was thirty-six now, older than a lot of first-time fathers.

In fact, mightn't the news serve to prompt the marriage proposal she was more than ready for? Wouldn't it make sense to seal the deal with a wedding, like Joan and Seamus had done, when Ellen told him of his impending fatherhood?

Her own father floated into her mind's eye. Ten years on, she could think about him dispassionately now. She could regret the fact that she was going to have his grandchild and he would never know, only because it meant that her child would be deprived of a grandfather.

His parents hadn't been told of Ivan's birth, and Ellen was equally disinclined to tell them about this pregnancy – or about a wedding, if and when it came to pass. What was the point?

It was sad, but it was life. Now she must look to the future, and leave the past in the past.

And the future was bright – wasn't it?

Reaction

ON FRIDAY, LEO ARRIVED AT THE FLAT TO TAKE HER out. Claire had already disappeared for the night, and Ellen had her speech ready.

He kissed her cheek. 'You look wonderful. I've missed you.'

'Me too. Let's not eat out,' she said. 'Let's stay here. I've got a casserole that just needs reheating.'

'You OK?'

'I'm fine, just . . . feel like staying in.'

Since her conversation with Claire she'd been anxious, her head full of what-ifs and buts and maybes. Every possible scenario had played out in her head, and she'd realised that she wasn't sure after all how her news would go down.

'Fair enough. Should I go out and get wine?'

'If you want some,' she said. 'Not for me.'

He smiled. 'Not for you? Why not? Don't tell me you're on a diet.'

'No, no diet.' She took a breath. 'Because, um . . . I'm pregnant.' And just like that, he was told. After the eloquent, heartfelt words she'd been rehearsing all week, out it tumbled, landing with a thump between them like a wet sponge.

He froze, his smile growing glassy. He stood for a minute, his eyes on her but his thoughts in a place she couldn't reach. 'You're pregnant? How?'

'Well, it might have been that tummy bug, or food poisoning or whatever, on the way back from Ireland. That could have messed up the pill. But it's not foolproof – Joan got caught, remember?'

Still no sign of how he was taking this. 'Are you quite sure?'

'I'm sure.'

He studied her. 'And how do you feel about it?'

'I'm happy, if you are.' She began to be afraid. 'I know it's a . . . surprise.' She'd been going to say shock.

'It certainly is.'

Now there was no sign of a smile. His face was tense, a gathering of lines between his eyes. He didn't look happy. Not remotely.

She thought of Ivan, and his clear blue gaze, and the way he'd wrapped his tiny hand around her finger the first time she'd seen him, and how it had caused a corresponding little tightening inside her.

Her speech arrived belatedly. 'I'm going to have it, Leo. I'm going to keep it. I want to be a mother, and I think I'm ready. I'd like you to be a father, and for us to raise it together, but—' she broke off, her voice threatening to break – 'if it's not what you want, I'll understand.'

It would kill her. Losing him would destroy her – and still some instinct told her not to put pressure, not to make him feel trapped.

He looked down at his hands. A car passed in the street below. 'We didn't plan it,' he said.

'No. It was nobody's fault.'

He lifted his head. 'Ellen,' he said, 'I'm not sure I want to be a father.'

Everything in her plummeted to the floor. Her hands were suddenly cold. 'But we've talked about children.'

'We decided nothing.'

'You'd be a good father,' she said urgently. 'You're a good man, Leo.'

He gave a faint smile. 'Not the same thing – and anyway, I'm not sure how good I am.'

'What do you mean? Of course you are.'

'I need to think,' he said. 'I need to be alone, Ellen.'

She had to resist an urge to grab him, to hold on to him. Not to allow him to go. 'What about dinner?' Stupid. Stupid. What did dinner matter?

'I need to think,' he repeated, already walking away. 'I'll call you.' And he was gone, pulling the door softly closed behind him.

In a daze, she sank onto the futon. She spent the night there, curled up tight, too shocked to cry, too anguished to do more than fall into moments of sleep, only to jolt awake again and again to the fresh realisation of what had happened. All the next day she remained where she was, wrapped in a blanket, shivering with cold.

'Look,' Claire said, putting a mug of tea into her hands when she got home from work, 'these things happen. I'll help you,' she said, setting a plate of beans on toast before Ellen. 'You won't be alone,' she said, going for a shower – but Ellen didn't want Claire, she wanted him. Were they over? No, no, no, no, no. She couldn't countenance it, couldn't see her life without him in it. Couldn't lose someone else.

'You want me to stay in tonight?' Claire asked, already dressed to go out.

Ellen shook her head. 'I'll have an early night.'

'Are you sure?'

'I'm sure.'

'It'll be OK. It'll work out, Ellen. I'll see you later,' she said, pulling the door closed behind her, and Ellen tried not to feel abandoned by her too.

She sat as the light left the room, imagining her mother's face when Ellen told her she was pregnant and single. Far worse than Joan, who'd had Seamus willing to marry her. And Frances – would Frances disapprove of single motherhood? Ellen couldn't be sure of her reaction. But even if the world in its entirety turned its back on her, she knew she wouldn't be able to do what Claire had done. She couldn't put an end to something conceived in love; she couldn't do it.

Just before ten o'clock the doorbell rang, snatching her out of a half-doze, making her heart thump. She looked out the window but couldn't see who was there. She pressed the buzzer and waited, telling herself not to get her hopes up. Telling herself it could be anyone.

She heard footsteps approach the door. She opened it.

'I'm sorry,' he said. 'I'm sorry, Ellen.'

She looked at him dumbly. She didn't know what he was sorry for.

He stepped inside and caught her hands and squeezed them. 'Let's do it, Ellen. Let's have a baby.'

She couldn't speak. No words came. 'My darling,' he said softly. He put a hand under her chin and kissed her lightly. 'I don't want to lose you. As long as you're happy, I'm happy.' He gathered her into his arms and she leant against him, breathing herself calm.

At length they drew apart. 'I need to eat,' she said, suddenly starving. No dinner the previous evening, nothing all day today.

'We can go out' – but she was in no condition to dress up. She dumped Claire's beans on toast, untouched and cold, and put more bread into the toaster. She cut cheese and placed the slices on the toast and slid it under the grill while he made tea and set out crockery, and she felt tender as a convalescent, and still half afraid to believe he was staying with her.

'You'll move into my house,' he said, pouring tea into two cups. 'Right?'

Breathe. Move in with him.

She put half a slice of toasted cheese on a plate and slid it across to him.

'I know my house isn't the most child-friendly, but we can work on that.'

'Yes,' she managed.

He stirred in milk for both of them. Gradually, she felt the tightness inside her beginning to loosen. They ate toasted cheese and tossed names about. He liked Oliver for a boy and Juliet for a girl; she preferred Adam or William for a boy, but liked Juliet too.

Marriage didn't come up. It wasn't mentioned. One step at a time, she thought. This would be more than enough for now.

She asked how he felt his mother would take the news, and he said, a little too enthusiastically, that he was sure she'd be happy. Ellen imagined again telling *her* mother: that would need serious courage, even with Leo still in the picture. A baby, but no wedding. No, that would not go down well.

They washed up. She showered and dressed, and wrote a note for Claire. They went out to the street and found a taxi to take them to Battersea. Lying in his arms later, listening to the little puff at the end of his sleeping exhalations, she thought about how quickly everything could change, and how terrifying that was.

BATTERSEA, LONDON
NOVEMBER 1987
THE THIRD MOVE

Rage

'YOU TRAVEL LIGHT,' HE SAID.

'Easier to pack,' she replied, frowning at the books she'd just placed on his shelves: did they look frivolous next to his, with their more colourful covers? Upstairs, she folded her sweaters into drawers he'd cleared for her, and her underwear (mostly new) into another.

She hung the rest of her clothing in the big old wardrobe, next to his suits. Her shoes and boots she tucked into the gap between the bottom of the wardrobe and the floor.

'You sure you don't want to swap?' His were lined up neatly on a separate unit behind the door.

'No, they're fine there.' Who cared where she kept her shoes?

In the bathroom she stuck her toothbrush into his mug, her shampoo and conditioner and soap on the shelf in the shower cubicle. She'd been wondering if his cast-iron bath was big enough for both of them; she would find out, first chance she got.

In his kitchen – rarely used by him – she tucked her folder of recipes in Frances' scrawled handwriting beneath a bundle of linen napkins in a drawer of his dresser. She loved his house, mainly because it was his, full of things he had chosen – and now she lived there too, and she wanted to dance with happiness. She would miss the fun of sharing with Claire, but this move felt so right.

Claire was also quitting the flat. She'd found the new business premises she was looking for, and would give up her lease on the sandwich bar at the end of the year. 'A deli,' she told Ellen, 'with a seating area.' It came complete with an upstairs apartment, which she was planning to move into, and which she was already calling her boudoir. Yes, she'd always been destined to have a boudoir.

The morning after she moved in with Leo, Ellen discovered that she could walk to work in just ten minutes. She gave her new address to Bella in reception, and broke the news to Lucinda that she would be looking for maternity leave in a few months.

'Oh – wonderful!' Lucinda exclaimed. 'You're entitled to sixteen weeks, and don't you dare do anything foolish like decide to become a stay-at-home mum!'

'Not a chance,' Ellen said. 'I love my job too much.' She did.

'You'll be godmother,' Ellen told Claire. 'You'll need to remember the birthdays – and don't pass on any bad habits.' A link with her child would keep them together, prevent them from drifting apart as their lives took different turns.

'No bad habits? Where's the fun in that?' The adventurous spirit was still there, underneath the businesswoman she was becoming.

Leo broke the news to his mother on the phone. 'She says congratulations,' he reported to Ellen. 'She's looking forward to becoming a *grand-mère.*'

'Really? She said that?'

'Well, not in so many words, but that was the gist.'

It wasn't the truth. He couldn't lie to save his life. Ellen was glad he'd spared her a face-to-face encounter with Marguerite, so she hadn't had to witness his mother's reaction. What did it matter to her? The woman lived in another country: in two years they'd met exactly once. Ellen could tolerate that much contact.

She told him she'd go to Ireland to break the news in person.

'I'll come with you.'

'It might be best if I went alone,' she replied. 'I'm not sure how Mam will take it.' But she was all too sure how it would go, and she was right.

'I don't believe it,' her mother said. 'I don't believe you're doing this to me too.'

'Mam, it's not—'

'Bad enough to have one daughter making a show of me – I'll be the laughing stock of the town when this gets out.'

'I hardly think—'

'At least Joan had the grace to get married.'

'Mam, it's 1987. Nobody cares about that any more.'

A mistake. Her mother's eyes glittered with anger. 'Nobody cares, she says – easily known you're living in London, where people do what they like. I'll have you know people still care about that sort of thing here, lady. You won't be around to see the sniggers, to hear everyone talking about poor Patricia Sheehan, whose husband walked out, and now—'

Ellen couldn't listen to any more. Without thinking, she retorted: 'All you care about is what people think of you – you don't give a damn about your own children! No wonder Dad left – I just wish he'd taken me with him!'

Her mother glared at her, white-faced. For a minute, neither spoke. Already regretting her outburst, Ellen searched for something, anything, to defuse the situation – but before she could find it, her mother wheeled abruptly and left the room.

Ellen slumped into a chair, listening to footsteps marching up the stairs. What now? Her back hurt, her legs ached. She regretted the burger she'd eaten in Heathrow that sat like a stone in her stomach.

In less than a minute her mother reappeared, holding a biscuit tin that she thumped onto the table. 'You might as well have this,' she said coldly, folding her arms.

The tin had a picture of a fox on it. 'What's in it?'

'Open it.'

Ellen prised off the lid and found a tumble of envelopes. She lifted one out – and with a shock of recognition she saw her father's handwriting, and her and Joan's names, and the address of the house he'd left. This house.

She pushed the rest of the envelopes about, and saw that they were all the same. All stamped, all unopened. All addressed to her and Joan.

She looked up. 'He wrote to us?'

No response. Her mother's mouth was a grim line.

'He *wrote* to us?' Ellen repeated, trying hard to contain the anger that bubbled up again. 'He wrote to me and Joan, and you kept them from us?'

'He *left* me!' her mother shouted suddenly, her face blotching. 'He walked away and left me with two daughters to raise – what did you expect me to do? That's nice thanks for trying to protect you!'

'You weren't protecting us, you were punishing us,' Ellen said sharply. 'You punished Joan and me because you couldn't punish him. You took it out on us.'

'What are you talking about? I was keeping you safe! I was making sure he couldn't hurt you any more! How can you not see that?'

Ellen looked down again at the letters. Was that really what she thought she'd been doing, protecting them? Could she seriously have seen nothing wrong with this? She knew, she must have known, that Ellen and Joan had craved a word from him. How could this have felt OK to her?

'I went out to work!' her mother insisted. 'Don't you remember? I got a job. I paid for everything with no help from him! He sent me cheques, not even the manners of a note in with them – I took great pleasure in tearing them up!'

Ellen regarded her in bewilderment, her anger seeping away in the face of this baffling new information. Cheques. She'd torn up his cheques. They'd scrimped and saved after he'd left, Ellen and Joan taking Saturday jobs to make pocket money, and still their mother had torn up his cheques.

She'd heard enough. She stowed the tin in her rucksack and pulled on her jacket. She left the room without another word as her mother said her name sharply. She closed the front door with a slam, and nobody followed her.

She walked the half mile or so to Joan and Seamus' house, praying she wouldn't meet anyone she knew. It had begun to rain; she felt the sting of it on her face as she put up her hood. It was almost December.

She reached the house. She rang the bell and Seamus answered. He took one look at her and stepped back to let her in.

Their father had written every few months. In the letters he hoped they were well. He said he missed them, and they were in his thoughts every day. He told them he was working in a school in Dublin, and gave his address. He said he'd love to hear from them, if they felt like writing back.

He sent separate birthday cards, into which he'd slipped money. Ten pounds until each of them had turned eighteen, twenty pounds after that. They piled up the notes as they opened the cards.

His last letter was dated April 1985, well over two years ago. He must have stopped writing because they'd never written back. He'd kept writing to them for years, hoping one of them at least would respond, but he'd finally given up.

Or died.

The thought was accompanied by a twist of pain, a violent lurch in Ellen's gut that caused her to draw in her breath with a hiss. Let him not be dead. Whatever hurt he'd caused, let him be alive.

'This explains the post box,' Joan said, and only then Ellen remembered her mother having one put up at the gate. Was it after he'd left? It must have been. So she could check the post before her daughters saw it. So she could intercept any letters he might write.

Joan regarded the envelopes, scattered across the kitchen table. Seamus was upstairs, putting Ivan to bed. 'At least she kept them. At least she didn't throw them out. I wonder was she ever planning to show them to us?'

'Joan, how could she have kept them from us? How could she have been so cruel?'

Joan lifted a shoulder. She was taking it so calmly. 'She must have thought she was doing the right thing. She was doing her best by us.'

The same thing Frances had said. Were they right? Was Ellen judging her too harshly? She couldn't think straight.

'I can't go back to her, Joan. Can I stay here tonight? I'm going to Galway tomorrow.'

'Of course you can. Will you see her again before you go back to London?'

'Why? What's the point? We've never got on – not the way you get on with her.'

'Ellen, she gets on with you as well as she gets on with anyone. She's not the easiest to live with, but it suited me to stay with her for as long as I did. And she's actually great with Ivan – better than she was with us, to be honest.'

'I just can't get past the fact that she drove Dad away.'

'I don't know,' Joan said. 'It takes two to tango – maybe the blame wasn't all on her side. I mean, he could have told us he was leaving. He could at least have done that. She's not a happy person, Ellen. I wonder if she and Dad were ever happy.'

'How do you feel about him now?' Ellen asked. 'Now that we've got the letters, I mean.'

Her sister gave another shrug. 'I honestly don't know, Ellen. It's good that he wrote to us, but I still hate the way he left, with no explanation – and he's still not told us why. I can't be sure what I'd say or do if he showed up.'

'We could make contact,' Ellen said. 'We have his address now.'

'No,' Joan said quickly. 'I don't think I want to do that. He should be the one to come and find us.'

Ellen imagined tracking him down, locating his house. She pictured herself ringing the doorbell and waiting for someone to appear, and she shrank from the prospect. What if that someone was a stranger who had to break the news to her that the previous owner had died? She didn't know if that would be easier or harder than coming face to face with him again.

She wasn't brave enough. Maybe some day, but not now.

'Will you tell Mam I showed you these?'

'I will. I'd rather be straight with her. I'm sure she'll guess you did anyway. At least they're out in the open now.'

Seamus reappeared and looked through the letters, shaking his head. 'It's sad,' he said. 'It's a sad state of affairs. Would you like a glass of wine, Ellen?'

She suddenly remembered why she was in Ireland. 'Actually, I have news,' she said, relieved to be able to turn the conversation in a different direction. On hearing of the pregnancy Joan hugged her, Seamus put the kettle on, and the evening ended on a more positive note.

'Congratulations,' Frances said the following day. 'I'm guessing you're both happy about it?'

'We are. Leo wasn't sure at the start, but he's accepted it now. I've moved in with him.' Ellen hesitated. 'Frances, we're not getting married – at least, we have no plans right now.'

'I see.' Her face gave nothing away, but there was none of her mother's anger. 'And you're alright with that?'

'I'd prefer to get married,' Ellen admitted, 'but if he doesn't want to, I can't do anything about it. We'll still be a family.'

'That won't have gone down well with your mother.'

'No, it didn't – and there's more.' She told her about the letters from her father.

Frances tutted. 'It was very wrong of her to keep them from you, but it doesn't surprise me. She's unhappy, Ellen. I'm not excusing her, I'm just saying.'

Ellen let a beat pass. 'You wanted to talk about her once. You started to tell me what she was like when she was growing up, and I stopped you. Will you tell me more now?'

She wanted to understand her, to hear something, anything, that might explain her mother's cruel concealment of their father's letters. She was so tired of the anger and the bitterness that were still colouring every interaction with her mother. She wanted, she needed, to let them go, and find some kind of peace between them.

Frances folded her hands and was silent for a bit. Eventually she spoke, words emerging slowly and deliberately. 'It's my belief that your mother's mental state was always . . . fragile. I don't know what name they'd put on it today; depression, I suppose. When we were young, nobody talked about that kind of thing. People were moody, or they weren't. Anyway, for whatever reason, she could be difficult to live with. I think I touched on that before.' She looked enquiringly at Ellen.

'You did.'

'It wasn't her fault: I don't think the poor thing had any control over it. Medication helps now, of course, but she was never prescribed anything, never even brought to a doctor. It just wouldn't have occurred to our parents.'

She stopped again. 'Ellen,' she said earnestly, 'there's no badness in her. There never was. Keeping the letters from you was wrong, but I'd bet anything she thought she was doing the right thing. And remember, there were two of them in that marriage, and we just don't know what happened to cause your father to leave, so I don't think it's fair to assign blame.'

She pulled at the red strip to open a packet of custard creams. It was sad she'd stopped baking her crumbly buttery shortbread, and her ginger biscuits with their pleasing snap. 'I'm guessing,' she said, 'that Kevin won't last. I know they're not living together, but I suspect he'll get tired of trying to keep her happy.'

'I should make my peace with her,' Ellen said.

'You should. Be the bigger one, Ellen. Be kind to her. At the end of the day, she's still your mother, and she's the one who stayed around.'

So that night Ellen wrote a letter, using Frances' writing pad:

Dear Mam,

I'm sorry we fought. I stayed with Joan and Seamus, but you probably know that by now. I was angry that you'd kept the letters from us, but I should have talked it through with you instead of walking out.

I know things have been strained between us since Dad left, and that's my fault. I feel now I was being unfair to you, and I'll try to make amends.

I hope you'll accept your grandchild when he or she is born. My due date is May sixteenth.

I'm not sure if I'll be home between this and then, but I'll keep in touch.

love Ellen x

And then she wrote another letter.

Dear Danny,

Big news! I'm pregnant, due in May, and I couldn't be happier, and Leo and I are both looking forward to becoming parents. I've moved into his house, which is lovely, even if it has far too many stairs – and the more pregnant I get, the harder the climb will be! It's a townhouse, narrow and tall, just a couple of rooms on each level. We're turning a bedroom on the first floor into the nursery, so it'll be right next to ours, and there are two rooms on the top floor that can serve as bedrooms when we have company.

Work continues to be wonderful.

Hope everything's OK with you and Bobbi. Write when you get the chance.

E xx

She made no mention of her father's letters. He didn't need to know precisely how messed up her family was.

Marguerite

MUCH TO ELLEN'S DISMAY, SHE AND LEO WERE invited to France for Christmas, just as they were on the point of booking a winter sun holiday. 'She says my half-brothers are going skiing with their father,' Leo told Ellen after a phone call, 'so she'll be on her own if we don't show up. Would you mind?'

What could she do but agree? He'd spent just one Christmas with his mother since he and Ellen had got together – and knowing that Marguerite wasn't exactly enamoured by her son's choice of partner, Ellen guessed that saying no to this invitation would be another black mark against her, so on Christmas Eve they flew to Nantes.

By now, Ellen's jeans were beginning to be difficult to fasten. Her ankles were puffy, and her calves ached when she climbed the stairs. Her initial queasiness had been replaced by heartburn, and she was waking up more frequently at night with a bladder demanding to be emptied.

'Wait till you get to the last three months,' Joan warned. 'You'll be waddling instead of walking, and your back will kill you, and you'll go to the loo a million times a day. Just wait and see.'

None of this bothered Ellen unduly. The thought that a baby, her and Leo's baby, was growing inside her was a continuing source of joy. Let the symptoms do their worst: she couldn't wait to be a mother, and she was certain that as soon as Leo saw his child, he would be just as smitten as her.

They were met at the airport by Marguerite's driver, Claude, who on being introduced to Ellen lifted her hand and touched it to his lips, and murmured '*Bonne Noel, Madame*'. He was silver-haired and dignified, and as upright when he sat in the driver's seat of Marguerite's enormous old Peugeot as a man forty years younger.

It was bitterly cold. Huddled into her red coat, Ellen looked through the car window at skeletal trees and bare hedgerows stiff and white with frost. She tucked the wool blanket that Claude had produced from the car boot more tightly around her, and yearned for blue skies and sunshine.

The house where Marguerite and her sons lived was located a few miles from the centre of Nantes. Ellen's first sight of it put her in mind of the Bennet home in *Pride and Prejudice*. Inside, it featured high-ceilinged rooms with large fireplaces where tiny fires flickered, and elegant sash windows whose insides were frosted over when Leo folded back the shutters each morning, and ancient radiators that clanked and groaned and did their best. Ellen shivered her way through the week in three layers of woollens, and clung to Leo in bed at night, craving warmth rather than passion.

But the bed linens were crisp and immaculate, the pillows feathery and deep, the mattress just the right balance of firm and soft. Their room had a view of rolling hills and patchwork fields, and the cook, Emmaline, wife of Claude, and as round and rosy as he was pale and straight, brought mugs of steaming hot chocolate up the stairs in the mornings that sent sugary heat rushing all the way to Ellen's toes.

And to be fair, Marguerite was gracious. She greeted Ellen civilly on arrival and congratulated her on the pregnancy, and enquired as to how she was feeling – and Ellen couldn't help wondering if Leo had had a word.

Marguerite instructed Claude, who seemed to double as a sort of manservant, to light a fire each evening in Leo and Ellen's room. She told Leo that Claude and the car were at their disposal for the week, and she brought them to a local hotel for Christmas dinner, and invited neighbours in for drinks another night.

But in her dealings with Ellen, particularly if Leo wasn't within earshot, she remained coolly distant – and once or twice Ellen thought she caught a look directed at her that felt antagonistic. She decided it was just the woman's default expression – and anyway, they didn't have to be best friends.

She was sorry the half-brothers weren't around to provide distraction. 'You'll meet them soon,' Leo promised. 'We'll have them over to London.'

In the middle of their stay Ellen developed a chesty cough which Emmaline treated with honey and ginger teas, and bowls of soup so spicy they made Ellen's eyes water, and by the time they touched down in London the cough had pretty much dried up. 'Could we coax Emmaline to come and be our nanny?' she asked Leo, and he laughed and said he wouldn't dare try to steal her away from *Maman*.

Frances had been right in her prediction that Kevin wouldn't last. 'He and Mam have split up,' Joan reported on the phone in early January. 'She didn't say why, and I didn't ask. It's tough on both of them, still having to work together. How was Christmas in France?'

'Lovely.'

Her mother hadn't responded to the letter Ellen had sent from Frances' house. At Christmas, a card had arrived to Ellen's old address with *Happy Christmas Ellen* written on it, and no mention of Leo. Apart from the Walkman that Ellen used daily on her journey to work, her mother continued to disappoint her spectacularly.

As her pregnancy advanced, they made preparations.

'Yellow,' she said, 'for the nursery. Works for a boy and a girl.'

'It'll be a boy,' Leo said. 'I can feel it.'

'What if it's not?'

'We send it back, of course, and demand another.'

They furnished the nursery with a cradle and a rocking chair and a chest of drawers, all cream. They found a mobile to hang above the cradle, zoo animals dangling. Lucinda came one Sunday afternoon and painted a moon on the ceiling and a cow jumping over it.

When the room was ready they stood in the doorway, taking it in. Ellen found his hand and lifted it to her lips and kissed it. 'Thank you,' she said.

He looked at her with a quizzical smile. 'For what?'

'For everything.'

At the end of April Ellen rang Laura at the employment agency. 'Do you supply nannies?' she asked.

'We certainly do. Are you in the market for one?'

'We will be, around the end of August, when my maternity leave is up. Someone mature,' she said, 'with lots of experience.' As it looked like neither grandmother would be involved to any great extent in the baby's life, she thought an older nanny might go some way towards filling that gap.

Two weeks before her due date she finished work, weary of the round-the-clock trips to the loo that Joan had promised, and a constant ache in her lower back that made it difficult to stay sitting for long, regardless of how many cushions she propped there, and the sheer effort of hauling her extra bulk around.

'Ring me,' she said to Lucinda, 'if you need to toss around ideas. I can still think, even if I'm physically useless.'

'Wouldn't dream of it – put your feet up and forget about us. We'll struggle on till you get back.' They sent her home in a taxi, with a stack of tiny unisex clothing from Harrods and a new bottle of Chanel No. 5.

Two days before Ellen's due date, Claire came to visit. The new deli was doing well, all pale wood and stainless steel. Cold, Ellen had thought when she'd seen it a few weeks earlier. Smart and sophisticated, but lacking the colour and warmth of the sandwich bar.

Claire seemed happy, though. She brought a trio of picture books and a giant bar of Cadbury's Fruit & Nut that Ellen immediately opened. Throughout the pregnancy she'd craved chocolate, which normally she could take or leave.

'Still no word from your mother?'

'No.'

Her baby would have two largely absentee grandmothers, a pair of great-grandparents who would probably never know of their existence, and a grandfather whose whereabouts were unknown. The rest of their relatives were separated by either the Irish Sea or the English Channel. Not exactly your typical Irish family.

They would grow up with English and Irish passports – a French one too, if they wanted – and they would probably have a hybrid, but mostly English, accent. They would be fluent in French thanks to their father, and they would ski from an early age if Leo had his way. Ellen had yet to decide if it was a battle she wanted to fight, already imagining a catastrophic accident on the slopes that would leave their child paralysed from the neck down before the age of ten.

But she would definitely do battle on the Eton front. Leo had been sent as a boarder there at twelve, an action which Ellen privately regarded as tantamount to child cruelty. Time enough for that confrontation.

'What does it feel like?' Claire asked.

'Being pregnant?'

'Not physically, mentally. Knowing you're going to be a mam.'

'It's scary. Such a huge thing, bringing a new person into the world, having it entirely dependent on you – but it's exciting too.'

'You'll be a good mother,' Claire said, breaking off another square of chocolate. Ellen wondered if she ever regretted the abortion. Her child would be five now, developing a personality, already showing signs of the adult it would become.

'Best of luck,' Claire said on leaving. 'Let me know when there's news.'

Five days later, there was news. On the nineteenth of May 1988, Juliet arrived, and the world shifted on its axis.

Motherhood

ELLEN WAS BESOTTED, SMITTEN, OBSESSED, LOVE-struck. As soon as her daughter – her daughter! – was placed on her chest, red and bawling, a new order was heralded in, with Juliet at its centre. Dark-haired and dark-eyed, creamy-skinned once the crying abated, and utterly adorable. In possession of all her fingers and toes – the tiny nails! The minuscule knuckles! Six pounds and thirteen ounces of perfection.

Three days later Leo took them home, and days and nights blurred as Juliet's demands to be fed and changed and bathed and fed again took over. When Leo returned to work after a week, Ellen spent nights on a day bed in the nursery so he could get the sleep he needed to function.

She and Juliet travelled through the days together, Ellen woozy with tiredness but still blissfully content. Everything was new, everything was miraculous. Leo came home with takeaway dinners, and sometimes Ellen ate them and sometimes she didn't. Food became something she snatched while Juliet slept, before tumbling into sleep next to her. In the two months following Juliet's birth she lost all the pregnancy weight, and the further half stone she'd long wanted to shed.

Leo presented her with a ring. It was a thin white-gold circle studded with tiny rubies, her birthstone.

'Thank you,' she said, sliding it on to her finger, smothering the voice that whispered *It should have been another.*

She sent photos to her mother and Joan and Frances and Danny. *We'd be happy if you'd like to come and see her,* she wrote to her mother, *and you'd be welcome to stay with us.*

Congratulations, her mother's brief response read. *I hope you and your daughter are keeping well, and you're getting enough rest.* No reference was made to Ellen's invitation – and again, Leo might not have existed.

She's a beautiful child, God bless her, Frances wrote. *Bring her home to meet us all as soon as you can.* She sent a tiny hat and bootees in soft pale green wool.

Can't believe you're a parent, Danny wrote. *I'm afraid to show Bobbi in case she gets broody. I'm far too young to settle down.* His card was accompanied by a set of Winnie-the-Pooh books, and the sight of them jolted a long-forgotten memory: the same set in Danny's family home, one of his older sisters reading them to Ellen and Danny.

Joan sent a rag doll with painted red circles for cheeks. *Ivan can't wait to meet his little cousin,* she wrote. *Come as soon as you can.* Ellen wondered how she could bring Juliet to see his cousin and not call to her mother's house in the same town.

In the weeks that followed Juliet's arrival Claire dropped around most Sundays, her only day off work, and ordered Ellen to bed for the afternoon while she and Leo attended to Juliet and made a roast chicken dinner according to the instructions Ellen had stuck to the fridge.

'You need a nanny,' Claire said.

'I've ordered one' – and ten days before she was due back to work, Maggie arrived for an interview.

She's a widow, Laura had told her. *She had five of her own kids and now they're grown and she's looking for nanny work. She was a nurse before she married, but she gave it up when the kids arrived. She's Irish too, from Mayo.*

Maggie was squat and square and buxom, with a mop of bleached hair that looked like it never saw a comb and a wide gap-toothed smile that narrowed her eyes to slits. She called Juliet a pure dote, and took her from Ellen and placed her against her shoulder, and Juliet settled as if she belonged there.

'Tell me everything,' Maggie said, so Ellen brought her around and pointed out all the baby paraphernalia, and told her of the feeding schedule she was trying to stick to, and showed her the list of emergency phone numbers on the fridge door, and all the time Maggie cradled Juliet, her free hand making slow circles on the baby's back.

Over tea, she told Ellen of her marriage to the Irish builder she'd met in a London dancehall in the fifties, and the children who were scattered now, and the death of the builder when he'd fallen from scaffolding five years ago, a few months before his planned retirement.

'I went back nursing then,' she said, 'just agency work, nothing permanent, but it wasn't the same. I think I was out of it too long, so I told Laura I wanted to be a nanny. I was bringing up children far longer than I was nursing.'

She was too good to be true. Juliet would be in the safest hands in London.

'Please come and work for us,' Ellen said, and Maggie told her she'd be delighted, and the next new regime beckoned.

'Am I glad to see you back,' Lucinda said on Ellen's return. 'There are three briefs waiting for your magic' – and Ellen shrugged off her guilt at abandoning Juliet and set to work, and found to her relief that motherhood and its attendant exhaustion hadn't robbed her of ideas.

In September, Marguerite came to view her new grandchild. She booked into a nearby hotel for two nights, and brought a stack of adorable little cotton dresses and a soft sweater in palest blue for Ellen. She called Juliet *ma petite*, and crooned softly to her in French, and in three days she managed to avoid being alone with Ellen.

Claire's Sunday-afternoon visits petered to twice-monthly ones. On rainy days she and Ellen would listen to music in the living room while Leo tended to Juliet; when the sun shone they would put the baby into her pram and wheel her across to the square's private little park so she could watch the neighbourhood children scampering about.

'So how's it going,' Claire asked one day, 'with you and Leo?'

They were sitting on their usual bench, Juliet propped in her pram. 'Fine,' Ellen said. 'Why?'

'Just wondered if a baby made any difference, or if you two are still madly in love.'

Ellen laughed. 'We don't have time to be madly in love these days, but everything's OK.'

It was true they didn't reach for each other in bed as frequently as they used to, but Ellen put that down to the turned-on-its-head world of new parents, both in full-time employment. 'Wait till you become a mam,' Ellen said. 'You'll understand how sex has to take a back seat for a while.'

'That'll never happen.'

'It'll never take a back seat? I think you'll find you won't have a choice.'

'No, I mean I'll never be a mam.'

Ellen looked at her in astonishment. 'Why would you say that?' Maybe the abortion had done damage.

'Because I like my single life too much.'

'Well, yes, for a while, when you're young, but eventually you'll meet someone you want to settle down with. Everyone does – or most people do.'

Claire shifted her gaze to the playing children. 'I did meet someone,' she said, 'but he was taken, so I've given up on that idea.'

'You met someone? Here in London? Was he married?'

A short silence – and then Claire turned to her and laughed. 'Your face! I'm joking. You're so easy to fool. But I mean it about never settling down: far too many men out there. I'll be footloose and fancy-free – *and* childless – to my grave. No offence, goddaughter,' reaching forward to stroke Juliet's cheek, 'but I'm glad you belong to someone else.'

Was it true? Did she really never want to make a life with anyone, never see children in her future? Ellen had always assumed both of them would marry – but now it seemed that neither of them might ever walk down an aisle on someone's arm.

She had Leo, though, and Juliet. Sad to think of Claire with nobody, just a series of never-ending one-night stands or short-lived flings. Who would want that kind of life?

When Juliet was five months old, Ellen and Leo took her to

Ireland. Joan had organised lunch at her house and invited their mother, to save Ellen having to visit the family home. When she arrived, she greeted Ellen cordially enough, if without any great affection, and she was stiffly polite to Leo – but she reserved the bulk of her attention for her granddaughter.

She took her on her lap and regarded her solemnly, and declared her to have the Sheehan chin. Ellen was grateful that at least she was being acknowledged, even if it was just within the four walls of Joan and Seamus' house. After lunch, Ellen and Leo moved on to Galway, where they were to spend the night after dining with Frances.

You can stay with me, Frances had said, but Ellen told her they'd already booked into a hotel. Frances' house wasn't set up for a baby guest – and although she seemed to have accepted the fact that Leo and Ellen weren't married, Ellen felt reluctant to spend a night with him under her aunt's roof, even if he was assigned the tiny boxroom. Better to stay in neutral territory.

When Frances opened the door, she was leaning on a stick. 'The hip is at me,' she said. 'It comes and goes.' She limped ahead of them into the kitchen and sat heavily at the table. 'Leo,' she said, 'set the table; plates are heating on top of the cooker. Ellen, give me the child and serve up, it's ready to go.' She held Juliet, who'd slept in the car and was still drowsy. 'Beautiful child,' she said. 'Some beauty you are.'

Leaving her later, Ellen asked if she'd consider taking a UCG student into the house. 'You could charge a low rent in return for her doing a bit of housework, and maybe grocery shopping, just to give you a break,' she said, and the old Frances reared up.

'What would I want a break for? I *told* you it's just the hip – I'm not helpless or senile yet! Next thing you'll be putting me into a nursing home!'

Ellen told her she wouldn't dare try, and promised to come back for another visit as soon as she could, and went away reassured. Under the frail exterior, the staunch heart and iron will were alive and well.

In London Maggie continued to be a godsend, and Juliet reached the usual milestones – sitting up, teething, crawling, moving onto solid food. Ellen bought half a dozen tubs of Babygloop yogurt, and a share of every tub found its way onto her daughter's hair, face and clothes.

'What was that about no messing in your ad?' Leo asked.

Ellen laughed. 'Good job I added the disclaimer at the end.'

A month before Juliet turned one, Joan phoned to tell Ellen she was pregnant again. 'We thought it was time Ivan had a brother or sister. I'm actually sorry we didn't start trying a bit earlier – would have been lovely to have them close in age like we were. You should go again soon, Ellen.'

'Give me a chance,' Ellen protested, laughing. 'I'm still learning.' But it wasn't that: despite the lack of sleep and extra work that went along with motherhood, she loved the idea of having another baby. It was Leo.

One is all we need, he'd said, soon after Juliet was born, and Ellen had been too full of bliss to argue. But she *would* argue. She would convince him, in time.

A day after Joan's phone call, Juliet took her first step. Ellen, in the act of putting a box of cereal away, turned to see her daughter, arms outstretched, put one tiny foot forward and connect it with the floor before thumping down on her behind.

'Oh!' She crossed the room and scooped up the startled child and danced around the kitchen with her, and told Leo in great excitement when he got home from the dentist what he had missed.

The day before her first birthday Juliet said *Mama* clearly – and Ellen, chatting with Maggie as the nanny put her coat on, promptly burst into loud tears, which in turn made her daughter cry.

'Hope Mama won't frighten Juliet every time she says a new word,' Leo commented when Ellen reported the incident. 'It might just give the wrong message.'

'Mama will try to contain herself,' she promised.

With a full-time job, and a small daughter waiting to occupy her out-of-work hours, time began to play tricks on her. Days galloped along, weeks tumbled into months, whole seasons whirled past without giving her a chance to grab onto them. Before she knew it, Juliet was turning two.

And once in a while, still, she would glimpse someone on a Tube or on the street who reminded her of Ben – the way he walked, the set of his shoulders, the sound of his laugh – and she would experience a tiny residual squeeze of her heart.

But Ben was in her past, and if her life was hectic now it was good too, and she was happy.

Finchley

IN FEBRUARY 1991, ELLEN GOT A LETTER FROM Danny.

Hey you,

It's finally happening. I suggested to Bobbi that I make an honest woman of her, so on Valentine's Day next year – her birthday, as it happens – we're going to go to church and do the deed. I'm letting you know in good time, so you can make what arrangements you need to make to come and throw confetti at us – and of course we'd love if Leo and Juliet could be here too. Bobbi's parents have already booked the golf club for the reception – I suspect they're thinking ahead to when they can't look after themselves any more, and they'll remind us of how our wedding nearly bankrupted them, and we'll be forced to take them in.

You can stay with us while you're here – everyone else has booked into hotels – and Juliet can learn to swim in the pool if she hasn't learnt already. Come for at least a week – it's a long trip.

Hope you can make it,

D x

PS My latest mobile phone – they're called cell phones here – can now handle international calls, so you'll have no peace. They're getting smaller and lighter all the time – and you'll have your own within a couple of years, guaranteed.

She wrote back saying she'd be there. *Between you and me (and possibly Bobbi, if you swear her to secrecy), I would love to marry Leo, but there's still no sign of a proposal, and I'm too proud, or too cowardly, to ask him, so I must accept it and be glad for what we have.*

She said she'd travel alone. *Bringing Leo and Juliet would involve far more organising, and we have a wonderful nanny who I'm hoping will still be with us this time next year (and for the next several years). Juliet will be three in May, can you believe it? Since Joan had Trisha she's been on a mission to convince me to go again too, and I will, some day.*

She told him of a second advertising award that had led to a salary hike and a job offer from a bigger agency. *Leo was all for it; they're very prestigious and it would have meant more money for sure, but in the end I decided to stay put. I love Creative Ways, and Lucinda and I work really well together, and I earn enough. Great that someone wanted me, though.*

In May, she tried again with Leo.

'I'd love another baby,' she said, 'and it feels like the right time. I know you grew up an only child, but I really think it would be good for Juliet to have a little brother.' No harm to plant the suggestion that the next child would be a boy, to carry on the Morgan name.

It took time, and quite a bit of coaxing – 'You're so good with Juliet; being a father comes naturally to you' – but by the middle of July she had finally won him over, and she came off the pill.

On her thirtieth birthday they got Maggie to babysit and went to see *The Mousetrap*. Ellen hadn't stepped foot inside a theatre since having Juliet, and feeling again the joy of watching a live performance, she vowed not to leave it so long before the next.

She was sad to leave her twenties behind. They'd been where she'd got to know Frances properly, and where she'd fallen in love, not once but twice, and found success and fulfilment in the working world. And of course she'd become a mother in her twenties too, easily her greatest achievement to date. Her thirties, she resolved, would be even better.

In August, assuming that another pregnancy was just a matter of time, she began quietly exploring the possibility of moving to a new house. Leo's was charming, and the location was great, but it wasn't a family home. It had no garden to speak of, just a little paved patio, and the two flights of stairs were definitely not child-friendly.

They were getting away with it so far, but when the second baby came along she felt it would quickly become unsuitable. So she began studying estate agents' windows whenever she was out and about, and noting the areas that featured what she was looking for. Just doing her homework. Just seeing what was out there.

In September, Joan rang to say she and Seamus would be moving to Cork before the end of the year. 'He's being transferred. It's a promotion; we decided he should take it.'

'That'll be a big change. What about your job?'

'Plenty of schools in Cork. I can sub for a while if I have to.'

'Mam will miss you.'

'She'll be OK. I'm sorry she won't be around to look after the kids, but you can't have everything.'

Ellen phoned her mother once a month or so. Trying, as she'd promised Frances, to reconnect, to bridge their gap, but the calls were brief, the topics general. They talked of the weather, and the latest political scandal, and Juliet's milestones, and Joan's children's goings-on. They limped through five or ten minutes and then disconnected, and Ellen felt no closer at the end of each call.

'We've put our house on the market,' Joan said, 'and we'll rent in Cork until we find one.'

'Best of luck. Let me know how you get on.'

'I will. Any news yourself?'

She'd told Joan that she and Leo were trying for another baby. 'No news yet,' she said. She said nothing about the covert house-hunting – better not, when Leo didn't know about it.

A few weeks later she decided to view a house in Finchley, just to get a feel for what sounded like a suitable family home, to walk through rooms and imagine herself there with Leo and Juliet. She took an afternoon off work, and sat on a train for forty minutes, and followed directions to the house.

It was bright, with nicely proportioned rooms and just one flight of stairs. The smallest of the four bedrooms held a child's bed, and a train set on the floor, and a poster of Spiderman on the wall. Ellen stood on the landing and looked down at the back garden that had a swing and a slide in it, and she imagined the flowers and herbs and shrubs she would plant there if it were hers. Yes, this was the kind of house they needed. As soon as she got pregnant she'd talk to Leo.

With time to spare she strolled through Finchley's main street. Halfway along, her attention was caught by a man walking ahead of her. Something in the way he moved . . . what was it? Yes, a little turn-in of his right foot when he planted it on the ground.

Exactly like her father had done; some long-ago knee injury to blame.

But it wasn't her father. It couldn't be him. His hair was grey, and he wore an anorak, which was all wrong. A sports jacket in summer, a heavy coat in winter; that was always what he'd worn. And the footwear was wrong too – he'd never owned a pair of runners.

And then he slowed to glance through a window, and she got a view of his profile – and her heart gave a little squeeze. He was so like him.

Was there any possibility? The height was right, the build was right. Hair turned grey as people aged, and clothing styles could change too.

She was ten paces behind him. She was probably wrong. She'd seen men over the past few years that had resembled either him or Ben, and none of them had turned out to be who she'd thought. People could look alike, especially when you hadn't seen them in years.

He pushed open a café door and entered. She held back and peeked in, and saw him cross the floor and embrace a young woman who had got to her feet at his approach. He took a seat facing the window.

Facing Ellen. She saw him clearly.

There was no doubt. It was him. After fourteen years, she was looking at the man who'd walked out on them.

She felt her breath quicken, her colour rise. A pulse pounded in her ears. Her mouth was dry. He was there, just yards from her.

People walked around her as she stared in at him – and then maybe he sensed her, because he glanced up and looked right at her. For an instant, their gazes held – and without thinking about it she strode to the door and pushed it open and entered the café on legs she could no longer feel.

He rose as she approached the table. It seemed to take forever. She bumped against someone's chair and kept going. She took in his startled expression – and now the young woman he was with was turning to look at her too.

'Ellen,' he said – and the sound of his voice saying her name stopped her dead. She stood rooted, feeling all the blood draining now from her face.

'Ellen,' he repeated, arms coming up – and she found her voice.

'Don't touch me!' Not shouted, more hissed, with quiet vehemence. 'Don't!' she repeated, although he had already dropped his arms. She couldn't think what to say next, her brain buzzing with a thousand questions that she couldn't articulate. She was aware of the woman looking fixedly at her, but she kept her eyes locked on his.

'Why?' she said. 'Why? Why?' She was like a robot that had malfunctioned, unable to move past the word.

'Ellen—' He seemed every bit as paralysed as her. 'Will you . . .?' He indicated a vacant chair – and that gesture unleashed something in Ellen.

'You left us!' Louder now, her words sharp and harsh, heedless of the heads that swung around. 'You left us, you just walked out! How could you do that? How could you *do* that to us? What kind of a father are you?'

She became aware that tears were spilling down her cheeks; she dashed a hand up to swipe at them but they kept coming. 'And who is *she*?' she demanded, pointing at the woman who shrank away. 'What are you doing with her? How dare you! I *hate* you! I *hate* you!'

And at that she swung around and marched blindly from the café, eyes still streaming as she stumbled again into chairs, pushing her way out, half-running down the street, almost tripping over an uneven kerbstone but somehow managing to stay upright, her only thought to get away, get away – but he was coming after her, he was calling her name repeatedly.

'Wait! Ellen, wait! Please, Ellen, wait! Please!' – and in the end she had to stop because the breath was gone from her body. She had to stop and lean into the stitch that was stabbing her, and take panting gulps while he caught up with her.

'Ellen,' he said, panting too, 'please let me explain. Please let me. Will you let me tell my side, Ellen?'

She shook her head, so forcefully it almost unbalanced her again. 'I don't want to talk to you – you've hurt me enough! Go away! Leave me alone!' She cast around wildly, but she'd lost her bearings and couldn't figure out the way back to the Tube station. She swiped at the tears that kept coming. 'Stay away!' she ordered. She couldn't let him get close. She was terrified of him getting close.

'Are you alright?' a man asked, glancing in her father's direction. 'Do you need help?'

She was mortified. He thought she was in danger. 'I'm OK,' she told him, knowing that her face told another story. 'It's OK,' she said, 'thank you' – and giving her father another swift glance, he walked on.

They stood facing one another. 'Will you let me explain?' he pleaded. 'Please.'

'I don't want to hear whatever you have to say,' she replied, but the fight was gone out of her. She was exhausted from emotion. 'Excuse me,' she said to a passing woman, 'where's the Tube station?' and the woman gave directions, eyeing Ellen curiously.

'I'll come with you,' he said. 'We can talk on the train. Please give me a chance, Ellen,' and she ignored him and kept going, and he kept following, and there was nothing she could do to stop him.

And on the train, he told her.

'Things weren't right for a long time. I'm not putting the blame on your mother; there were two of us in it. She was . . . troubled, and I didn't have the patience to deal with it. I stayed for you and Joan, long after your mother and I had run our course.'

Ellen looked stonily at him.

'Ellen,' he said brokenly, 'you have no idea how happy I am to see you now.'

'You walked out,' she said, some of her fire returning. 'You never once came back. In fourteen years you never came back.'

'Your mother said I wasn't to. She said if I left her, I had to leave you both as well. All I could do was write to you.'

'We didn't know that. Mam only handed them over a few years ago.'

His face changed. 'What? She kept them from you?' She saw the devastation her words caused. 'I waited,' he said, so quietly she had to lean in. 'Every day, I waited for you and Joan to write back.'

'You could have visited,' she insisted, determined not to weaken. 'Even if you couldn't live with her, you could have come and spent time with me and Joan.'

He shook his head. 'She said if I ever came back she'd tell you why I went.'

Ellen stared at him. 'You've just told me why you went.'

'No. There's more.'

He broke off and looked through the window, giving Ellen a chance to study the features that had been so dear to her. The face as well known as her own had new lines in it, fanning out from his eyes, pleating the skin around his mouth. Skin pouched beneath his eye sockets, tiny blood vessels scribbled over his cheeks. His hair was longer than she remembered, touching the back of his collar.

And then he said, so softly she barely heard above the hum of the train, 'Ellen, I met someone. She worked in the newsagent's beside the school.' He drew in a breath, blinked rapidly. 'I'm sorry, Ellen. We had an affair.'

She sank her face into her hands. After all the pain, all the tears, all the lonely years, it came down to this. A sordid little affair with a woman behind a counter in a newsagent's. She remembered the shop dimly; she'd been in it. Couldn't remember who worked there, had taken no notice of them.

'It wasn't what broke up your mother and me, Ellen. We were over by then, honestly.' He halted. 'I want you to know the whole truth. Can I go on?'

She looked up slowly. There was more?

He took another breath. 'We had a child. It wasn't planned, it was an accident. You saw her in the café.'

'She's your *daughter*? You had another daughter?'

'I did.'

She struggled to take it in. She and Joan had a half-sister, had had her for years without knowing it. 'How old is she?'

'She was nineteen in January.'

Nineteen. He'd been gone fourteen years.

'She was five when you left,' Ellen said. 'You had another child, and you stayed living with us for five years after that.'

'It was unforgivable. I couldn't bear the thought of leaving you and Joan.'

She ignored this. 'Where did they live?'

He gave a small lift of a hand. 'A flat,' he said, 'on the other side of town.' As if it didn't matter – and she supposed it didn't.

'Did people know the child was yours?' She couldn't believe she was having this conversation. It felt like a parallel universe.

'Nobody knew. She told nobody who the father was, not even her parents. Not until—'

She finished it for him. 'Not until you left us, and went to live with your new family.' She saw him flinch, and was glad.

'I tried, Ellen. Honest to God, I tried to stay. I couldn't. Making that decision was hell,' he said quietly. 'It was pure hell.'

'We were there first,' she said angrily. 'We were your first children – but that didn't matter when another one came along.'

'It wasn't as simple—'

She cut him off. 'Did our mother know? Did you tell her?'

'I told her I'd met someone else. I didn't tell her about the child.'

'So you took your new family and moved to Dublin.'

He just nodded. A short silence fell.

'But you live in London now,' she said.

'No, I'm still in Dublin. I'm just over visiting Iris. She works in an art gallery in Covent Garden.'

Iris, her half-sister. The daughter he hadn't deserted. She smothered a pang of jealousy.

'Does she know about me and Joan?'

'Yes. I told her last year.' He paused, closed his eyes briefly. 'After her mother died.'

She wasn't prepared for that. She said nothing. She wouldn't tell him she was sorry for his trouble, because she wasn't.

'She was knocked down by a drunk driver, the week before Christmas. She was out for a walk.'

Still she held her tongue. It was nothing to her.

'Ellen,' he said then, 'I've thought about you and Joan every single day since I left. I've agonised about my decision, wondering if I made the right choice, or the most selfish one. I never stopped loving you and Joan, I love you both to bits, you must believe me, but I couldn't go on the way it was.'

'She tore up your cheques too,' Ellen said. Wanting to hurt. 'Joan and I had to get Saturday jobs.'

She saw the wounds her words caused. 'I'm so sorry, Ellen.'

They were nearly at her stop. She felt drained.

'I tried to make contact,' he said, 'after . . . Iris' mother died. I rang the house and Patricia answered. She told me you'd both moved out, and . . . she said you didn't want to hear from me.'

Listening, Ellen felt a surge of rage. Yes, there was fault on both sides, she could see that now, but even after all these years, her mother remained determined to punish him for leaving, and to punish her daughters in the process. What was the point in trying to move on from the past when her mother seemed bent on keeping it alive?

'I tried contacting Frances, I thought she might help, but I had no address, and there was no number for her in the book.'

That much was true. Ellen remembered asking Frances why she wasn't in the phone book, and Frances replying that she gave her number out to people she wanted to have it, and that was enough.

'What about you?' he said. 'Do you live here now?'

'Yes.'

'Are you married? Do you have children?'

She ignored the first question. 'I have a daughter,' she said.

'A granddaughter,' he said softly, eyes glistening.

'You have three grandchildren. Joan has two.' She felt a kind of sadistic satisfaction saying it. She got to her feet as the Tube approached her station.

'Will you keep in touch, Ellen? Will you take my number – or give me yours? Can I ring you sometime?'

She looked at the man who had meant the world to her. She looked at the yearning in his eyes.

The train stopped. The doors whooshed open.

'No,' she said. 'I won't keep in touch.'

Without waiting for a reply she stepped off the train and walked rapidly from the station. When she got home she heard Maggie and Juliet in the kitchen. She checked her watch and saw that there was still half an hour before she normally got back from work. She tiptoed upstairs and sank onto her bed and cried for the lost years, and all he'd missed.

After wishing to see him again for so long, she bitterly regretted the encounter. She should never have gone to Finchley. She wouldn't tell anyone about bumping into him, not even Joan. What was the point? She had no intention of making contact with him again – and Joan, she was sure, wouldn't want to meet him either if she knew what Ellen now knew.

All these years, their mother had known about the other woman. Little wonder she'd been bitter, even if, as he'd claimed, their relationship had already died. Not surprising she'd torn up his cheques, secreted away the letters to his daughters, denied him the chance to reconnect with them when he'd finally made contact with her. Wrong, but not surprising.

The half-sister, though. Iris. Should Joan be told about her? And how could Ellen tell her without revealing how she knew? Oh, it was complicated. It was too hard.

She would do nothing. For now at least, she would say nothing.

Families

NEARLY SEVEN YEARS AFTER HER FIRST ENCOUNTER with Leo in Paris, Ellen finally met his half-brothers. How had it taken so long? Never having lived with them, Leo had confessed to having no real bond when Ellen had expressed a curiosity about them. *We get on,* he'd said, *but there's a big age difference. We have little in common.*

You have a mother in common, Ellen had pointed out – but considering that the mother was ice-cold Marguerite, maybe the lack of brotherly connection was understandable, so she hadn't pushed him until Juliet's arrival. *They should be part of their niece's life,* she'd said, but it had still taken Leo a long time to issue the invitation for them to spend Christmas in London. They'd invited Marguerite too – they could hardly exclude her – but she'd already made arrangements to spend the day with a newly widowed friend so the boys, Henri, eighteen, and Louis, sixteen, travelled alone.

And right from the start, Ellen warmed to them.

'*Enchanté*,' they murmured, brushing her cheeks with shy kisses and presenting her with a bottle of Chanel perfume. 'Our mother say to us you like,' Henri said, and blushed and apologised for his poor English, and Ellen told him in French not to worry, her French was also poor, and it broke the ice.

They declared Juliet to be a princess, and gave her a picture book that was written in both languages, and a doll whose name was Madeline in a white dress and bonnet, and they won her over as quickly as they'd won Ellen. She was soon chattering to them in the French Leo used with her – and Ellen, watching, thought, *At least she has two lovely uncles, even if she mightn't see a whole lot of them.*

In early January she went shopping in the sales for an outfit for Danny and Bobbi's wedding. 'Days will be mild but not hot,' Danny had said on the phone, 'and cool in the early morning and evening,' so she settled on a jade green dress with a matching coat, and said no to the hat the salesperson suggested. A hat might not survive the trip, and she wasn't sure anyway she had the head for it.

She stood on the pavement outside the boutique. She was less than five minutes' walk from Covent Garden. In her pocket was a list of London art galleries that she'd photocopied from the Yellow Pages at work. She went into a phone box and began ringing the ones located nearby.

'May I speak with Iris?' she said each time her call was answered, and it took five calls.

'This is Iris,' a soft voice replied. Ellen opened her mouth and closed it again, suddenly out of words. She hung up quickly and found the gallery, and saw her half-sister inside behind a desk.

'Good afternoon,' Iris said brightly at Ellen's approach – and then her smile slipped into uncertainty as recognition dawned. Her eyes were a striking green, and outlined in black. There were little green studs in her ears. She wore her pale hair in a side ponytail that draped across one shoulder, and a dress the colour of autumn. Her figure was neat. She had a delicate kind of prettiness.

Was there a faint resemblance to their father? Ellen wasn't sure. 'I rang just now,' she said.

'Yes.' Calm. Quiet.

'I didn't know about you. I didn't know you existed until that day in the café.'

'I didn't know about you either, or your sister, until . . . recently.'

After her mother had died he'd told her. Ellen shifted her bag from one hand to the other. 'I said to him I didn't want to keep in touch.'

Iris made no response.

'I was angry,' Ellen said. 'I spoke in anger.' To her dismay, she felt her eyes filling. She blinked hard.

Iris reached up to touch her ponytail briefly. Her nails were perfect ovals, painted pale pink with white tips.

A sound made them both turn towards the window. A toddler was slapping his hand on the glass: a woman pulled him away and led him off, mouthing an apology.

'Will you give me his phone number?'

'Of course.' Iris scribbled on a notepad and ripped off the page. She knew his number by heart, because she'd grown up in the same house as him. It had been her number too, before she'd moved to London.

Ellen folded the page without looking at it. 'Thank you.' She hesitated. 'I'm not sure when I'll use it, or . . .' She trailed off.

Iris nodded. 'You'd rather I didn't say anything.'

'I would, yes. If that's OK.'

'Sure.' She touched the end of her ponytail again. 'I don't know if you'd like to, well, meet me sometime?'

Ellen thought about that. 'Maybe,' she said, and Iris gave her another number, and the face of her half-sister accompanied her all the way home.

A week before she left for California, Joan rang.

'Mam was on the phone earlier. She's not feeling well. She's been to her doctor and he's sending her for tests. I thought you'd want to know.'

'What's wrong with her?'

'She has a cough she can't shake, and no energy. It's probably nothing.'

'Right.'

She thought again about telling Joan of the encounter in Finchley, and the existence of Iris. Was she wrong to say nothing? In refusing to keep in touch with him she'd been trying to hurt him, but it had also left her conflicted – and now she had a secret she was keeping from her sister.

She decided to wait until she came back from the wedding and tell Joan then. Maybe. 'Let me know how the tests go.'

It was cowardly. It was the best she could do.

California

SHE FLEW FROM LONDON TO BOSTON ON WED-
nesday evening and fought sleep in the airport for three hours
before boarding a flight to San Francisco. She'd taken a week off
work: Leo had suggested a longer break, to give her more time on
her first trip to America, but a week was as much as she wanted
to be apart from him and Juliet.

Enjoy yourself, he'd said as she was leaving. *Don't worry about us, we'll
be fine.* Maggie would hold the fort by day like she always did until
Leo got in from work, and Claire had promised to call around on
Sunday afternoon like she used to. The deli was doing well – so well,
in fact, that she now operated it as a wine bar on the weekends, which
left her with even less time off. *I'll get a manager,* she kept promising,
and Ellen wished that she would. She missed her friend.

Danny was waiting in the arrivals hall when she emerged. She felt
crumpled and tired and headachy from unfamiliar food at the wrong
times, but he caught her in one of his bear hugs, and it was worth the
discomfort to see him again.

He drove a little dark green sports car with a roof that folded
back. 'There's money in computers,' she said when she saw it, and
he laughed and said just a bit.

'Roof up or down?'

'Down, of course' – and she pulled a scarf from her bag and wrapped her hair in it, and they sped along the highway, and she'd forgotten how good sunshine felt on her skin, and how wonderfully spacious a blue sky made the world seem, and by the time they arrived she felt euphoric as well as exhausted.

His and Bobbi's apartment was in a complex of just a dozen, with a communal pool and two tennis courts. Bobbi was there with her mother; the four of them sat under a big umbrella on the deck and ate French toast and drank coffee while Ellen showed photos of Juliet and Leo and answered questions about her job – advertising always fascinated people – and tried to swallow her yawns.

'Taste this,' Bobbi said, handing her a little chocolate thing in a bun case.

'What is it?'

'Peanut butter cup. Addictive.'

She bit into the chocolate and found the peanut butter. The combination of sweet and salt was irresistible. She had another. She was glad they weren't available back home.

Finally Bobbi showed her to her room, which was small and simple and all she needed. A thin window blind had been pulled down: behind it the sun still shone. 'We're all going out to dinner tonight,' Bobbi said. 'Both families, so it'll be noisy. I know you'd probably rather sleep, but his family are dying to meet you. We'll let you sleep as long as we can.'

Tomorrow was their wedding day, and Valentine's Day, and Bobbi's birthday. Ellen had wanted to book into a hotel for the wedding night, but they wouldn't hear of it. 'We've been living together for nearly ten years,' Danny had said. 'We'll be newlyweds in name only.'

She slept without moving, sinking into a deep dreamless state until Danny tapped on her door and told her she had half an hour before they needed to leave for dinner. 'My parents are here,' he added. 'We're meeting everyone else at the restaurant.'

She showered and dressed hurriedly and went out to find them, and his mother hugged her and declared that she'd know her anywhere – 'I was so delighted when you and Danny met up again!' – and his father shook her hand, and their faces were strange and familiar all at once.

There were twenty-six of them at dinner, gathered around a long table. Sixteen on Danny's side, nine on Bobbi's, and Ellen in the middle. She was touched to be the only non-family member there.

She ate lobster, dipping the chunks into a bowl of melted butter. She sat between Danny's eldest sisters, whom she barely remembered – the gap had been too wide in her childhood – but who chattered nonstop between mouthfuls. She was still tired, but glad to be there for him.

Halfway through the meal she excused herself to go to the ladies', where she found the youngest of Danny's sisters washing her hands. 'Wouldn't you know it,' she told Ellen cheerfully, 'my period has just arrived. Great timing.'

'Oh no' – and even as she said that, Ellen thought, *Hang on.* Sitting in the stall, she tried to remember when she'd last had a period. She'd been so busy in the run-up to Christmas, with presents to buy, and work hectic, and the two French boys to get ready for, and her father and Iris on her mind. It hadn't occurred to her to keep track.

Could it have been as long ago as November? This was the middle of February. And now that she thought about it, hadn't she been feeling a little off in the mornings? She'd put it down to overwork, and the head cold she'd picked up just after Christmas that had hung around, but . . .

She tried not to allow excitement in. She might be wrong. But just in case, back at the table she pushed her wine glass aside and drew her water glass closer. For the rest of the evening she spooled back over the previous weeks, hunting for more clues, only half-listening to the chat around her.

She'd get a pregnancy test tomorrow. The wedding wasn't until two: in the morning she'd ask Danny to direct her to a chemist, and she'd pick one up. She'd say nothing to anyone else.

Tomorrow she'd find out. Tomorrow she'd know.

An hour later she was lying in bed, trying and failing to sleep, despite her exhaustion. She hadn't rung Leo like she'd planned, afraid her voice might give her away. If the test told her what she wanted to hear, she'd change her flight and go home sooner. Danny would help with that.

She got up and wandered in pyjamas out onto the deck – and started when a figure turned from the table at her approach.

'Snap,' Danny said. He patted the chair next to him and she sat.

'Pre-wedding nerves?'

'More like too much lobster.'

The night was cool, as he'd warned: she rubbed her hands together, wishing she'd pulled on a sweater.

'Hang on,' he said, and came back with a soft throw that he

placed over her shoulders, and a jug with two tumblers. 'Juice – unless you'd prefer water, or something stronger.'

'Juice is fine.' It was orange and pulpy and delicious. She gathered the throw around her and inhaled the scent of some fragrant flower. 'This is lovely,' she said.

'It's nice,' he agreed. 'Peaceful. We're lucky.'

They lapsed into a comfortable silence. She thought of Leo and Juliet. London was eight hours ahead, so it was morning there. Leo would have dropped Juliet to the crèche and travelled on to work. She thought of his face when she told him she was pregnant again, if it turned out that she was.

'Danny.'

'Yes.'

'Is there a chemist nearby?'

He turned to look at her. 'Next block. What do you need? We might have it.'

She had to tell him. She wanted to tell him. 'A pregnancy test.'

'Seriously?'

She nodded. 'I mightn't be right – but I think I am. We've been trying, but I'd lost track, with Christmas and everything. It only struck me tonight that I'm late.'

'Wow. I suppose I won't congratulate you until you confirm. I'll take you first thing in the morning: it's two minutes in the car.'

'Thanks. And . . . if it's positive, would you mind terribly if I changed my flight and went home a bit earlier, maybe Sunday instead of Tuesday? I'd prefer to tell Leo in person.'

'Sure. I'll sort it.'

'Thank you.'

Another silence fell. She sipped juice, felt its tang on her tongue. 'The Winnie-the-Pooh books,' she said. 'I remember your sisters reading them to us in your house. Juliet loves them.'

'I'm not surprised. A child of yours would have to love books.'

'True.' She took another sip. 'I told someone once that I'd like to write a book, or try to.'

'Definitely you should. For children or adults?'

'Adults. A novel.'

'Why don't you?'

'Oh, part laziness, part fear – and partly because I'm so busy all the time. And if there's another baby, it'll be even more difficult.'

'Hey, if you really want to do something, you'll find the time.'

Pretty much what Ben had said. Setting down her glass, she yawned. 'Sorry.'

'Don't be sorry,' he said, getting up. 'Go to bed and go to sleep. See you in the morning' – and in the morning Ellen did two tests and got two clear lines on each wand, no mistaking them.

Oh boy.

Danny, bless him, sorted new flights in fifteen minutes – and when Bobbi, still in dressing gown, came in to find out what he was doing, they told her. 'Hey, congratulations!' She pulled out drawers till she found a rabbit's foot keyring. 'For luck,' she said, pressing it into Ellen's hand. 'We'll always remember the day you found out.'

The wedding went by in a blur. The golf club was very fancy indeed, with the ceremony under a gazebo in the immaculate grounds, a fountain in the background. Ellen dreaded to think of the bill, although the crowd was small, just a dozen or so more than the dinner guests of the night before. She pretended to drink the champagne poured for the pre-dinner toasts, all the time imagining breaking the news to Leo.

A boy, she thought. A miniature version of him. Two children would be enough, if he didn't want more.

As they waited for the meal she rang Leo using Danny's cell phone. Just before eleven in the evening in London: Juliet would be in bed, but he should still be up. She couldn't tell him, not over the phone, but she suddenly needed to hear his voice.

He took a long time to answer. 'Hello?'

'Did I wake you?'

'Ellen. No, no . . . I was in the bathroom. Everything OK?'

'Yes, everything's fine. I'm just ringing to say a quick hello. I'm at the wedding, it's very posh. How are you getting on?'

'All fine here too. Juliet's in bed.'

'I hope she's not missing me too much.'

'She's . . . no, no, at least yes, she misses you, of course, but she's OK.'

He sounded distracted. She guessed he'd fallen asleep in front of the television. 'Love you,' she said. 'I'd better go. Kiss Juliet for me in the morning. See you soon.'

'Yes, have fun. Goodnight.'

Next day she slept late, waking to silence and a note on the kitchen table: *We've snuck out to meet some leftover wedding guests for brunch – if you wake and feel like following us, address on the reverse, along with cab number. If not, raid the fridge and we'll see you soon – D x*

She stuck a bagel into the toaster and spread it with cream cheese. She nibbled it slowly on the deck – a faint queasiness, not too bad – and wondered how her mother would take the news of her second pregnancy.

The following day, Sunday, Danny brought her back to the airport. On the way she told him about bumping into her father, and the discovery of a half-sister.

'Wow, that's big.'

'It was. Very big.'

'Will you stay in touch?'

'With him, I don't know. With Iris, maybe.' She thought it funny – not funny, that wasn't the right word. Sad? Strange? – that her children would have half-uncles on one side of the family and a half-aunt on the other. Common enough in these days, of course, with lifelong marriages not the certainties they once were. There was even vague talk of a divorce referendum, but Ellen couldn't see divorce ever becoming a reality in Ireland.

She also told him about her mother being sent for tests. 'I don't know if she's had them yet or not – it was Joan who told me about them. Mam and I had a bit of a falling-out when I broke the news that I was pregnant with Juliet.'

'Oh, shame. Hope the tests show nothing bad.'

The sky was blue again. Such a deep, wonderful cloudless blue. Maybe she and Leo should move their family to America.

'Keep me posted on all fronts,' Danny said at the airport, 'particularly on the baby front. I'm pretty much an honorary uncle, in at the start like this – and Bobbi and I might be able to provide a cousin or two at some stage.'

'That would be great – definitely our kids will be honorary cousins. Thanks for everything, and sorry for making you take me to a chemist on your wedding day.'

'Only for you.'

The flight, the flights, seemed endless. In Boston airport she tried to read her book but her mind was miles away. Conceived in December probably, so the due date would be sometime in September. Joan's birthday was in August, Frances' in September. Nice if it arrived in the middle.

She thought again about the tests her mother was to have. She'd be sixty-six in May, not old by any standard. She'd ring Joan tomorrow evening to see if there was news.

Her flight landed in Heathrow just after seven on Monday morning. By the time she'd retrieved her luggage and got through the checks it was five to eight. Should she splash out on a taxi? No – the Tube would be just as quick at this hour, or quicker.

The train was full. She sat on her suitcase, eyelids drooping with tiredness. She regarded the other newly arrived passengers and wondered if any of the females were pregnant too. She hugged her secret to herself and ignored her bladder, which needed to be emptied. She should have gone in the airport, but now she would wait till she got home.

She walked from the station to the house, every step increasing her desire for a toilet. Juliet would be in crèche, Leo at work, so she planned to turn up at the bank at lunchtime. She'd rather tell him at home, but she couldn't possibly wait all day, so his office would have to do.

But first a shower, and sleep.

Shock

AT THE HOUSE SHE FISHED HER KEY FROM HER pocket. She opened the door and dropped her bag in the hall before making a dash for the downstairs toilet. As she was washing her hands afterwards she thought she heard footsteps descending the stairs.

She emerged from the loo and looked around. The front door was still open, her key still in the lock, her bag precisely where she'd dropped it. Hallucinating, she decided, from lack of sleep. She pulled out her key and closed the door. She'd make tea and have it while she was getting ready for bed.

There were two cups on the kitchen table, a coffee pot between them. He and Maggie maybe, although Maggie was more a tea person. As she crossed to the table, rapid footsteps sounded suddenly on the stairs. She froze, heart hammering. Had she disturbed thieves? Should she make a dash for it, out through the back? But the key to the back gate—

The kitchen door opened and Leo appeared, tucking shirt tails into trousers. 'Ellen – you're back. What's up? What's happened?'

She let out her breath. 'My God – you scared the life out of me. Why are you here? Why aren't you at work?'

Instead of answering, he swept her into a hug she wasn't expecting, causing her to stumble a little.

'Sorry,' he said, still holding her, his voice travelling over her shoulder, 'you caught me having a sneaky nap – Juliet was a bit restless last night.'

She eased from his embrace to study him. 'Is she OK? Anything wrong?'

'No, just overtired or something. She was fine going to crèche.'

'But shouldn't you be at work?'

'I decided to take the day off. Didn't I tell you?' His shirt was buttoned wrongly. Why had he felt he'd have to get dressed before seeing her?

'So,' he said, clapping his hands – he never clapped his hands – 'let's make coffee and you can tell me everything.' As he spoke, he whisked the cups from the table and deposited them in the sink.

'Were you entertaining?' she asked.

He laughed. 'Hardly – unless you count Claire as a visitor. She was here yesterday. I was being a slob, leaving them there.'

Claire. She'd forgotten Claire's promise to drop in on Sunday.

'I was going to do a clean-up before you arrived,' he went on, his back to her as he sluiced the cups out with water. 'So – was the wedding called off?'

'No, it went ahead – I phoned you while it was going on, remember?'

'Oh ... yes, of course. Sorry, I think I'm still half asleep.' He turned to her then, drying his hands on a towel. 'So why did you come back early?'

There was something wrong with his smile. It wasn't sitting right.

'I took a test,' she said. 'In America.' Disappointed at how her big news was falling flat.

He set down the towel. 'Oh yes?'

'A pregnancy test, Leo.' Maybe he'd drunk too much last night. He seemed fuddled, not with it. She crossed to him and undid his buttons and fixed them. 'I'm pregnant,' she said.

For a second he didn't react, and then he embraced her again, wordlessly.

After a minute she drew away again, frowning. 'Leo,' she said, her palms against his chest, his heart beating beneath it, 'you're acting oddly. What's up? Did something happen? Is Juliet really OK?'

He laughed. It was too loud. He grabbed her hands. 'Juliet is fine, never better! Everything's fine. You worry too much. Everything's fine.'

'And what about the baby? Are you happy I'm pregnant?'

'Of course I am!'

No. Something was wrong. He couldn't lie. He was trying, but he was failing. 'Leo,' she began, 'was—' She broke off. She wet her lips and started again. 'Was someone else here?'

He frowned. 'Was – what? I told you, Claire was here. Yesterday. You knew she was coming, right?'

She shook her head. 'No, I don't mean Claire. I mean now, this morning.'

'What are you talking about?'

'Just now, when I came in. I heard someone coming down the stairs when I was in the loo.'

She waited for him to say she'd imagined it, of course nobody else was there, but he didn't.

And he had come downstairs just minutes later.

No.

No.

Please.

His shirt buttons.

His odd manner.

No. Please. No.

He looked trapped. Her heart fell. It dropped all the way to the floor. No.

'Say something,' she begged. 'Tell me I'm wrong. Say whatever it takes to make this go away.'

Still he remained silent. She felt like she might vomit.

She drew her hands from his. 'Was someone here this morning? Was someone with you?' She stepped away, already knowing the answer he wouldn't say.

'Ellen—'

'Who? Who was here?'

'I'm sorry, I'm so sorry—'

She covered her face with ice-cold hands. 'Oh God, oh God, oh God.' She kept saying it, kept repeating it. She felt him trying to take her hands again and she leapt back, hip colliding painfully with the edge of the table. 'No! Stay away – don't touch me!'

'Ellen, please, it was a one-off, it meant nothing, a stupid impulse—'

'Who is it? Do I know her? Have I met her?'

'Ellen, it doesn't matter—'

'It doesn't *matter*?' she shot back, hip throbbing. 'It doesn't matter that you – that you – *Jesus*!' A new and horrible thought struck. 'Was Juliet here? Did you bring someone in when our daughter was in the house?'

'No, I swear it, Ellen. Juliet knows nothing – she came after I brought Juliet to crèche. Please believe me.'

'And you took the day off to be with her.'

He said nothing.

'Who is it?' she demanded again.

'Someone from work, you've never met her. Please, Ellen—'

She'd had enough. She left the room, stunned. Leo followed, still pleading. 'I'm sorry,' he said. 'I'm so sorry. I was stupid.'

She opened the front door.

'Don't go, Ellen – don't leave like this, please.'

'I'm picking up Juliet,' she said through lips that felt stiff. 'Don't try to stop me,' and she was pulling her bag behind her, walking out into the rain that had started while she was inside, shaking with cold and fright and exhaustion, fighting not to wail like an animal, not to bellow like a bull. She was walking away from him, away from his house, away from their life, and she had no clue where she was going.

Juliet. She must get Juliet. Back on the High Street she flagged down a taxi and gave the address of the crèche. The driver darted an enquiring look at her but said nothing. In the back of the taxi she tried to compose herself for Juliet, and whatever adults she'd have to deal with.

'A family emergency,' she said. 'I have to take her,' and one of the assistants went off to get Juliet, and she was brought out in her outdoor clothing, and she said 'Mummy!' and flung herself into Ellen's arms, and Ellen held her close and squeezed her eyes shut for a few precious seconds before bundling her out and into the waiting taxi.

'Where to?' the driver asked, and Ellen gave the name of the deli. Claire would help. Claire would know what to do – but all she found there were two young staff members in olive green aprons. 'She had errands to run this morning,' one of them told Ellen. 'Said she'd be late.'

'I need to make a phone call,' Ellen said. 'I'm a friend of hers.'

'There's a phone in the back room,' she was told, so she left Juliet with them and dialled Maggie's number.

'It's Ellen,' she said, her voice cracking. 'Maggie, there's been – I'm – I have Juliet, and we need a place to stay for a day or two. I just got home from . . . America, I came early, and Leo—' She broke off, unable to say it.

'That's no problem at all,' Maggie said. 'Are you coming now?'

'Yes, I'm at – a friend's deli, but she's not here. I know it's a terrible imposition, but I—'

'You have my address, haven't you?'

'Not on me. Remind me.'

Maggie told her the street and the number, and Ellen pulled a pen from her bag and scribbled it on her hand. 'Thank you so much,' she said, and hung up, and leant against the wall to steady herself before reclaiming her daughter and setting off again.

'We're having an adventure,' she told Juliet on the way. 'We're going to Maggie's house.'

'Is Daddy coming?'

She swallowed a lump in her throat. 'Daddy's busy with work, so it's just you and me.' How long would that lie last?

'I want Madeline,' Juliet said, and Ellen realised that she had nothing for the child, no clothes, no toys, no doll that her new uncles had brought her from France at Christmas.

'We'll get her, darling. We'll get Madeline soon.'

The sight of Maggie, so kind, so capable, so unquestioning, made Ellen want to burst into tears. 'Sorry,' she murmured. 'I didn't know where else to go.'

'There's a bed ready,' Maggie replied, indicating the stairs, 'second door on the right,' drawing Juliet away. 'Come on, pet, we'll make buns while Mummy has a nap.'

Ellen trailed upstairs, too numb for even a thank you. She was sure she wouldn't sleep, despite her exhaustion. She would lie on the bed and try to collect her thoughts – but she did sleep, soundly and deeply, and when she woke it took a few minutes to understand where she was, and for the nightmare to come crashing back.

She looked around. The wallpaper had flowers on it. The carpet was tan, with more flowers. A knob was missing from one of the dressing table's drawers. A basketball sat on the floor under the window, whose curtains – yellow – were apart. The sky outside was white.

She wished to be back in California, under a perfect blue sky. She wanted to be eating peanut butter cups with Danny, or catching the bouquet that Bobbi had thrown right at her, knowing that Ellen yearned to be married to Leo.

The thought of him brought back the ugly scene in the kitchen. She saw again his panicked face, the wrongly buttoned shirt. She heard his forced laugh.

A one-off, he'd said. *A stupid impulse.* He'd slept with someone else in their bed. Had it really happened? Had he really done that to her? Maybe she was still asleep. She pinched herself, and felt it.

Everything was unpredictable now. Nothing was stable any more. She understood why people talked about having the rug pulled out from under them.

Downstairs she ate the poached egg on toast that Maggie made for her, and a bun afterwards that she didn't want, but ate because Juliet had made it.

'I have a camp bed,' Maggie said while Juliet watched cartoons in the sitting room. 'We can put it into your room for Juliet.'

'He had someone in the house, Maggie.' Her chin wobbled. 'I came home early because I wanted to tell him I'm pregnant. I did a test in California.'

'Oh, lovey,' Maggie said, covering Ellen's hand with hers. 'Oh, lovey.'

'I'm going to find us a place to rent,' Ellen said. 'Will you still come? I'll try and get somewhere not too far away.'

'Of course I'll still come. You'll need me more than ever when the second little one arrives.'

'Thank you.' She'd have to get another week off work so she could sort things out. Could she afford crèche fees on top of rent, and Maggie's salary, and groceries, and bills, and whatever else she wasn't thinking of?

Leo would want to help. He'd want to salve his guilty conscience – but she didn't want him to. She wanted nothing to do with him. She thought of her mother, tearing up the cheques her husband had sent, and she felt solidarity. They'd both been betrayed.

She looked at Maggie in despair. 'How did this happen? I thought we were happy. I thought he was happy.'

Maggie just shook her head, and they fell into silence. This should have been such a happy day, Ellen thought. This should have been a day of love and planning. She'd been going to wait a week or two, and then broach the subject of looking for a more suitable house.

'This will be just for a few days,' she said. 'I'll find someplace else.'

'You stay as long as you need. You know all mine are moved out, there's plenty of room.'

'Thank you. Thank you so much.' Ellen gripped her hand. 'I need to ask you to do something else, Maggie. I need you to go to the house and get a few things. Would you do that? I'll get a taxi to take you there and back.'

'Make a list,' Maggie said, and after she'd left, Ellen sat with Juliet in her cluttered sitting room, imagining the meeting between Maggie and Leo, and how the conversation would go.

'He's sorry,' Maggie reported on her return, when Juliet had been tucked up with Madeline in her new bed. 'He said to tell you he's sorry. He looked terrible.'

'I can't trust him again, Maggie. I can never trust him again' – but even as she said the words, she couldn't imagine life without him. How could it be possible? How could she go on?

In the morning she left Juliet with Maggie and got the Tube to the deli, where she found Claire.

'I heard you were looking for me,' Claire said, bringing her upstairs. 'I phoned you, but I only got Leo.'

'He told you?'

'He did. I'm so sorry.'

'Did he tell you why I came home early?'

'Yes. I'd say congratulations, but . . . Where are you staying?'

'With Maggie, just for the moment. What time did you leave our house on Sunday?'

'Around six.'

So it had happened after that. After Claire had gone, after Juliet had been put to bed. He must have rung to tell the woman that the coast was clear. Because of course she'd stayed the night; of course she hadn't just dropped by after he'd come home from bringing Juliet to the crèche. She'd stayed the night, with Juliet in the next room, and then she'd lain low while he got Juliet up and out. She'd waited in bed for him to come back from the crèche – or maybe she'd got up and made coffee. Maybe that was when they'd had it, before going back upstairs.

'I need to phone Frances,' she said. 'Can I use the downstairs phone?'

'Use mine here,' Claire said. 'I'll leave you alone.'

'Hello?'

The sound of the familiar sharp tone was wonderful. 'Frances,' she said, 'it's me, Ellen. I'm back in London.'

'You were talking to Joan.'

'What? Joan? No.' She tumbled out the events, the pregnancy discovery, the changed flight, the shock of Leo's betrayal. 'We're staying with Juliet's nanny. I'm not going back to him, Frances. I'll find somewhere to rent.'

'Oh, God love you, my pet. I'm so sorry to hear that.'

There was a pause. Ellen's sluggish brain rewound to something that had snagged there. 'Why did you mention Joan?'

'She rang me yesterday. She was waiting till you came home from America to ring you.'

'What did she—?' And abruptly, she remembered. 'The tests my mother was having.'

'Yes. It's not good, Ellen. It's cancer that started in her lungs, and it's spread too far for them to do anything.'

'Oh, God.' Ellen bowed her head. It was too much. She would break; she would snap in two under the weight of it all.

'I'm going to go and stay with her,' Frances said. 'She needs someone to look after her' – but even as she spoke, Ellen could see what would happen. It was the only thing that made sense, although the thought of it dragged her down even further.

She'd have to talk to Leo. She shrank from the prospect, but it was unavoidable. He'd have to agree before she could do what she knew was inevitable.

'I'll come,' she told Frances. 'Juliet and I will come home.'

HOME
FEBRUARY 1992
THE FOURTH MOVE

Mother

THE LAST TIME SHE'D SLEPT THERE WAS THE NIGHT of Joan's wedding, seven years ago. The wallpaper was the same, strutting peacocks against pale blue that she'd been allowed to choose at the age of fourteen, when her father had decided both girls' bedrooms needed freshening up.

The dressing table, the wardrobe, the armchair and the bookshelves were still there. The frilled bed linen, the yellow rug by the bed, the stain on the floorboards under the window where Claire had dropped a bottle of nail varnish remover once.

She found places for her things and Juliet's as best she could, the opening of drawers and the hanging of clothes reminding her cruelly of moving in with Leo. She recalled how happy she'd been as she'd installed her belongings in his home, how sure that she'd found the man to spend the rest of her life with.

So many of her belongings were still in his house – her books, her portfolio, her summer clothes – and some of Juliet's stuff too. *Tell him to pack it all up*, Maggie had said, *and bring it to my house. I'll store it in one of the bedrooms; it'll be fine there. Keep in touch*, she'd said, *let me know what's happening. I'll get temp work for a while, so I'll be free to come back to you, whenever that is.* Maggie, her rock.

She opened the cabinet above the bathroom sink and saw bottles of pills that were new, all with her mother's name on them. She left her things in her toilet bag and propped it on the end of the bath.

You didn't have to come, her mother had said, but the fire had gone out of her voice, and already Ellen fancied her face looked thinner. *I wanted to come,* she'd replied, and it was only half untrue.

The days passed, and life settled into its new routine, with tears never far away. She wept for her mother, and for herself and her situation, and for her children who would not after all grow up under the same roof as both their parents. Tears ambushed her at every opportunity, and the opportunities were many.

The sight of Juliet sitting on her grandmother's knee like she belonged there, thumb plugged in her mouth as her grandmother read *The Tiger Who Came to Tea* in a slow, careful voice.

The knobs of her mother's spine pushing against paper-thin skin as Ellen helped her to get dressed each day.

The sound of the racking cough at night, every night, from the bedroom next door. The way her mother looked at Ellen when Ellen came in to help her sit up for some water. The mouthed, barely audible *Thank you* after she'd sipped.

There was no reconciliation, not as such. No big emotional scene, no apologies or professions of love, nothing that would make it into a Hollywood story. But as the weeks passed, Ellen was aware of a persistent chipping away of old hurts and resentments, a small calmness settling into the place where they'd been.

When she reached the stage where she could put it into words, she wrote to Danny and told him everything. He wrote back.

Oh God. I am so beyond sorry. What a nightmare time for you. I wish I was there to help. Sending long-distance love. Hugs to your mam. Sorry, sorry, sorry. xxx

A week or so later a small box that weighed practically nothing was delivered to the house with her name on it. Inside she found a beautiful silk square, light as a wisp and big enough to wrap around herself twice, and the colour of Californian skies.

My favourite shade of blue, she'd told him, as they'd flown along the highway under glorious sunshine with the roof of his car down, on the way to Palo Alto and his wedding. How was that only a few weeks ago? It felt like another lifetime.

He would never have cheated on her. She knew that without question. At the bottom of the box she found two packets of Reese's Peanut Butter Cups. *With you in spirit, old friend – love D xx* she read in the card that had a hummingbird on it.

Juliet was taken in by a local playschool, where she quickly made friends. Ellen also put her name down in the same primary school that she and Joan had attended. She'd felt obliged, in case they were still there when the time came for her daughter to start school in September.

In case Juliet's grandmother was still alive then.

Every day she grew weaker, every day there was less she could do, but still she insisted on getting up and getting dressed each morning, even if it was only to make her torturously slow way down the stairs on Ellen's arm, to move from her bedroom to the chair in the sitting room that had always been hers.

And inevitably, the time came when she couldn't manage the stairs, so Ellen borrowed a fold-up bed from a neighbour for Juliet, and Seamus came from Cork to help Ellen dismantle the bed in

Joan's room that Juliet had been using, and reassemble it in the dining room that hadn't been used in years. When they had dressed the bed Seamus carried his mother-in-law downstairs, and seeing her so limp and wasted in his arms, Ellen again fought tears.

Frances came and went during this period, staying a few days each time, doing what she could for the sister who should be outliving her. Joan arrived from Cork for a few hours whenever she could get away, ordering Ellen out for a walk or to her bed for a nap.

Every so often, Ellen would remind herself that she hadn't yet told her sister about the encounter with their father, or the existence of Iris. Events had taken over, and the time never seemed right for the conversation. Still, she must find an opportunity.

Claire phoned weekly from London. 'Thinking of you,' she said to Ellen. 'Wish I could do more.'

She did more. She sent chocolates and bath salts and toys from London. She had bouquets delivered, and a silk pillowcase for Ellen's mother. She got her own mother to call to the house with the homemade brown bread Ellen used to love.

And Leo rang twice weekly, every Sunday and Wednesday at five o'clock. It had been the only condition he'd put on agreeing to let Juliet go to Ireland, but Ellen would have given him the number without his asking, because she didn't want her daughter, or their next child, to grow up without a father. She wouldn't let that happen to her children.

She still loved him. Love, she discovered, didn't have an off switch. Despite what he'd done it was still there, lodged stubbornly within her, pressing up against the anger and the disillusionment and the pain. As she and Juliet had taken a taxi to the airport she'd felt a huge sense of loss. It was as if he had died, or part of her had.

When the phone rang at the appointed time each week she answered, and they had a brief, agonising exchange of words.

How's your mother?

She's weaker.

Sorry to hear it. How are you?

. . . I'm managing.

Please come back. I'm so sorry, Ellen. I miss you. I love you.

Here's Juliet, she would say then, because she couldn't cope with that, couldn't cope with anything emotional between them.

Lucinda had been wonderful. *You can take leave of absence,* she'd said, *and we'll use you on a freelance basis, if you're agreeable. I can email you briefs, and we can discuss on the phone, and see how we go.*

Email had been spreading across the globe, so Ellen had invested in a computer and Danny had guided her through signing up for her first email account, and she grabbed whatever time she could to work. It wasn't ideal. Her internet connection was weak, and documents from Lucinda could take a long time to load up. In addition, she missed the brainstorming and the buzz in the studio where ideas were born every day.

Meanwhile, her second pregnancy moved through its stages, interrupting precious sleep with jabs of pain and insistent urges to pee, causing her to drag her way through the days with aching back and swollen feet and heartburn. It would all be worth it, she told herself. She would love this child every bit as much as she loved Juliet.

One evening she had an email from Danny.

News. All going well, Bobbi's going to make me a father in November. Thinking of you a lot, wish we weren't so far apart. Hoping you're coping. Hold on, pal. It won't stay bad, I promise you. xx

She emailed her congratulations. She must look to the future, as he was doing. She must find a way to be happy again.

Reconciliation

ON HER THIRTY-FIRST BIRTHDAY IN JULY, IN HER eighth month of pregnancy, the hospice nurse who had been dropping in every day for the past while told Ellen to prepare herself. 'A week or so,' she said, 'two at the most.' After she'd left, Ellen went into the dining room and sat by the bed there and looked down at the wasted face of her mother. She saw small jerking movements behind the closed eyelids, little twitches of the cracked, bloodless lips.

She reached out and touched a bony shoulder. 'Mam,' she whispered, and after her third attempt, the eyelids fluttered open.

'Mam,' she repeated, and then stopped, not knowing where to go next. Not knowing what she wanted to say, after years of saying nothing of any consequence.

She lifted a corner of the bedclothes and found her mother's cold, white hand. She took it in both of hers and cradled it. 'Mam,' she said again, 'I wasn't always . . .' stopping to push down a sob, beginning again '. . . I know I was hard on you after Dad left.'

Her mother's gaze roamed about. Ellen had no idea whether she could still see. She hadn't asked the nurse, afraid of the answer.

'I'm . . . I just want to say I'm sorry, Mam. I treated you badly. I blamed you for everything.'

She felt, or thought she felt, a tiny pressure from the hand she held, a hardly-there pressing of fingers into her palm. Maybe it was another involuntary movement.

'You did the best for us, for Joan and me. You did what you thought was right, and I couldn't see that.' Tears ran freely down Ellen's face now, dripping onto the blankets. 'I just wanted to say sorry, and thank you. Thank you, Mam.'

Her mother closed her eyes, and again Ellen felt a small movement from the hand she held. Had her words been heard, and if so, had they been understood? She sat on, listening to the shallow breathing, seeing how the ravaged body took up such little space in the bed, its bulk hardly affecting the line of the blankets.

Eventually she relinquished her mother's hand and tucked it back in. She wiped her eyes and blew her nose, and decided the time had come to phone her father. He needed to know, whether he deserved it or not. She had to tell him – which meant she also had to tell Joan about their chance encounter.

'I can't believe it,' Joan said. 'I can't believe you didn't tell me.'

'Sorry, Joan. I wasn't sure you'd want to hear.'

There was silence on the line for a minute, and then Joan asked, in a different voice, 'What's he like?'

'He's still . . . himself.'

He was still their father. Whatever he'd done, he would always be that. She told Joan about the affair, and the child that had resulted from it, and there was more silence while Joan digested that.

'Joan, I think I need to tell him about Mam. I think he should know.' She braced herself for an angry retort, but it didn't come.

'Phone him,' Joan said. 'Tell him to come,' so Ellen did, later that evening.

'Ellen,' he said. 'I'm glad to hear from you.'

'It's Mam,' Ellen said, and told him.

'Oh,' he said quietly. 'Oh.' She heard a catch in his breathing, and thought he might be crying.

'Do you want to come and see her?'

'I do.'

He arrived the next day, while Juliet was in playschool. He sat by the bedside of the woman he was still married to, and he bent towards her and spoke in words that Ellen, standing uncertainly in the doorway, couldn't hear. She closed the door softly, and didn't ask him anything when he emerged later, swollen-eyed.

They sat in the kitchen waiting for Joan to arrive from Cork. Ellen felt terribly conflicted, wanting so much to find the father she'd loved again, but needing now to forgive him too. She didn't know where to start.

She told him about Leo's infidelity, feeling an explanation was needed for her presence here.

'I'm so sorry that happened.'

'He's the father of this baby too,' she added. Even if she didn't know how she felt about him, she realised that she didn't want him to think her promiscuous. 'He'll still have contact with his children.' She stopped. 'I didn't mean—'

'I know,' he said quickly. 'You're doing a wonderful thing, looking after your mother.'

'I owe her,' Ellen replied deliberately. 'I didn't make life easy for her when you left. She was the one I blamed.' *When it should have been you.* It sounded in her head, every bit as loudly as if she'd said it.

'Can you forgive me?'

'I don't know,' she replied honestly. 'I want to, but . . .'

'If there's anything I can do, tell me. If I can help in any way—'

She nodded. He was trying to make amends, she could see that. She must figure out how to meet him halfway.

When they saw Joan's car pulling into the driveway her father went out to meet her, and when she stepped from the car Joan walked straight into the arms of the man she'd said she never wanted to see again, and they stood close together like that for a long time, as Ellen watched them through the kitchen window and thought about how complicated and unpredictable and devastating love was.

Farewell

LEO CAME TO THE FUNERAL.

Ellen had thought he might – she'd asked Maggie to tell him about the death, not able to ring him with the news herself – and in spite of everything, the sight of him after months of absence brought a flood of feeling, a rush of persistent love that caused her to burst into fresh tears, a wild sobbing that didn't seem possible, given all the weeping she'd done over the past months.

She was hardly aware of his arms going around her, of him cradling her head and murmuring her name and calling her his darling as she cried out her heartbreak, as it poured out of her in a torrent.

'Come back,' he said, when her tears were spent, when they sat together on the patio, everyone having left them alone. 'Forgive me and come back,' and she looked at him and wanted to, so badly it hurt.

'How can I trust you not to do it again?'

'I don't know,' he replied, 'but I hope you can, because I swear it'll never happen again.'

'Why did it happen? Wasn't I enough?'

He closed his eyes briefly. 'You were. You are. I was weak, I gave in to temptation.'

She'd grown stronger: his betrayal had done that much for her. The old Ellen, the one who'd scarcely believed he could be interested in her, was gone. She was tougher now, able to look after a dying mother and a small daughter while making her way through a pregnancy without the love and support of a partner, and managing some freelance work too – but the thought of bringing up two children largely on her own, trying to compensate them for their father not being around, was still a prospect she hated.

She wanted so much to believe it could work – and moving back to London would mean returning to Creative Ways, the company that hadn't deserted her when she'd left them so abruptly.

'We'd need a bigger house,' she said, 'with a garden. I won't go back to yours.' She couldn't bear the thought of entering it again, of walking into the bedroom where he'd betrayed her.

'I'll find one,' he promised, taking her hands. 'Can I come here when the baby is born, just to see it?'

'. . . Yes.'

She was afraid. She was terrified to give him a second chance, but for the sake of their children – and yes, for herself too – she must find the courage to risk it.

She introduced him to her father, forgetting that she'd never told Leo of their encounter in Finchley all those months before. She didn't explain – let Leo think he'd simply seen the death in the newspaper. The men were stiffly polite with each other. Leo called him sir, and hid the surprise the sight of him must have caused. Her father called him nothing at all.

To her great surprise, Danny showed up at the funeral too. 'Mam saw the death notice,' he said. 'I was due a visit home.' His hug was warm, and lasted longer than usual. She closed her eyes and leant into him.

'How are you?' he asked.

'Sad. Scared. Trying to be hopeful.'

'You'll be OK, pal,' he said. On being introduced to Leo he simply nodded and kept his arms folded, and Leo was equally distant. Her oldest friend and the man who'd betrayed her had little to say to one another.

Among the other mourners was Kevin, the one-time companion of her mother. She'd never known what title to give him. 'I'm so sorry,' he said, shaking Ellen's hand, and she couldn't tell if it was an apology for deserting her mother – and never once ringing to enquire about her when he knew she was sick – or the usual words of condolence.

Claire didn't come to the funeral. *Better if I leave it till after,* she'd told Ellen on the phone, *when everyone else is gone. You'll need someone then. I'll come next week, and I'll stay a few days.*

She stayed three days, spending the nights in her family home and the days with Ellen and Juliet. Telling Ellen of the assistant at the deli who'd been stealing from the till, and the new signage she'd organised, and the glowing review she'd got from a restaurant critic, while Ellen did her best to concentrate as her almost-born child kicked against the walls of her womb.

'I'm coming back to London,' she told Claire, when she got a chance. 'Leo and I are going to try again. He's convinced me to give him another chance.'

Claire gave no immediate answer. Ellen watched her topping up the gin she'd poured, adding ice cubes, stirring with a finger.

'What do you think?'

Claire lifted her glass and took a sip. 'Obviously I'd love to have you back, but are you sure you're doing the right thing?'

'I don't want my children growing up without their father. And I still love him, and he seems genuinely sorry.' She told her of his promise to sell his house and buy one more suited to a family. 'Surely that proves he wants to start again?'

'Selling and buying houses takes time, Ellen.'

'I know. I'll wait.'

'Well, it's your life, I suppose,' Claire said slowly. 'But I want nothing to do with him, not after what he did to you. We can see each other, you and me, when he's not around.'

Silence fell. Ellen would have liked her to be a little more encouraging, but she could understand her concern. They sat on deck chairs while Juliet and a friend from playschool lay on the grass beneath the same gnarled apple tree that Ellen and Claire had climbed as ten-year-olds.

'Have you help for when the baby arrives?' Claire asked.

She had. The day after Claire left, Frances moved in with her suitcase. She was almost seventy-eight, and she'd taken the bus from Galway and a taxi from the station, the blue Beetle having finally been surrendered to a used car dealer. She looked worn out by the journey, but she hadn't listened when Ellen had told her she'd find someone else – and truth to tell, Ellen hadn't wanted her to listen.

'So,' she said, after she'd been installed in Ellen's mother's old room, and she and Ellen were sitting with glasses of lemonade in the garden, 'how are you getting on?'

'I'm OK.' Ellen hesitated. 'Frances, there's something else.' She told her of her plan to move back to London, and watched her aunt as she digested the news.

'I won't tell you what to do,' Frances said eventually. 'I'll just hope for the best.'

'It won't happen again, Frances. He's really sorry. He's going to look for a bigger house for us.'

'Is he indeed.'

And the very next day, ten days before she was due, Grace was born, and the world slowly started making sense again – and when Leo came to see his new daughter a few days later, Frances left him in no doubt about her feelings towards him.

You'd better behave yourself, she said, Ellen overhearing from the sitting room where she and the girls were waiting to see him. *You'll have me to answer to if you hurt her again* – and Ellen was grateful that there was at least one person in the world who would always, always be on her side.

Two, she corrected herself. Frances and Danny.

Changes

'ELLEN,' HER FATHER SAID, 'I'VE BEEN THINKING about this house.'

She'd rung to tell him of Grace's arrival, and he was back to meet his new grandchild, and to get to know Juliet a little too. 'What about it?'

'I'd like to sign it over to you. I thought you might want to stay living here.'

'Thank you, but I don't.' She told him of her plans, and saw the doubt in his face. Everyone doubted this move.

'Are you sure it's the right thing to do, Ellen?' he asked. 'You've been under a lot of strain in the past while – maybe you should wait a little before you make this big decision.'

Frances appeared just then with a tray. Ellen remained silent while her aunt poured tea and cut slices of the fruit cake someone had dropped to the house in the wake of her mother's death. He had a nerve to try and be a father now. He hadn't earned that right back yet.

'I think you should sign the house over to Joan and me,' she told him after Frances had left. 'I'm assuming Iris will inherit your place in Dublin.'

'Yes . . . if that's what you want, I'll do that.'

'I'll talk to Joan about it.' She couldn't bring herself to call him Dad. 'Could you look after my computer when I go back to London?'

'Of course.'

'We should put the house up for rent,' Joan said later, when Ellen relayed the conversation with their father. 'No point in leaving it empty. We could sell it, but let's get tenants in for a while and think about it. When you're ready to go back to London, we can put an ad in the paper.'

Leo came every other week, and stayed a few hours. He never suggested an overnight visit, and neither did Ellen. It was different between them, he more conciliatory, she quieter. He brought books for the girls, and the nougat that Ellen loved.

Just before Christmas he told her he'd found a house. 'It's in Lambeth, so not too far from your work. I have photos.'

She leafed through them. Two storeys, with a good-sized kitchen and two reception rooms, and a sunroom jutting from one side. Upstairs were bright and airy bedrooms, and a bathroom with his and hers sinks and a claw-footed bath and a separate shower.

The garden had a tree in it that she couldn't identify, and more than enough space for children's playthings. Outside the sunroom was a little patio for warm evenings.

The price was higher than she'd been allowing during her covert investigations, but Leo would have calculated what he could afford. What they could afford.

'Like it?'

She nodded. 'How's your house sale going?'

'Hopeful. One of the people who viewed it last week wants a second viewing.'

Hopeful. She would remain hopeful.

LAMBETH, LONDON
JUNE 1993
THE FIFTH MOVE

Return

SHE HUMMED ABSENTLY AS SHE LIFTED TINY clothes from a suitcase and tucked them into the cream chest of drawers that had come from the old nursery. She added her toothbrush to Leo's in the mug on the bathroom shelf, feeling a shiver of *déjà vu* as she did. Her clothes now had a wardrobe to themselves, her shoes their own rack. He'd added to the furniture from the old house: wicker seating in the sunroom, a second small bed for when Grace would need it, a chaise longue and a piano in the sitting room.

'A piano?' Ellen asked.

'I thought the girls might want to learn when they're older.'

It brought her back. *I play a bit of piano*, Ben had said. *I'd like to see what a music degree might feel like.* Had he followed that dream, fulfilled his side of the pact they'd made, she to attempt a novel, he to study music? Just as well they hadn't set a deadline, with her no closer to starting a book.

It was early June, the house sale having taken until May to close. Ellen returned to London with two daughters, nearly sixteen months after she'd run away from it with one. Leo met them at the airport and took them to their new home, and now she was settling them in.

'Thank you,' he said, 'for coming back. I don't deserve you.' He presented her with a watch that had diamonds for numbers. It was flashier than she'd have chosen, but she thanked him and put it on.

The house was located in a cul-de-sac of eight, three of which were occupied by other young families, the rest by older couples whose children had grown and left, and one tiny, elderly woman living alone who glared at Ellen when they encountered each other, and reminded her of Frances.

The girls spent summer in the garden. Grace, looking like a little ghost in a generous layer of sun cream, crawled about the lawn, stopping every so often to sit and pull the head off a daisy while Ellen grabbed the chance to replace the sun bonnet she persisted in yanking off. Juliet and Sally, her new friend from two doors down, had doll tea parties, and pushed each other on the swing, and jumped in and out of the paddling pool as Maggie, reinstated on their return, kept an eye out.

And over the summer, Ellen and Leo reconnected.

'Every Saturday night,' he said. 'Just you and me, out to dinner.'

'What about the girls?'

'Maggie says she'll babysit' – and it felt like in the early days, when he would call to the Notting Hill flat once a week and take her out.

When she turned thirty-two in July Maggie moved in for the weekend while he and Ellen flew to Paris, where they'd met. This time she made it to the top of the Eiffel Tower and visited the Louvre, and on Saturday afternoon he brought her to Shakespeare and Company, where she browsed among the bookshelves for two happy hours.

'Never hurt me again,' she said in bed that night.

'Never again,' he promised.

'Swear on your children's lives.'

'I swear.'

Little by little her faith in him was restored, until there were days when she could almost believe he'd never been unfaithful, never crushed her heart.

It was wonderful to be properly back at work too, to have designated working hours instead of struggling to fit them around her other demands. In her absence Creative Ways had expanded, with a clutch of new clients, an extra team in the studio and two more account handlers.

Within a couple of months of Ellen's return, a press ad that she and Lucinda had created won a big award. Shortly afterwards, she was headhunted again by the same agency in central London that had tried to poach her before, and again she said no, rejoicing in the evidence that she was still good at what she did.

The only blot, the only downside, was that she hardly ever saw Claire. 'Busy, busy,' she'd say when Ellen phoned. 'Some day I'll get my life back. How are the girls?' She never asked about Leo.

Still single, and presumably still dating, although she was vague when Ellen enquired. 'Oh, the usual,' she'd say, or 'Nothing new,' leaving Ellen no wiser.

She came just once to see the house. It was a Sunday in September, and Leo had taken the girls to Brighton for the day. 'It'll be just you and me,' Ellen had said on the phone, so Claire had agreed, and brought a bottle of Pimm's.

'Here we are,' she said, 'like old times.' Ellen walked her through the kitchen and the bright sunroom, and pointed out the newly planted shrubbery in the garden, and she admired it all. In the sitting room she ran a finger along the spines of books, and picked up photos and set them down, and paused to study the latest advertising award that Leo had insisted on framing and putting on the wall.

'I'm happy for you,' she said, back in the sunroom, watching as Ellen filled their glasses. 'Perfect home, perfect children, perfect job. Perfect life, really.'

Ellen noted the absence of Leo in the list. 'Hardly perfect: some days I'm so busy I nearly forget to breathe, and most of the time I feel like I could do with a week of uninterrupted sleep. And look at you – successful businesswoman, footloose and fancy-free. Men still panting around you, I'm sure.'

Claire laughed as she raised her glass. 'True enough. God's gift to mankind, right here.'

In January, Ellen finally called the number Iris had given her. 'I didn't mean to leave it so long,' she said. 'Our father probably told you why.'

'He did, I'm sorry. I hope things are better now.'

'They are. I was wondering . . . would you like to meet my girls? Juliet is five and Grace is one. I suppose they're your half-nieces, if such a thing exists.'

'I'd love to' – so Ellen gave her the address and told her to come for Sunday lunch, when Leo would be in Leeds on one of his conferences. Claire might join them, Ellen thought on the way home – but when she rang, Claire told her she was being taken to Hampshire for the weekend. 'Shame,' she said. 'Next time.'

Iris brought two jigsaws and a bottle of sparkling wine. She shook hands solemnly with Juliet and kissed Grace's cheek, and insisted on setting the table and helping with the washing-up, and over lunch she told Ellen that she shared a flat in Finchley with two friends from school, and had an Irish boyfriend who managed a Covent Garden café, and she clapped loudly when Juliet sang a French song that Leo had taught her.

'Your children are delightful,' she said afterwards, when she and Ellen had put both of them down for naps.

She was delightful. 'You must come again when Leo's here,' Ellen said. 'Bring your boyfriend.' Generous with her invitations, now that she was happy again. Pleased after all to have another sister, another aunt for the girls.

In March, her father turned seventy. After thinking about whether she should acknowledge it, Ellen decided to send him a book of war poetry, because he used to like reading Wilfred Owen. In the accompanying card she wrote *Happy Birthday from Ellen* and followed it with a single, cautious *x*.

They'd taken to writing to one another. He'd started, a week after Ellen had moved back to London, and she'd let a month go by before responding. It struck her, as she struggled to fill a page with polite, banal phrases, that she was now writing the kind of letter to him that she'd written to her mother. The thought made her sad.

He rang the day the book arrived to thank her.

'How are you?' he asked, and she said everything was fine.

'Iris told me you had her to lunch,' he said. 'I'm so glad.'

Easy, she thought, to have Iris to lunch. Iris hadn't walked out on her without a goodbye. It remained the stumbling block between them, the obstacle she hadn't figured out how to get past.

In summer of the following year Leo and Ellen took the girls to France for a week. They crossed on the ferry from Dover to Calais and drove down the west coast, taking their time, stopping for a night in Rouen and another in Le Mans until they reached Nantes, where they were to stay for three nights with Marguerite and her sons before retracing their steps to Calais.

Ellen felt more than the usual wariness at the thought of meeting Marguerite – had Leo told her the true cause of her flight from his house? – but on meeting her she was cordial as before, kissing Ellen, sympathising on her mother's death, welcoming the girls and enquiring about their trip thus far. The reserve was still there, but Ellen felt she was making an effort.

Louis and Henri were as charming as she remembered, happy to see Juliet again and to make the acquaintance of Grace. 'We must take the girls to the kitchen,' Henri said. 'Emmaline waits to see them,' and off they went.

After dinner, Leo having brought the girls up to bed, and the boys out with friends, Ellen found herself alone with Marguerite on the patio to the rear of the house, with its remembered view of hills and fields.

'I will get cognac,' the older woman said, and Ellen thought of the brandy Leo had ordered for her the day they'd met in Paris. When Marguerite returned with glasses they sat in silence for a while, listening to squeals of Juliet's laughter floating from an upstairs window. Whatever else he'd done, Leo was a good father.

Ellen lifted her glass and took a sip, enjoying the hot trail of it. They must have it at home more often, an after-dinner treat on weekend nights.

'My son was unfaithful to you,' Marguerite said then. Quietly, her voice thoughtful, her gaze on the vista before her.

Ellen's heart sank. She'd hoped it wouldn't come up. Maybe if she made no response, that would be the end of it – but it wasn't.

'It will happen again,' Marguerite went on, slowly and calmly, turning her head now to regard Ellen dispassionately. 'I know him. I am sure of it. You will leave him again. You will take his children from him.'

Her words, delivered with such little feeling, appalled Ellen. Had the woman no heart? How could she say such things? 'No,' she replied, as evenly as she could. 'He's not like that. He made one mistake; he swore it won't happen again.'

Marguerite turned back to the view. She raised her glass and sipped. 'I hope you are right,' she said, and nothing further. At that moment, Ellen hated the older woman. Jealous, she thought, of what Ellen and Leo had, and what she did not. She resolved to forget the remark, but for the rest of the night, and the remainder of their stay, his mother's words echoed in Ellen's mind, lingering like a bad smell.

You will leave him again. You will take his children from him. As much an accusation as a prophesy, even as she'd acknowledged that any future separation would be Leo's fault. Ellen said nothing to him of the exchange, not wanting to come between mother and son.

It will happen again.

Crèche

IN DECEMBER SHE SLIPPED A LETTER IN WITH Frances' Christmas gift. *Iris has become part of the family*, she wrote. *She's great with the girls, so gentle and kind, and she babysits every now and again too . . . I hope you like the thermal vest. I know how you feel the cold, and this one has silk in it, so it should be lovely and soft . . . News from Cork is that Joan is expecting again, due in May . . . I'll come and see you soon, when I can organise a weekend off. I'll leave the girls with Leo and we can relax, just the two of us.*

A few days later, Frances phoned.

'The vest is the best thing I ever put on me, I'm as cosy in it. Thank you so much.'

'I'm delighted to hear. How are you?'

'I'm slow but I get there, which is good going for eighty-one. I've been thinking about your idea to take in a student. I might do it next year.'

Ellen smiled. She'd come round to it in her own time. 'I think you'd be right.'

'Your father phones me,' Frances said. 'Now and again, just for a chat.'

'Does he?'

'He says you write to each other.'

'We do.'

'I'm happy about that, Ellen.'

'I'm trying, Frances.'

'Good girl.'

And three days before Christmas, an email arrived from California:

Hope life is good with you. News – we're going to catch up with you and become a family of four in May, all going well. When are you coming to see us again?

She responded:

Wonderful news, congratulations! High time Cormac got a brother or sister. Hope Bobbi's feeling OK. Joan's going again too, due in May as well. Must be something in the water. I'll be out to see you right after Grace's 18th birthday.

Everything's good. Long may it last. Sometimes late at night I'm scared that it mightn't, but most of the time I'm OK.

And he came back:

Bobbi's fine, sailing through pregnancy like she did first time around. Congrats to Joan and Seamus – we'll race them to the finish line. Cormac says hello to Juliet. As soon as I teach him how to send an email he'll be in touch.

I know it's easy to say, but try not to worry. Understandable to be wary when it happened once, but I feel everything will work out this time.

Even though he had precisely no grounds on which to base this feeling, Ellen was comforted by it. Marguerite's prophesy of Leo offending again haunted her, however much she tried not to let it. She resolved to put her trust in Danny, and believe him instead.

'More babies on the way,' Leo remarked when Ellen told him. 'I hope it's not giving you ideas.' But he smiled as he said it, and she thought she could probably get around him if she wanted a third. Did she want a third? She decided that a family of four would do her nicely, at least for the moment.

In May Joan gave birth to a sister for Ivan and Trisha and called her Daphne, after the character in *Frasier*. Four days later Danny emailed to announce the arrival of their second son, Matthew, named for Bobbi's grandfather.

'Books,' Leo said when Ellen wondered what she should send, so she parcelled up two Beatrix Potter collections and posted them off.

In September of that year, four-year-old Grace began attending a crèche, but kicked up so much they took her out again after three tearful days. 'She's not ready,' the director told Ellen and Leo. 'Give her another year and try again.'

They'd had no such problem with Juliet at the same age. The girls were very different, Grace more stubborn, more prickly and more prone to tantrums than her quieter big sister. They'd got off lightly with their first.

Ellen travelled alone to Galway the following Easter to spend a couple of nights with Frances. She'd already emailed the UCG Students' Union, asking them to add her aunt's address to their accommodation list for the following academic year. *One female student*, she'd written. *It's an old lady on her own, looking for a bit of company, and maybe some light housework in return for a reduced rent.*

After lunch on Sunday, Frances went for a lie-down and Ellen strolled into the city centre. On impulse she decided to visit the bookshop, Sunday shopping now being a thing, to find to her dismay that it no longer existed. In its place stood a music store, pumping Thin Lizzy out into the street. The bar she remembered was still next door, but Piles of Books was gone. She wondered where Jasper and Edwin had ended up.

Inevitably she thought of Ben, who could be anywhere in the world now, or right back here in Galway. She imagined bumping into him on the street, seeing how both of them had changed in the years apart. Would they even recognise one another?

Yes, she thought. They would. They always would.

Daughters

WHEN LEO TURNED FORTY-SIX HE ACCEPTED A redundancy package his bank was offering, and set himself up as an independent financial advisor. Thanks to his years of experience and network of contacts he quickly built up a client base, and soon he was spending most of his time making house calls.

Ellen asked why his clients couldn't come to him. 'You could make an office out of the small bedroom – or we could extend. We have the space.'

He shook his head. 'Someone willing to go to them is what they want. It's paying dividends – I have a waiting list.'

'That's good, but your hours are so long. You're hardly ever home before the girls are in bed.'

'It'll be worth it, wait and see. Just have faith, Ellen.'

Yes, having faith was the way to go. She must keep the faith.

'Thank you,' she said.

'For what?'

'For making it easy to come back.' *For not doing what your mother said you'd do.* 'Claire said I have the perfect life,' she added with a laugh.

'Claire said that? When was this?'

'Oh, ages ago. That day you took the girls to Brighton, and she came to see the house. I thought it was funny.'

'You don't see her much any more,' he remarked.

'I don't – we mostly talk on the phone. She's always so busy.' She said nothing about Claire not wanting to meet him; that would be cruel. 'I feel sorry for her, not having anyone special. I thought she sounded a bit envious of me and my perfect life.' She looked at him teasingly, but he gave just the briefest of smiles before getting up.

'I told *Maman* I'd give her a ring. Better do it' – and he was gone. As little interested in Claire, it seemed, as she was in him.

In August, Ellen and Joan agreed to put the family home on the market. The tenants they'd found for it had handed in their notice, in the process of buying another house, and both sisters felt the time had come to sell. The thought of letting it go didn't faze Ellen. For a long time she'd felt no connection with it.

In September, they tried again with Grace and the crèche, and this time Leo brought her, and after another few iffy days she settled, much to Ellen's relief. At Juliet's parent–teacher meeting in October, Ellen and Leo were told that she showed artistic leanings.

'I think she'll become a brilliant painter,' Ellen said on the way home. 'People will pay millions for her works.'

Leo laughed. 'And Grace?'

'She'll take after you, and become a successful businesswoman.'

'Poor thing.'

In November, Joan rang with the news that someone had bid the asking price on the house. 'Are you happy to say yes?'

'Absolutely,' Ellen said.

Sold

FOR CHRISTMAS LEO, ELLEN AND THE CHILDREN returned to France. Marguerite, now approaching eighty, had been in failing health for some time, and had requested their company. 'I know you're not exactly great friends,' Leo told Ellen, 'but I feel she doesn't have too many Christmases left,' so they went, and Ellen was forced to put on a polite front, and hide the resentment she now felt towards the older woman.

They found her thinner, paler and quieter than before. She didn't appear until lunchtime each day. She ate sparingly and spoke little to the adults, but murmured in French with her granddaughters.

Emmaline was still employed there, nursemaid as well as cook these days, but her husband Claude had died the summer before. The big old Peugeot was nowhere to be seen. No more outings for Marguerite.

The house was cold as ever. Ellen spent much of her time in the kitchen, the warmest room, with Emmaline and the girls. *Mes petites belles*, Emmaline called Juliet and Grace, giving them little cups of the hot chocolate Ellen remembered from her first visit with Leo.

They returned to London a day before 1997 became 1998. In February, Joan rang to say that the tenants had vacated the house and the sale was near closing. 'You want to come and stay a night there for old times' sake?'

Ellen felt no such inclination, but it sounded like Joan did. 'I'll book flights and let you know.'

That night she rang Claire. 'The house is sold,' she said. 'Now I have no more ties with the town.'

'End of an era,' Claire said. 'I must tell Mam when I'm talking to her.'

'How are they keeping?'

'Fine, all well.' She didn't ask about Ellen's father.

'How's life with you?' Ellen asked.

'Good. Busy as ever. How are my goddaughter and her sister?'

'Both great. They'd love to see you, whenever you have time.'

'Give them hugs from me,' Claire said.

Ellen rang her father to tell him the news. 'Good to know,' he said. 'Good to draw a line under it. You should come and see me sometime,' he added, 'if you'd care to.'

'When I get a chance,' she said.

Leo, when she told him of the sale closing, said she should spend longer than one night in Ireland. 'Couldn't you take a few days off work? Go and see Frances – and your father, if you want. You could fly into Shannon and come back from Dublin. Maggie and I can hold the fort.'

He was still spending much of his days calling on clients. They hadn't been seeing enough of each other since he'd gone out on his own. 'We should have a mini break when I get back,' she said to him. 'Just the two of us. We could go to the Lake District or the Cotswolds. Somewhere scenic, with nice walks.'

'We can think about that,' he agreed.

In the end she just took one night in Ireland, not wanting to use any more of her holidays at such a cold time of the year. Joan picked her up at Shannon and drove them to the house, and they dressed the beds before walking into town for dinner.

'Let's go for a drink,' Ellen suggested, so they went to Claire's family's pub. It was just before six, and the place was quiet. Claire's father was behind the bar, plumper and balder than Ellen remembered. 'The wanderer returns,' he said when she went up to order. 'You're looking great. London is suiting you.'

She'd always liked Claire's parents. They'd come to her mother's funeral, and Claire's mother had hugged her and kissed her cheek.

'See much of our girl these days?'

'Not as much as before. We're both so busy.'

He dropped a lemon slice into a glass. 'Turned into a right yuppie, she has. Wish she'd settle down with someone, or come home.'

She heard the sadness in his words. He was older than Claire's mother, heading into his eighties by now, if he hadn't reached them already.

'Tell her to come for a visit, next time you're talking to her. Say her mother misses her.'

'I will,' she promised, and he refused to take payment from her. She would ring Claire on her return to London and urge her to take a trip home: surely she could spare the time for that.

Later, after a mediocre dinner in a new Chinese restaurant, she lay in her old bed for the last time, and was glad. The only thing she'd taken from the house, before the tenants had moved in, was the note her father had left. She'd retrieved it from beneath the mattress, meaning to throw it out, but instead she'd tucked it into the little pocket at the back of Ben's notebook, unable to let it go.

She closed her eyes and slept.

Again

IT WAS AFTER SIX THE FOLLOWING DAY WHEN SHE got back. The ten-minute walk from the Tube station had been difficult, with sleeting showers and an icy wind. She let herself in with her key, damp and shivering. Hot chocolate, as soon as she'd said hello to everyone and given the girls the presents she'd bought in the airport, and a hot shower directly afterwards – or maybe the other way around.

'I'm home!' she called, and heard only silence. She pulled off her gloves and hung her coat – and turned to see Leo standing at the kitchen door.

'You're back,' he said, making no move towards her.

'I'm back. Where are the girls?'

'They're at Angela's, they're fine.' Angela, mother of Juliet's friend Sally, lived two doors away.

'Grace is there too?' Grace never went to Sally's house.

'Just for a bit.'

Ellen went to him and put her arms around him. 'Missed you. I'm frozen.'

'Ellen,' he said – and something in his voice made her draw away to look at his face.

'What's wrong?' He hadn't returned her hug. His arms hung by his side. She felt a clutch of fear. 'Are the girls OK?'

'The girls are fine,' he repeated. 'Come into the kitchen. We have to talk.'

She didn't move. She flashed back to her return from America, and felt an unpleasant heave in her gut. 'What is it? Tell me here. Tell me now.'

He opened his mouth, and said nothing.

The world stopped.

Time stopped.

She didn't want to hear, because whatever it was, it was bad.

She had to hear. 'Quickly,' she said.

'Ellen,' he repeated, 'I'm so sorry. I've . . . been having an affair.'

She stood rooted, frozen, staring at him.

What?

What?

Then, without thinking, she stepped towards him and slapped his face hard, so hard it made her palm sting. 'You *fucker*!' she shouted. She never used the F-word, never. She raised her hand to hit him again; he caught her wrist and held it.

'Please,' he said. 'Please don't do that.' His cheek reddened as she watched. Her breathing was harsh, ugly. Out of nowhere, she heard Marguerite's words. *It will happen again. I am sure of it.*

Fuck Marguerite.

'You swore!' she cried, yanking her wrist free. 'You swore on your children's lives! You *bastard*!' She swung at him again – he ducked, and avoided the blow.

'Who?' she said, her voice not hers. Too loud, too guttural to be hers. 'Who is it?' She made fists of her hands and punched him as hard as she could, wherever she could – face, chest, stomach, arms. 'Was she here, in this house?' She wanted to hurt him, hurt him. 'Did you bring her to this house?' She lashed out with a foot, connecting hard with his calf. 'Tell me! Fuck you, tell me who she is!'

He shrank from her, curled and twisted to avoid her, raised his arms to protect his head. And when she stopped, breathless, blood racing, nothing left in her, he straightened and stepped away, and folded his arms.

'I'm sorry,' he said. 'I'm leaving. I have to leave.'

Every part of her was shaking. She leant against the banister, needing its support.

'Who is it?' she demanded again. 'Tell me!' And when he made no response, she repeated it. Roared it in his face, bellowed it with every ounce of her remaining energy. 'Tell me who it is! Tell me, you fucker!'

'It's Claire,' he said in a low voice.

'Oh Jesus!' she shouted. 'What's wrong with you? You know that's not true! Why are you lying? Why would you say such a stupid thing?' She swiped at him again, but now he batted her arm easily away and stepped further from her.

'I'm sorry, Ellen.'

'Tell me the truth! Be a man, for Christ's sake!'

'I *am* telling you the truth,' he said in the same quiet tone. 'I never meant for it to happen, and neither did she. We both tried—'

We both. No. *No!* She shook her head violently. 'Do you think I'm stupid? I know it's not Claire – it couldn't be Claire!'

'I'm sorry.'

Claire? No. Not Claire. Never Claire.

Claire?

I prefer them more rough and ready – but he's perfect for you.

Claire, her friend.

Juliet's godmother.

She slumped onto the stairs, her brain still refusing to accept what he was saying. How could it be true? How could it? It made no sense.

But . . .

What had Claire told her once, when Juliet was a baby? Something about meeting a man she could have settled down with, but he was married. No, she hadn't said married, she'd said taken. And then she'd laughed and said she was joking.

What if it hadn't been a joke?

She never came to the house. One time she'd visited, when he'd brought the girls to Brighton.

I'm happy for you. Perfect home, perfect children, perfect job. Perfect life, really.

No. Not Claire. Not her friend Claire.

She raised her head and looked at him. She thought of Claire telling her she was being taken to Hampshire for the weekend, when Ellen had phoned to invite her to lunch to meet Iris. The same weekend that Leo was supposed to be at a conference in Leeds. Did conferences even happen at weekends?

Claire. Could it be Claire? It could. She realised that it could. Of all the women in the world, it could be the last one Ellen had thought would betray her.

'How long?' Her voice empty, her throat hurting from her earlier shouting.

'. . . A few years.'

Roisin Meaney

She stared at him. 'A few *years*? How many years?'

'It started when you went to Danny's wedding.'

'Danny's *wedding*? Six years ago? Jesus Christ!'

Another realisation dropped. It hadn't been some random woman last time, someone Ellen had never met, as Leo had claimed. It had been Claire who'd been in bed with him that morning. Claire, who could have virtually any man she wanted, had taken the one man Ellen had made a life with.

She'd probably helped Leo to put Juliet to bed on Sunday night, and then she'd stayed. When they'd heard Ellen returning the next morning, she'd run downstairs and fled while Ellen had been in the loo. If Ellen hadn't needed the loo, she'd have discovered her there.

And when Ellen had rushed to her closest friend after finding out that Leo had been unfaithful, the girls in the deli had told her that Claire would be late in that morning. Errands to run, they'd said.

For six years they'd been having an affair. For six years Claire had done that to her, and Ellen hadn't had a clue. She thought of the gifts that had arrived from Claire while Ellen was in Ireland. She thought of Claire coming to stay a week after Ellen's mother's funeral.

Salving her conscience, while she'd been sleeping with Leo. *I want nothing more to do with him*, she'd said when Ellen had told her of her plan to return to him. *Not after what he did to you.*

But she had no conscience, had she? Pretending to be Ellen's friend, pretending to be on her side. How cold-blooded did you have to be to treat anyone, let alone a friend, like that?

She found her voice. 'Why did you want me to come back? Why didn't you just leave me in Ireland?'

321

'I wanted us to work,' he said. 'I didn't want to be that man. I wanted the girls, and I wanted you. I told her—'

'You wanted both of us,' she said dully. 'You wanted me and Claire,' and he didn't deny it. 'So why are you telling me now? What's changed?'

'She wants me to end it. She said I had to choose.'

Claire had made him choose, and he'd chosen her over the mother of his children. Of course he had. Ellen had never stood a chance when it was Claire she was up against. All the times they'd gone out as teens, and in London too, no boy or man had ever given Ellen a second look once they'd clapped eyes on Claire.

'Your mother said you'd do it again, and I didn't believe her,' she shot at him. 'She said she knew what you were like.' Launching it like a grenade, because it didn't matter any more. 'I said you weren't like that, you'd made one mistake and you were sorry. I *defended* you, like a fool.'

'Ellen—' He took a step towards her; she darted back.

'Don't you *dare* touch me! Don't you touch me ever again!'

He put his hands up in surrender. 'I'll move out,' he said. 'I'll make sure you and the girls are provided for. I'll want to see them, Ellen. I'm entitled to see them.'

'I *know* that,' she snapped, even as something pinged in her, some echo, some parallel. Her father telling her, on that day in Finchley, that her mother had forbidden him to see Ellen and Joan. He'd had entitlements too. He could have insisted on seeing his daughters, taken her to court if he'd had to, but he'd done nothing.

She shook the thought away – this was not the time for it, and Ellen was not her mother. However much she wanted to kill Leo this minute, however much she itched to take a kitchen knife and ram it into his heart, his cheating, soulless heart, she would not attempt to fight him on this.

'Just go.'

'Angela will—'

'Get out!' she shouted, and without another word he lifted his coat from the hallstand and left the house. She listened to the diminshing tap of his footsteps, and when she could no longer hear them she lowered her head into her hands and sobbed, unable to believe what had happened. Unable still to comprehend that it was Claire who'd come between them. Now he was gone, and they were finished as partners, connected only through their children.

When her tears were spent she dragged herself upstairs to their room, woozy with tiredness. She opened his wardrobe and saw only empty hangers.

He'd already moved out. That was why he'd dropped the girls to Angela, so he could move his things to Claire's apartment, or wherever they were planning to live.

He and Claire were going to live together.

She felt a wave of nausea, a heaving in her gut. She raced to the bathroom and threw up the insipid egg sandwich she'd eaten on the plane. She eyed the defeated woman in the mirror. Twice betrayed by the man she loved, and the friend she'd trusted. How had she not seen, not guessed? How had they fooled her for so long?

She had to get the girls. She rinsed and spat, and dabbed foundation under her puffy eyes, and went to reclaim her daughters. Angela gave no sign that she saw anything amiss. Back in the house Ellen phoned for a pizza and got the girls washed and changed for bed, and they ate it in front of the television.

'Where's Daddy?' Grace asked after Ellen had tucked them up in their twin beds. 'I want Daddy to read the story.'

'He had to go away for a while, but he'll see you soon.'

'When?'

'Soon.'

She read *Goodnight Moon* too brightly. She turned off the main light and left on the little lamp in the shape of a toadstool that Juliet's godmother had given her for her first birthday. She tiptoed from the room and entered her and Leo's bedroom – no, her room – and as soon as she closed the door she broke down again.

She stripped and remade the bed, swiping tears away. She undressed and climbed in without brushing her teeth. She desperately needed sleep, but her mind refused to stop spinning. She lay in the darkness, trying to figure out what to do, where to go from here.

She'd had it with London. London was tainted now. It would mean saying goodbye to Maggie, which was awful, and handing in her notice at Creative Ways, horrible too, but she couldn't stay.

She would have to bide her time until the girls got their school holidays in July, nearly five months away; she couldn't subject them to more disruption – and then what? Would she be able to move back to Ireland? Would Leo agree to her taking his daughters out of the country?

He hadn't stood in her way when she'd gone there with Juliet the last time, but this was different. Now there was no dying mother who needed looking after, and no possibility of Ellen ever returning to him.

She hated the thought of having to get his consent, but the law was the law, and she wanted to keep things civil for the girls' sake.

They would need to discuss it, a prospect she dreaded. She thought of the scene they'd had in the kitchen, the ugly language she'd used, and she felt ashamed.

But even assuming he agreed to the move, where could they live in Ireland, with the family home sold? She would have to rent, with all its uncertainties and limitations – and they'd also need a stop-gap place while she settled on a location and found a suitable property.

What about Frances? She'd take them in, Ellen was sure, and the UCG student who rented a room there now, Marie or Maria from Roscommon, would be gone home in the summer – but then she dismissed the idea. Frances wasn't able for two young children in her house any more, even for just a few weeks. It wouldn't be fair to ask her.

The other possibility was one she was reluctant to consider. Her father lived alone in his Dublin house, and she knew he'd help if she approached him, but could she live under the same roof as him again? She might have to, in the short term.

She turned her damp pillow over and pressed her face to its welcome coolness. This would be the end of her and Creative Ways: she couldn't expect them to go on using her remotely like they'd done before, not indefinitely. She would look for other freelance work in advertising, or failing that, she would find a job in a bookshop again, or in any kind of shop.

She stretched out a hand and felt his side of the bed, cold and empty.

Never again. Never again. Tears again.

The thought of him with Claire was unbearable. She imagined the girls meeting her with him, and her pain turned to cold fury.

She was *not* to have contact with them; under no circumstance could that be allowed to happen. Ellen would demand it, would be as intransigent as her mother on this point. There was little danger of the girls asking about Claire – Juliet scarcely remembered her godmother, so long it was since they'd met, and Grace didn't know her at all.

Leo's mother had been right, and Ellen hadn't believed her. She would never see Marguerite again, never endure another stay in her chilly house. She was sorry that Henri and Louis were out of the picture too – she would have liked the girls to have some kind of contact with them growing up.

Of course, in years to come, if Leo stayed around for his daughters, he would be the link to their lovely uncles – but she couldn't think that far ahead, with the immediate future bleak enough to need all her energy.

She'd see more of Frances in Ireland, even if they didn't end up in Galway. That was one good thing. Ellen would take driving lessons, and buy a secondhand car when the money from the family-home sale came in, and make her way to Galway as often as she could from wherever they lived.

The night passed, cruelly slowly. She cried some more, wishing for Frances, craving her aunt's reassurance.

And finally, towards dawn, she slept.

Showdown

LEO PHONED THE NEXT DAY. ELLEN SAW HIS NAME on the screen of the mobile phone he'd got her for Christmas, and nearly didn't answer.

'Hello.'

'Hi. Are you OK?'

She closed her eyes, hating the careful note in his voice. Waiting for her to swear at him again. 'What do you want?'

'I'd like to take the girls for a few hours on Saturday.'

She couldn't say no. 'Don't bring them to her. I won't let you take them if she'll be around.'

'I promise.'

'Your promise isn't worth a curse. If they tell me you brought them to her I'll fight you in every court in the land to get you barred from seeing them.' Could she even do that?

'I won't, Ellen.'

'I've told them you're busy at work. I need you to say the same.'

'I will.'

'They'll be ready at ten.'

Every day Grace asked where he was, and every day Ellen told her he'd see them at the weekend. Juliet, turning nine in April, needed more of an explanation.

'We've decided to live in different houses for a while,' Ellen told her, 'and see how it goes,' and Juliet's face crumpled and Ellen held her while she cried, and felt fresh hatred towards him for ripping their family apart.

When the doorbell rang on Saturday, Grace rushed to the hall and flew into his arms as soon as Ellen opened the door. Juliet followed, giving him a more cautious greeting, and turning to hug her mother before she left.

'I'd like them back by five,' Ellen said stiffly.

'Yes.' He seemed about to say something else, but she closed the door before he had a chance. After they left, she stood in the hall and listened to the silence of the house.

'I'm so sorry,' her father said on the phone. 'I'd like to kill him. I wish you were here. Of course you can stay with me. I'd love to have you and the girls for as long as you want.'

'I was afraid for you,' Frances said. 'I can say it now. I didn't trust him one bit, or that Claire. I knew she was bad news, I wished she wasn't your friend. You're well rid of them both. What will you do?'

'I want to move home with the girls, but he'll have to agree, and it won't be before the summer.'

'Ring me as often as you want, and I'll ring you. You'll manage, you're strong like me. I know you'll manage.'

Was she strong like Frances? She didn't feel it. She felt broken in pieces – but for the girls' sake she would have to go on.

'Oh, Ellen,' Joan said, 'I don't believe it. Not again. How could he do it? And with Claire Sullivan, just to make things worse. That's just horrible. I have to say I never liked her. I always felt she looked down on me.'

I don't know what to say, Danny emailed. *It's unbelievable, the worst thing. I could kill him for hurting you. We're thinking of you, pal. Don't lose heart, you have the girls and you'll always have them, and your aunt and your father and Joan – and you'll always have me in your corner too. Stay strong and keep in touch.*

And then, three Saturdays later, Leo having called and collected the girls as usual, Ellen answered another doorbell ring an hour after they'd left and found Claire standing there.

'Ellen,' she said quietly, 'can we talk? Please?'

Ellen felt the blood rushing to her face, flooding it with heat, pulsing in her temples. Her legs shook; she went to close the door, but Claire planted a foot in the way.

'Please, Ellen.'

And then she found her voice – and with an effort, kept it under control. 'How dare you come here. How dare you come to this house.'

'Ellen, I just – this wasn't meant to happen. I would never have—'

'Wasn't meant to happen?' Ellen shot back, anger flying in. 'You make it sound like an accident!'

'I mean, I didn't set out to—'

'To what – seduce Leo? When you could have any man in London, you decided to take mine? You couldn't bear to see me happy and settled, so you made it your business to sabotage it. What did I ever do to you to deserve that?'

Claire winced. 'Nothing. You did nothing. Look, it's not as—'

'I trusted you. I never in a million years thought you'd hurt me – you of all people – but you have hurt me in the worst possible way. You lied to me, for years you deceived me. You pretended to be on my side when you weren't.'

'Ellen, I swear—'

'You made him choose, because you knew he'd choose you. You didn't care that you were taking him from his girls. That meant nothing to you. You don't care about anyone but yourself. You never have.'

As she spoke, it felt like a veil was being pulled away. How had she never seen the real Claire? All the clues were there. All the evidence was in full view. She always got what she wanted, whoever she had to walk over to get it.

'Ellen—'

'You make me sick. Your parents would be mortified, they'd be disgusted if they knew the kind of person you really are.'

She thought of them, those two kind, decent souls who would die of shame if they had any idea what their precious daughter was capable of, what she had done.

Ellen could tell them about the abortion. She could throw that little bombshell at them, see how Claire liked it – but of course she wouldn't do that to them. She wasn't Claire. She was altogether better.

'Don't come here again,' she said. 'Never come here again.' She closed the door, this time without any resistance, and leant against it. The end, she thought. The end of them. It brought no comfort.

'I want to take the girls to live in Ireland,' she said to Leo that evening, Juliet and Grace having been sent in to wash their hands for dinner. 'In July, when the school holidays begin. My father has said we can live with him in Dublin until we get sorted.'

'Ellen, London is their home, pretty much the only home they've known. And your work is here.'

'You've ruined London for me. I can't stay here any more. I have to give up a job I love because of you.'

'But Ireland is another country.'

'It's an hour on a plane,' she said. How cold she sounded. How unfeeling she had to sound, so she wouldn't break down. 'And the girls are half Irish. I know you can stop them from leaving, and I'm asking you not to. I'm asking you to do the decent thing.'

'When will I see them?'

'As often as you want, in Ireland.'

He made no reply to this, and she had to hope he would agree. After destroying what they'd had, after wronging her so cruelly for so long, she prayed he would do the right thing now.

'We'll miss you,' Lucinda said when Ellen handed in her notice. 'We're so sorry this has happened. We might continue to use you as a freelancer, if you're happy,' and Ellen said that would be marvellous. She'd been lucky with her jobs in London: shame she'd been so unlucky in love.

In July, Leo having consented to the move, they packed their bags. Her father travelled on the ferry from Ireland and filled his car with their luggage and brought it back to his house in Dublin while Ellen and the girls took a plane.

And Ellen, almost thirty-seven, left London with a hardened heart, knowing she would never live there again.

DUBLIN
JULY 1998
THE SIXTH MOVE

Restart

SHE THOUGHT OF THE SINGLE RUCKSACK THAT
had held everything she needed when she'd moved to Galway, and
later to London, and marvelled at the belongings she'd accumulated
since then. She had the girls now, of course, with their share of
luggage, but still it seemed excessive.

She managed with some difficulty to fit their clothes in the
wardrobe of the room he'd prepared for them. He must have got
the bunk beds specially – and was that a fresh coat of paint on the
walls, or had they already been pink?

Her room across the landing had cream wallpaper printed with
yellow rosebuds, and pretty matching furniture. Iris' room, had to be.
Ellen's computer, which her father had been looking after, sat on a
small folding table by the window. She hadn't thought she'd need it
again, and was glad she hadn't sold it or donated it to a charity shop.

She fitted her things where she could, and pushed her empty
suitcase under the bed. Her box of books could live at the bottom
of the wardrobe; no point in unpacking them when they'd be
moving again as soon as she found their own place.

The house was part of a small development in Rathfarnham,
just two minutes' walk from a big park. Semi-detached, painted

cream, with a pair of bakers living next door, one of whom had already called around with a plastic container of gingerbread men. *Welcome*, she'd said. *Your father's been so looking forward to your arrival.* Ellen wondered exactly how much he'd told them.

'I suggest,' he said to her that evening, 'that you enrol the girls in a local school – I mean local to here, and then, if you still want to rent a place you could get one close by, and I could be on call if you wanted me for anything. I could do school runs, or take the girls for a few hours in the afternoons to let you work. Anything, really.'

He was trying to help, she had to acknowledge that. She did need to sort out a school before the new year started in September, and she couldn't deny that it would be useful to have someone to call on if she needed to. But did she want to live in Dublin, or move closer to Frances in Galway?

'I'd love you to stay here in this house,' he said, reading the doubt in her face. 'It makes more sense. I won't expect rent, and it'll give you a chance to concentrate on finding work if you don't have to look for a place to live too.'

It did make sense. The girls could get to know their grandfather. They'd have a male role model in Leo's absence. Still she was slow to commit to something more permanent. 'I'll look for a school,' she said. 'I'll start with that. I'd rather pay something, though, while we're here.'

'How about you help with the meals then?' he said. 'I'm not much of a cook, and Frances tells me she turned you into one when you were with her.'

'I could do that.' She remembered his French toast. They'd loved his French toast. She opened her mouth to ask if he still made it, and closed it again. 'I'll organise the evening meal, and buy what food is needed. We can take it from there.'

She found a school within walking distance whose principal agreed to take the girls in. She wanted to admit that it might not be for long, but said nothing in case he decided to give the places instead to children whose parents had no plans to move out of the area.

She approached ad agencies in the city and slowly began to pick up freelance work, and Lucinda was in touch as she'd promised too. After some hunting around, Ellen found a narrow writing bureau to replace the small table in her room, and got to work.

As she'd known he would be, Leo was generous with his financial contributions, depositing a sum into her Irish bank account each month that more than covered the girls' expenses.

She never spent a penny of his money on herself. What she didn't need for the girls she used for groceries and to pay the house's electricity bill that she insisted on covering too.

He flew from London every other weekend to spend the day with his daughters. He took an early flight on Saturday morning and turned up at the house around ten. At the sound of the doorbell, Grace would dash to the hall.

'Hello,' he would say, giving Ellen a little smile as he lifted his younger daughter into his arms, and for the sake of the girls she would force herself to smile back.

'All OK?' he would ask as Juliet got into her coat.

'Fine.' She never asked how he was. 'See you later, girls.'

Even-tempered Juliet took the visits in her stride, but Grace would be sulky with Ellen afterwards. Six since August, she made it clear to her mother that she held her wholly responsible for the split. The irony wasn't lost on Ellen.

To her relief, her father avoided all contact with Leo. She had to acknowledge the benefits of living with him, the hours he freed up so she could work. And once, she'd overheard him remonstrating gently with Grace. *Mum is doing her best, pet*, he'd said. *Try and be a bit nicer to her*, and Ellen was reminded of Frances saying much the same to her. How history repeated itself.

In September the girls started in their new school. She'd been dreading it, remembering Grace's difficulty with the crèche – and sure enough the first few days were tricky – 'I want *Dad* to bring me!' she would wail – but with Juliet's help, and a sympathetic teacher's support, her younger daughter eventually settled and found friends.

Later in the month Ellen left the girls with her father and went to Galway to celebrate Frances' eighty-fourth birthday. 'I'm so glad you're back,' Frances told her, 'and isn't it great to be finished with all that other nasty business?'

'It is.'

But Ellen saw with dismay how frail her cherished aunt had become, how firm a hold the arthritis had now, making her wince as she climbed the stairs or stooped to add coal to the fire.

'When does your student get back? When is college reopening?'

'Next week. You wouldn't know she's in the house, she's that quiet – but she makes herself useful, doesn't wait to be asked to do anything. That was a good idea of yours. I'm looking forward to having her back. How are things between you and your father now?'

Ellen considered. 'They're better – at least, on the surface we get on fine, but . . . I'm not sure we'll ever be as close as we were.'

'That's up to you,' Frances replied. 'That's within your gift, Ellen.'

'What do you mean?'

'I mean talk to him. Open up to him, tell him what you're thinking and feeling, and give him a chance to respond. If you're both honest with one another, that will help.'

Ellen looked at the woman who'd taken her in, who'd made her feel welcome, who'd taught her how to cook, and how to tell a flower from a weed. The woman who'd guided her when she'd needed it, who'd supported her in everything, and praised her when she'd earned it. The woman who always told the truth, and expected it from others.

'Frances, I don't know what I'd do without you. You've been so good to me.'

For once, Frances didn't flap away the compliment. 'I'm glad we had the chance to get to know one another properly. You learnt that my bark is worse than my bite.'

Ellen smiled. 'I certainly did.'

When Ellen was leaving, Frances packed up a batch of homemade flapjacks, one of the few things she still baked. She pressed a twenty-pound note into Ellen's hand and instructed her to pick out books for the girls. 'Come and see me soon again,' she said. 'Bring my grand-nieces,' and she stood at the front door, leaning heavily on her stick as Ellen walked the familiar path to the gate.

Talk to him. Open up to him. Easier said than done.

Peace

SHE WAITED TILL THE GIRLS WERE IN BED ONE evening, and her father was behind his newspaper in the sitting room. When she asked if she could have a word he lowered the paper.

'What about?'

She took the armchair opposite him. She paused, unsure of where to start, half-regretting that she'd taken this step – but she *had* taken it, so she would continue. 'I think we need to talk about when you left, because I'm finding it hard to let it go.'

He folded the paper then and set it on the coffee table, and something in his expression told her he'd been waiting for this. She let a pause go by while she collected her thoughts.

'I kept waiting for you to come back,' she began. 'I was sure you'd come back. It messed me up, I couldn't sleep, I did all sorts of stupid stuff . . . but the thing was, I blamed Mam. I told you that, just before she died. That day you came to see her.'

He nodded. He remembered.

'I was never mad at you. I was sad and confused, and I missed you all the time, but I never held you responsible. I got it into my head that she must have been the reason you left.'

She shook her head. 'I know she wasn't easy to live with – and Frances helped me understand a bit more about that – but you were the one who had an affair, and you were the one who lived a double life for years, and you were the one who finally walked out on us.'

She was careful to keep her voice neutral. She didn't want to attack him, not when he'd done so much for them in the last while. 'I was too hard on Mam, and now she's gone, and . . . I never really told her I was sorry for how I treated her, how I shut her out. I tried, towards the end, but I think I left it too late.'

She stumbled on, conscious of his eyes on her. 'And even if you didn't love Mam any more, I can't understand how you could have left me and Joan. Whatever about meeting someone else, and even having a child with her, if you had really loved us like you said, you couldn't have walked away like that and never insisted on contact. And I want to get past this, I want to move on, but I don't know how.'

She sat back – and as if they were connected by some invisible thread, he leant towards her.

'Ellen, first of all, you looked after your mother when you were going through your own terrible time. You were there for her when she needed you. I think that was your way of saying sorry, and I'm guessing she knew it.'

He paused, and seemed to be collecting his own thoughts.

'You're right about me,' he said. 'I was completely selfish. I told myself it was for the best that I left, but of course it wasn't, not for you and Joan. I was just trying to justify my actions. I hurt you unbearably, my first two precious daughters, and I'll bring that regret to the grave with me. But let me assure you—'

He broke off, got abruptly to his feet. 'No, let me show you something,' he said, and left the room, and a memory flashed of her mother going to get the biscuit tin of his letters she'd kept from Ellen and Joan.

He didn't bring back a biscuit tin: he brought a plastic bag. He set it on the coffee table and drew out a sheaf of pictures. Drawn by childish hands, her and Joan's hands. The usual houses and stick figures, the usual yellow ball of sun sitting in a scribbled blue sky with thought-bubble clouds, the usual red and green flowers poking from grass. *Daddy*, she read, underneath the stick figures, and *Mammy*, and *Ellen* and *Joan*. Their earliest pictures, in crayon or paint, putting her in mind of her daughters' artworks.

The bag held cards too, early homemade ones with *Happy Birthday Daddy* in the same childish script. Inside one she read *I love you Daddy, from Ellen xxx*. Later ones had been bought in a shop, some from her and others from Joan, *Daddy* becoming the more grown-up *Dad* in the messages inside.

And photos, lots of photos. Ellen and Joan sharing a pram, then two toddlers, then in tiny school uniforms, little bags strapped to their backs. Blowing out birthday candles, opening wrapped presents, standing on a stage in the school hall with their classmates. Sitting on his shoulders or cradled in his arms, or leaning into him as older girls. He'd held on to them all through the years.

'I missed you both too,' he said. 'Every single day. I'm the one to blame, Ellen. I'm entirely to blame, and if you can't forgive me for that, I understand.'

'I think I can forgive you,' she said carefully. 'It might take a while to get back to where we were, but I really want to try.'

'I'd love that' – and it was the start of a beautiful kind of peace between them.

Promise

ONE DAY IN MAY, TEN MONTHS AFTER THEIR MOVE back to Ireland, the three of them still living in her father's house, Ellen was rummaging through her writing bureau when she came across Ben's notebook. She'd never written a word in it; all she'd used it for was to store letters and clippings in its back pocket. She opened it now and read again the message he'd written on the flyleaf: *To Ellen, for the book ideas. All my love, B xxx.*

Even after the passage of so much time, she could see twenty-year-old him clearly in her head. He'd been full of fun. They'd been perfect for each other. If he'd stayed, if only he'd stayed. She thought of the heartbreak she would have been spared. She'd never have gone to London, never met Leo in Paris.

But if he'd stayed, she'd never have had Juliet and Grace, and that was unthinkable – so maybe after all it was best that he'd been her first fleeting love.

She flicked through the empty pages of the notebook. *You have a go at a novel,* he'd said, *and I'll give a music degree my best shot. Promise me you'll try,* he'd said, and she'd promised.

She jumped on in her memory to the time, years later, when she'd sat on the deck with Danny, the night before his wedding when she thought she might be pregnant. She remembered telling him someone had said she should try writing a book. *Definitely you should*, he'd said – and when she'd countered that she was too busy, he'd told her that if she wanted to do something badly enough, she'd find the time.

She thought it might have begun then, the story that had been coming together bit by bit whenever she had an idle moment. She hadn't jotted it down, so full her London life had been, but she was aware of it, curled up quietly within her, growing slowly, waiting patiently for her to pull it out and put some kind of shape on it, and give it a voice.

Since returning to Ireland she'd been preoccupied with settling the girls into their new lives and sorting work for herself, but now that things weren't so hectic, maybe she should begin to explore this. Maybe the time had come to keep her promise.

What if you try and don't fail?

She would use the notebook, even though typing on her computer would be quicker. Somehow, the notebook felt like the right place. She opened it again and found a biro and started scribbling, the words rushing out as fast as she could form them.

Prologue: An ill-judged one-night stand that results in a pregnancy, an infant girl given up for adoption by a frightened new mother, scarcely more than a girl herself.

Main story: The parallel lives of mother and daughter over the ensuing years, their near-encounters and mutual acquaintances – they live unknowingly in the same town. The accidental reunion as they lie in adjoining hospital beds twenty-five years after the adoption, each having given birth to new babies. A chance remark in a conversation leading to the discovery of their identities.

Maybe an epilogue, the two babies growing up together?

Nothing very groundbreaking in the premise. A story of love and heartbreak and serendipity, a testament to the enduring power of love with a note of hope at the end, the closing of a circle and the start of another. The kind of warm story she herself liked to read. What did she have to lose by giving it a try?

After playing around with her plot for a week or so, she opened a document on her computer and began writing the story. Over the weeks and months that followed, whatever else she was doing, she devoted at least an hour a day to it. Every day she wrote a little more, every day her word count rose.

It wasn't plain sailing, far from it. There were times when she read over the previous day's words and deleted every one. There were nights she lay in bed, unable to sleep because of a stubborn plot glitch, wondering how she'd ever thought she could write a book. But there were days too when her fingers flew over the keys, and her characters did her bidding, and she felt she might have something worth holding on to.

She told nobody except Danny, who she figured was far enough away to keep the secret.

You're writing a book – how fantastic is that! Yes, I remember you saying something that night – what took you so long?? Best of luck, and keep me posted. I have a good feeling . . .

All fine here, Cormac and Mattie running rings around us like true American kids. Bobbi's father is in hospital having a hip replaced – all that's worrying him is how long he'll have to stay off the golf course.

Love to your dad, and hi to the girls, look forward to everyone meeting up some fine day,

D xx

By early December she had a first draft, or thought she had. The story felt like it was finished. She titled it *Norma and Caroline*, the names of her main characters, and then thought it sounded too like Thelma and Louise, and changed it to *What the Heart Believes*.

She would set it aside till after Christmas. She'd forget about it for a month and then read it again, like she'd seen suggested somewhere. If she was still happy with it, she'd think about showing it to someone.

The notion was truly terrifying.

Frances

'IT'S MARIA,' SAID THE VOICE.

Maria. Did Ellen know a Maria?

'I'm renting with Miss O'Shaughnessy in Galway.'

Miss O'Shaughnessy. It took a second to realise that she was talking about Frances. Ellen felt a sudden swoop of fear. 'Is everything OK?'

'I didn't know who else to call. Your name and number were by the phone.'

'She's my aunt. What's happened? Is she OK?'

'She – I'm sorry, she had a – I heard a noise, in her room, I was downstairs, and I heard – and I found her on the floor. She must have fallen, getting out of bed—'

Ellen wanted to scream with impatience. 'Is she OK? Where is she?'

'I called an ambulance, I couldn't lift her, they took her to the hospital. They said – they said it looked like a stroke.'

Ellen closed her eyes. 'Which hospital?'

'I'll drive you,' her father said when she told him. 'I'll run next door and get Jesse to bring the girls home from school.' Jesse was one of the bakers, with a daughter in Grace's class. 'She'll hang on to them till we get back' – but Ellen was throwing things into a bag.

'I'll get the train. I'll stay the night, and maybe longer. It's better if you're here – Grace could kick up with Jesse. You can drop me to the station.'

On the train she told herself there was nothing to worry about. People had strokes every day; they were commonplace. If they were caught on time, people got over them. Life went on. Frances had years ahead of her, at least ten. People lived well into their nineties now if they were healthy – and Frances had hardly ever been sick. You couldn't count arthritis; that wasn't life-threatening in the least. She'd be fine. She'd be sitting up in bed when Ellen arrived, complaining that everyone was making far too much fuss.

The train pulled into Galway in the middle of the rush hour. It was the first week in January, and a sleety rain was falling as Ellen searched for a taxi. She'd forgotten her gloves; her hands were quickly frozen.

The journey to the hospital took an eternity, her taxi crawling through the streets as she sat hunched over her bag, the knot in her stomach tightening with every minute that passed, wanting to scream at the driver to go faster, even though she knew he couldn't.

When the bulk of the hospital came into view she couldn't bear it any longer. 'This will do,' she told the driver. 'I'll get out here.' She paid him and ran, bag thumping against her, dodging people, splashing through puddles, the rows of lighted windows beckoning her on. *I'm coming*, she told Frances. *I'm nearly there.*

She was too late.

'A massive stroke,' a doctor told her. 'There was never a hope of recovery. She slipped away quietly about an hour ago. She wouldn't have known anything. I'm very sorry. I can take you to her.'

She sat by the bed, too numb to cry. Someone had placed a wooden crucifix on the sheet over Frances' chest. Ellen pressed the hand that was still warm. She bent to kiss the pale forehead and whisper her goodbye, and her thanks.

She rang the house and passed the news on to Maria. 'I'm on the way,' she said, 'I'll be with you as soon as I can.' She couldn't leave the girl on her own in the house that night.

Maria was tall and thin, a heavy fringe of chestnut hair stopping just short of large grey eyes that were now rimmed with red. 'You're welcome to stay for the rest of the academic year if you want to,' Ellen told her. 'The house will only lie empty otherwise.'

'Would it be OK if a friend moved in?' she asked in a tremulous voice. 'I'd be nervous on my own.'

'Yes, of course, if they don't mind using the little bedroom.' Better to have the place occupied – and Frances' will wouldn't be read until the summer, if then.

She knew her aunt had made a will, because it was one of the things she'd advised Ellen to do. *Always best to have one made,* she'd said. *You can change it as often as you want, but if you die with no will, you'll have no control over who gets what – and it could cause all sorts of rows and delays.*

She spent the night in Frances' room, surrounded by all her aunt's things, remembering the happy times they'd shared, the cooking, the gardening, the crosswords. When she was leaving in the morning she locked the bedroom door and pocketed the key. She would return after Maria had left, and do whatever needed to be done then.

Frances was buried four days later, on a bitterly cold morning. Ellen's father drove them from Dublin, leaving the girls in the care of Iris, who'd come home specially. Seamus appeared too, in place of Joan who'd stayed in Cork with their latest child Gary, just two weeks old.

Frances' brothers flew in from Australia, uncles Ellen hadn't seen since her mother's funeral. They told her that Frances had always been full of praise for her in her letters. 'She called you the daughter she never had,' one of them said – Ellen kept forgetting which was Patrick and which Peter.

She wept her way through the mass, her arm tucked into her father's. She stood shivering by the open grave in the cemetery where her grandparents were buried, and watched as Frances was lowered in to join them.

On her return to Dublin a letter waited for her in Leo's handwriting. She opened it and read that his mother, Marguerite, had died peacefully in a French hospital. Another death. She wrote him a formal reply, expressing condolence, and wrote a second longer letter of sympathy to Henri and Louis. *The girls and I would love to see you in Ireland*, she wrote, *if you ever feel like visiting*. She gave them her phone number and said to ring anytime. She wondered if they would, or if they'd fade away, never to be seen again by her.

In March she called into the local library and found a list of Irish-based literary agents. Not that many, so she emailed each one and asked if they'd care to read part or all of the novel she'd written.

In April she got two polite refusals, each citing too many clients to consider taking on another.

In May, a third refusal.

At the end of the month Maria rang from Galway to say she'd be moving out of Frances' house after her summer exams. On the appointed day Ellen took the train to Galway to say goodbye and

to reclaim the keys, and she stayed two nights after Maria's departure, putting the house in order for whoever would take possession
of it.

It was horribly empty without Frances in it. She stripped beds
and washed linens and towels. She swept and mopped floors.
She polished mirrors and cleaned windows. In Frances' room she
perched on the edge of the bed, lonely and sad. The drawer of
the bedside locker was half-open – she went to push it closed
and saw a photograph, sepia with age, lying inside. She took it
out.

A young man was dressed all in white, trousers, shirt, apron, his
clothing in stark contrast to the darkness of his skin, even with the
faded colouring of the photograph. His hair was cut close to his
scalp. His smile was wide.

She recalled Frances speaking of a man who'd worked in the
hotel kitchen with her for a few years. He'd had a bibilical name –
Abraham? Jacob? – and an Irish missionary mother and an African
father. *A heart of gold*, Frances had said, or words to that effect.
Was this him? Ellen thought it might be.

And years later, on the night of Joan's wedding, she and Frances
had sat at the kitchen table, and she'd asked Frances if she'd ever
met anyone, and the answer coming, truthful as ever: she had, but
it wasn't to be. Too much went against it, she'd said, something
like that, and Ellen remembered wondering what that meant, and
thought she understood it now.

Too much went against a white woman and an African-Irish man
in the Ireland of fifty years ago. Too much went against love
between people of different skin colours in the Ireland that had
yet to realise that love knew no boundaries.

But she'd kept his photograph. All her life she'd kept him close to her.

Ellen sat on as a soft drizzle fell outside, and she thought about how much she'd miss Frances. She remembered her arrival there, finding her aunt on her knees by the rockery, digging out the weeds. She smiled as she remembered how sharply Frances had spoken that first day, how taken aback Ellen had been to be attacked, it had felt like, when she'd done nothing wrong.

A shaky start – but what a firm foundation they'd eventually dug.

Legacy

'I'D LIKE TO LEARN TO DRIVE,' SHE TOLD HER
father, so he took her for an hour each weekday to an industrial
estate, and he put her behind the wheel and told her what to do,
and she ground the gears and flooded the engine and revved uselessly
in neutral, and slowly began to learn the right way to do everything.
Within a month, he said she was ready to apply for her test.

It took two attempts to pass it, and when she did, they hunted
around until they found an eight-year-old Beetle without too many
miles on the clock. Not blue like Frances', but orange. Like a lady-
bird, she thought, and there and then it was named.

Towards the end of August, two official-looking envelopes
arrived at her father's house with her name typed on them. She
steeled herself for more rejections, but was wrong on both counts.
In the first, an agent called Dorothy O'Connell asked for the
opening and closing chapters of her book, and a more detailed
synopsis than she'd already sent.

The second letter was from a solicitor named Robert Fitzsimons
who told her he was representing the late Frances O'Shaughnessy,
and who asked that she contact him at her earliest opportunity in
relation to a bequest. A personal visit would be preferable, he said,

so she rang and made an appointment, and drove to Galway on her own, slowly and carefully, trying to remember everything she'd been taught. *Ring me when you get there*, her father had said, probably every bit as nervous as she was.

She parked in Frances' driveway, her car occupying the ghost imprint of the blue Beetle. She walked into the city and found the office she needed, where she was told that her aunt had willed her the house.

'She also left this for you,' the solicitor said, handing Ellen an envelope. Inside was a letter dated two years previously.

My dear Ellen,

I'm assuming I'll go before you, long before you, and hopefully I will. I want you to have the house, because it makes sense in my head for you to live in it with your girls, and my brothers certainly don't need it. You always felt right in it when you were staying with me. You may decide, of course, that you'd rather someplace more modern, or if you're still in Dublin, you might not want to move west. It'll be yours to do with as you want, and I won't be back to haunt you if you sell it.

Thank you for all you did for me. I know I wasn't the easiest to live with, but I enjoyed our time together, even if I didn't often show it. You reminded me of me a bit – I'm not sure whether you'll take that as a compliment or not, but I mean that you have a good heart, as I hope I do too.

I'll leave it at that before I get boring. I wish you a long and happy life. As I write this you're going through your troubles but I feel better times are coming for you, and as you know I'm never wrong.

Your loving aunt,

Frances

Dear Frances.

She showed the letter to her father. 'What do you think?' she asked. 'What should I do?'

'Whatever feels right,' he replied. 'You know you're welcome to live here as long as you want, but you can work anywhere, and you might like having your own place – and you know Galway from your time there. It was very decent of Frances. Think about it. Don't rush to a decision.'

She thought about it. Next year Juliet would be moving to secondary school, and Grace would be turning nine. It would mean another upheaval for her girls, but against that they'd have their own house, with their own rooms, in a city that Ellen had grown to love while she'd lived there, and their grandfather would only be a drive away.

She would move, she decided, next summer. She'd tell the girls soon; she'd ease them gently into the notion of relocating, so they'd have lots of time to get used to the idea. She'd enrol them in new schools in Galway, and have everything set in place for the move.

She would also extend the house, if allowed. A two-storey extension, with a bigger kitchen leading into a sunroom at ground level and an extra bedroom above, possibly ensuite. They'd need another bedroom for guests, and the sunroom would be a useful teen space in later years. They'd still have plenty of garden.

Frances' garden belonged to her now. She could hardly believe it. In latter years it had fallen into neglect, but she would resurrect it. She would take great joy in bringing it back to its former glory.

Her father got an architect friend to draw up plans, and she applied to Galway County Council for planning permission. Hopefully, with a year at her disposal, the building would be done by the time they were moving in.

She told the girls, making it sound as appealing as she could. 'A house of our own,' she said, 'and a lovely garden.'

Predictably, Grace objected. 'I don't want to move again' – so Ellen had to resort to bribery.

'We could get a kitten,' she said. Grace had pretty much adopted the bakers' cat from next door, sneaking it regularly into her grandfather's house. 'You and Juliet could name it' – and that did the trick.

She rang Leo to tell him. 'It will be a good thing for the girls,' she said, 'to have our own place. It would mean you flying to Shannon or Knock airport instead of Dublin.'

She no longer loved him. She wasn't entirely sure when this realisation had hit her: all she could say for certain was that she knew it to be true, and her overwhelming reaction was relief. It made it easier to be in his company.

He didn't protest. He simply thanked her for letting him know, and asked her to pass on the new contact details after they'd made the move. He enquired about schools, and Ellen told him she'd already sorted them.

'When they're a little older,' he said, 'I'd like them to come and stay with me sometimes, during the holidays' – and she had to say yes to this, although she still dreaded them meeting him and Claire together, and discovering that it was Claire who had taken him away from them.

Grace would no doubt attack Ellen for not telling them – Ellen was always her punchbag of choice – but Juliet would be hurt too that they hadn't been told. It was so hard to know the right thing to do. She missed Frances, who would have known what the right thing was.

In the meantime, she sent the first chapters and synopsis of her book to Dorothy O'Connell. A month later, when she'd convinced herself that she'd never hear from the agent again, she received a reply by email.

Ellen,

I'd like to read the rest of your manuscript. Feel free to send it electron-ically at your convenience.

   Best,

   Dorothy

At her convenience. With difficulty she waited till the morning, and then emailed it off. She watched it loading slowly as an attach-ment, her two hundred and twenty precious pages, and imagined it landing in the agency, and Dorothy O'Connell printing it and reading it. She felt almost unbearably excited.

She told her father.

'I can't believe you wrote a book,' he said. 'That is some achieve-ment, Ellen. All this time I thought you were writing ads. Best of luck with it.'

She emailed Danny with the news.

An agent reading your manuscript – how fantastic is that? My fingers are so tightly crossed I can't eat my French toast, that's how supportive I am. Keep me posted on EVERY development. Booker here we come.

In the days and weeks that followed she checked her inbox constantly, smothering disappointment when another day passed with no response from Dorothy. Finally, after six weeks, the message she'd been waiting for arrived. Things moved slowly, she was discovering, in the literary world.

Ellen,

Will you come to see me? I like your story and your voice, and I'd like to talk to you. Please ring my secretary to make an appointment.

Best,

Dorothy

She rang there and then, unable not to, and was given an appointment for the following Thursday, two days away. Two eternities away. To keep herself busy she mowed the lawn that didn't need mowing, and cleaned the bathroom, and changed the sheets and pillowcases on every bed.

She washed the bed linen and hung it out to dry. She emptied the fridge and scrubbed it, and moved on to the oven, and vacuumed and mopped every floor in the house. She took in the laundry and ironed it, and after that she baked a chocolate cake, because she'd run out of things to do.

'I love it,' Dorothy O'Connell said. 'It's well structured and fresh in tone. It's got plenty of emotion, which is always good, and you can certainly write. Women readers will identify with the subject – and it's the kind of story that would translate easily to the screen.'

She was short, shorter than Ellen, and plump, and dressed in a pinstriped jacket and skirt, and her hair was cut tight to her scalp. 'I'd be happy to represent you, if you're agreeable.'

Represent her. Ellen was fairly sure that meant become her agent. 'Yes,' she said. 'Very agreeable. Thank you.'

'Well done. I'll have my secretary mail you my contract. Take a few days and let me know. If you're still happy to be signed up, I'll begin talking to editors. In the meantime, start thinking of a plot for your next – we'll be chasing a two-book deal.'

A two-book deal. She walked all the way from Harcourt Street back to Rathfarnham, as euphoric as she'd been when Tim at Marketing Solutions had offered her a three-month trial. Once she signed along the dotted line – and she'd sign whatever arrived – she would have an agent. She would be a writer with an agent, and her agent would be talking to editors about her. So far, so good.

She thought about how happy Frances would have been at the news, how much faith she'd always had in Ellen. And Ben, whose suggestion it had been to write a book.

Maybe one day he would walk into a bookshop and see a book with her name on it, and recall what they'd had, and smile.

Deal

DOROTHY'S CONTRACT ARRIVED IN THE POST. TWO copies, one to keep, one to sign and return. Dorothy was to hold back ten per cent of everything Ellen earned, which might yet prove to be nothing at all. She skimmed over the rest before signing and returning the document with a thank-you note.

At Christmas, Iris came home with her boyfriend Ultan, who had graduated to the position of fiancé over the summer. The following week, Henri and Louis, now twenty-seven and twenty-five, visited Dublin for two days, staying in the nearby hotel Ellen had organised, and she replicated Christmas dinner, complete with crackers, in their honour.

In the spring, building started on the Galway house, planning permission having finally been granted. The builder, Fintan, was the husband of one of Frances' friends: his name and number had been sellotaped to her fridge from the time she'd had a leaking chimney.

'All done,' he told Ellen at the end of June, so she got into her car and came for a final inspection. She walked with him through the bigger brighter kitchen, its newly plastered walls waiting for paint, and into the adjoining sunroom with its expanse of glass that looked out on the garden, now featuring a new patio.

They climbed the stairs and turned left at the top, into the new ensuite bedroom. Nice, she thought, to have her own bathroom. She would put Juliet into Frances' old room, and Grace could take the one that had been Ellen's.

The garden was smaller, but still big enough. After Fintan left, Ellen planted a camellia outside the sunroom in memory of Frances. 'Not that I need a reminder,' she told her aunt later at the cemetery. 'Not that I'll ever need one, dear Frances.'

As soon as the school holidays began, Ellen, her daughters and her father piled into his car and made their way back to Galway, armed with brushes and rollers, masking tape and overalls, ground sheets and lots of paint. For a week they worked, Ellen and her father doing the edges and borders of each room while the girls tackled the centre areas with rollers.

This arrangement required covert supervision and furtive redoing, and nightly scrubs in the bath, but she figured it was worth it to give them a sense of ownership of the house. 'This will be our last move,' she promised them.

And at the start of August, a week after her fortieth birthday and as they prepared for their move to Galway, she took a call from Dorothy telling her she'd been offered a two-book publishing deal.

GALWAY
AUGUST 2001
THE SEVENTH MOVE

Frankie

A SMELL OF PAINT LINGERED. SHE FLUNG OPEN windows as she moved through the rooms. The house felt familiar and different. She had to keep reminding herself that it belonged to her. Her very own home, her name added to the title deeds.

'Can Grace and I have the new bedroom?' Juliet asked.

Ellen looked at her in surprise. 'You don't have to share here, you can have a room each' – but it turned out they liked sharing, and because Juliet rarely asked for anything, Ellen said yes. 'Our own bathroom!' Grace exclaimed, and Ellen thought it a small price to pay for harmony, and moved into Frances' old room.

They spent the rest of the day unpacking, folding sweaters into drawers, hanging clothes, arranging shoes on racks and books on shelves, attaching posters – Westlife, Alicia Keys, Backstreet Boys – to the freshly painted walls with Blu Tack. When suitcases and boxes and rucksacks had been stowed in the attic, Ellen used the new oven to reheat the chicken casserole she'd brought from Dublin, and they had their first family meal in Galway.

'Come soon again,' she said to her father when he was leaving. 'We'd love to have you stay anytime.'

'Be careful what you wish for,' he replied. He'd turned seventy-seven in March, and they'd found their way back to one another, and she knew she had Frances to thank for that.

'You said we could get a kitten,' Grace reminded her at bedtime.

'We will,' Ellen said, 'but let's get you and Juliet settled into your new schools first. You need to be happy there before we look for a kitten, because kittens won't be comfortable in a house unless everyone is happy in it.' She'd learnt a few coping strategies when dealing with her temperamental little daughter.

Two weeks later, both girls seeming content with their new schools, they went to the local cat sanctuary, where Grace picked out a round-bellied calico kitten that mewed loudly all the way home.

'You need to think of a name,' Ellen told the girls.

'Frankie,' Juliet said, 'because of Frances, who gave us our house.'

Ellen waited for Grace to object, but instead she repeated 'Frankie', and the matter was settled. Maybe they'd already decided between them.

From day one the new arrival created havoc, clawing her way to the top of curtains, leaping onto kitchen chairs and from there to the table at every opportunity, leaving tiny but definite scratches on furniture legs, scattering litter far and wide every time she used the tray.

But from day one she was also Grace's, choosing her lap over the others' when she finally ran out of steam, sleeping at the end of her bed – a battle Ellen had fought and lost – and generally making no secret of her preference.

In the meantime, Ellen's agent, Dorothy, was negotiating the terms of the publishing contract, and in October it finally arrived for Ellen's signature. Publication date for the first book was set for June of the following year, the second two years later. The money offered sounded generous to Ellen, but she had no yardstick, no author friends to compare notes with. Payment would be doled out in stages, with the first cheque due on contract signing.

She flicked through the pages, seeing *territories* and *rights* and *typescript*, and other terms that meant little to her, but that presumably made perfect sense to Dorothy. She signed and returned it, and a week later was invited to meet her editor – who was, to her surprise, a man called Tony. She'd assumed a woman would handle what felt to her very much a woman's book. 'He's good,' Dorothy told her. 'Your book will be in safe hands.'

Your book. The most thrilling words in the universe. Again she thought of Ben, and the possibility of his coming across the book somewhere.

Tony was in his sixties, and fond of bow ties. He told her these two facts in his deep rumbling voice within a minute of meeting her. He also told her he wanted to change the title of her book. 'Are you attached to it?' he asked, and Ellen said not particularly.

'I'm thinking *Mother and Daughter*,' he said, giving a sweep of his arm, as if the title were there in front of him, in neon lights possibly. He looked like he might be fond of neon. 'Your story is full of heart, full of emotion, and *Mother and Daughter* says that – and it's simple and memorable, like all the best titles. Yours, forgive me, is a little dated, a little clunky.'

She forgave him. They were having lunch in a Michelin-starred restaurant in Dublin. It felt surreal, lunching with her editor. He told her, over roasted guinea fowl, that he'd been in the business for forty years, 'since I was a callow youth'. He was given to pronouncements, accompanying them with a big smile that sent his face into a thousand happy creases.

He told her that her book was wonderful. A triumph, he declared, that needed only a few minor adjustments to be completely perfect. He predicted a film deal, and suggested that her second book would follow the fortunes of mother and daughter as their children grew up. 'Readers adore sequels,' he pronounced, smiling hugely over a bowl of sticky toffee pudding that he told her, with further glee, his doctor had strictly forbidden. By the end of the lunch, she fancied herself a little in love with him.

Over the months that followed, she revised her opinion. He had been sent to torment her, returning each version of her edits with a note that started by praising her latest submission, and continuing with *just a few more tweaks* ... It took until the end of February for him to declare himself satisfied. 'Onwards!' he pronounced. 'To copy-editing, which I feel sure will be plain sailing.'

Ellen's heart sank. More editing – but the copy-edits proved far less traumatic than Tony's, requiring her only to check the practical adjustments that had been made – correction of dates, elimination of commas, substitution of repeated words and the like.

By the end of March, *Mother and Daughter* was ready. 'Ready for proofreading,' Tony told her. 'The final furlong. Nearly there now, won't feel it till we're done and dusted,' so Ellen awaited the manuscript's return yet again – the manuscript she now despised – and when it showed up she trudged wearily through it, telling herself it was really, definitely, the last time.

'The cover!' Tony announced, a week or so later. 'Don't you love it? Isn't it perfect? So eye-catching on the shelves – it will *jump* out at readers!'

Was it perfect? Did it jump out at her? She liked it well enough, a line drawing of a woman leaning over a cradle – and of course the sight of her name beneath the title was wonderful – but it might not have been the cover she'd have chosen. She decided to trust Tony's judgement – and Dorothy's, who liked it too.

A photographer was summoned to Ellen's house, and she was photographed in the sunroom and in the garden, and seated at the little writing bureau. 'Just look natural,' the photographer said. 'Pretend I'm not here,' and she grimaced her way through the ordeal and cringed at the results, but Tony was pleased, or claimed he was. 'You look very lovely,' he pronounced, and she forgave him the months of torture in return for the lie.

In June he organised a launch in a Galway bookshop, timed for a week after the official publication date, and posted Ellen a bundle of invitations to distribute. She sent them to everyone she could think of, including Henri and Louis in France, and Iris in London – and after some deliberation, Leo. She didn't think the overseas invitees would come, but she thought they'd like to be asked.

They came. Everyone she invited turned up, and lots of people she didn't know appeared too, in response to the poster the book-shop had displayed in the window. 'People love a book launch,' Tony told her on the night, resplendent in a spotted dicky bow and three-piece suit.

He gave a short, hilarious speech, littered with pronouncements and dramatic gesturing, and Ellen gave an equally short and far more nervous speech – basically thanking everyone she could think of, particularly Tony, and her agent Dorothy, also in attendance.

Everyone gave her gifts. Champagne and chocolates from Tony, a framed print of the cover from Dorothy, a gold locket from Henri and Louis into which she put photos of the girls. Her father gave her a silver bookmark on which he'd had inscribed *To Ellen love Dad* and the publication date.

Leo, keeping a low profile, gave her an old hardback copy of *Great Expectations*, her favourite Dickens. From America Danny sent more peanut butter cups, and a little rubber duck holding an open book. *Wish I was there*, he wrote. *With you in spirit, as always xx.* She'd mailed him and Bobbi one of her advance copies, and everyone they knew in California had read it, and allegedly loved it.

A week after publication, *Mother and Daughter* went to number ten in the Irish bestseller list, prompting another bottle of champagne from Tony and a beautiful bouquet from Dorothy. The following week it had dropped to number twenty, never to climb again, but one week in the top ten was enough, more than enough. Ellen clipped the list from the newspaper and slipped it into the pocket in Ben's notebook.

I wrote my book, she told him in her head. *I did it. I kept my side of the pact.*

Waking up a couple of weeks later on the morning of her forty-first birthday, she made a mental list of things to be thankful for.

Two healthy daughters.

A mortgage-free house of their own, where she felt completely at home.

A book that had made the charts.

An agent and editor she liked and respected.

Financial security.

Equilibrium in her dealings with Leo.

Her father back in her life, and a new sister she'd grown to love.

Danny always there, removed geographically but in her corner at all times, and her truest friend.

Such a lot. So many blessings.

Funeral

ON A SATURDAY IN SEPTEMBER, IRIS AND ULTAN were married in a Dublin church, Juliet and Grace their brides-maids. Ellen watched her father walk his youngest daughter up the aisle, and saw how proud and happy he was, and felt a stab of quiet sorrow that she'd never had the chance to be the bride on his arm.

Iris' family on her mother's side were polite on being introduced, but largely kept their distance from Ellen and Joan. The exception was Iris' grandmother, who sought Ellen out to tell her she'd read and enjoyed *Mother and Daughter* – a gift from Iris – and expressed delight when Ellen told her she was writing a sequel.

'I loved all the twists and turns you put in along the way,' she said. 'Real life is full of them, isn't it? I remember the shock we got when Sarah told us she was pregnant.'

'Sarah?'

'Iris' mother,' the older woman said quietly. 'My daughter,' and in this way, Ellen learnt the name of her father's mistress.

'Of course. I'm so sorry. You must miss her terribly.'

'Yes, every day . . . but now Iris is such a blessing to us.'

'She's a sweetheart,' Ellen agreed. Twists and turns, indeed.

Joan told Ellen, over slices of lemon drizzle wedding cake – baked, as it turned out, by the same grandmother – that she and Seamus were thinking of having a fifth child. 'Are we mad?' she asked, jiggling two-year-old Gary on her hip, and Ellen said no.

They weren't mad, they were lucky. They'd found one another, she and Seamus, and they'd lasted.

In November, Danny's father suffered a heart attack and didn't survive it. Ellen's father rang to tell her he'd seen the death in the paper. 'I thought you'd want to know,' he said. 'He was only seventy-nine.'

She emailed Danny.

I've just heard about your dad. I'm so sorry. I'll see you at the funeral xxx

She remembered his father saying a few words at the wedding in California, welcoming Bobbi to the family. How long ago that seemed now, with so much having changed.

Danny was quiet and sad when they met. She hugged him and Bobbi, and she said hello to Cormac and Matthew, ten and six, who had their mother's eyes and their father's height, and who looked tired after flying all the way from California to the funeral of a grandfather they scarcely knew.

'I talked to him a few days before,' Danny told Ellen later. 'He was planning to replace the boiler. When Vincent rang to tell me he'd died, I thought he was joking. I can't believe he's gone.'

Vincent was his oldest brother. She didn't know what to say. It was after the mass, after the burial. They were sitting on the stairs of his family home, people milling about below. She took his hand

and they sat in silence, listening to the clatter of teacups and the disjointed conversations that floated up. Funerals really were sociable affairs in Ireland.

'I'd like to move home,' he continued after a while, 'but Bobbi wants to stay in the US.' Bobbi was downstairs, talking to her in-laws.

'You don't like living in Palo Alto any more?'

He shrugged. 'It's not Palo Alto. I feel I've been in America long enough. I miss Ireland – and I'd prefer the boys to grow up here. And now Mam's on her own, I'd like to be closer to her.'

'And you could carry on with your job?'

'I could work anywhere there's internet, and so could Bobbi, but if she wants to stay put . . .'

More silence fell. Their silences had always been easy.

'Your boys are lovely,' she said finally.

He smiled. 'They're the two best things in my life right now.'

No mention of his wife.

'Hey,' he said, 'we haven't even talked about your book. I was so delighted for you, and sorry I couldn't get to the launch. How's the new one going?'

'Halfway through, going OK I think. You should meet my editor.' She described Tony, just to cheer him up. She exaggerated the bow ties and the drama. 'He's very kind, and always there if I need him.'

He lifted an eyebrow. 'Married?'

She laughed. 'Very happily, for years: his wife came to my launch. And if that wasn't enough, he's closer in age to my father than he is to me.'

'That's a shame. And how are things between you and Leo?'

'They're OK. He stays with us now when he comes to see the girls.'

She'd offered the accommodation, feeling that she should, with two empty bedrooms in the house, and knowing the girls would love it. He slept in the room that had been Ellen's, and they shared the main bathroom, but had yet to bump into one another on the landing.

Two Saturdays a month he came, sometimes three, and he stayed just one night. In the mornings he made pancakes like he used to do on Sunday mornings in London, and she saw how good he still was with the girls, and was glad to see it.

He'd made no more mention of Juliet and Grace going to stay with him. He rang them often, every few days. The girls took it in turns to talk to him, and sometimes he and Ellen spoke briefly too. They'd moved on, both of them. She'd survived her second broken heart.

'And Claire?' Danny asked.

The name brought a dull twist of pain. 'Never spoken of. She still sends presents to Juliet on her birthday and at Christmas, and puts something small in for Grace too.' Never a note for Ellen. 'I'd prefer she didn't, but for Juliet's sake I say nothing.'

'I'd forgotten she was Juliet's godmother. Any romance for you in Galway?'

She shook her head. 'Not really looking, to be honest. I'm busy writing – and I still do the odd freelance job, for Creative Ways and a couple of Dublin agencies – and since I don't have Dad around here to help out with the girls, they take up the rest of my time.'

'That's a pity. That you have nobody, I mean.'

'Not really. I'm fine.'

Another little silence. Out of nowhere, the memory came to her of Danny telling her he had feelings for her, and wanting to act on them, and her turning him down in favour of Ben. Who knew how it might have gone between them?

Someone called him from downstairs then. She remained where she was for a while as people passed her on the way to and from the bathroom.

She thought they would have made it, like Joan and Seamus.

Joan

THREE DAYS INTO 2003, JOAN HAD A MISCARRIAGE. Ellen left the girls with her father, who'd been spending the Christmas holidays with them, and drove to Cork. Seamus answered the door, looking worn out.

'She won't let me do anything,' he told Ellen. 'I can't get her to rest. She keeps saying she wants to stay busy.'

Ellen gave him a hug. He looked like he needed one. 'Where are the children?'

'My sister in Limerick has taken them for a couple of days. Joan's in the kitchen.'

She was peeling potatoes in her dressing gown, eyes glittering and red-rimmed. 'There was no need for you to come,' she said, making it sound like an accusation. 'I'm fine. We're fine.'

'I wanted to come. I want to help. Give me a job, because I'm not going away' – and at that Joan dropped the potato peeler with a clatter and slumped into a chair and laid her head on her hands and wept hard, angry tears. Ellen sat next to her and drew slow circles on her sister's back and remembered her mother's spine, and how the jutting bones had cracked her heart.

When the tears were spent Ellen coaxed her upstairs and ran a bath. She added oil from a bottle she found on a shelf, and Joan sat in the scented water and cried some more while Ellen returned to the kitchen and got a dinner together. When her sister didn't reappear, Ellen brought a tray upstairs to find her asleep in bed, so she brought it down again and covered the plate with tinfoil.

'It might be a sign,' Seamus said, cutting into his chicken. 'She's getting older.'

'Forty isn't too old, not when she's already had four healthy babies. See how you both feel when she's a bit stronger.'

Ellen stayed the night in Trisha and Daphne's room, finding a stray red sock between the sheets, and under a pillow the copy of *Matilda* she'd sent Daphne for Christmas. In the morning she poached eggs for Seamus and Joan before driving back to Galway.

In May, Joan announced she was pregnant again. 'Due in November,' she said. Ellen crossed her fingers when she heard. Thankfully all went well, and on the last day in November, two weeks late, and following two days of labour, Philip joined the family.

'Never again,' Joan said.

Tony

THE FOLLOWING YEAR, FIFTEEN-YEAR-OLD JULIET
sat her Junior Cert exams, and Ellen's second book, *Promises to
Keep*, appeared on the shelves. It was reviewed in three newspapers
(two were favourable, one lukewarm) and made it to number nine
in the charts before slipping again.

One position higher than *Mother and Daughter*. She was going
in the right direction.

A few weeks after publication, Tony invited her to lunch. 'I'll
come to you,' he said. 'Choose your favourite Galway eatery and
book us in for Thursday, if that suits you.'

He travelled by train – 'I'm not fond of long car journeys on my
own' – and Ellen met him at the station and drove them to the
restaurant. She wondered if he was going to offer her a new publication deal, although she would have thought anything like that
would have to come through Dorothy.

Over slices of blue cheese quiche he told her of the arrival of
a first grandchild the week before that had served as great
comfort to him and his wife following the recent death of a
beloved dog, and he asked her about the new book she'd begun
writing.

And finally, over a shared portion of bread and butter pudding – 'my doctor would be apoplectic if he could see me!' – he told her the real reason he'd taken her out to lunch.

'It's so silly,' he said, dabbing his mouth with his napkin. 'I mean look at me, in my prime, a mere boy of seventy, and they're telling me I must stop driving, and give up work, and basically sit under an umbrella in the garden for the rest of my days.'

He appeared to be in perfect health, clear-eyed and rosy-cheeked and well able to eat. Today's bow tie was maroon, a matching handkerchief slotted into his jacket's top pocket.

'Are you sick?'

'Not in the least. They've just found some complicated heart thing – I can't even remember the name – that apparently makes any kind of stress out of the question, so Judy has hidden my car keys and is insisting I tender my resignation at work, because she doesn't fancy being a widow. My father dropped dead aged fifty-nine, and everyone's afraid I'll follow in his footsteps, even though I've outrun him already by eleven years.'

'I'm sorry to hear that,' Ellen said. By this point, she'd confided in him about Leo, and about her father's departure and subsequent reappearance. He'd become her friend as much as her editor. 'I hope you'll be OK.'

He smiled. It took years off him, so full of merry, twinkle-eyed joy. 'Oh, I intend to. I'm determined to prove them all wrong. Sorry we won't be a team any more, but I'll make sure my replacement treats you well.'

In the middle of September the Junior Cert results came out, and Ellen was relieved when Juliet's were satisfactory. Her older daughter had grown up artistic and dreamy, every bit as much a bookworm as Ellen, and with the same fondness for theatre. The two of them went regularly to plays, leaving Grace in the care of seventeen-year-old Angie from a few doors down.

'I don't need a babysitter,' Grace would complain every time – poor Angie – but Ellen thought eleven too young to be left alone. Grace continued to be the unpredictable one, the discontented and mulish one, given to sudden bursts of rage and slamming of doors. The brighter one too, flying through homework while Juliet sat with head bent for far longer.

On the evening of the exam results, Ellen and Juliet sat on the patio after Grace had gone to bed, Juliet having shown little interest in a special disco at the school. At fifteen she had yet to bring home a boyfriend, or even speak of one. The light was waning, but the air was heady with the last of Frances' roses that bloomed faithfully every year.

'Still thinking about art college?' Ellen asked.

Juliet nodded. 'Graphic design. I like the idea of illustration, maybe for children's books, or graphic novels. I'd love to study in Dublin, at the National College of Art and Design, if I could get in – and maybe I could stay with Granddad.'

She'd been thinking about it – and much as Ellen would hate to see her leaving home, moving in with her grandfather made a lot of sense. When Juliet left school in two years he would be eighty-one, and Ellen liked the idea of someone in the house with him at night. It would also give Juliet a secure place to stay.

'Let's find out about entry requirements, and we'll talk to Granddad nearer the time. Of course I'd miss you madly.'

Juliet smiled. 'I'd be back for all the holidays.'

'Well, I should hope so.'

They would grow up and leave her. They would begin lives without her, as she had done aged twenty. She remembered the heady excitement of boarding the Galway bus, the thrilling thought that at last she was free. Never once had she considered her mother, without a partner as Ellen was now. Never once had she wondered how she might be feeling at her elder daughter's departure, and now it would soon be Ellen's turn to be left behind.

She shook her gloomy thoughts away. Juliet would be back after college, and Grace was going nowhere, not for years – and when it eventually happened she would deal with it, and life would go on.

College

WHEN ELLEN FINISHED WRITING HER THIRD BOOK, Dorothy sent the manuscript to the publishers who'd brought out her first two, they being entitled, according to the terms of Ellen's contract, to first refusal of her next. A month later, an offer came back that Dorothy wasn't happy with. 'Leave it with me,' she told Ellen. 'I'll see what other interest is out there.'

Within a month she'd found a different publisher. 'Two more books,' she announced. 'More money for you, and they have better overseas connections too,' so Ellen signed along a new dotted line.

Her editor was Vanessa, glamorous and beautifully spoken, with a list of household-name authors and none of Tony's warmth. But within a short time of working with her Ellen could see that she was very, very good at what she did, editing with cool precision, steering tactfully, turning a rough first draft into a polished manuscript without seeming to have done very much at all.

In September, Grace started secondary school. Ellen was glad that three of her primary school friends were also enrolled there. 'You want me to go with you on the first day?' she asked, and Grace said, 'Most definitely not,' and went off with her friends.

Ellen thought of Claire in her teens, swiping things from shops, smuggling bottles of cider from the family pub, learning how to smoke – and while Ellen at that age had been thrilled to have such an adventurous friend, she hoped fervently that Grace would not meet someone similar. Her younger daughter, she suspected, would need little encouragement to let her wild side out. Ellen braced herself for teenage storms ahead.

She didn't have long to wait. At mid-term, Grace dropped an entirely unexpected bombshell.

'I want to go to London,' she said. 'I want to live with Dad.'

Tread carefully here, Ellen told herself. Stay calm. Stay reasoned. 'Grace, you're only twelve. You really can't expect me to let you move to another country.'

'I've lived in London – it's not exactly a foreign land. And my *father* still lives there.'

'He works full-time—'

'Mum, I'm able to look after myself. Anyway, I'd be at school when he was at work.'

Ellen caught at this. 'You're not enrolled in any school there.'

'I could find a school – or study at home. I don't need teachers.'

This was getting ridiculous. 'It's not going to happen, Grace,' Ellen said firmly. 'You're far too young.'

Grace adopted the mulish look Ellen knew so well. 'He wants me to live with him.'

'Has he said that?'

'No, but I know he'd like it.'

Ellen was too tired for a battle. She was in the middle of her latest edits, and at the familiar stage of beginning to hate the manuscript. She had a job from Creative Ways waiting to be tackled, and one of the kitchen taps had started leaking. 'Maybe in a few years we can talk about it again.'

Grace glowered at her. 'I'm going to ask my dad. I'm ringing him now.'

'Do.' Ellen knew he'd back her up, and maybe Grace would listen to him – but after a brief conversation in the hall Grace returned to the kitchen and said, 'He wants to talk to you.'

'Maybe we could do a deal with her,' Leo said.

'What do you mean?'

'She could come to me for a week at Christmas. That might keep her happy for the moment.'

'Leo, she's twelve. What would you do with her? She has no friends there any more; you'd have her all the time.'

'Exactly. In a week she'd be delighted to go home again, and get away from her boring dad.'

He might have a point. 'What about—?' She broke off, unable to say the name. 'Are you still—?'

'No,' he said quickly. 'I live alone.'

So they hadn't lasted. At least she wouldn't have to contend with that. 'Have you said it to Grace about Christmas?'

'Not until I ran it by you.' An edge of impatience to his words. 'Credit me with a little more sense, Ellen.'

'Sorry. Juliet might want to go too – how would you feel about that?'

'Fine. I'd be happy to have both.'

He was due time with them on his own. He'd been good about coming to Ireland to see them for so long, and he hadn't pushed about them coming to him. She agreed to his plan, and three days before Christmas she put Grace on a plane to London, her heart in her mouth. Juliet had opted to stay at home, much to her mother's private relief.

'See you in a week,' Ellen said to Grace, resisting the impulse to hug her tightly, contenting herself with a ruffle of the hair. Grace didn't do hugs – or at least she didn't hug her mother. 'Be good for your dad.'

Contrary to Leo's prediction, Grace wasn't happy to come home. One look at her scowling face as she walked into the arrivals hall at Shannon a week later told Ellen that she was far from happy.

'Frankie missed you,' Ellen said, and all she got was a shrug. 'Grace, you can go again. As long as your dad agrees, I'm happy for you to spend part of your holidays with him. And when you finish school, if you still want to, and if he's is OK with it, we can talk about you moving there.'

'That's *years* away – and anyway I'll be able to do what I like after school.'

Ellen let that go. 'I'm sorry, love.'

'I *hate* Ireland!' Grace declared. 'London is much cooler!'

Ellen recalled her own determination to leave the city after finding out about Leo and Claire. She remembered how endless the weeks had seemed till the girls got holidays from school and they could pack up. All she could think about was going home – but had she been wrong to uproot his daughters so thoroughly, to force them to live in a different country to him?

They could have found a little house to rent in Bath, or somewhere equally lovely. The girls could have had far more contact with him, even if it had meant them finding out about Claire, and Grace mightn't have harboured such resentment towards her mother – but what was done was done.

To Juliet's great delight, on leaving school she was offered a place in the National College of Art and Design. Ellen drove her to Dublin in September, conflicted. Proud to have a daughter going to college, sad to be losing her.

'No Grace?' her father enquired when they got there.

'She's staying the night with a friend. She says hello.'

In the morning she hugged Juliet goodbye, her daughter having opted to travel to college by bus, refusing her grandfather's offer of a lift. 'Start as I mean to go on,' she said, tweaking the cherry-red beret Leo had bought her on his last visit to Galway. 'It's a straight run into town.'

She was so pretty, Ellen thought, with her creamy skin and Leo's dark eyes. The boys would find her gentle femininity irresistible; they'd flock around her. By Christmas she'd have found someone, hopefully someone decent like Danny or Ben, even if he was also destined to be a penniless artist. It was time for her first real love – and possibly her first heartbreak. Ellen hated the thought of that, but protecting her daughter from it was beyond a parent's power.

At the start of October, a letter arrived with Creative Ways' logo on the envelope. This was surprising. Lucinda always communicated through email, not letters.

You are invited, Ellen read on the card she pulled out, *to our celebration of twenty years in London.*

Twenty years? Twenty years since she'd walked through the doors of Creative Ways as a new employee? Impossible. Unbelievable.

Twenty years, two decades. She sat on the bottom stair, spooling back over all they'd brought. Getting together with Leo, having Juliet and Grace, her mother dying, her father returning. Finding Iris, losing Leo, and Claire.

The event was taking place on a Friday evening at the end of November. She could stay with Leo – he'd stayed with them often enough. She could bring Grace, who'd love the chance for an extra weekend with her father.

She cast her mind back to the house in Lambeth where she and the girls had been so happy, and where he still lived. She didn't know, because she hadn't asked, if Claire had lived there with him after Ellen and the girls had vacated it. One part of her longed to see it again, to walk through its rooms and remember the times they'd enjoyed – but could she bear it, given the circumstances of their leaving? And was she ready to return to London?

She'd been to the company's ten-year anniversary party. She'd been working there at the time, having reunited with Leo after their first split. He'd accompanied her to the party, and it had been a great night – but this time she'd be going alone, and meeting her old colleagues who no doubt would be full of questions, and while she was proud of the books she'd brought into being, and happy to be where she was now – well, half happy, half lonely – she wasn't sure she wanted to be back in that world, even for one night.

She wrote an email:

Lucinda,

I've just got your invitation, and I'm so touched to be invited. I have nothing but happy memories of working at Creative Ways; it was wonderful to have been there at the start, and to be part of that exciting time. I'm not at all surprised that you've made it to twenty years, and I have no doubt there'll be many more – but I'm going to pass, if you don't mind. I'm not sure I want to be in London again, not yet . . . maybe I'll make your thirtieth! I hope you understand.

And one came back, almost immediately:

Dearest Ellen,

Justin and I will miss you on the night, and so will everyone, but I understand completely. Did I tell you how much I loved Promises to Keep? *So looking forward to the next.*

There's a new job coming in shortly that you'll be perfect for, if you have the time. I still haven't quite forgiven you for spoiling me for any other work partner – you and I were made to create great ads together!

L xx

Eugene

'I'D LIKE TO BRING A FRIEND FOR CHRISTMAS,' JULIET said on the phone. 'Her parents live in Spain, but she'd prefer to stay in Ireland. Would that be OK?'

'Of course it would. Grace is going to London again, so you can take her room. You'll have the twin beds and the ensuite.'

'That would be great, thanks, Mum. We'll travel with Granddad.'

Rosie was as fair as Juliet was dark, hair cut to frame her small face, eyes blue as cornflowers, a lilting Cork accent in her speech. She brought Ellen a poinsettia, and a delicate angel bauble for the Christmas tree that she'd made as part of her ceramics course.

She gravitated towards Frankie, grown fat and content on Ellen's leftovers. She placed her on her lap and the cat made no objection, although Grace's was usually the only lap she'd tolerate.

'Mum's Spanish,' she told Ellen over dinner. 'They spend winters there: she hates the cold.'

'And you weren't tempted to get a burst of December sun?'

'Not really – I like Christmas in Ireland.'

Two days after Christmas, Juliet asked Ellen to go for a walk. 'Just the two of us,' she said. 'Rosie wants to watch *Willy Wonka*.' And arm-in-arm with her mother, the two of them swaddled in hats and scarves, she told Ellen that she liked girls. That she liked Rosie in particular.

Ellen was astonished. She'd had no inkling, none at all. Had there been clues she hadn't picked up on? Juliet hadn't had boyfriends, but neither had she herself at that age.

'You think you're gay?'

'I know I am.'

'You're young,' Ellen said. 'At your age I hadn't a—'

'Mum,' Juliet interrupted gently. 'I've known for years, and so has Rosie. You might think we're too young, but could we just see where it goes? Would you be OK with that?'

'Whatever makes you happy, sweetheart. That's all I ever wanted, for you and Grace to be happy.'

Juliet squeezed her mother's arm. 'Rosie makes me happy.'

'And have you told your father how you feel?'

'Not yet.' She looked at Ellen. 'Would you tell him, Mum?'

' . . . I will.'

She wondered how that conversation would go. It wasn't something she and Leo had ever discussed – she supposed they'd always assumed their kids would be the same as them.

To Ellen, love was love, whatever form it took – but she couldn't say she wasn't worried. What about other people? What about those who couldn't countenance the thought of a same-sex relationship? What if Juliet and Rosie suffered as a result?

Again, it was something she couldn't protect her daughter from, much as she would want to. She would have to accept the path Juliet was on, or was trying out, or whatever, and hope for the best.

Leo took the news equably. 'Let's wait and see,' he said. 'She's young. She might be experimenting.'

'Maybe so.' But she'd seen the way Juliet and Rosie were together, and she was glad her daughter had love in her life, even if it wasn't the love her mother had anticipated for her.

And what about her own situation?

She enjoyed living in Galway, with its strong arts culture and vibrant community spirit, but while she knew a good share of people here – neighbours, parents of the girls' friends, librarians and others she encountered routinely – she couldn't say she was close to anyone, male or female, and romance had been a stranger since her return to Ireland. Next July she'd turn forty-five: was that it? Was that side of her life over? The thought was disheartening.

Two weeks later, the doorbell rang. It was mid-morning and she was alone in the house, Juliet, Rosie and her father having returned to Dublin, and Grace at school. Ellen opened the door to a man she'd never met.

'Eugene?'

'That's right.'

'Thank you for coming.'

He was scruffy, his jeans bagging and stained, his shirt collar fraying. He could do with a shave and a haircut, and with reducing the gut that strained his shirt buttons. She'd got his name from a noticeboard in the supermarket. *Plumbing services, no job too small.*

The open neck of his shirt revealed curling hairs. There was a scatter of grey in the dark hair on his head. His eyes were between green and brown. He smelt of the cream she'd rubbed on an aching shoulder last year. His bootlaces were undone. He was her age, or close to it. If he were a character in a film, or in one of her books, he'd be the bit of rough with a heart of gold who died tragically towards the end.

He shut off the water under the sink and took apart the dripping kitchen tap. 'The seal is gone,' he pronounced. 'I have one in the van.'

Afterwards he cleaned his hands with washing-up liquid while she made tea. He stirred in three heaped spoons of sugar and told her of a married son in Canada and an unmarried daughter in Dublin. He didn't mention a partner, but she got the sense he was alone. My son, he said, not our son.

She put Ginger Nut biscuits on a plate. She told him she wrote books. He said the only thing he read was the racing section in the paper. 'I should be ashamed of myself,' he said, clearly not.

She enjoyed him. 'Do you win?'

'Fifty-fifty. I don't go mad, but I get a kick out of the flutter. So,' he said, helping himself to more from the teapot, 'what's your guilty secret?'

She thought. 'I have an occasional glass of wine in the evenings.'

He guffawed, dunking a biscuit into his tea. 'Come on, you can do better than that.' He put the entire biscuit into his mouth.

She couldn't – could she? She thought harder. 'Sometimes I stay in my pyjamas all day,' she said. 'Would that be classed as a guilty secret?'

'Only,' he said, taking another biscuit, 'if there's someone with you.' Holding her gaze, dipping another biscuit blind into his mug, moving it up and down slowly in the hot liquid. The hint of a smile on his face.

Good God. Was he flirting? She laughed. 'You're an awful man,' she said.

'Ah no,' he said. 'I'm a good man. I'm a very good man.'

There was a new feeling in the room, a tension that wasn't unpleasant. She felt an inner tingling, a stirring of something long dormant. 'Are you married?' she asked.

'Nope. She got sense and left me years ago. I'm footloose and fancy-free.' He looked at his watch. 'And I have a bit of time before I need to be at my next job.'

He didn't ask if she was married. He didn't care. She left the kitchen and he followed her upstairs, and in her room he unbuttoned and unzipped her, the feel of his rough hands on her bare skin making her tremble with desire.

There were no niceties, no kisses, no soft touches. He teased her, bringing her to the edge and drawing back, making her wait, making the end, when it came, intense enough for her to cry out.

Afterwards he pulled up the jeans he hadn't waited to take off fully. 'Well,' he said, 'that was unexpected.' Pushing feet back into the boots he'd kicked off. 'Must be my lucky day.'

Downstairs she felt the after-throb of her orgasm. 'Twenty euro,' he said, and she wanted to pay more, just a call-out charge would be more than that, but didn't say it in case he laughed at her.

After he left she showered, filled with growing disbelief. How could she have let it happen? Was he in the habit of targeting lonely women? Was she just another one?

They hadn't used contraception. She could be pregnant. The thought was shocking until she calculated, and realised it was a safe time of the month. Then she thought about sexually transmitted diseases, and put *condoms* on her shopping list, just in case.

Condoms, in case a man she'd only just met, but had already had sex with, showed up again. What on earth was happening to her?

Two weeks later he phoned. 'How's that tap behaving itself?'

The sound of his voice, the easygoing way he said the words, made desire rise shockingly in her, and sent caution flying out the window.

'You might need to have another look.'

'I'll be there in ten minutes.'

She brushed her teeth and changed into her prettiest underwear, and a dress that didn't need much undoing. She let him in. He wasn't impressed with the condom, but he went along with it. They did it on the landing, the carpet chafing her buttocks, her dress bunched above her breasts. He ripped a seam of her knickers pulling them off.

Every so often he rang. From the random nature of the calls, she figured it was probably when he was already on a job in the area. If she gave him the go-ahead he called around. He parked his van on the next road, so the neighbours wouldn't guess what she and the plumber were up to.

She bought the kind of underwear that made her feel sexy: bits of lace, stuff he could see through. It was always intense with him, always animal in nature. He wasn't tender or affectionate. She didn't want him to be.

They were hurting nobody. It pushed the loneliness away for a while. It made her feel alive.

Grace

HER THIRD BOOK, *HIS AND HERS*, WAS PUBLISHED the year she turned forty-six. Two weeks later it went to number two in the bestseller list, and stayed in the top five for ten weeks.

Dorothy sent flowers and a case of French wine.

Vanessa sent a voucher for a spa day for two.

Publishers from Germany, Italy and Croatia expressed interest. 'All reputable,' Dorothy said. 'The advances are small, but it's a foot in the door. I'd advise you to accept,' so Ellen signed three new contracts.

She was asked to do radio interviews. *His and Hers* received glowing reviews in several publications. Danny created a website for her.

'You need to join Facebook,' he said on the phone. He'd taken to calling her from work now and again.

'Never heard of it.'

'It's a social networking service, aimed at connecting people. It started a few years ago in Harvard, and now it's worldwide. It would be great for spreading the word about the books.'

'Danny, you know what I'm like with technology.'

'Ellen, you're living in the second millennium.'

'But my heart is in the first,' and he gave up, and promised to spread the word through his own Facebook account.

Grace, almost fifteen, flew alone to London the day after school closed for the summer. 'Feed Frankie,' she ordered her mother, and Ellen resisted the temptation to point out that she was usually the one who fed her, whether Grace was there or not. Leo took two weeks off work and he and his younger daughter went to France and stayed with Henri and his wife, Sabine, who were living in the old family home in Nantes with their infant daughter, Esme.

Grace rang Ellen every few days, probably at her father's insistence, and spoke excitedly about a swim in the local pool or a hike in the hills, and Ellen rejoiced at how happy she sounded, and wondered how on earth she'd settle back in Galway.

'Mum,' she said when she reappeared, 'you know how I said I wanted to go to live with Dad in London?'

'Yes.' Here it came, the next round of the battle.

'Well, I've decided I'd rather live in France.'

'What?'

'Hang *on*, Mum. I've said it to Henri and Sabine, and they say I could live with them, and go to school in Nantes. I could help Sabine look after Esme too.'

'Grace, sweetheart, you're still—'

'I know I'm too young now, I *know* that. Just *listen*. I'd stay here and do my Junior Cert, and then I'd go and do the last two years of school in France. Mum, I could, Henri says he could get me into a school. I'd *really* love it. I'd be as good as gold, I'd study really hard, honestly.'

Ellen looked at her pleading face.

'Please, Mum. Just think about it, at least.'

'Does your father know you want this?'

'Yes, and he's OK with it.'

She rang Leo. 'You told her you're OK with it?'

'Ellen, Grace is a good kid. She's bright, she's got a mind of her own.'

'You can say that again.'

'I know you and she can spark off one another—'

'She said that?'

'She didn't have to. I can see it myself when I'm there. Listen, it's not a problem. You want what's best for her, I get that, and so do I. But she has a strong will and she knows what she wants, and she's not afraid to go for it. You have to admire her for that.'

'She's still a child, Leo. Even if we wait a year, she'll only be sixteen.'

'A switched-on sixteen who won't take any crap. And she'd have Henri and Sabine looking out for her. She got on great with them – she was like a little mother to Esme – they'd love to have her, she could teach Esme English. And I could pop over every other weekend, make sure all was well.'

'She'd have to come home, every holiday.'

'Of course she would.'

So she agreed, with so many reservations, to think about it. Grace was her baby: the idea of her living in another country, without either of her parents around, was terrifying. Then again, Henri was pretty much family, and dependable – and so, hopefully, was his wife.

In the meantime, Juliet and Rosie packed rucksacks and went travelling around Europe for the summer, ending up on a Greek island for their last week and coming home tanned and too thin.

They stayed with Ellen for the month before college reopened, and she fed them until they filled out again.

In October, her phone pinged with a text. *Is the coast clear?* Eugene asked. She hadn't seen him since Grace had come back from France. She looked at his name and conjured up his face and waited to feel something, and felt nothing.

She'd outgrown him. He'd been a wild antidote to her solitary state. She deleted his text, and he got the message and didn't contact her again.

She joined a book club that met in the library. She made new friends, had coffee with one or other of them during the week, went back to the theatre, which she'd neglected since Juliet's departure. Life resumed its even keel.

Success

A WEEK BEFORE THE PUBLICATION OF HER FOURTH book, Dorothy told her the publishers had made an offer for two more. New translation offers came from Austria and Sweden and Norway.

In August, after sitting her Junior Cert, Grace packed up for France. Following some municipal to-ing and fro-ing on Leo and Henri's parts, and a pedagogical assessment that Grace had afterwards pronounced to be dead easy, she'd been accepted into the same *lycée* that Henri and Louis had attended, located in the centre of Nantes.

Ellen and Grace flew to France the day before the new school year began, and Henri met them at the airport. Although Ellen hadn't seen him since her first book launch, they were in regular written and phone contact, so he didn't feel unfamiliar. He was still the same lovely Henri, welcoming Ellen warmly, telling Grace that Esme was waiting for her at home.

Ellen stayed one night with them. They'd transformed Marguerite's house, overhauling the central heating, laying thick rugs on the old floors and adding heavy lined curtains to the windows, in addition to the shutters that they'd retained. The sweeping view that Ellen loved was the same: she stood at her bedroom window and remembered Marguerite, and the thorny road they'd trod together.

In the morning Henri drove them to the school, which was small and made of red brick, with big wooden doors through which teenagers were streaming. Ellen got out of the car and made to walk in with Grace, but her daughter said, 'I can do this on my own, Mum,' so Ellen contented herself with a quick hug and stood, eyes brimming, as her strong, brave, obstinate, beloved daughter walked away from her.

Look back, she begged silently. *Look back before you go in* – and reaching the top of the steps, Grace turned and gave her mother a cheerful wave, and Ellen forced a smile and waved back. And Henri, standing beside her, put an arm around her shoulder and squeezed. 'We will look after her,' he promised, and she thought *You'd better.*

Grace's letters – her first letters to Ellen – were full of news and full of joy. By Halloween she'd found a boyfriend called Luc – no qualms about telling her mother – who was in her class, and who called her *tigresse* – 'which means tigress in English, in case you don't know!'

Tigress. Dear God. Ellen rang Leo. 'Did you know she has a boyfriend?'

'I did. I met him last time I was there.'

'Thanks for telling me.'

'Don't worry: I told him he'd better not sully my daughter's virtue, or I'd be forced to shoot him.'

'Leo.'

'Ellen, this is why I didn't tell you. He's fine, very mannerly, and she's happy. They're sensible – and Henri is keeping an eye out.

He says she's flying it at school. You really don't need to worry about her.'

Grace came home for Christmas, her hair cut into a bob, her fringe short and blunt. She wore eyeliner, and she'd ditched her beloved Diesel jeans in favour of a tartan miniskirt. 'Two euro in a charity shop,' she told Ellen. She looked like a young woman, not the child Ellen had accompanied to France just four months earlier.

She spoke in rapid French on the phone with Luc. She washed up after meals without being asked, and took Ellen's shopping list to the supermarket, and readily agreed to surrender her bedroom to Juliet and Rosie, arriving on Christmas Eve. Ellen wondered if Grace had been kidnapped and a changeling sent back to Ireland in her place.

'Do you want me to tell Grace about you and Rosie?' she asked Juliet when they arrived, and Juliet said Grace already knew, and Ellen realised that her daughters were no longer the children she still fancied them to be, and it saddened her that the day would come when they no longer needed her.

Her father joined them for Christmas, as he did for all their Christmases in Galway. At eighty-four he was tired. Ellen could see more small deteriorations, more little signs of ageing, every time they met. She was glad Juliet hadn't moved into student accommodation in second year, glad that she'd opted to remain in the house with him so he'd have someone at night. Rosie stayed with them most weekend nights, which seemed to work too.

'Would you consider coming to live here with me?' Ellen asked him one evening. They were alone, the three young people having gone to the cinema. 'I need company, with the girls moved out.'

'What about Juliet? I couldn't leave her on her own in Dublin.'

'Of course you could: she's very responsible. And she could always ask Rosie to move in, if you were OK with that.'

'I'd be fine with that, but you don't want me here. I'd only slow you down.'

'How would you slow me down? I'd still write during the day, and you could do whatever you wanted, and I'd feel safer with someone else in the house at night. Think about it.'

'I will,' he promised – but nothing happened until the following summer, when Juliet was in Spain with Rosie and her parents, and he fell in his back garden and lay there for almost a full day, unable to get himself up, before a neighbour spotted him from her window. Miraculously he'd broken nothing, but he was cut and bruised and shaken, and kept in hospital overnight for observation and tests.

A few days later Ellen drove him and his luggage from Dublin to Galway. Juliet and Rosie remained in his house, continuing to live there after graduation, with Juliet picking up the occasional illustration job, and painting murals on shop windows and children's bedroom walls, and Rosie working in an artist's co-operative. They'd never have afforded rent in Dublin, scarcely one salary coming in between the two of them, so the house was a blessing.

Iris, Ultan and their twin girls were frequent visitors to Ireland, dividing their time between Dublin and Galway. Ellen loved seeing the little girls toddling around the garden with their grandfather, the three of them moving slowly among the shrubs and flowers that Ellen loved to tend whenever she got the chance and the weather obliged.

Grace thrived in France, during which time Luc was replaced by Jacques. At eighteen she graduated with exam results that were more than good enough for her to study veterinary medicine, which she'd decided was the career for her.

'I'd like to go to college in London,' she told Ellen. 'I could live with Dad and save on accommodation.'

'As long as he's happy to have you,' Ellen replied, already knowing Leo wouldn't object. He and Grace had always been close, their bond weathering their separations.

She wondered if Leo had met anyone after Claire. If he had, he was being discreet about it. She hadn't seen him since both girls had moved out of home, but every so often he phoned her or she phoned him, just to keep in touch, and it was pleasant to hear his voice.

She'd always loved his voice.

She continued to write, one novel following another, the only interruption the occasional job coming in from Lucinda, Ellen having tapered off the rest of her freelance work. As long as Creative Ways needed her, she would make time for them. Every day after breakfast she would switch on her laptop and spend the morning putting words onto the screen while her father went for a gentle walk around the block or read the newspaper in the sunroom, or just sat and dreamed, the way old people did.

In the afternoons she'd meet friends or go shopping or potter in the garden, or curl up with a book until it was time to prepare dinner. Occasionally she was invited out on a date, and sometimes she accepted, and other times she found excuses.

In 2011 she turned fifty. Both girls came to Galway for the occasion, and she took them and her father out to an early bird dinner in a newly opened French restaurant, just so Grace could show off her fluency with the waiters.

Later that evening Joan phoned her to wish her a happy birthday. The sisters didn't see a lot of each other, Joan busy with work and children, Ellen with her writing commitments, but they kept in touch by phone.

'How's everything?' Joan asked. 'How's everyone?' And Ellen filled her in, and then heard about Seamus' promotion to area manager – 'finally!' – and twenty-four-year-old Ivan's romance with a work colleague that looked like it might last.

'Any love life yourself?' Joan asked, and Ellen told her that she hadn't time for a love life, and didn't add that she continued to miss it. Maybe she'd already had her quota of men she might have grown old with; maybe Ben, Danny and Leo had been her three possibilities.

Happy 50th, Danny's card said. *Happy to report I'm still 49*. He enclosed a fifty dollar bill – *a dollar for every year* – and for his fiftieth a week later she sent him a dozen lottery scratchcards, and he returned one that had a €5 win. *Buy yourself a new hat*, he told her, and she put a colander on her head and emailed him a photo. *A steal at €4.99*, she wrote.

Two years later, twenty-five-year-old Juliet was commissioned to illustrate a new children's book series, which took months of work but which paid handsomely. 'I feel rich,' she told Ellen. 'I'm going to splash out on a new hairdryer,' and Ellen thought how little it took to make her happy.

For Grace's twenty-first in August of the same year she asked Ellen to come to London. For the first time she hadn't come home for the summer holidays, and Ellen knew why.

'It's time you met Tom,' Grace said. The Tom she'd started seeing shortly before the previous Christmas, the Tom who had littered her communications to her mother ever since. Ellen knew he must be important. 'Dad says he'll take us all out to dinner. Juliet and Rosie are coming, and Iris and Ultan – and how about Granddad?'

'I don't think he'd be able for the flight, love, but I'll say it to him.'

'You go,' her father said. 'I'll be fine here.'

Eighty-nine now, and soldiering on. Getting himself out of bed in the mornings, dressing in the soft tracksuit bottoms Ellen had got for him, his arthritic fingers no longer able for zips or buttons. Negotiating carefully the stairs he insisted he was still able for.

Ellen called to the house next door. 'I'll be away on Friday night,' she said to Kay, a widow in her sixties, an empty-nester like Ellen. 'I'll leave a cold dinner for him, but could you think of an excuse to call around on Saturday morning?'

'I could, of course,' Kay promised. 'And I might just find myself in possession of a hot apple tart on Friday night to share.'

'Thanks Kay.'

They'd had keys to one another's houses since the time Ellen had locked herself out and borrowed Kay's extendable ladder to get in through her open bedroom window.

Leo looked good, and younger than his sixty-two years. Navy suit, white shirt, hair cut tight to his head, the dark sprinkled now with grey, a neatly trimmed beard a new addition. 'A bit too busy,' he said, when Ellen asked how work was going. 'Looking at retirement next year.'

'And then what?'

He gave her the smile that in the old days would have made her want to touch him. 'Thinking about France.'

'Moving there?'

'Maybe.' He nodded in the direction of Tom. 'Looks like our baby has made her choice.'

Ellen regarded the fair young man seated next to Grace. 'Early days,' she said. 'At her age, I didn't know who I wanted.' Or rather she had, but he'd gone off to see the world and left her behind.

'At forty-five, I didn't know who I wanted,' Leo said, too low for anyone else to hear.

She looked at him. They were seated together at the end of the table. Forty-five. The age he'd been when he'd told her about the affair with Claire. The age he'd been when she'd left him for the second and final time.

'I thought I did, but I was wrong,' he went on. 'I had what I wanted, but I couldn't see it. I was a fool.'

She couldn't argue with that. It should have made her happy to hear it, but it didn't. 'History,' she said. 'Water under the bridge' – and back came the waiter with dessert menus, and the topic was dropped.

What might have been, she thought. The saddest phrase in the world. She would have been happy with him. They could have grown old together.

Bakery

ELLEN DROVE SLOWLY, LOOKING FOR A PARKING space. In the twenty years since she'd spent her last night in the family home with Joan, there had been a lot of changes in the town. Unfamiliar shopfronts, new pedestrianised streets, a roundabout she didn't remember, a one-way system that had almost caused her to drive towards oncoming cars.

But the shop she was heading for, Flannery's Bakery, was still there. She'd been delighted to find it in the phone book when the idea had occurred to her. Still family run, the man on the other end of the phone had told her, the next generation in charge now.

'A coffee cake,' she'd said, 'for a ninetieth birthday,' and she'd given him the message to write on top.

Her father's favourite cake. It had come back to her out of the blue, when she'd been wondering what to do for his ninetieth. Every birthday without fail, her mother had got him a cake from Flannery's, always coffee – and now Ellen was back to do the same.

The bakery might be still there, but it had changed too. It was bigger, having expanded into the premises next door – a sports shop before, she thought – and a seating area had been introduced. Half a dozen little wrought-iron tables and chairs, people sitting and chatting.

Ellen gave her name, and the young man behind the counter produced the cake. *Happy 90th birthday Dad*, she'd put, even though his granddaughter Juliet was coming for the party too. No matter – the cake was from Ellen, and he was her dad.

She paid and turned to go, stepping aside to allow a woman in a pink coat to enter the shop. The woman thanked her and came in – and then stopped.

'Ellen?'

Ellen looked at her, and felt a shock of recognition. For a second she couldn't move, the cake box between them.

'It's Ellen, isn't it?' Claire asked, but she knew it was Ellen. They would always know one another.

She hadn't aged well. Her face was lean and hollowed out, the skin puckered and leathery from too much sun. Her hair, which Ellen had always envied, was bleached and dry, its gloss gone. Her spark, her bloom was missing.

'Long time no see,' she said, a tentative smile on her face as she moved aside to allow someone else into the shop. 'How are you?'

'Fine.' Ellen's mouth was stiff. Of all people to bump into.

'Would you let me buy you a coffee?' Claire asked, gesturing towards an empty table.

'No, thank you.' Ellen made to pass her, and Claire put a hand on her arm.

'Ellen, please, don't be like this.'

She bit off a sharp retort. The anger was still there after all this time, just waiting to rear up. 'I need to go.'

'Let me walk with you then, just for a little while.'

She made no response to this. Claire held the door open and followed her out. They moved along the path, Ellen staring straight ahead.

'You're not back living here?' Claire asked.

'No.'

'How's your aunt?'

'She died.'

'Oh . . . sorry.' Claire pulled a pack of cigarettes from her pocket, reaching in again for a lighter. 'I hear you've had books published. Well done.' She gave a little laugh that had a chesty rattle in it. 'You were always the smart one.'

She wouldn't have read them. She'd never been a reader.

'The girls are well?'

'They are.'

The cards to Juliet had petered out eventually, and Ellen had been relieved. Maybe, she thought now, that decision had been made when her affair with Leo had ended. No more obligations to his daughters.

They got to the car. Ellen opened the passenger door and sat the cake box on the seat. She turned to face Claire.

'You and Leo didn't last,' she said. Calmly, not in anger.

Claire exhaled smoke with another rattling laugh. 'We didn't. Good enough for me.'

At forty-five, I didn't know who I wanted.

Ellen studied her. 'Was it you?' she asked. 'Did you make the first move?'

For a second, Claire made no reply, holding eye contact. 'It was mutual,' she said then. There was lipstick on one of her front teeth.

'I was the forbidden fruit, and he was . . . well, he was forbidden too, I suppose.'

No sorry. No trace of apology in her voice. There was something wrong with her, Ellen thought. It was more than just self-centredness; it was a coldness, a lack of sensitivity. She truly seemed to have no regrets.

'You told me he wasn't your type,' Ellen persisted. 'You said you liked them more rough and ready, but that he was perfect for me.'

Claire nodded. 'And I meant it at the time. But . . .' She trailed off, one shoulder lifting, and again Ellen saw that it meant nothing that she'd done the damage she'd done.

'You told me once you'd met a man you could see yourself settling down with, but he was taken. Did you mean Leo?'

'Yes. I fancied him for years before anything happened.'

Ellen thought about that. She thought about the kind of person who'd get a kick out of telling a friend, however cryptically, that she wanted the man the friend loved. She remembered Claire laughing, right after she'd said it. *Your face*, she'd said. *I'm joking*, she'd said.

'Are you still in London?'

'Not for a long time. I sold the deli. I live in Spain now.'

'Alone?'

She shook her head. Of course she wasn't alone. 'With Simon. He's English, good-looking. We own a bar in Malaga – well, I do.'

'Are you married?'

'No.' She lifted an arm to rake fingers through her hair, and her coat sleeve rode up to expose a series of small dark bruises on her wrist. The kind of bruises, Ellen thought, a gripping hand might leave behind.

Claire drew hard on her cigarette before flicking what was left of it onto the path. 'His mother can't stand me,' she said, expelling smoke with the words, grinding the butt into the cement. 'Cow.'

Ellen was aware of a creeping sense of pity. She'd had her chance with Leo, and she'd failed to hang on to him. Her looks were gone, and it seemed like her Englishman might be abusing her. Her life hadn't turned out well.

'I have to go,' Ellen said, moving around to the driver's side.

Claire regarded her over the car. 'Are you happy?' she asked – and for a moment, Ellen thought she saw the old Claire, or the Claire she thought she'd known. The daredevil, the ally, the friend she'd have done anything for.

And then the moment passed.

'That's none of your business,' she said, and got in, and drove away without a backward glance. Four miles out of the town she pulled into a lay-by and cried, hardly knowing what the tears were for.

Danny

IN LATE SPRING OF THE FOLLOWING YEAR, DANNY emailed to say he was coming home for a while. *I'll explain when I see you*, he wrote. *I'll take a trip to Galway. Tell me when you can take a break.*

He didn't say he was coming alone, but it sounded like he was. She told him he'd be welcome any time he liked. *I'm already on a break, just handed over my first draft. If you want a bed for the night, I have it.*

'Mam hasn't long,' Danny told her when he came. His mother had been diagnosed with cancer a year earlier, and deemed not strong enough to withstand the severe treatment it would require. She lived now with one of Danny's sisters. 'I'm going to stay until her time is up.'

'I'm so sorry.'

They sat in the sunroom. It was May, the air soft and kind, the garden coming into bloom again. Ellen's father was lying down.

Danny had lost a little weight. Small pouches of skin sat beneath his eyes; hair slowly receded from his temples. She remembered the surprise of his long hair when they'd met again in Galway, the sideburns that were almost a uniform among young men then. He was still in the jeans they'd all lived in, except now they were narrower in the leg.

'So tell me,' she said, refilling their mugs with the Californian coffee he'd brought, 'how are the boys doing? How's Cormac getting on in college?' At twenty-two, his elder son was following in his footsteps, halfway through his computer science degree.

'He's doing fine – but Matthew has just announced he wants to take a gap year with his girlfriend, much to his mother's disapproval.' Matthew was about to graduate high school.

'Oh dear.' Ellen told him about her reservations when Grace had gone to live in France. 'It worked out fine,' she said. 'I worried over nothing. And travel broadens the mind.' A brief flash of Ben then, giving the news that had broken her heart.

Danny sat back, cradling his mug. Ellen heard the soft call of a robin somewhere nearby, the only birdsong she was sure of, despite Frances' patient attempts to teach her to identify others.

'We're kind of on a break,' Danny said then. 'Myself and Bobbi. No big bust-up, just . . . we're gone a bit stale, I suppose. When Christine rang to tell me about Mam, it seemed like Fate was giving us an opportunity, a bit of time out for both of us.'

'I'm sorry.'

'It's fine. It might be all we need. Tell me about this Christmas book you're writing.'

He stayed a night in Frances' old room, Ellen having finally commandeered the ensuite when Grace had gone to live in London. Over the weeks that followed he returned every so often, always staying over. One day he and Ellen paid a visit to the UCG campus, almost unrecognisable from his days there.

'The student bar,' she said. 'Cheap drink every Wednesday night for us.'

'Happy days,' he said.

'I'll stay another while,' he told Ellen after the inevitable funeral in October, after Bobbi and the boys had flown to Ireland and gone back without him. 'I should stay to help sort things out,' and the while turned into months, with him living alone in the family home, and the boys flying over at holidays to stay with him, and Ellen didn't know what that meant for his marriage, or what it might mean for him and her.

The more time that passed without a sign of a reconciliation between him and Bobbi, the more she wondered if there was a possibility, even now, of her and Danny turning into something stronger than friends. Might they finally be the ones to grow old together? He was still married, and the last thing she wanted was to come between him and Bobbi. Nothing to be done but let events take their course.

As Christmas approached she went to the library, bringing her and her father's books to exchange. She greeted Helen and Carmel behind the desk, both known to her from her many visits.

'There you are,' Helen said. 'We were just talking about the new bookshop that's opening up.'

'I hadn't heard – where?'

'Where Music Station was, next door to Ryan's pub. There used to be a different bookshop there, years ago.'

'Piles of Books,' Ellen said. She hadn't been down that street in a long time. 'I worked there for a while before I moved to London.'

'Did you really? Small world. They're opening in the new year –

you'll have to go in and introduce yourself, so they'll be sure to keep you in stock.'

'I definitely will.'

Nice to think it was going to be a bookshop again. No doubt it would be completely different to what had been there before, but it would still be interesting to look in and see what the new owners had done. And she might well drop into Ryan's pub too, have a coffee for old times' sake.

Christmas came, and with it Grace and Tom. He taught violin in a London music school by day and busked in underground stations at weekends. Grace ran her own small-animal veterinary clinic in a premises leased with a little help from her father, and she and Tom lived in the flat above it.

Juliet and Rosie seemed happy as ever, still living in Juliet's grandfather's house, making a little more money these days thanks to Juliet's commissions, but in no imminent danger of being rich. They'd gone to Spain for Christmas, but promised to ring in the new year in Galway.

On Christmas evening, after dinner had been eaten and presents exchanged, after her father had gone up to bed and Grace had brought Tom out for a walk, Ellen sat in the sunroom listening to a carols concert on the radio and watching the lights she'd strung on Frances' camellia winking off and on. When her phone rang she looked at the screen and saw Leo's name. He'd been living in France, close to Henri and the others, since his retirement.

'Hi. Happy Christmas.'

'Happy Christmas, Ellen. How did it go?'

They spoke a little. He told her of the goose Henri had cooked, and the scarf Sabine had knit for him. She thanked him again for the Chanel perfume that had arrived unexpectedly a few days before Christmas. They hadn't exchanged gifts at Christmas since they'd split up: she hadn't known what to make of this one, and had texted her thanks.

'I want to say something,' he said. 'Can I?'

'. . . Yes.'

'Ellen, I still love you. I never stopped, I just lost sight of it for a while. These last few years . . . I've tried to forget you, but I can't. I probably shouldn't say it, but life is too short, and if there's any chance at all that you would – that we could try again, I want you to know that I would really like that.'

'Leo,' she said, and stopped. She watched the lights, off, on, off, on. She listened to the choir singing about shepherds and angels. 'You hurt me so badly,' she said. 'You broke my heart twice.'

'I know, I know I did. I'm so sorry. Give me a chance, and I'll spend the rest of my life making it up to you.'

She couldn't answer. Words literally failed her. Years after he had shattered her life, this.

'Think about it,' he said. 'We could live anywhere you like, Ireland, France, wherever. Will you think about it, Ellen? Will you please just consider it?'

'I'm hanging up now,' she said, and did, and switched off her phone. She continued to sit, wrapped in a soft blanket, as the voices of the choir filled the air.

At length she heard the sound of the front door opening and closing, and the dull thumps of steps on the stairs. Grace and Tom going up to bed, probably assuming she was already in her room.

She sat on, remembering what she'd thought to be forgotten.

Bookshelves

'I'M GOING INTO TOWN,' SHE TOLD HER FATHER after breakfast. 'There's a new bookshop opening, and I want to have a look.'

It was three days into 2016. Grace and Tom had flown back to London; Juliet and Rosie were still upstairs. *Grand opening January 3*, Ellen had read on a giant poster in the window when she'd walked by the bookshop, the soon-to-be-bookshop, on New Year's Eve.

Leo had not rung back. Instead, he'd texted.

I won't push you. I'll wait for your decision. Please think about it. I meant every word. L xx

She hadn't deleted the text. Could she love him again, could she risk it for the third time? The questions spun around in her head, tormenting her. Fool me once – what was that saying? Something about shame.

She needed to live with the possibility for a while. Consider the repercussions for her and the girls. In the meantime, she would fill her days.

The shopfront was blue instead of the dark green she remembered. *Bookshelves* was written in gold script above the window, a quill emerging from the last letter. She looked at the window display and saw books by Colum McCann and Niall Williams and Donal Ryan and others. On the door was a large sign that simply read *We're Open!* in triumphant blue lettering.

Inside, it was buzzing. People milled around, some with wine glasses in their hands, despite it being mid-morning. A tall smiling young man approached her with a tray of glasses half filled with golden liquid that sparkled.

'Hello there!' he said brightly to Ellen. Australian accent. 'Welcome to Bookshelves – do you fancy a little New Year tipple?'

She began to say no, and stopped. She wasn't writing today. 'Thank you.'

'You can add orange juice and make it a Buck's Fizz if you prefer,' he said, gesturing to open cartons on the front desk, so she did.

'Good luck,' she said. 'I'm a big fan of bookshops.' To her surprise, it was remarkably similar in layout to Piles of Books. Same display tables, same little crannies – and was that the same spiral staircase? She thought it was. 'You're not local.'

He grinned. 'How could you tell? I'm half Irish, so I'm coming back to my roots.'

'And this is your shop?'

'It is – with a little help from my father. It's a big gamble, one I've been thinking about for a while. I'm Hugh.'

'Ellen. Nice to meet you – and best of luck.'

'Thanks.'

'I'm actually a writer,' she said. May as well get that in.

'You are? What do you write?'

'Novels.'

'Ellen what?'

'Sheehan, just in case . . .'

His face lit up. 'Ellen Sheehan? No way – we have you in stock! You might sign them for us?'

'Thanks so much, I'd be delighted.'

He set down his tray and took a pen from his breast pocket. 'This is great – an author visit on my very first day! We'll have to get a snap too. Hang on till I find the books. Hey, Dad!' he called to someone behind Ellen. 'Guess what – this is Ellen Sheehan, the author!'

She turned to see a man approaching. Shorter than his son, tanned and freckled. Jeans, check shirt, glasses. Thinning sandy hair.

He drew closer, looking at her wonderingly.

Her mouth dropped open. She felt a rushing inside. A whirling, a chaos.

'Ellen Sheehan,' he said slowly, 'as I live and breathe.'

She found a smile. 'Hello, Ben,' she said.

OUTSIDE GALWAY
OCTOBER 2019
THE LAST MOVE

Happiness

BY THREE O'CLOCK, THE FINAL PIECES OF FURNI-
ture from Frances' old house have been unloaded and brought in.
When the sound of the removal van has faded, Ellen opens one
of the book boxes and starts to fill the large bookcase they'd chosen
together for the sitting room.

From the kitchen she hears humming. He has volunteered to
cook the first dinner in the new house: *You can do the unpacking;
I'm hopeless at it.* The arrangement suits her perfectly. This way,
she gets to decide where everything goes.

As she opens a second box he appears in the doorway, sleeves
rolled. 'Any idea where the knives are?'

'There's a box that says crockery and cutlery,' she tells him. 'You'll
get plates and cups too, and glasses.'

'Yes, ma'am. How's it going?'

'I'm not sure they'll all fit. We might have to build an extension.'
Between them, they have a ridiculous number of books.

'We can leave some of yours in the attic for now,' he says, and
ducks as she feigns flinging a book at him, and retreats again to the
kitchen. When the bookcase is full she pushes the remaining two
boxes under the window. More shelves are definitely needed – but

where can they fit them? The couch takes up most of the adjoining wall, leaving just enough room beside it for Frances' little china cabinet, which Ellen couldn't bear to part with.

She moves upstairs, happy to leave the books question for later. The stair carpet is worn in parts: another job for them to do. No rush, they have all the time in the world now. This brings a wave of happiness as she lifts a suitcase onto the bed in their room and begins to take out clothes.

Presently, the smell of frying onions drifts up. He's making pizzas, he told her. *My own secret recipe, so no peeking.*

There might be peeking, she'd said. *I might have to steal the recipe,* and he'd threatened the wooden spoon if she came within ten feet of the kitchen.

You haven't got a wooden spoon. It's still packed.

I'll find it, missy.

Oh, they will have so much fun together.

Last night's launch in Bookshelves went smoothly, with her biggest turnout yet. In addition to the usual local crowd, all her own old faithfuls showed up to celebrate the arrival of her tenth novel. Juliet and Rosie, of course – and Grace turned up with Tom, much to her mother's relief.

Sorry, Mum, Grace whispered on seeing her. *Sorry for getting mad at you on the phone,* and Ellen pressed her lips to Grace's cheek and told her it didn't matter at all.

Her sister Joan came from Cork, along with her daughters, Trisha and Daphne, who have made it their business to distribute their aunt's books among all their friends – *and sometimes,* Trisha told her, *we give your books better positions on bookshop shelves,* and Ellen had to pretend she hadn't heard that, knowing from her own days in Piles of Books that booksellers didn't appreciate customers moving the books around.

Henri and Sabine and fourteen-year-old Esme travelled all the way from France. Iris and Ultan flew from London with their twins. Ellen's editor, Vanessa, and her agent, Dorothy, both made speeches, and afterwards Ellen saw them together, heads bent in conversation, Dorothy, no doubt, negotiating better terms for the latest offered contract.

And seeing all the faces she loved around her, she was inevitably reminded of the ones who weren't there.

Her mother, who might be proud of her daughter now if she could see her.

Her father who left them last year, his three daughters gathered at his bedside as he slipped away. Buried now beside Iris' mother, Sarah, the woman he should have married.

Frances, still missed every day.

Tony, her first editor, who'd phoned her earlier in the day to wish her well. *Still here*, he'd said. *Still going strong, after all their dire predictions.*

Danny, her oldest friend, reunited after all with Bobbi, and busy looking after their first grandson, child of their son Cormac. Danny, who came close, but not close enough.

Leo, father of her children, breaker of her heart, currently living in the south of France with the ex-wife of one of his old banking colleagues. Leo, who after all only wanted what he couldn't have.

She's hanging the last shirt in the wardrobe when the doorbell rings. 'I'll get it,' she calls, and flies down. She opens the door and there they all are.

Rosie and Juliet, Grace and Tom, Iris and Ultan with the twins, Henri and Sabine and Esme – all of whom stayed last night in the rental house Ellen had booked for them. They'll stay there tonight too, because she insisted on them all being here for the first dinner in the cottage.

Boxes are moved from the kitchen to the hall. As folding chairs are unfolded, Hugh arrives from the bookshop. Places are found, some at the table, others at the worktop.

The chef distributes pizza slices, which are well received. 'This can be your signature dish,' Rosie says, 'whenever we have an occasion.'

'Just as well,' he says. 'The only thing I can cook.'

When the food has been eaten and coffees poured, he gets to his feet and pats his pockets. 'Now,' he says, 'there's a little thing I must do.' More patting. 'Hang on, I know it's here somewhere.' Eventually he casts around, frowning. 'Where did I put it?'

'What are you looking for?' Grace asks, and he holds up a hand and goes on scouring the room.

'Ah!' he says then, and opens the fridge and sticks his head in, and emerges with a little box.

A little blue velvet box.

At the sight of it, everyone goes still.

Ellen puts a hand to her throat as her first love, Ben McCarthy, drops to one knee beside her chair. Ben McCarthy, married in Australia, divorced when his son Hugh was twelve.

I should have come back then, he said, after they reunited. *I should have come back and hunted you down*, and Ellen said no, she wouldn't have been there, she would have been in London. *It wasn't our time. Now is our time.*

They didn't need to fall in love again; they simply stepped back into the old love, and it still fit perfectly. Within weeks of meeting, they were spending nights together; within months, he'd given up the lease of his flat and moved in with her and her father. And nothing in her life has felt so completely right as here and now, their own place together at last.

They've planned a pup, and Ellen fancies a kitten or two, and maybe a pair of donkeys to eat the grass in the field that came with the house – and he's threatened to squash a piano into the cottage. No music degree after all, just plinking along like he always did – but marriage wasn't mentioned by either of them. Marriage, she thought, wasn't in their plans.

He opens the little box now, all eyes on him. He looks at Ellen, nobody else, as he shows her the ring.

'Ellen Sheehan,' he says, 'will you for God's sake make an honest man of me?'

She nods, too full for words, and the room erupts in cheers as he slides the ring onto her finger and pulls her to her feet to embrace her. 'We got there in the end,' he whispers.

And safe in his arms, she knows she has finally come home.

Acknowledgements

Thanks to my invaluable editors Ciara Doorley of Hachette Books Ireland and Molly Walker-Sharp of Sphere UK, both very good at keeping me on track. Much appreciated.

Thanks to my agent Sallyanne Sweeney of MMBcreative, vigilant, attentive and always professional.

Thanks to my copy editor Aonghus Meaney, and to my proofreader Emma Dunne for their careful checking.

Thanks to those who helped when I came to them with a query during the writing of this book: Hope and Verna in O'Mahony's Bookshop in Limerick, Geraldine and Jackie in UCG's Special Collections Reading Room, Gabrielle Monaghan and Siobhan Ryan, and blushing apologies to those I've forgotten (every time).

Thanks to my family for their unwavering support, in particular my sister Treasa and my mother Rose.

Thanks to you for being kind enough to choose this book: I really hope you enjoy it.

Roisin x
www.roisinmeaney.com
Twitter (never X): @roisinmeaney
Bluesky: @roisinm.bsky.social